A Pour of Rain

A POUR *of* RAIN

STORIES FROM A WEST COAST FORT

HELEN MEILLEUR

RAINCOAST BOOKS

Vancouver

Raincoast Books gratefully acknowledges the support of the Government of Canada, through the Book Publishing Industry Development Program, the Canada Council for the Arts and the Department of Canadian Heritage. We also acknowledge the assistance of the Province of British Columbia, through the British Columbia Arts Council.

First published in 1980 by Sono Nis Press, Victoria, B.C.

Published in 2001 by
Raincoast Books
9050 Shaughnessy Street
Vancouver, B.C.
V6P 6E5
www.raincoast.com

1 2 3 4 5 6 7 8 9 10

NATIONAL LIBRARY OF CANADA CATALOGUING IN PUBLICATION DATA

Meilleur, Helen, 1910–
    A pour of rain

    ISBN 1-55192-422-6

1. Port Simpson (B.C.)—History. 2. Meilleur, Helen, 1910–
—Childhood and youth. 3. Trading posts—British Columbia—Port
Simpson—History. 4. Hudson's Bay Company—History. 5. Indians of
North America—British Columbia—Port Simpson Region—History.
I. Title.
FC3849.P68M45 2001   971.1'1   C2001-910848-6
F1089.5.P58M45 2001

Photo credits: the first thirteen images in the insert are courtesy of the British Columbia Provincial Archives. All other images, courtesy of the author.

At Raincoast Books we are committed to protecting the environment and to the responsible use of natural resources. We are acting on this commitment by working with suppliers and printers to phase out our use of paper produced from ancient forests. This book is one step towards that goal. It is printed on 100% ancient-forest-free paper (100% post-consumer recycled), processed chlorine and acid-free, and supplied by New Leaf Paper; it is printed with vegetable-based inks by Houghton Boston. For further information, visit our website at www.raincoast.com. We are working with Markets Initiative (www.oldgrowthfree.com) on this project.

Printed and bound in Canada

To the memory of my parents
Robert Boyd Young and Eva Ina Young

Contents

Foreword

ALTHOUGH THE ORAL TRADITIONS of British Columbia reach back to the origins of the world itself, the literary voice of Canada's westernmost province remains relatively recent — less than 150 years old discounting the correspondence of Spanish military commander Don Pedro Alberni from Nootka Sound in 1790, the scant journals of explorers like Alejandro Malaspina, George Vancouver, Alexander Mackenzie and Simon Fraser. Ledgers from isolated fur trading outposts and the narratives of a few eccentric wayfarers like R. Byron Johnson or Walter Butler Cheadle, unwilling sojourners like John Jewitt or determined settlers like Susan Allison supplement the record. And, while the province has produced its share of literary genius, from Earle Birney to Sheila Watson, from Dorothy Livesay to Douglas Coupland, from Patrick Lane to George Clutesi, from Jack Hodgins to Joy Kogawa, much of this work falls across the latter decades of the twentieth century. Even the writing of Helen Meilleur, whose *A Pour of Rain* reaches back to the beginning of the last century and beyond, establishes its unique point of view from a vantage point far closer to our present sensibilities. Indeed, of the literary output included in *Skookum Wawa*, the watershed anthology of writing from and about the Pacific region published in 1975, better than 60 percent of the writers did the bulk of their work after mid-century. This is even more true of its successor anthology, *Genius of Place: Writing About British Columbia*, in which the proportion of writers who did most of their important work after the Second World War jumps to 75 percent. Yet these anthologies are probably fair reflections of the evolving history of the literary landscape west of the Rockies. Travel back beyond 1960 and, like the early human settlements themselves, those literary expressions rooted in a strong sense of place become less and less frequent. The numbers of writers are fewer and the publishing opportunities narrower in a province where 80 percent of the population was dispersed into a rural hardscrabble economy. Many of those who wrote did so from a sensibility shaped by the colonial mindset that dominated life at the outermost fringe of a great globe-straddling empire in which all points of view tended to the assumed cultural superiority of London, Paris and Berlin — or even Toronto and Montreal.

The West Coast was often portrayed as an exotic contrast to civilization, an assumption that lies behind even Martin Allerdale Grainger's *Woodsmen of the West*, a powerful and stark 1906 evocation of life in the float camps and A-frame logging shows of the mid-coast. Or it was perceived as an ethnological treasure house to be looted by the likes of eminent anthropologist Franz Boas before First Nations culture vanished. Those early artists who did attempt to root themselves and their expression of the world firmly in the place they inhabited tended to be marginalized as eccentrics. Emily Carr found herself simply ignored, as was Susan Allison, whose stunning portraits of life on the frontier of the 1860s didn't extend beyond occasional newspaper accounts until Margaret Ormsby collected, edited and published them in 1976. Hubert Evans' 1927 novel about a First World War veteran returning to a life battling the wilderness earned such scant notice that he didn't write another for twenty-seven years.

Then, in the 1930s, a new generation of writers began to shake off these colonial constraints, finding their characters in the world around them and setting their narratives in the place they knew best. Howard O'Hagan would write about Indian legends from the Rockies and frame them into a still compelling novel of mythic proportions that propelled him to the forefront of Western letters when it was reprinted. Arthur Mayse would begin publishing short stories and novels that were set in and drew upon a contemporary reality that seems simultaneously remote and eerily prescient — drug smugglers, logging accidents, ghosts from the Great War and remembrances of the early Russian presence on the coast — and find a ready audience, first in London and New York, and then farther afield in Germany, Norway and the Netherlands. Bruce Hutchison would write his epic history of the Fraser River and tap into a new Canadian nationalism. Roderick Haig-Brown would begin creating a global awareness of the natural history of B.C. rivers and forests. R. S. Patterson would enthrall British and American readers with his experiences homesteading in the Peace River and venturing up the Nahanni River through the Funeral Range to the mysterious Headless Valley and beyond, through the canyons and into the hidden Backbone Range.

It is to this explosion of talent and its vigorous celebration of an emerging culture here on the wet, fecund coast and in the austere mountain valleys of what Charles Lillard has called the "Sitka biome" that Helen Meilleur rightfully belongs. She was born at the beginning the twentieth century and, like many of her peers from that period, her literary work didn't even begin in earnest until after the century's mid-point had been reached. *A Pour of Rain* wasn't realized in print until 1980, when she was seventy years old. But it was quickly recognized as an indispensable classic of British Columbia lore, a perceptive window into the vanished world of a coastal trading post that was itself a lingering echo of the days when newspaper reporters were expected to know the Chinook trade jargon and the canoe people still ventured out on the *skookum chuck*.

More than ninety years ago, Helen Meilleur's mother arrived at Port Simpson, not far from where the Nass River ends its descent to the sea. The river meanders back through the rustling cottonwood groves of its alluvial fan, back past Anhluut'ukwsim Laxmihl Angwinga;asanskwhl Nisga'a, the jumbled lava bed where two thousand Nisga'a are said to have been entombed in molten rock one night, past the austere uplands of the Mats'ii'aadin, all the way to its headwaters on cloud-plumed Magoonhl Lisims, home of the creator. In the year of Helen's birth, the Nisga'a Land Committee — an organization of chiefs, elders and other tribal leaders assembled to resist the wholesale parcelling out of aboriginal lands to the K'umsiiwa, as white newcomers were known — had travelled to Prince Rupert to petition Prime Minister Wilfrid Laurier with their grievances. The prime minister was sympathetic, promising to settle the aboriginal land question in British Columbia once and for all.

Who among those leaders would have imagined that they would all lie mouldering in their graves before the promise was fulfilled? Or that the newborn baby girl would live to see the Nisga'a Treaty signed and herself become a living bridge between the time of spirits and supernatural beings and a time of science and technology, between an age when Raven still shaped the cosmos with his jokes and the Sea Grizzly walked with ghosts of the drowned entangled in its hair and an age of satellite mapping, jetboats and e-mail that jacks the most remote tribal group into the electronic pulse of the world.

But Helen Meilleur's eloquent, beautifully modulated literary voice is that bridge, the more important because she reaches back from her own experiences to those of a generation as far from her present as her birth is from ours. *A Pour of Rain* is a document of great importance to British Columbians precisely because it weds the narrative sensibilities of the oral cultures that surrounded her childhood to the historical perspectives of the new culture to which they became fused by economics, politics and the more pragmatic bonds of love, marriage and those friendships that endure in spite of prejudice and folly. Her own memories of the dying embers of the Victorian era — not quite extinguished at the farthest edge of an empire which would soon be transformed and swept away by the Great War — are melded with those gleaned from the journals, ledgers and log books of Hudson's Bay Company traders. The resulting alloy is at once lustrous with the texture and hue of human sense and sensibility while sharp in its understanding of the historical context. It forms a unique portrait of the origins of this province, a birth that occurred right at the interface between worlds, the world of myth and the world of empire, the world of rain on cedar and the world of steel and telegraphs, the foreign country of the past and the unknown country of the future.

This edition will be the third impression of *A Pour of Rain*, which was first published in 1980 and went through two printings. It will surely not be the last. As long as British Columbians wish to know from whence they came, whether First Nations, newcomers or descendants of settler peoples, these stories will have currency and the power to expand horizons so that we might know once again those fog-shrouded landscapes at the beginning of time when Thunderbird reigned in heaven and how they were changed forever by the coming of the K'umsiiwa, a spirit people of another kind.

—Stephen Hume

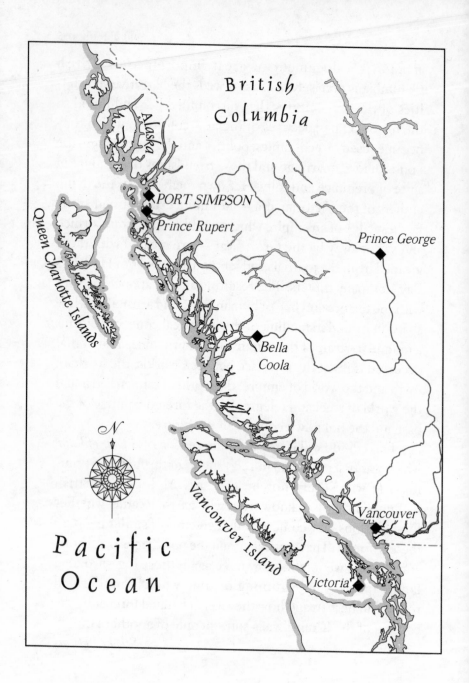

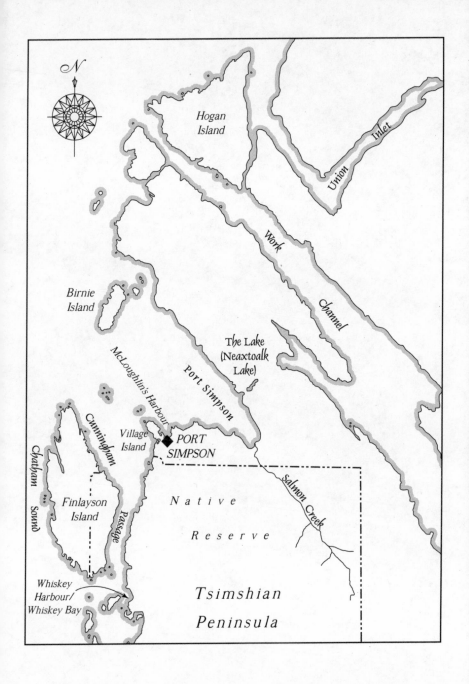

N

Hogan
Island

Union
Inlet

Work
Channel

Birnie
Island

The Lake
(Neaxtoalk
Lake)

McLoughlin's Harbour

Port Simpson

Village
Island

◆ PORT
SIMPSON

Chatham
Sound

Cunningham

Finlayson
Island

Passage

Native

Reserve

Salmon Creek

Whiskey
Harbour/
Whiskey Bay

Tsimshian

Peninsula

Preface

A POUR OF RAIN WAS CONCEIVED in my childhood. My father returned to Port Simpson from one of his annual business trips to Vancouver and Victoria chuckling over the stories of Simpson's stockaded past. He had gone to the office of Mr. C. H. French, the Hudson's Bay Company's district manager, to discuss foreshore rights, discovered that Mr. French shared his enthusiasm for historical tidbits and ended the session with the two of them huddled over a reading glass trained on an 1839 Fort Simpson journal. I don't know what happened to the foreshore rights but the thought of that journal implanted itself in my mind where it outlived most of the educational and occupational ideas of a lifetime.

Once, in the 1930s, I tried to track down the Fort Simpson journals only to learn that Mr. French had retired and that all such materials had been housed in London. And still the thought of them, well out of reach, tantalized me. In 1973 I learned of the Hudson's Bay Company's priceless gift to Manitoba — the Hudson's Bay Archives. My life did not permit me to pack up and leave for Winnipeg that day. In fact, by the time I reached my goal and *A Pour of Rain* was born, the pregnancy had been of more than fifty years' duration.

This book is an attempt to share my delight in the journals. It is made up of the little known and often astonishing details of early life on Canada's mainland West Coast. In the few instances, including the title and some chapter headings, that I have used quotations without identifying their source, they belong to the journals. I have taken one liberty with the quotations; I have standardized the spellings of First Nations tribal and personal names and a few others. The journal keepers wrote them as they heard them and they heard with Scottish, Irish, English and Bostonian ears. Not only did each man have his own spelling for a name but he was likely to have a variety of spellings for it. I chose the forms that most nearly reproduced the words I heard as a child and apologize to those who may have heard them differently. I am aware that my use of the word *tribe* to designate units that ranged from family to nation may offend some who have delved into the intricacies of tribes, clans and totems. I use it because the First Nations people of my Port Simpson days used it thus, as did the journal keepers in their day.

I am convinced that the journals reported well and truly but there is one area that requires a little skepticism, the area of Indian-Fort relations. The Hudson's Bay men, though they probably knew the First Nations people better than any white men since, wrote from the Hudson's Bay viewpoint. Please bear in mind there was another viewpoint — unrecorded.

While many published works were of valuable assistance in providing background and alternative perceptions, my chief sources, in addition to the Fort Simpson journals, were primary ones: personal diaries, letters, reports and ships' logs. And so I am indebted to the British Columbia Archives and its staff and especially to the Hudson's Bay Company and to Shirlee Anne Smith, its obliging archivist. Thanks should also go to the staff of the Hudson's Bay Company Library in Winnipeg and to the staff of the New Westminster Public

Library who coped with many strange requests.

Concerning the chapters that deal with my family's life in Port Simpson, I am grateful to my late brother, Loyal Young, whose enthusiasm for the project breathed new life into many a faltering chapter; to Edith (Raley) Graham who shared her memories, knowledge and family papers and photos with me, and to Frances Tait who generously and frankly filled in gaps in my understanding of Tsimshian attitudes and thinking. "The Life and Times of My Father's 74" (Chapter 34) is printed with the kind permission of *Cycle World*. Finally, thanks go to Alice Frith whose encouragement extended even to working with me in both archives, and to my niece, Helen Young, who shared some night shifts with me.

A Pour of Rain is an experienced book. It was published in 1980 and had been out of print for a few years. I am grateful to David Stouck and Mylar Wilkinson for returning it to life through their anthology, *Genius of Place*, and to Raincoast Books for being kind to it and sending it out again to "tell it as it *was*."

—*H.M.*

PART I

Arrivals

CHAPTER 1

At Port Simpson

THE CENTURY WAS in its seventh year and already racing headlong into change when my mother rolled over the gunnel of a Tlingit dugout onto the beach that fronted the Hudson's Bay post at Port Simpson. For twenty-six years thereafter she and my father and their family were to know Port Simpson as home, while an era fell to pieces about them.

In the ooze and beach grass of low tide Mother hiked her dress and two petticoats above her kid boot tops and faced the unknown country of Canada. It looked good to her. She had not seen so much evidence of civilization in all the eight years she had spent in southeastern Alaska. The forest had been beaten back seventy years before and now Port Simpson rolled down from its backdrop hills, green as only perpetual rainfall could colour it, soft as overzealous vegetation had shaped it. And the buildings were *painted*.

Mother turned to wave goodbye to the Native girl sitting on the bow of the anchored fish boat that had brought her from Ketchikan. Then she started up the beach, her handbag on one arm, a Tlingit basket on the other. The hand-bag bulged, the basket bulged and so did Mother — she was nine months pregnant. Charlie, her Tlingit boatman, strode ahead with two suitcases, never glancing back, in the accepted manner of a Native man walking with a woman, and thus they reached the main road where Mother, puffing, called a halt.

"All that broken glass we walked through, why is it there, Charlie?"

"Hotel. Bar," and Charlie's arm swung out to indicate a three-storey building set on pilings.

Even as Mother stood admiring its balconies topped by a tower and a flagpole — it was not the flimsy, false-fronted hotel of western lore — a window flew up, voices leapt out and a bottle exploded on the rocks below. Mother, a zealous advocate of teetotalism, sighed and turned her back on the hotel, which meant that she was then facing the Hudson's Bay post.

"I thought it would have a stockade."

"Gone long time."

"Why is the flagpole in the middle of the wharf approach?"

"Flagpole very old. Wharf more new."

"Those huge gateposts just stand there all by themselves?"

"Nobody take down."

"There are lots of buildings."

"Mebbe eight, nine."

The store building was unmistakable. It was narrow, not more than twenty-five feet wide, but it extended back from its railed porch some one hundred and twenty-five feet. Its Hudson's Bay Company white paint and red trim had been kept in glistening condition. The only other large building entirely visible from the road was settling under moss and age. Mother noticed lace curtains at its windows.

Charlie did not need to designate the reserve. Mother sniffed the westerly breeze and realized that a Canadian Tsimshian village smelled exactly like an American Tlingit village. Fish, smoke, offal, dogs, tar, low tide, all the familiar elements were there. But the village was larger than those she knew in Alaska and among the rough shacks she glimpsed many partially painted houses complete with Victorian cupolas, bay windows, verandahs and bric-a-brac.

"And where's the hospital?"

Charlie pointed upward in the opposite direction, to what looked like a large dwelling pinning down a hilltop. Mother studied the sudden rise with some dismay as they walked toward it but as they reached its foot Charlie swung right onto another gravel road.

"Hill no good. We go long way," and they began a more gradual climb. A three-plank sidewalk branched off that road, and after Mother had taken off her cape and her hat and switched the handbag and basket from one hand to the other, and gasped for a while, they started off on it across a sea of muskeg.

"Isn't this a mission hospital?"

"Yes."

"Well, it must be a mile over and up from the Indian village. How do sick Indians get to it?"

"Walk."

"But if they can't?"

"Men carry on stretcher."

"That must be hard on the men as well as the patient," said Mother and kept on walking.

The sidewalk ended at the hospital porch. Charlie placed the suitcases by the door, lifted his cap as Mother had taught him to do six years before in the Native school at Saxman, and was gone. Mother twisted the iron handle of the doorbell. A young nurse opened the door. Her hands, head and starched apron all made a small jump of amazement. Six hundred miles from the nearest city, with no steamer due for five days, an unknown white woman on one's doorstep was something in the nature of a materialization. The girl murmured and flew down the corridor. Mother waited at the open door, savouring the heavy carbolic odours — she had been living in and about Native villages for eight years.

A nurse, whom Mother knew to be the matron by her grey hair and the authoritative crackling of her uniform, emerged from the corridor. She showed no glimmer of astonishment; after years of outpost nursing she had graduated from surprise.

"Come in," she said. "And when are you expecting your baby?"

"Now," said Mother.

That is how the Young family came to the settlement in the large bay off Chatham Sound, north of the Skeena River, south of the Nass and behind the barrier islands of Finlayson and Birnie. How Port Simpson came to be there is another story.

CHAPTER 2

On the Nass

WHEN MOTHER LANDED at Port Simpson she knew where
she was — some arrivals were less certain, for Port Simpson
was cursed with confusion about its name and location. Its
final shift in identity had taken place some twenty years
before when the federal government had officially changed
it from a fort to a port. The first arose out of its beginnings, which were made forty miles to the north under the
temporary name of Fort Nass.

Fort Nass was a mistake that came about because it was
such a fine day in August 1830 when Captain Aemilius
Simpson, seeking a site for the Hudson's Bay Company's
north coast trading post, coaxed the brigantine *Cadboro* as
far up the river as the southerly breeze, tides, currents, depth
and the conformation of the land would allow. He anchored
about fourteen miles from the mouth. Two armed ship's
boats pulled away from the *Cadboro* at four in the afternoon
to continue the exploration upriver. What with canoes of the
Nisga'a, reputedly unfriendly, hovering about, and the sun
making its way westward as the boats made their way eastward, it is not much wonder that the officers quickly decided
upon a location on a point that thrusts out into the river in the
vicinity of the old grease village. How could they imagine on

a warm summer day, with the river rippling gently, that when winter attacked that exposed point it would hurl an icy wind straight off blue, Nass glaciers, blasting through the stockade posts as though they were bamboo shoots, ripping off roofs, capsizing boats, gobbling fuel and sending otherwise intrepid men cowering to shelter? On the company's records the fort was found unsuitable because of Russian opposition and navigational difficulties, and doubtless those were great. But anyone who has tried to stand upright on that particular finger of land when a Nass blow was in progress has his own idea of why the fort was moved lock, stock, and all but one rum barrel, to McLoughlin's Harbour, well to the south of the Nass River.

Before the move and before that cask of rum was presented to the Natives as a farewell gift, the first name change had occurred. In May of 1831, along with Peter Skene Ogden who was in charge of the land party, Captain Simpson returned to establish Fort Nass. In less than four months he was dead. Fort Nass became Fort Simpson in his honour. Thus began the second confusion, for some nine years before, Captain Simpson's illustrious relative, George Simpson, Governor of Rupert's Land, was similarly honoured by the renaming of the fort at the confluence of the Liard and Mackenzie Rivers. To those who live south of Queen Charlotte Sound or Williams Lake, the north is the north and whether Fort Simpson be located on the coast of British Columbia or six hundred miles inland in the Northwest Territories is of little consequence. And so, almost a hundred years later, sometimes items of our mail wintered over on the bank of the Liard River and sometimes my father opened a packing case to discover snowshoes or fur caps intended for a frozen rather than a sodden north. This particular confusion was transported to the new location along with the company's personnel, furs, trading goods, records, provisions, building pieces, gate fittings, a bitch and her pups and Captain Simpson's disinterred body.

Fort Simpson's moving day was the last Saturday in August 1834. It proceeded with the smoothness of a tornado. In the forenoon an officer traded rum to the Natives and from that point onward the Company's people had a small war as well as a large move on their hands. The Nisga'a for the three years of the fort's existence had proved themselves cooperative and, considering that this was a period of rum-selling, peaceable. But they were loath to allow all the metal and trade goods so urgently needed by them to be whisked out of their reach forever. Outside the locked gates there were milling Natives and muskets, knives and pike poles. There were whoops and yells and attempts to batter down the temporary fence replacing a bastion that had been disassembled and shipped. There was a barrel of goods seized at dagger point and recovered at cutlass point. There were up to twenty muskets trained directly into the fort yard from the hill behind, and there was a shot from the bush that whipped past the head of a workman who had gone to the beach to load a boat during one of the calmer moments. When a few Nisga'a were taken into the fort for strategic reasons, a bloody battle with dagger and fists broke out among them.

Toward the end of the day, even the imperturbable Hudson's Bay gentlemen had completely lost interest in packing and loading. They threw open the gates and marshalled their men, women and children through the agitated crowd. When the last of the fort people crossed the threshold outward, the first of the Native mob crossed it inward. The Nisga'a set about stripping the premises while the entire fort company was ferried to the safety of the *Dryad*, which stood off in the stream to await the morning tide.

Then the fort was demolished by means of that twenty-five-gallon barrel of rum that had been conspicuously left behind. No sooner were the Hudson's Bay people packed into their crowded quarters aboard ship and breathing normally again, than the shore erupted in probably the fiercest farewell party that ever took place on the coast. Shots and shouts and shrieks and thuds of destruction lacerated the northern night. Whether someone with a fine sense of fitness had picked the date or whether it was merely a coincidence has not been recorded, but it was August 30th, 1834, four years to the day after Captain Simpson had chosen the Nass site.

CHAPTER 3

At McLoughlin's Harbour

FOUR OBDURATE RUSSIANS and a gunboat were responsible for the *Dryad*'s sailing south instead of north to the new fort site.

When the Hudson's Bay Company made its Pacific beginnings in 1821, Russia and Britain shared the northwest coast of the American continent without benefit of boundary; in other words, the Russian American Company and the Hudson's Bay Company shared it. They had a loose arrangement of treaties and expired treaties and understandings by which they traded warily on the edges of one another's rich fur territories. The Hudson's Bay was a tough company made up of tough men. So also was the Russian American Company that had evolved from survival days on the Aleutian Islands. They were mutually respectful. In trade they were avowed enemies but in other matters, particularly opposition to American traders, their interests were so similar that they cooperated readily. Neither cared to face what its government might do to its unpublicized trading habits in a hard and fast boundary settlement, so they continued to step delicately around the issue. But in 1834, the Russians, without warning, tramped heavily — on the toes of the British company.

Three months before the *Dryad* transported Fort Simpson (Nass) to Fort Simpson (McLoughlin's Harbour), she made the thousand-mile coastal run from Fort Nisqually, now Tacoma but then the Company's southern port, to Stikine Sound. She rode low in the water because she carried building materials for a fort and a land party of thirty-five men and three officers. She was bound for the Stikine River to establish an upriver post in what was acknowledged British territory. The coast, deemed to extend ten miles inland, was acknowledged Russian territory.

There was enthusiasm aboard the *Dryad*. Peter Skene Ogden understandably shared it; he had lived through three Nass winters. Once again he was in charge of the land party.

The *Dryad* anchored in Stikine Sound, preparatory to making the run up the river. A few miles from the anchorage a Russian post stood on Point Highfield. It was not impressive in appearance but it bore the name Redoubt St. Dionysius. Even as the gentlemen trained their glasses upon it a whaleboat left the shore and headed for the ship. It brought a mounted gun and an emissary carrying an official scroll inscribed in English, prohibiting trading in those waters. The whaleboat and emissary returned to the shore while a baidarka, a sealskin craft of the Aleuts and Inuit, made the journey out to the ship. It brought two officers. One spoke enough English to convey the information that the Russians would attack should the *Dryad* try to enter the river. He drank a pint of the brigantine's brandy without showing any sign of relenting, and then the baidarka paddled off. Soon after, the whaleboat and swivel gun returned with yet another Russian and an interpreter of *Spanish*. The Hudson's Bay gentlemen had to use some Latin and much imagination to glean his message which seemed to be that a boat was being dispatched to Sitka for further orders. The next move came after the lapse of a day, when Mr. Ogden

was summoned to visit the Russian commander. He sent
two other officers who were so hung with pistols and knives
and guns that, had they fallen overboard, they would have
plummeted to the bottom. Their gig rounded the point and
suddenly the comedy hardened into drama. There, off the
fort, rode the brig *Chichagoff* mounting four swivel guns
and twelve cannons and manned by a crew of eighty-four,
armed almost as heavily as the visitors. This was a message
that needed no translation. The two officers met the commander aboard the brig. In spite of politely proffered wine,
he had only "no" to say. It seemed redundant.

The *Dryad* swung at anchor for ten days awaiting a more
favourable word from Sitka but it did not come and the
commander's stance did not soften. A Tlingit chief added
his warning to the Russians' and Ogden heeded his words;
Tlingit practised the art of massacre. Loaded to the gunnels
with the materials and personnel for a new fort, the ship
weighed anchor and headed south. For once, the
indomitable Hudson's Bay Company had come out second best. Even the *Dryad's* departure was ignominious for
the weather was against her and, after setting sail, she made
no more than a mile's headway in two hours and had to
anchor again, still in sight of the fort.

Apparently Peter Skene Ogden was familiar with the sheltered waters then known as McLoughlin's Harbour. There
the *Dryad* was bound, through fog and foul weather, to found
the new fort. If it could not be built on the Stikine it would be
built south of Nass Straits and east of Dixon's Entrance. It
took thirteen days of waiting and working to cover the approx-
imate one hundred sixty miles. Those were days of inaction
and tedium for the people of the land party but the last inaction and tedium they were to know for weeks to come.

Fort Simpson's second site was chosen almost as speedily but far more fortuitously than the first. An evening and

a whole day were squandered on the exploration for it. The *Dryad* entered the bay at 5 p.m. on July 12th. Before her anchor was out, one boat was launched to investigate the shoreline; immediately after, a second. By dusk, Captain Duncan and Dr. W. F. Tolmie, aboard the second boat, had located a possible site. Further search next day confirmed it.

At 4 a.m. on July 14th, the land party went ashore to commence levelling the wilderness, and to devise shelters for themselves and their baggage. The gentlemen had tents; the men had boughs. Class distinctions were never allowed to become fuzzy. That night and thereafter they slept ashore — fortunately the rain held off until the 18th.

Next day, provisions and trade goods were landed, a temporary store was fashioned out of oilcloth, Dr. Tolmie was appointed Indian Trader and another post was in operation. On that day also, the party began what was to become an almost constant occupation for the next half-century: the cutting of pickets for the stockade. A picket was a log twenty to twenty-two feet long, one to two feet in diameter, squared and sharpened to an uncomfortable point at the top. Hudson's Bay personnel took the matter of pickets seriously, and on the 15th of July, 1834, behind a hastily thrown-up barricade of downed trees and bush, the thought of a stockade must have been comforting, especially as the *Dryad* sailed off to the Nass, leaving the camp unprotected.

By the seventh day of the encampment, clearing and cutting pickets and watching and existing had become such a routine that, in spite of the complication of rain, Dr. Tolmie's diary remarked nonchalantly, "Nothing of note."

Something of note was recorded on July 23rd, however, for the *Dryad* returned from Fort Simpson (Nass) bringing pieces of lumber from a house and the store. This transportation of boards and materials from one building to another miles distant, was already a well-rooted custom on the coast. The tribes in their nomadic travels from winter to summer villages and back again, carried their cedar boards with them in their canoes. At their destination, they fastened the boards back onto the permanent posts of the houses and were immediately at home. Prefabricated buildings are not entirely a twentieth-century development.

During July 24th and 26th the lumber was rafted ashore from the *Dryad*'s anchorage. All hands and backs turned out to carry it up the beach. The Hudson's Bay Company built solidly; those timbers were hand-squared trees. It was on the 24th also that the fort was measured out, one hundred fifty feet of new stumps by one hundred fifty feet of underbrush.

While Mr. Ogden flitted between old and new Fort Simpsons aboard the *Dryad*, supervising the dismantling there and the planning here (he even worked in a trading voyage to Tongass in this period), James Birnie took charge of the new project. Clearing and building were his first concerns since he had to be prepared to receive everything that could be transported from the Nass post by the end of August. But protection had a high priority too, so part of his contingent was always off in the woods cutting pickets, or in the bay rafting the pickets toward camp, or wrestling those logs up the beach. And then, there were the complications; life in the encampment was not entirely a summer idyll.

The most obvious complication was the weather. There were some fine days and more wet days. Rain in Port Simpson in July and August is not necessarily a gentle summer rain. It is just as likely to be a pounding fall rain or a driving winter rain. Mr. Birnie's exasperated note of August 24th suggests that he was experiencing the latter. With water dripping into the food and through the men's bowery quarters, filling the trenches dug for pickets, making mud of the clearings and keeping clothing, blankets and possessions soggy, even Hudson's Bay fortitude must have been slightly taxed.

Mr. Birnie had personnel problems, too. The men worked long hours on a diet mainly of salted fish and meat. They worked with materials that were logs or roughed out of logs; even boards were often two inches thick. They used the most basic tools — anything as refined as a crosscut saw had to be borrowed from a ship — and the most basic power, their own tired muscles and sinews. They often worked for a day at a time in seawater. If you think those living and working conditions added up to more than the human body could endure, you are correct. By July 18th, the fourth day of building, there were four men too sick to work and by the 25th the number had risen to six. These illnesses were not one-day indispositions but lasted for weeks, there, under the dripping branches. On August 7th, after a day of discharging pickets, three men were "disabled by strains" and as many of the sick as were able to lift an axe were set to peeling pickets. Then there were the accident cases. One man survived (in what condition we are not told) a timber falling on him. Another fell from the top of the frame of a house, breaking a thigh bone and sustaining other injuries, while two men were laid up, one with a cut foot, one with a cut hand. Dr. Tolmie was present to look after the first of these wounds but by the time the second occurred he had left to make a house call on a couple of accident cases at the Nass fort, taking with him four men as crew, an additional drain on Mr. Birnie's depleted workforce.

Mr. Birnie could allot only so much frustration to his camp's declining health, for the fur trade took precedence over all else in a Hudson's Bay fort, even in an infant fort. Therefore, when the brig *Bolivar Liberator* anchored in the bay she was a complication that had to be investigated and assessed. She fell into the category of "Boston Trader" and enemy of the Company. She turned out to be a pleasant complication, for Captain Dominis was a likeable fellow who entertained the officers aboard ship in a luxury they had renounced two weeks before; besides, he had traded most of his cargo at Sitka and offered only slight competition.

Then there were the unforeseen disruptions, great and small. In Port Simpson, a boat has always seemed nearly as necessary as arms or legs. At this time when picket cutters were going out in two directions and spending long days rafting home, the fort's one boat must have been rarely at anchor. However, one evening she was sent out to anchor in the care of a Tsimshian. Next morning she was nowhere in sight. An obliging Captain Dominis provided one of his ship's boats for the search; rival traders on the coast in those days always rallied to the aid of one another in the face of a marine disaster. The shoreline around Port Simpson is a succession of charming bays and coves and indentations. The searchers must have put into thirty of them during the 8th of August and all to no avail. A reward for the boat's return was offered to the Natives but it continued missing.

As the end of August and the final move from the Nass approached, there was a push to complete the stockade consisting of a full one thousand fifty pickets. And so, on the 26th and 27th of August, how were a number of builders employed? They were repickling the salmon. You can be sure this was no mere whim; the entire complement was doubtless living on that salmon.

Mr. Birnie dealt with his difficulties with one hand while he waved his builders on with the other. On a Monday logs were laid for the store foundation. On the Tuesday "filling logs" and part of the rafters were raised. On Wednesday the roof was put on. It was a Native-type roof of bark, some used bark from the Nass, some traded from the neighbouring tribes. On that day also, the first storey was planked. On Thursday the store was finished as far as Mr. Birnie was concerned and on Friday the trader folded up his

draped oilcloth and moved in, protected by a special barricade of logs from one of the Nass houses. Other projects
proceeded at a similar clip.

The Nass evacuees, heavy-eyed after their harrowing
night at anchor in the river, came ashore on the beach in
front of the new fort on August 31st, right on schedule.
And, right on schedule, there stood a stockade to receive
them, a store to receive their stock and a shed, complete
with cut alder for the forge, to receive the blacksmith's
shop — forty-seven days from rainforest to primitive fort.

I am glad the people of Port Simpson have a beautiful,
green monument to James Birnie. It is Birnie Island that
forms a breakwater against the seas of Dixon's Entrance.
With Finlayson Island to the south, it furnishes a frame
for Simpson's sunsets and is the main and most intriguing
feature of any seaward view north or west.

PART II

Family Neighbourhoods

CHAPTER 4

Background to Reserve Living

IN PORT SIMPSON I was a member of a minority group; I was a white child living on a reserve. I knew the sensation of walking through curious stares, of hearing myself being discussed in an unknown tongue, of watching a fascinating game without any hope of participating. My parents were aware of the situation and never regarded it as even a slight problem. Both had served apprenticeships in minority groups of *one*, among the Tlingit of southeastern Alaska, and to them our lives in the Native village, with an eighty-year-old white community at hand, were well balanced and even spacious.

My parents had reached Alaska from the extreme edges of the continent and the extreme edges of the American approach to life. My father came from a long line of Presbyterian ministers. He was four when his mother died and his father deposited him in a Presbyterian manse in a Pennsylvania town and then hurried off to Alaska to serve as a lay missionary under his brother who was in charge of his church's missions in the new territory. My father, growing up in the care of his minister grandfather and a maiden aunt, was pressed into a puritanical mould and stamped with propriety. Upon graduation from high school he found himself in the depression of 1893 and faced with an ecclesiastical future. He broke the mould rather violently and began to make his way to Alaska and the father he did not know. By taking strange jobs along the way, he reached Seattle in the days when ships overloaded with goldseekers sailed frequently out of that port. The trip north plunged him into the miners' raw world and released him from his childhood (perhaps too completely, according to my mother) although fragments of the mould stuck to him for his entire life.

If nineteenth-century missionaries were supposed to be as poor as church mice, lay missionaries were supposed to be poorer. Dad's father found he could sustain life by operating a small store wherever he was stationed. By this time the Tlingit were demanding white men's weapons, tools, clothing, household goods and foods. I am sure my grandfather's store hustled his flock into our civilization, an absolute requisite of mission work of that era, faster and further than did his prayer meetings. At any rate, the store had grown to such proportions that Grandfather was happy to turn it over to his young son while he retired to his volumes of sermons that occupied the whole kitchen table.

My father built up a rival library with such titles as *Business Methods* and *The Rural Store in the Community* but his chief interest in his new life was the fur buying. With crews of Natives, in their canoes or the small sailboats that were replacing them, he travelled the coast — up shadowed inlets, through hidden channels, to beaches where Native houses clustered and white men rarely came. Sometimes he would be gone for weeks at a time, to return in a state of awe at what he had seen. Butler, Pennsylvania had not prepared him for such grandeur, nor for the lice that outraged his Presbyterian body by the end of a trip. Eventually, since the gold fever raged all about him, he added prospecting to these excursions.

While my father was still a *chechako* ("tenderfoot" in Chinook jargon), the government of the United States belatedly realized that it owned a territory sparsely furnished with schools. Half-heartedly it sent out a call for teachers that my mother wholeheartedly answered. She was the daughter of covered-wagon pioneers who had pursued their dream from Iowa to California and thence into Oregon. Having conquered one segment of that magnificent wilderness they would load the wagon with the older children and a couple of new babies each move and be off again in search of wider rivers, sunnier valleys or higher hills. The zest for challenge and the unknown never left my mother, so it is no wonder that at twenty she dropped her chalk in an Oregon schoolroom and sailed north on another gold-rush steamer to become the only white person and the very first teacher in a Tlingit village.

Into the new schoolhouse in Gravina crowded children of all ages and adults of all ages, too. Unlike most tribes of the north coast to whom schools were merely a warm place to pass a winter's day, the Tlingit had somehow been inspired with an insatiable craving for the white man's education. This inspiration might have come from William Duncan's New Metlakatla on Annette Island, which was a dramatic demonstration of the results of literacy. During the winter months Mother taught all day and all evening, and then went home to her teacherage, a shack on the beach just above high tide line. She never had one moment's fear of her Tlinglit neighbours but she had a shaking terror of the white men who sometimes landed on her beach from passing boats.

Since Mother was a natural explorer and Dad a self-taught one, it is not surprising that they discovered one another. Their courtship was conducted by rowboat across the channel that separates Gravina Island from Revillagigedo Island and their marriage took place after Mother's fourth year in Alaska.

By this time Mother had taught in several different villages and was deeply involved in her work. She would have continued it but the times and my father's upbringing were so scandalized at the thought of a married woman's working that she became a dedicated homemaker instead. This was not easy since their first home was the *Mabel*, a twenty-eight-foot steam and sail sloop. My father took the mail contract for their end of the Alaskan coast and their lives became entirely waterborne. Most of their mail run was in sheltered waters but each trip they had to skirt the west coast of Prince of Wales Island, which is as exposed as the west coast of Vancouver Island and closer to the fury of Aleutian storms. My father from an inland, eastern town became a superb seaman and navigator and my mother from an inland western farm became an accomplished deckhand, quartermaster and engineer.

Within two years my parents had saved enough to have the *Tidings* built to their design and specifications. She was built in an Edmonds, Washington shipyard and they ran her up the Inside Passage and into Ketchikan harbour with a pride that was never duplicated in their lives, unless, perhaps by the births of their children. The *Tidings* was thirty-six feet long, beautiful of line and the first gasoline-powered boat in those waters. When they emigrated to Canada my parents felt misgivings about relinquishing their United States citizenship, but they felt real grief at parting with the *Tidings*.

CHAPTER 5

On the Mission House Hill

MOTHER TOOK HER FIRSTBORN home from hospital to what is known in family history as Dan's house. Dan was an enterprising Indian who had built a two-storey frame house designed on the utilitarian lines of the Hudson's Bay Company buildings rather than the rickrack architecture so popular at that time. Having finished off a few rooms and painted the front white with red trim, Dan found his funds depleted and fishing season almost a year away. He was delighted to rent his house to the young white couple who were setting up a store on the reserve. Mother was happy in Dan's house and took pleasure in ruffling curtains for the windows and planting flowers beneath them. She did have one complaint though: when the wind whistled down from the Nass Valley in winter, it found cracks in Dan's unfinished back walls and froze the diapers, freshly washed or unwashed, into ice cylinders in pails and tubs.

Dan's house was in what my father referred to as a good neighbourhood. The Methodist mission house was next door, beyond that was a residential mission school for boys, and at a discreet distance from the Boys' Home, the Crosby Girls' Home, well fenced.

The Methodist church itself formed the western boundary of this complex. It had been designed by Thomas Trounce of

Victoria and built by the Rev. Thomas Crosby and his enthu-siastic Tsimshian converts, in 1874. It was Gothic in style and buttressed and, eighty feet by sixty, it could seat eight hundred. Its spire rose one hundred and forty feet toward heaven and was made of hand-hewn and hand-fitted pieces. An important feature was that it rivalled in size and magnificence the Anglican edifice that William Duncan had built at Metlakatla, which had once been famous as the largest and finest church west of Chicago and north of San Francisco. The Tsimshian, trained in the grand manner by their potlatches, gave lavishly toward their church's building. In 1874 currency was still a novelty on the north coast; they gave blankets and furs and muskets.

When Dad first attended church there he was impressed by the lofty interior. Up and up it rose until the highest braces looked like an etched design. The choir's music rolled around up there and so did whatever heat was provided. The Natives never seemed to notice the chill that brought numbness to the white congregation just ahead of the doxology.

Dad's second Sunday in Port Simpson was a stormy one and once again his gaze ascended, this time in terror. The whole building groaned and the faraway top of the structure swayed. What distressed him most was the sight of the lamps, suspended from the ceiling, swinging like censers. Just as the long prayer reached the passionate exhortation there was a sharp report. His bowed head jerked upward but the beams above him were intact. He added a thanksgiving to the long prayer and after the service went out to inspect the founda-tions. In that rain-soaked soil cedar foundations could rot in as few as six years and these had been in place for thirty-two. On the east side of the church they had given way completely and stringers had collapsed, leaving joists without any support whatever. My father never contributed to any cause as eagerly as to the repairing of the church.

By the time I was old enough to be curled and buttoned

tightly and sent off to church with my father, repairs had brought the building under control. The temperature and the services had hardly changed at all, however.

We sat in the pew directly behind the pupils and teachers of the Crosby Girls' Home. Though the six-year-old Home girls must have had chilblains under their prickly woollen stockings, even as I had, they never scratched. And though the eighteen-year-olds had swains seated somewhere behind them, they never twitched so much as a cherry on their T. Eaton hats.

A choir was seated behind the minister. It always sang one anthem and according to Port Simpson standards sang very well indeed. (My opinion of anthems as I squirmed on the hard pew was that they were rather slow in getting to the point.) The choir by no means led the congregational singing. This was done by an important lady, widow of the chiefest of Tsimshian chiefs, one of the very first and certainly the most influential of Christianized Natives of Thomas Crosby's mission. She had taken as her own particular duty the braking of every hymn to what she considered a suitably solemn tempo. Her voice pierced and held — and held. "Onward Christian Soldiers" became a dirge and "Abide with Me" a long wail. Successive organists and ministers battled her voice but never won.

The hymns seemed always to deal with death in the last stanza. During the Tsimshian interpretation of the sermon, which often lasted longer than the sermon itself, I would leaf through the hymnal in search of one that defied this morbid tradition. My father did not sing the hymns. Though out in the boat, in a good sea with the bow slapping, he would bellow strange leftovers from his inhibited youth, in church he riveted his eyes to his hymnbook, emitting a sound of strangulation only in very loud bars and on the amens. But the psalms were another matter. Here he had an advantage over the chief's widow and he wrapped his voice around those voluptuous phrases and sent them right up to the top rafters.

The Boys' Home, at the time my parents lived near it, housed twenty-five young Tsimshian who learned something of carpentry and other basic skills as well as classroom subjects. They were taught entirely in English. Now that the Native languages have been all but lost, there is bitter criticism of this system. And yet, without the immersion method, how could Tsimshian children, who arrived without a word of English, have learned enough in a few years in the Boys' Home to supply the white men's knowledge that the villagers so earnestly sought? And though our First Nations lore does not tell us this, the great impetus toward Christianity and twentieth-century ways came no more from the missionaries than from the Indians themselves. And had you been a Tsimshian, would you not have welcomed an escape from the tyranny of the medicine man, the terrors of witchcraft, the inexorable class system, slavery and retaliatory killings?

Behind the Girls' Home fence four teachers laboured mightily to inculcate Victorian standards of morality, cleanliness and English spelling in forty-six girls of assorted ages. "Home Girls" were recognized by their starched Alice-in-Wonderland pinafores; by their correct if limited conversation: "Yes, Mrs. Young," "No, Mrs. Young"; by the wondrously fine darns in their cotton stockings and by the aura of self-conscious superiority that flickered about them as they passed "village girls" on the street. They passed in a crocodile, two by two, the smallest girls in front, the sizes carefully graduated to the tallest girls at the end, flanked and backed by teachers. None of them was ever heard to shout or seen to push, run, leap, or even deviate from the line, and these were children come straight from seashore and forest. Most of them appeared to be happy in their lives; female Natives had a long and horrifying history of docility behind them.

Every Sunday morning my father righteously attended church and my mother, a nonbeliever, just as righteously refrained from attending church. This did not impair her friendship with the mission people on the hill. They exchanged seeds and newspapers and recipes, shared gifts of venison and salmon, and rallied to one anothers' household crises such as broken clotheslines, frozen water pumps, unroofed wood-sheds, straying children and unexpected company. The mission house of those years specialized in all kinds of company. Its front door opened to admit couples for counselling, church stewards for instruction, chiefs for ceremonious visits, mischievous boys from the Home for reprimand, or the entire church choir for a party. That door opened to everyone in the white settlement, too, and to visitors from all over the coast. The bridge and engine-room staffs of the *Princess Sophia* were entertained when fog held the ship at the wharf for hours; local ladies gathered for tea; whole families from other northern missions descended for days, and children came to elaborate birthday parties. The most illustrious of all the company was the viceregal party, which arrived to grace Port Simpson with its presence for a day. The event was both an honour and a disillusionment to the eight-year-old daughter of the house who dropped by Mother's kitchen to confide, "The Duke of Connaught is handsome and the Duchess is lovely but Princess Patricia — she has darns in her stockings. My first princess and she has a darn on her heel."

It was while she lived in Dan's house that Mother was introduced to Port Simpson society. In those years, 1906-1910, several families besides those of the fort and mission lived in Simpson for the town was the centre of north coast commerce, politics and culture. The whole contingent of ladies was led by the Anglican rector's wife who resided, of course, in the Rectory and presided over her drawing room in the manner prescribed by the English novels of the day. Queen Victoria's reign had only recently ended and propriety prevailed. Over the muskeg, through the bush, raising their skirts delicately above the garbage of the reserve, gloved, hatted, and sometimes veiled, the ladies made their rounds, leaving a calling card here, sipping tea there, and on their appointed days they were "at home."

The ladies' entertaining was never casual in a place where supplies depended upon infrequent steamship arrivals and steamship arrivals depended upon weather, the Skeena cannery pack, a logging camp opening far down the coast, or any of a dozen vagaries of northern life. If the sugar was short-shipped the ladies served oatcakes and if the butter arrived rancid they served bread and cheese, that is, if the yeast held out. There was never fresh meat except for venison in season or a dubious roast of porcupine or bear. Other than the staple oranges, lemons, apples, potatoes and onions, fresh fruit and vegetables were rare and wondrous. Generations of children grew up without ever tasting fresh milk because cattle brought in immediately foundered in the muskeg.

Port Simpson families were not altogether deprived, however. They enjoyed delicacies that the modern gourmet might envy. The Natives were their teachers in good eating and salmon became the mainstay of their diets. A salmon, up to about fifteen pounds, cost twenty-five cents and that price remained unchanged for most of my childhood. The most desirable salmon to those connoisseurs was a white spring and any salmon whose flesh was not still quivering was regarded as not strictly fresh. There was rejoicing when the oolichans came into the Nass River in March. They were fished through the ice or between the ice floes and reached us springy and glittering and crammed with their almost nutty flavour. Smoked oolichans were available all year round. Hard and dark and oily, they looked repulsive to the novice but they became almost addictive after one greasy session on the kitchen table. Crabs and clams loitered about all the beaches, waiting to be caught or dug.

Port Simpson's spring festival was not of cherry blossoms but of herring eggs. The Tsimshian seemed to relish fish eggs above all other foods and the non-Native village partook with mixed reactions. One day the water over a whole bay would be in gentle, silver turmoil while above it clouds of seagulls screamed their greed. The herring came into the bay in front of the town at recess time one year. Every last school child rushed to the beach to push spruce boughs or planks or kelp out from shore. The teacher rang the end-of-recess bell, and rang and rang while children pulled out their laden boughs, munched and waded. Not one of us felt the slightest guilt — surely the teacher knew the herring had spawned. Fish eggs were eaten fresh, cooked or dried. Those dried on seaweed were considered most desirable; they could be popped into the mouth container and all. Seaweed for food was harvested carefully. Dundas Island was said to have the best. The Natives usually dried it across boards nailed to uprights. They stored it in boxes so that it came out in compressed blocks from which one pulled a leaf to chew. It was an uncomfortable child who pulled too large a piece for, as it was reconstituted in the mouth, it grew and grew. Seaweed was an acquired taste.

Oylets, on the other hand, were popular with everyone. They are the tender, young shoots that salmonberry and raspberry canes thrust upward in early summer. They were a Tsimshian snack food to be peeled and eaten as one came upon them — not too small, mind, or they would have little flavour; not too large or they would be woody.

There were numerous other foods common to the coastal peoples that most of the white community tried and rejected, among them octopus, salmon heads, Hudson's Bay tea (known elsewhere as Labrador tea), the rice-like corms of the chocolate lily and sopalalie berries dried and beaten by hand in water till they made a fine froth, unfortunately bitter to European tastes. Indian rhubarb, called cow parsnip in other parts, was irresistible to Native children who ate it until their mouths broke out in sores and then continued to eat it.

In Dan's house, Mother balanced such indigenous ways and Port Simpson society but she never did get around to having calling cards printed. Instead she engaged Martha, a prize graduate of the Girls' Home, to take care of the baby, Ruth, in the afternoons, and escaped to the store where her help was sorely needed. As she took more responsibility in the business and her life was further complicated by my arrival, the family solved some major problems by moving into a house in the very centre of the reserve, within waving distance of the store. This accounts for my earliest memories being well wrapped in the smell of drying salmon.

CHAPTER 6

Opposite the Bandstand

THE NEW FAMILY HOME stood tall on one corner of the village square, which was not really square but oblong, being a substantial widening in a main road. Chief Swanson's house stood noticeably taller across a side street.

Our windows looked out upon the bandstand. It was as light and graceful as "The Waltz of the Flowers" that issued from it on occasion. In those years before the first war, it was often filled with bandsmen and music. The Port Simpson Band was an amazement to visitors. It played with both spirit and precision. Few years had intervened between blankets and band uniforms and many Tsimshians had learned to read difficult classical music before they learned to read more than basic English. Their ancestral music and dances led them into the works of Haydn and Mozart as naturally as a river falls into the sea. It was a marching band in red and gold, much gold, and kept a busy schedule during the winter months. It escorted bridal processions and funeral processions, welcomed boatloads of visitors from neighbouring villages, accompanied similar junkets from Simpson, played for special events, of which there were many, and gave concerts.

The second most interesting building on our road was the firehall. It hauled its front end out onto the square while its rear sprawled along the shoreline. It was ugly and its glory was in the past but I never passed it without pausing, in hope and dread, to put my ear to the black space that gaped between its double doors. In the late 1800s it had been headquarters for a sixty-man fire brigade, resplendent in navy pants and scarlet tunics. A brass band had practised all day inside its walls while a rival band practised all day inside the Rifle Company's hall. By 1913 it was dark and empty, except for a few axes and buckets and coils of rope. Still, Rosie had heard the dance of the dead there.

Rosie, wiry and excitable and voluble, an atypical Tsimshian, often appeared at our kitchen door with a salmon for sale. One evening she came just as Mother was lighting the lamps.

"Rosie, you're all out of breath and you're shaking. Are you sick?"

"No, Mrs. Young, I scare. I just come past the firehall and I scare."

"What scared you?"

"I walking past and I hear sounds in the firehall. I look in crack but all dark in there. But sounds very loud, drum sounds and singing the old song, and rattle, and stamp, stamp, stamp. It was the dead people — dead long, long time — doing their dance. My grandmother tell me sometime they come on a beach and dance but they never come to firehall before. I don't know what it mean. I scare for this."

Who cared if the firehall was ugly?

The firehall faced the wide entrance to the bridge. Five hundred feet of piles and planks and railings, the bridge traversed the sandbar that joined the Island to the mainland at low tide. On one side, storefronts lined a third of its length, while on the other side there was a small landing stage for boats. That was where one stood to look far down the channel, southward, when a storm was blowing and some boat was long overdue from Prince Rupert.

My father's store stood first in the line of bridge buildings. The other stores were owned by Natives and were operated casually: when they contained some stock, when their owners were not elsewhere, and when there was nothing more pressing going on in the village. One of them survived on this basis for my entire life in Simpson and for it I felt a distinct affection. It carried violet gum and, though there was no currency smaller than a nickel in Port Simpson, penny candies. "Coloured plaster of Paris," my father snorted, regarding these treasures.

Dad's store was prosaic by comparison. It was there because the Hudson's Bay Company was unwilling or unable to adjust from the molasses-rice-and-blanket trade to the revolution taking place in the Tsimshian way of life. The coastal peoples were leaping headlong into our culture and Dad was equipping them with the most modern materials he could procure. Barrels and barrels of dishes he brought in, and there was always demand for more. Hardware, particularly the more specialized tools such as hacksaws and drills, crossed the counter straight from the packing case. The ribbon and Valenciennes lace that Mother measured off would have totalled a few miles. When a modern Tsimshian deplores the passing of his own culture, as we do also, he needs the missing history to show him his people's surge to overtake our civilization. It came like a tidal wave and it swept away old attitudes and arts, customs and crafts, beliefs and behaviour, more relentlessly than did the lesser tides of government and missions.

My father's business revolved around boat days. All boat days brought activity and excitement and tantalizing glimpses of the elsewhere world, but one, out of our pre-1915 years on the reserve, still blazes away in my mind. Cannery season was ending. Some of the Natives had returned to the village, eager to spend their summer's pay. Others would not be back for a week or more. After lunch, Dad left the house hurriedly, because he was shipping oil drums and had to roll them to the wharf. He was hardly out the door when Mother called to Ruth, "Bring me the plums from the pantry. They won't keep till tomorrow. I've got to make the jam before boat time."

"When's the boat due?" asked Ruth.

"According to the tides, she'll be working the Skeena on the way north this trip. Evening, I guess."

Mother filled the kitchen with jars and utensils and steam and good odours. Her jamming procedures were at their climax when outside our window the voices of village boys rose in that cry that spun the town into action, "Steambo-o-at."

Mother's large spoon, sheeting red syrup above the preserving kettle, dropped into the jam. In one continuous motion she shoved the kettle to the back of the stove, peeled off her apron and propelled Ruth and me out the door. We all ran in the direction of the store.

Dad was waiting for us, his hat on his head, a sheaf of papers under his arm. "You can finish Jeffrey's order, all but the copper paint. That'll be in on the boat," and he was off to the wharf to check his incoming freight.

When the steamer arrived the white people gravitated to the dock but the Natives made their way to the store to savour the excitement and assess the new stock. Though the store filled rapidly the crowd was quiet and unhurried. Mother moved from counter to counter, weighing candies on the small scale, potatoes on the large scale, pumping coal oil out of a drum, counting buttons out of a box.

The *Princess May* whistled in, and Ruth and I dashed to the warehouse window to watch her dock. The *May* had cranky steering gear and docked awkwardly; she had once sliced right through one end of the wharf. Her landings were suspenseful.

The *May* had been tied up perhaps half an hour when I perceived, bearing down upon the store, that phenomenon of summer boat days, a party of tourists. There were six in the group. I knew they were tourists by their clothing. The men's suits were of a cut not yet seen in Port Simpson and the women's frocks were sheer and fluttery and matched their hats and parasols. Travelling coast people simply did not look like that. The tourists sailed into the store with exclamations of surprise, "Look at this. Why, it's just like an ordinary store."

One gentleman had a pencil and notebook. "Large stock, clean and well laid out," he muttered as he wrote. A woman approached the counter where Mother was measuring off lamp wicking for Sarah Adams.

She stared and suddenly said, "You're not Indian at all, are you?"

Mother murmured to Sarah, by way of apology, "Pelton wawa," (foolish talk), and Sarah giggled with her shoulders.

The woman persisted, "My, you must find it interesting here. We've seen so many queer things already. There are lots of houses without any people in them, aren't there?"

Mother, totalling Sarah's bill, said, "Away at the canneries."

"We came to one house that looked really nice. We're interested in how Indians live, you know, so we knocked on the door. There didn't seem to be anyone home and the back door wasn't locked so we opened it. We're very interested, you know. And would you believe, those strange people had gone away — to the canneries, you say — and left a pot of jam on the range?"

Blue fire shot across the counter from Mother's eyes. "Two dollars and seventy-five cents," she said to Sarah.

One of the tourist gentlemen said, "But where are their teepees?"

The *May's* whistle blasted out a warning and the sightseers were gone. Dad arrived soon after, pushing a two-wheeled cart with a load of boxes and sacks. Jack, the store's handyman, followed with another cart of heavy freight. He would make many such trips before boat day was over.

Ruth and I sat very quietly on nail kegs, out of the way, so that we would not be sent upstairs. (The fur chest was upstairs and in the heat of summer its padlock did not confine the odour of the bearskins.) Noises erupted all about us; nails screamed as Dad opened wooden crates; Mother's voice called to Jack in the warehouse; the hand truck rumbled back and forth and the even tones of many Tsimshian conversations made a humming background to everything. And then, from outside, came another sound and all the store noises were cut off as though a conductor had brought his baton down sharply. It was the clamour of the firebell. Through the show windows we could see it, at the top of its log tower across the street, tossing like something gone mad. The store was empty in seconds. Mother grabbed a pile of galvanized buckets and ran, the buckets still jammed together. Dad grabbed the heavy fire extinguisher and ran. They joined the general surge across the bridge and Ruth and I followed until we came upon a wall of people standing almost motionless.

Beyond and above this wall flames shot into the sky and sometimes a burst of sparks. Below us on the beach the line of bucket passers was in formation, moving with the rhythm that had once impelled war canoes. Momentarily the wind shifted and smoke enveloped us so that we coughed and gasped and covered our eyes. The people were silent except for an occasional shout from a firefighter and a few low Tsimshian phrases, but waves of dread and despair flowed through the crowd, even to two little white girls shivering at the farthest edge.

At last there came a crunching sound, followed by a sigh from the crowd. Then the wall of people began to show gaps and Ruth darted forward. "It was Billy's house," she said over her shoulder and there were tears in her voice. Of all the rotund, smiling, swaggering, shy little Native boys, Billy was our family's favourite. A young woman turned round to say to Ruth, "Not bad now. Isaak get Billy and Joe out before the roof go down."

Mother had to wake me to take me to bed at the end of that boat day. I said goodnight to Dad deep in his armchair, sorting out a week's Vancouver newspapers so that he wouldn't read Friday before Wednesday. Mother led me upstairs, one hand holding mine, the other in her apron pocket fondling her letters from Oregon. In later years I, too, learned to refer to boat day as mail day.

Life on the reserve changed abruptly for me when Ruth started school. I stood at our side gate and watched the children from Chief Swanson's house at play. They were sons and daughters, nephews and nieces, grandchildren and adopted children and friends. Esther looked after them all. They regarded me with little interest and though sometimes I knew they were talking about me they never approached. Esther in her thirteen-year-old maturity, was different; to her I was another little girl who needed her ministrations. She offered me jelly beans from her pocket, retied my shoelace, drove off the horseflies that harassed me, and hauled me out of the deep, wet ditch when I slid into it. Sometimes she sat beside me, leaning against our fence, and plucked long dry grasses to weave into play baskets for me. The motion of her fingers held me spellbound — Native women's hands often seem more expressive of themselves than their faces. She tried to teach me a little Tsimshian but when it became apparent that I would never master the basic "kg" consonant that was formed somewhere near the bronchial tubes and rose deliberately to be emitted in a slight explosion she smiled her rare, serene smile and said, "I guess we talk English."

It was Esther who saved me from the reserve dogs. They came in all dog sizes and colours and combinations of breed and they came in packs. What they had in common was hunger, neglect and hostility toward the human race. They learned early in my life that I was the most terrified white child on the Tsimshian Peninsula. It seemed that the moment our gate clicked behind me they converged from all parts of the village and advanced upon me, heads low, barking their red-eyed hate. Esther turned me round to face the dogs and taught me to glare and stamp my foot and bark "unduh" (go away) right back at them. Miraculously they gave ground and behaved as though they had just happened by. The word *unduh* has not been of much use to me since I left Port Simpson but turning to face my fears is still my best defence. Thanks, Esther.

CHAPTER 7

On the Fort Site

I WAS SNATCHED AWAY from Esther and the bandstand when I was in my fifth year. The family walked to its new home in five minutes but I felt uprooted because the house was on the *white* side of the street that separated the two communities. We moved as the result of a fire.

The Hudson's Bay post burned to the ground in 1914. The fire levelled even the haughty old gateposts. It left a great gash of an excavation that had been the store cellar, some rock piles that had been chimneys, and a depth of ashes everywhere. A row of cottonwood trees on the west boundary survived, and the curlicued iron letter press that had been obsolete and in everyone's way for years but was too heavy to move.

The fire was the last in a series of indications that the town had reached a turning point in time. Prince Rupert, instead of Port Simpson, had been selected as the terminus of the Grand Trunk Pacific Railway and blasting powder was shaping it into the new centre of north coast life. Furs were no longer abundant; sea otters were practically extinct, fur seals no longer to be seen and beavers strictly protected by law. The less valuable skins were still to be had for the trapping but fewer and fewer Natives trapped. They found trapping and the twentieth century incompatible. The Hudson's Bay

Company did not rebuild.

Port Simpson people had hardly become accustomed to the burned scar in the heart of their town when Dad signed a sort of caretaker lease covering the Hudson's Bay property for ninety-nine years. He engaged a young Tsimshian carpenter and set about building what was considered a modern 1915 store. The building proceeded with Tsimshian deliberateness and stopped completely for fishing season, hunting season, and the days following feasts. Dad moved his stock into the skeleton store and paced. By the winter of 1916 it was almost finished and Dad was drawing plans for a dwelling that would extend it to the cottonwoods and would form a second storey. Meanwhile the family lived in a house that adjoined the Hudson's Bay lands. It was nearly two years before we moved into our new, unfinished rooms to live to the sounds of sawing and hammering that might cease at any moment for a day or a month or a season. The plans and the carpentry did not always jibe so there were a few odd nooks that seemed to be architectural leftovers and were never finished.

I gave scarcely a thought to my parents' building frustrations for I had discovered a fascinating new world. Because the Hudson's Bay acres sprawled out and back from the waterfront where the store stood, my family had no very close human neighbours. We had some extraordinary inanimate neighbours, however, most of them ghostly.

The nearest house along the road was empty. In its lean-to there was a full-scale Japanese bath sunk five feet into the ground and tightly lined with boards all greyed by water. This had been the house of Sako, the Japanese boatbuilder, until a prop collapsed and he died under the hull of a new troller. At his funeral, rice was placed on his grave, and lights, and each guest received a white silk handkerchief.

Within shouting distance of the store stood the Hotel Northern, as solid as the rock ledge that footed its pilings and only slightly more weatherworn than when Mother first saw it. High tide sucked and sighed just below its floor. Having been recently vacated by its last operators, it was empty, too, except for the memories it housed of the turn-of-the-century riverboating years. At that time the Hudson's Bay Company operated steamers on the Stikine and Skeena and Port Simpson was a lively transshipment centre. Some said the hotel housed an active ghost as well. In an upstairs room, one of its original owners had blown his brains out, for love of a Tsimshian girl who spurned him. When the building reverted to the Hudson's Bay Dad had to maintain it but he could never adapt it to his business. He did make some use of it for storing shipments of lumber and heavy goods and for the coffins that were an all-too-necessary part of his stock. They did not improve the atmosphere of the hotel for my small brother, who dreaded Dad's "Time to take a load of pop empties to the hotel, Loyal." He and his fox terrier and the sack of bottles would stand for a long time on the hotel verandah before he would unlock the door and push it open a crack. Then he would try to persuade the dog to enter ahead of him. Tim went out of his way to tackle German police dogs but, faced with the hotel's interior, his neck hairs bristled, he emitted an unearthly whine and backed off. Sometimes it took Loyal and Tim an hour to get the bottles into the storeroom and I never offered to help.

Two of our neighbours were retired riverboats. The *Tahltan* was beached just across the road from our living room windows. When the short Stikine tide of gold and adventure ran out, it left her high and dry. The *Tahltan*'s hull was barge-like, being square, bow and stern, and flat-bottomed. There was not much romance left to her, in fact we played anti-I-over across her peeling cabin. But the *Port Simpson* was different; we would not have thrown a ball over her upper works even if we could have. She had been winched up on ways into a cut in the hillside, her stern wheel overhanging the road.

There she towered, still white and mahogany and queen of the fleet. In 1908 she had been launched from a Victoria shipyard to add a touch of elegance to the rambunctious steamboating on the Skeena. In 1912 she lined her way through the canyon for the last time. The new railway had put an end to the river run.

The fort site abounded in playplaces. There was a fifteen-foot platform that had been layered, flat stone upon flat stone, so carefully that it had survived the fire though the clay mortar had been burned out and the stones themselves had been left with an unnatural asperity to small fingers, and shattered if dropped. It was my theatre, my playhouse and my refuge. Once my parents came upon me there as I mixed a skunk cabbage leaf salad. Mother sniffed and asked, *"What* are you playing with?"

My father answered, "She's playing with history," and gave that old hearth a loving kick.

In fact, most of my play was with history, though Ruth and I had no intention of getting involved with history on the day that we reluctantly set out to pick berries.

CHAPTER 8

The Hudson's Bay Garden

MOTHER HUNG SMALL LARD pails around two stiffly protesting necks. "Now," she said with satisfaction, "those are nearly as good as the baskets the Indian girls wear for berry-picking. You'll have to stand on your heads to spill your berries."

Ruth and I looked wistfully toward Finlayson Island where we had planned to row that afternoon, then turned in the opposite direction. We were only a short distance beyond the old excavation where a tangle of vegetation pushed on to the roadside when Ruth asked, "Are those raspberries?" as she poked an arm into the thicket. They were. Ruth broke through at breast height while I wiggled in along the ground. Inside the jungle, a raspberry patch was fighting and winning a territorial war against salmonberry, thimbleberry, alder, some ancient trees that might have been apple, salal, grass and weeds that grew in mats. The berries were typical, voluptuous Port Simpson raspberries. We picked in high glee; we would have our tins full in no time and then we would get out in the boat. But while the raspberry canes emerged from their enemies only slightly twisted and bent, we fared worse. By the time our cans had begun to pull slightly on our necks, our arms and faces were scratched, Ruth's skirt was torn and one of my black stockings was without a knee.

"Perhaps we'd better stop," I called to Ruth who was charging on ahead, on the other side of the green wall that faced me.

"Not until we see how far this berry patch goes."

"My hair ribbon's gone. My face hurts and I'm hot."

"Well, look for a place to sit down."

I had not seen a clear spot big enough to sit down upon since we left the road, but now I began to scrutinize the ground. Surprisingly, there was a mossy hummock under one of those dead apple trees. I broke off a couple of branches that snapped like spaghetti and eased myself into the resulting dark hole. I began to feel better immediately and my hands dug into the deep, damp moss with appreciation. They encountered an interesting piece of wood, which I rubbed on my dress and studied. Then I looked all about my comfortable seat.

"Ruth, I think I'm sitting on a grave."

Through the bush came back the answer, "That's not nice. Get off it this minute."

Ruth was intrigued enough to come crashing back to me. I had cleared some of the weeds from my mound. Its shape and size were unmistakable. Around its perimeter, deep in the growth, were glimpses of white. When we dug for them they were revealed as whitewashed fence pickets. There was not much whitewash and not much picket left, to most of them, but they, too, were unmistakable. We attacked a stand of alder shoots growing up through the lower branches of the old apple tree and a few feet into it came upon a square whitewashed post. The alders had uprooted it and then, as though they were sorry, supported it in an almost upright position. My cleaned piece of wood fitted a notch in the post. I handed it to Ruth. Its carved letters read, "Lieut. AE Simpson, R.N."

We would have started then and there to tell Dad about our discovery, had I not tripped over an entanglement of roots and fallen headlong into a patch of salal. As I struggled out of the crushed leaves and stems, Ruth spied in the wreckage another wooden plaque. This one was smaller, but had been smoothed and carved in the same manner as the first. It bore only the words, "Infant Manson." Silently Ruth and I tore at bushes and weeds until a tiny mounded grave took shape. It lay directly in line with Captain Simpson's, and hardly three feet from it. I glanced at Ruth. She was kneeling, having been pulling grass, but she was not getting up. She was just looking at that oval bit of ground. Then I realized that I, too, was kneeling.

What Ruth and I did not know that summer's day was that one of us must have been kneeling on a second baby's grave, dug on the same day as the two we saw. When Captain Simpson's remains were disinterred at Fort Simpson, Nass, so also were those of two fort babies for reburial close to their own kind. Nor did we realize that we were picking berries in a graveyard that contained at the very least a score of similar miniature graves and as many more full-sized ones. No one in the Simpson of our day seemed to know that this wild thicket concealed the plot that for thirty-one years received the fort's dead, as well as the remains of other white people who met death in that region, and of chiefs and tribes people of high rank and those held in special regard by the Hudson's Bay people. The men of the fort made the coffins and dug the graves. The Natives seemed to accept burial as quite fitting though they had other customs concerning disposal of the dead. One was to cremate the body and later, sometimes much later, bury the bones and ashes, or place them in boxes to be attached to trees in the woods. Another, thought to have been reserved for people of the highest rank, was to place the body in the fetal position in a square cedar chest and consign the chest to a cave. There was such a cave on Birnie Island. Those corpses were mummified. Whether this came about by some forgotten Native process or by the effects of the limestone cave was always a subject for dispute at Port Simpson. By the time I was old enough to be allowed to scramble to the cave mouth, the boxes and the mummies had been shamefully vandalized by white people. No Tsimshian would ever have touched them; they were protected by a shaman's fierce curse.

Nobody really planned the first cemetery. It grew around Captain Simpson's grave as naturally as the garden grew in that bit of loamy ground. The new fort was only five months old when a Native girl who had been with Dr. Kennedy's family for three years, died. That same month the young son of a French-Canadian workman died. These deaths were only the beginning of the tragedy of the fort children. All over the nineteenth-century world infant mortality was high, but it seems that at Fort Simpson conditions were particularly discouraging to life after birth. The little survivors found other barriers to growing up, a major one being European childhood diseases to which they had no immunity. And so the rows of small graves in the garden grew and grew.

Two of the men from the Sandwich Islands were buried in the cemetery with apple trees instead of palms to wave over them. Mr. Gaskill, an English gentleman who had taken passage on the *Pandora*, apparently for the sake of his health, came to the end of his journey there. The half-Native wife of Captain Swanson gave birth to twins but died on Christmas Eve. Her body was not interred until nearly a month later; perhaps, since it was winter, it seemed possible to await the Captain's return on the spring trip of the supply ship. The Native wife of a French-Canadian workman was buried there, and several women of the Tsimshian encampment. One was called "Legaic's old wife" (chiefs often had a variety of wives, simultaneously). She had succumbed to smallpox in four days. Then there were the murdered chiefs.

Coaguele was the first. He was from a neighbouring area and was frequently a messenger for the fort people and always a friend. It was Coaguele who found the bitch and pups at the wreck of Fort Simpson (Nass) and delivered them by canoe to the new fort. Two years later a canoe of young Tsimshian from a Skeena tribe arrived at Fort Simpson with the news that their chief, Nashot, had died of smallpox. He was supposed to have contracted it from a member of Coaguele's tribe. That night the young men plied Coaguele and his companion with rum and then shot them. Another chief, Saloway, died with more justice but no less violence. He had killed a Stikine in a quarrel. The Stikine, of course, would have to kill someone of equal rank in Saloway's tribe. Saloway's brother, the likeliest victim, relieved the tension and saved his own skin by shooting Saloway. Haiash, a Haida chief, died for a similar reason. He was shot by a fellow Haida chief to atone for the death they had jointly dealt out to a Tsimshian chief's brother. If this sounds complicated and gruesome today, you can be sure it was even more complicated and gruesome in 1856. Out of their turbulence, all these people came to rest in the comparative calm of the Company vegetable garden.

The three disinterred bodies that began the Fort Simpson cemetery were not the only ones to enter it. Actually, it was a disinterred body that closed it. By 1864 the fort journal no longer spoke of burying the dead in the garden but now spoke of "sowing seeds in the graveyard" and there was barely room for seeds. In April 1865, a message came from Father Duncan at Metlakatla, requesting the interment of a body at Fort Simpson. After laying one of his flock to rest with solemn Anglican rites, he had been shocked to find that the burial had come undone. Mourning friends had sought consolation in rum and had become so consoled that they wished to share the source of their good feelings with their deceased fellow. They did. But Mr. Duncan, who seemed like stone against the savagery he had challenged, was shaken by this incident and dispatched the corpse to Fort Simpson. There was another death at this time, and those two coffins were the last to be squeezed into the pleasant little apple-tree cemetery.

Over the years, Alexis and Antoine had made many coffins and dug many graves. By 1865 these two survivors of the old voyageur days formed a little unit among the men, usually working together on their jobs. On a day in May, Alexis died. His grave had the distinction of being the first in the new burial ground adjoining the garden but outside it. Antoine built a small picket fence around it.

Whether or not it was a mark of progress, some time in the latter 1800s Port Simpson's white population ceased to commit its dead to the plot next to the vegetable garden and began to lay them away in a churchyard. The Anglican church was built on a bluff well behind the fort. It was a typical English village church in a typical British Columbia north coast setting. The two styles blended admirably; long after the walls of the church had lost their alignment it gazed out of its bower of second growth, like the English gentlewoman of literature, composed and serene. But the churchyard — in my mind ancient savagery lurked there.

The Anglican funerals followed a pattern: the church bell tolled; the procession mounted the wide steps that led to the top of the bluff; the service was read in the church and then, on the leeward side of the hill among scattered tombstones, another grave was covered. There was a surprising number of graves for the size of our town. Much of the population of the white village was descended from the mixed blood of the early fort days and these people were apt to retain the indigenous susceptibility to tuberculosis.

Some time in the 1860s the slow swirl of Hudson's Bay servants from fort to fort brought a Norwegian blacksmith to Fort Simpson. In his latter years there he had a great distinction — he was the only man who won outright praise in the Fort Simpson journals. Besides, his trade he could handle any job in the fort and do it well. He was apparently a man of intelligence and integrity. His Native wife bore him several children and most of them lived. Hans must have chosen his wife as well as he did everything else, for his children grew into dependable people, respected by both the Native and white communities. One son married a girl from an Interior fort, also of mixed blood. Once again the family discernment was infallible. This was a woman of gentle and refined character. She chose to favour the Native half of her heritage, a fact she proclaimed by wearing the black silk head handkerchief and shawl, the costume of Native women, well into the 1920s. Hans' son worked at the post until the Company left Port Simpson. On the highest hill overlooking the town and harbour, he built a home (we used to speculate on whether his house really did have twenty rooms) and he and his wife filled it with happy, healthy children. But when the oldest boy was in his teens he died a lingering, consumptive death and was laid in the Anglican churchyard. As the attractive daughters reached womanhood they followed. It was the fourth of these funerals I attended, for Lizzie had been a schoolmate of mine, though a senior while I was still in the primary class. It was Lizzie who chose me for her team in the game Run Sheep Run, though I was obviously a detriment.

The funeral service did not disturb me; it was almost a year since I had seen Lizzie and in no way could I associate her with the grey-covered casket. At the graveside the coffin was lowered out of my sight. Chilling as a loon's call, a cry out of the aboriginal past cut through the Anglican words and fell among us. On the edge of the grave there were struggling figures. They were holding Lizzie's mother who was straining toward the open grave.

Afterwards Mother tried to reassure me: it was the old Native way, a sort of playacting that relieved grief, something like the paid wailing that we understood. But I saw that mother's face and her eyes. She would have jumped.

Port Simpson was well segregated in death. The Tsimshian

had their own graveyard at the extreme opposite edge of town, on the seaward end of Rose Island. Evergreens encircled it and isolated it completely from the village. The paths between all but the newest graves were white with crushed clamshells, and standing companionably about were upright, granite tombstones in all shades of grey and one dark shade of pink. The older ones were not quite upright and their inscriptions were difficult to read through the moss and discoloration. The others made interesting reading since the custom of inscribing last words prevailed. Apparently no one had been allowed to die in silence and even the stone for a six-month-old infant bore such a pious message as, "I go to be with God."

We saw only the cemetery where a Methodist missionary conducted a Christian burial, but, when we lived on the reserve, we knew that after dark that same cemetery became the place where Tsimshian spirits were sent on their way with what they would require. Sometimes lights flickered here and there and a lantern burned all night on the new grave, while a fire flared on the beach, turning the deceased's possessions into smoke that could accompany his spirit. One night, from our house near the bandstand, we listened to wheelbarrows trundling toward such a fire and watched the silhouettes that moved in and out of its glow. A visiting mission lady sighed and said, "Such a dreadful pagan custom."

"Such an excellent custom for TB-ridden people," said my mother.

Not all possessions were burned. Sometimes special tools or trinkets or toys were placed inside the coffin. And sometimes a saucepan, or a cup, a teddy bear, or a jackknife would be seen beside a new grave. No one, white or indigenous, has ever been able to make me understand the inconsistencies of the Tsimshian beliefs concerning death; but then, no one has been able to make me understand the inconsistencies of the Christian beliefs concerning death.

Though the Native graveyard was always of shuddering interest to me, it was the drama in the tall dark trees enclosing it that drew me to the window each day as the afternoon sun headed for the horizon. Elsie, Mother's Tsimshian helper, explained it to Ruth and me. Mother was working at the store. Elsie had just given us a snack of bread and jam and stood looking out the bay window.

"Why do you always look out the window at this time, Elsie?" Ruth asked.

"I watch the dead people," said Elsie.

Ruth and I, bread in hand, were at the window before Elsie had time to turn her head.

"Where?"

"The trees around the graveyard. The crows are the dead people. Look at them all. They're mad today. Somebody in the village has done a bad thing and they're mad."

Hundreds of crows filled the circle of treetops. And they *were* angry. They rasped out their fury and beat their wings and darted back and forth. Next day Ruth and I were at the window ahead of Elsie.

"They have a meeting today," said Elsie.

The meeting was quiet and orderly. One by one crows spoke and the others swayed silently on top branches.

"They say what Tsimshian people should do," Elsie said.

Some days the crows broke up into small discussion groups and some days they seemed to be devoting themselves to merrymaking. "The dead people are very happy with us," was Elsie's comment on such a day.

"Where do the dead people go when they aren't at the graveyard?" Ruth asked.

"You see crows all over."

"But they aren't dead people, are they?"

"Sure. My cousin was getting wood down near Lacoo. A crow came to him and told him, 'Go home. Go home.' He jumped in his boat and rowed home as fast as he could. And when he got there his mother was dying. He just had time to speak to her. That crow was his uncle that died long time ago."

About 1930 the crows' graveyard was entirely filled. Then the Tsimshian cleared an area on Finlayson Island and made new clamshell paths. Instead of crossing the bridge, the funeral processions crossed the channel and, as the gas boats chugged away in a sweeping curve, there was a feeling of harmony about the seaborne farewell to a seaborne life.

On its route from church to embarkation, the long funeral cortege undulated noticeably as it neared the wharf approach. Here each person was forced to step over a protrusion in the road. It was the nub of a three-foot kingpost that had once marked the northwest corner of the stockade. Cross-grained and rounded, its edges worn level with the road, it had defied whatever force took down its section of posts, and the fire, and it continued to defy the weather and Simpson's foot traffic. In my day it was the only reminder of the stockades and of their posts, which Hudson's Bay men called pickets.

PART III

"Rain. Employed as Usual"

CHAPTER 9

Pickets and Other Logs

PICKETS WERE THE FIRST concern of the blacksmith's axes and a prime concern of all Fort Simpson's personnel until the stockades were abandoned in the latter 1800s. You might think that when squared logs up to two feet across were planted in the earth, the side of one pegged to the side of the next, and were reinforced with crosspieces and braced, they would be permanent. But no, those huge stockade pieces were as impermanent as willow wands in the face of their enemies. The walls of Jericho won everlasting fame because they tumbled once, but the stockades of Fort Simpson were in a constant state of tumbling.

The most insidious enemy of the pickets was rain. In Port Simpson, rain not only "falls upon the place beneath," it also washes over the ground and settles in a quagmire under the ground. In the low-lying areas of the fort, the footings of posts could rot in two years, toppling their twenty feet of solid height.

Storms, vicious enough to flatten a section of pickets, occurred indiscriminately throughout the year but the extreme tides that came ravening ashore belonged to the equinoxes. When they were blown inland by gales, they lashed at the stockades, hurling pickets and crosspieces out to sea.

The Natives stole the squared logs regularly. They needed them for building purposes and, more urgently, for firewood. They had little sense of future and, other than storing food, no instinct whatever for preparing for the winter. Even in my day, no one went out from the village for wood until the weather turned unbearably cold. Then, what they brought back was green and watersoaked and produced only smoke when it could be induced to burn at all. Naturally they regarded the Hudson's Bay stockade and garden fence (built of only slightly shorter pickets) as the Great Spirit's answer to their cold misery. During the summer they had no need to steal the pickets. Then they merely pushed them down so they could gain entry to the garden to dig Hudson's Bay potatoes, which the Great Spirit had also supplied against their hunger. They were adept at grabbing seagull eggs from the nest and making off before the gull mother could attack, so it is no wonder that their raids on the pickets were so successful. Hardly had a fence been completed around the first garden patch when Mr. Work wrote, January 16, 1836, "… commenced getting short Pickets & ribbons to enclose our Potato field as we find we are not able to keep the cedar fencing from being destroyed and burnt by the Indians." The change made little difference to the Natives and for the next twenty-two years a succession of journal keepers wrote exasperated notes concerning their losses.

Then Mr. McNeill, the Resourceful, commented, "Indians stealing pickets, say fifteen per day," and accepted the challenge. He hired two Tsimshian watchmen to be responsible for the pickets. The scheme worked as efficiently as most McNeill devices. The following January he recorded, "We have not as yet lost *one* garden picket. All former winters from 200 to 300 were stolen."

Perhaps Hamilton Moffatt, the factor who followed him, did not approve his tactics. At any rate Mr. Moffatt wrote in an 1861 letter, "Seven hundred pickets have been torn down and

stolen beside other little injuries too numerous to mention."
After a lapse, the tribes had returned to their picket operations.

No matter how the Company personnel battled to keep
their stockade intact, there was always the element of the
unforeseen; for instance, one winter night a large tree demolished a section of garden pickets by falling upon it, and on a
June day in 1852 a fire that started in the smokehouse burned
down fifty feet of stockade. And so the men went logging.

Logging was a home-based operation in the earliest days of
the fort. Considering the one thousand fifty pickets, in addition
to the logs for building that were cut in the first few weeks, it
is not surprising to find the picket cutters moving farther and
farther away from the fort. They set out by canoe with axes
freshly sharpened, provisions, usually for a week, and precious
little else by way of equipment. On a long operation their families went, too. Once, a factor inspecting the logging site at the
end of the first day was indignant to find that his men had
squandered part of the day in setting up shelters for themselves
— this was in winter. Other officers, though timing their expeditions no more humanely, showed a little more feeling for
their men. During the November storms of 1839, while eight
of his hands were putting together a raft on Finlayson Island,
Dr. Kennedy wrote "... have for these three days past sent them
a Glass of Rum each which I doubt not is very acceptable to the
poor fellows as they are in the water all Day."

At the end of each week the foreman returned for a fresh
supply of provisions, and, as the work neared completion, for
lines for the lashings of the raft. The men themselves were the
engines that dragged and carried the logs to the water's edge.
Then when the tide floated them they waded in to build the
raft, a job that often stretched over agonizing days of wet
numbness.

Once secure — and the workmen did build securely, for
only once was a breakup reported — the raft set off for home.

There were three possible sources of power: canoes to tow it, great sweeps fashioned from logs to propel it, and sail. Rafts varied in size from one made up of thirty posts to one which was one hundred twenty by seventy feet (larger than many city lots) and two tiers deep. That raft was composed of firewood, which one fort workman and forty Tsimshian had cut and rafted home in thirteen days. Some time about 1841, the Company began to send out large parties of Natives with a few of their men and occasionally the Tsimshian ran a logging show of their own, having first helped to create the demand, no doubt. In one three-day period they delivered thirty-six hundred pickets. Their pay was "2 Leaves Tobacco or 2 balls [ammunition] per picket, a gill of cannon Powder for every 10, a pint mixed Rum for every 20 or a 1/2 ounce of Chinese vermilion for every ten."

The Hudson's Bay Company made no concessions to weather. If logs were required, men were sent out to get them. Over and over again the journals tell of crews camped out, cutting and rafting in brutal cold and dangerous gales. In late October of 1837 a raft from Finlayson Island was caught in the wind and carried to the far side of the bay. As night came down a rescue party was sent out from the fort but in the dark and storm it could not locate the raft. Meanwhile, the loggers, hungry, exhausted, wet and aching with cold, abandoned the raft and made their way back to the fort in their canoes. Next morning, though the weather had not improved, back they went to work the raft right around the shoreline of the bay, mile after mile of shoreline; it was still too rough to cross the harbour. Once again they reached home in the dark. And so, three days later, the storm still raging, it was noted, "Sent off ten men to cut wood to raft home for fuel."

The next year, at the same season, nine fort men and thirty Natives, bringing in a raft, were caught in a blow that flung them in the opposite direction, out to the open sea. This was an "all hands" situation and with them thirty Natives in large canoes were dispatched to the aid of the rafters. Even this flotilla had to battle the gale for hours for possession of the raft.

There was a crew camped out on Finlayson Island in December of 1841:

December 5 — "froze very keenly during last night —"

December 7 — "Snowing all day."

The factor thought about his men suffering from exposure; he sent them four days' rations of fresh venison. And again, in March 1842:

"Weather gloomy and disagreeable, wind strong from the South East attended with frequent showers of snow. 9 men and 13 Indians started from here this morning to make a raft on the Island."

Dirty weather was only one of the hazards that the loggers dealt with. Those unwieldy rafts were inclined to hang up on rocks. Usually high tide would float a raft free but high tide could be many windswept hours in coming. And there were accidents in the woods, then as today, though proportionately fewer. The blacksmith's axes were certainly less deadly than modern equipment. Gashed feet seemed the commonest accident. Victims were paddled back to the fort as speedily as possible. The Natives, on occasion, turned logging expeditions into high adventure for the men, although there is no account of any of the loggers actually being harmed. In 1837, the Natives threatened that the men would not be allowed to bring logs out of the woods. The men of that expedition carried muskets as well as logs, but those logs were brought out and rafted home as usual. In July 1839, a party of wood squarers was summoned back to the fort in haste. That summer Haida raiders had been "skulking about" Fort Simpson for some time when finally, well armed, they landed near the fort. White men working in the woods would have been easy prey and most desirable slaves. There were many other unsettled times when the men were rushed home to the safety of the pickets. In 1861, Mr. Moffatt, the unfortunate factor who seemed to draw the Tsimshian's ire, reported on the hazards of coming home from work, "... and our canoe, as she was returning from rafting, received a shot from Legaic, the head chief, which fortunately did no damage."

The loggers' shift, though it lasted through days and nights of working the raft home, did not always end with the beaching of the logs in front of the fort. If the Natives evinced a particular need for wood, if storms threatened or if some project was held up for special logs, all hands turned to, then and there, and discharged the raft.

The logs were piled about the fort according to their purposes, pickets, spars, lumber, but the wood yard received the highest piles. Winters came early and stayed late and many summers were not summery. It was in the wood yard that the fire logs were chopped into fuel for every stone-and-clay chimney in the post. And then the men continued to chop and split alder to be burned into charcoal for the blacksmith's forge and to fuel the lime kiln and the steamer's insatiable fireboxes.

Storybooks depict the occupation of woodcutter as a philosophical, healthful one. At Fort Simpson it was neither. Axes and clothing were coveted by the tribes encamped about the fort and the wood yard was located outside the stockade. The woodcutters contended with more than knots:

March 26, 1836 — "Traded from the Nass Indians 4. Beaver Skins. 3 of the fellows seized one of our men today while cutting wood and took off his vest and Handkerchief but on our remonstrating with some of them on such conduct, they shortly afterwards returned the articles."

May 4, 1836 — "The Indians still continue about the Fort. Some of them were rather insolent and abusive while in an intoxicated state and one of them went so far as to trip one of our men while [he was] cutting wood and took the axe from him but [the axe] was almost immediately returned by the lookers on or by the sober Indians."

Sixteen years later the Natives still regarded woodmen as fair prey. Mr. McNeill's terse style denies us the details: "We had an axe stolen this day from one of our wood cutters, which nearly caused a rupture." Once, in the earlier days, the Haida chief known as Mr. Charles was murdered by a Haida when he tried to return to the fort axes stolen by his people.

In spite of near ruptures, the men chopped and split in the wood yard, day after day, until the summer of 1862. It was then that they began to carry coal, instead of wood, to the various fort buildings. Grates were added to the fireplaces and coal boxes were built for the houses. The cook seems to have resisted change, since the men continued to cut wood for the kitchen.

The saws rasped and sighed in the saw pit almost as regularly as the axes chopped. The saws were some ten feet long, one foot wide, single-bladed affairs. Two men at different levels pulled alternately on them, up, down, up, down. How they produced with them the boards and planks required to build, rebuild and then build again is a puzzle to machine-age people. In 1835 the sawyers produced ten boards in a day from squared logs. The lumber pile must have been seriously depleted in 1862 when Mr. McNeill set "all hands and four Indians" to sawing.

CHAPTER 10

Building

SHAPING THE PRODUCTS of the axes and saws into a fort was an ongoing process that became a way of life. By the time personnel, equipment, stock, furs and food were adequately housed, the earliest foundations were rotting and it was time to start again.

The arrival of the Nass River complement in 1834, at the month-and-a-half-old fort, doubled the encampment, which woke next morning to rain and the realization that it was September, the threshold of north coast winter. Nobody needed encouragement to plunge into the business of building.

Like the house that Jack built, 1834 Hudson's Bay construction began at the beginning. The blacksmith made the axes to fell the trees to square into timber to saw into lumber. That is why, on the second day of September, the blacksmith's forge was installed in a makeshift fashion, ahead of a thousand necessities. The blacksmith produced the axe heads and Natives from the Interior traded the handles, which they had fashioned from birch.

The rest of the workforce had to go to sea before they could begin building. Three days they spent rafting ashore the *Dryad's* cargo of dismantled buildings. Then, on September 6th, there was a triumphant entry in the fort journal: the lower storeys of the bastions were being assembled and the stockade gates were locked at night. Again the blacksmith was the hero of the day; he adapted the gate fittings from the Nass fort.

The first living accommodations to be put up were houses for officers, one to the west of the gates and one to the east. Dwellings had to have chimneys, and while there was no scarcity of stone around Fort Simpson there was a total lack of cement. A gentleman was dispatched to prospect for clay, which is not common in those parts. Being accustomed to carrying out orders, he promptly located a deposit on nearby Rose Island — if he had been sent for diamonds he probably would have found them. Once again, the masonry did not begin with stones and clay. It began with the purchase of a canoe for the price of three blankets. The clay was paddled to the fort beach, and five days later one chimney was completed. Three days after that, on September 30th, Mr. Birnie and Dr. Kennedy took possession of their hearths and homes.

October's undertakings were more diverse. While one crew was laying foundation logs for the men's houses, another was finishing the front of the gallery. (Eventually the gallery, twelve feet above ground and four feet wide, was to traverse the entire stockade perimeter.) While one gang was cutting one-inch cedar planks in the saw pit, another began squaring logs for a fourteen-by-fourteen-foot blacksmith's shop to replace the first open shed. October 17th marked a spirited climax. "Today hoisted flag staff & flag, saluting the latter with 5 Guns, returned by ship." Even more significant was the closing entry for the day, "a dram to all hands." Drams were not lightly dispensed.

Apparently the Hudson's Bay people worked to a monthly schedule, for the last days of August, September and October each concluded a building project. October's was not easy to achieve because of the rain that delayed the work. However, one job must have been abetted by the rain — that was the mudding of the men's houses. At any rate, on October 31st, the journal keeper remarked with satisfaction, "Men all housed." The men's reactions are not noted as they moved indoors one day ahead of November.

Housing, at this time in Fort Simpson, meant a roof above, foundations below, a chimney, walls and, of course, mud. Other buildings were as basic. From this point, until the fort burned down, the process of adding refinements was continuous; there was scope. And the journals, in their own terse style, told the whole story. For instance, on November 28th, 1834, the gentlemen's water closet was finished. Five years later, the building program got around to the men's "little houses." On December 27th, 1839, the blacksmith was making locks for them — presumably a delayed Christmas gift. In January of 1835 the kitchen chimney and oven, of stone and clay, were finished and the cook came in out of the winter weather. In March, posts and beams of the Big House were erected. The Big House of a fort contained the factor's living quarters as well as the officers' mess, rooms for unmarried gentlemen, and a sort of communal social centre and office. On March 10th the rafters were raised and on March 12th the rafters were lowered — to the ground by a vicious southwest gale. By July, however, the men were laying the upper and lower floors and in November plastering the walls. The plaster was home grown. It was harvested by canoe from the neighbouring reefs where clamshell deposits had been accumulating through time. At the fort, the shells were burned in a kiln and the resulting lime used for both plaster and whitewash. A bark roof must have been put on temporarily for it was November of 1836 before the Big House was shingled.

Not until the summer of 1835 do we hear of any furniture in the fort. Presumably the officers brought a few pieces from the Nass but the men could have had nothing but their wooden chests, which contained their entire worldly possessions. It is a relief to learn that on an August day the men were busy making bedsteads, tables and chairs.

When the fort was not yet two years old the men began replacing, repairing and expanding the most hurriedly assembled buildings. As you might guess, the blacksmith's shop was first on the list. The saw pit was removed to a safer distance from the new site, then a stone forge and chimney built and a shop erected around them. A few months later there was a casual entry: "Men ... righting the store which had a list inwards." Another year passed before we find the sequel: "Had the store raised and secured where the foundation had given way." It was August of 1840 before two men commenced "fitting soles" for a new store, thirty by twenty-four feet, and October before the new store was "arranged" while the flooring of the upper storey proceeded above the workmen's heads. A store of this size was adequate because the actual trading took place in the Indian shop. This shop must have been one of the earliest and most primitive structures because the crew that set about adding such niceties as flooring, "flat boarding" and plaster, in the winter of 1838, discovered the sleepers "much decayed." That same crew hung the door of Dr. Kennedy's house. What Dr. Kennedy had been using for a door for four years is a matter of conjecture. Probably it was a cedar mat, woven by his Native wife, though a blanket might have been more effective against the wind.

For nearly twenty years buildings rose and rotted. It was 1851 before the cycle was jolted off its track by a factor who was experienced in jolting. He was William Henry McNeill. His name is less familiar than that of many Hudson's Bay factors but his character and perception tugged and shoved at the company, the Natives, the land itself until he had shaped much of the west coast development and life of that century and the next.

Captain McNeill came to the coast as a Boston Trader, a term used by the Company with extreme distaste. Its implications did not apply to him since he was a man of principle rather than an unscrupulous ruffian. In 1831 he and his brig

Lama were known favourably to the natives from Oahu to Sitka to San Francisco and his trade was known to the Hudson's Bay Company as a problem. In the young Columbia District, problems were for solving, summarily, so the Company purchased the brig *Lama* and employed Captain McNeill and his experience. Why he gave up his career as an American ship's master and trader to become an employee of a British company, at a lower salary, we do not know but we do know that for thirty-one years he was a fiercely loyal and conscientious one. True, his independent spirit sometimes bristled on the pages of the journal that he wrote up in the manner of a ship's log. He never bristled more obviously than when he took command of Fort Simpson in 1851, with orders to rebuild the fort.

"I will however remark that some good man is required here to put up the new buildings. One 'head' man that understands building should be sent … we have a most miserable set here at the present called men," he wrote to James Douglas on November 20th. Nonetheless, by January his men were squaring wood for one of the corner houses and preparing posts for another. By the middle of the month his recorded objections contained a note of despair, "We make a poor show in putting up houses and if this Corner house is to be a specimen of the work, no one need think of building a new Big one … We have not *one* man that can square a piece of wood properly and who is to put up the new buildings required, is to be found out."

By the end of January his doubts were confirmed:

"As for the Corner house God knows when it will be finished. We have made one *new* base and cut *it*, after everything had been fitted cut one post three times after all were in their places, and to finish the lot we were obliged to put a piece on top of *the* post to make it equal to the others. I mention this, as people may think a Big House could be erected with the men we have here at present. There is no one to mark out the work, and I cannot be with one set of men, *all* the time, as we have lots of work to look after, and I must be an overseer for all of them. McN"

At the same time the weather became persuasive, "... heavy gusts during the night which made the old house tremble. I expect some time to see it tumble about our heads," and "Rain coming thro all the roofs in all directions." That was when Mr. McNeill decided to turn his "miserable set called men" into carpenters and make the fort shipshape. They blocked up the kitchen, reroofed houses, made wooden water troughs for the roofs and travelled twenty miles up Work's Canal to cut logs for the new Big House. Mr. McNeill proclaimed his final submission to his orders and the weather by building a carpenter's shop under the gallery and writing this note in the journal: "... gave the men & women of the establishment a dance in the Big House as it will be pulled down shortly."

The men progressed from dance to dance. November 4th, 1852, "No work done the men being out of sorts from dancing last night, we gave them a turnout to try the new floor in the new house etc." Mr. McNeill was obviously a psychologist as well as sea captain and factor. By this time his Big House project was into the finishing stages and he was producing refinements such as Fort Simpson had never seen. A man spent three days searching Finlayson Island for a suitable hearth stone for one of the fireplaces. The workman, who somehow managed to load and unload the huge stone, was given a day of rest. Then Mr. McNeill's critical eye discovered a crack in it and deemed it rather small, and the workman was dispatched to Work's Canal for a more perfect one. The neo-carpenters fitted mouldings around the doors, added a verandah, built in a closet for medicines, hung wallpaper in a sitting room and bedchamber, erected a stand for the hall clock, installed ventilators in the various apartments and, as a crowning glory, the blacksmith made a chandelier.

That Big House, started so reluctantly in 1852, was the centre of fort life until the post was consumed by fire. Mr. McNeill and his miserable set had built well.

The transformation from crude existence to nineteenth-century gracious living did not take place suddenly; it was accomplished over seven years during which Mr. McNeill and his men rescued, restored and rebuilt the many other fort structures, as weather and circumstances demanded. The diverse work on these buildings was done with the same McNeill thoroughness. One day the men roofed the outside oven with bark, another day, the saw pit. They built a new store, one hundred and ten feet long, that did not list inward and even installed a glass window in it. They made water runs out of grooved logs and a chute for dirty water from the kitchen. They put "facing pieces" on the men's houses, renewed the gunsmith's house under the gallery, made bricks for an oven, plastered inside the cellars, put new "covering boards" on the Indian shop. They put up two new houses, the third blacksmith's shop and new bastions. They constantly repaired the gallery, which the rain quickly turned green and slippery and rotten. They applied much Hudson's Bay Company white and red paint (red on the big gates and the ridges of the houses) and whitewashed all four sides of the fort. They took down the flagstaff that had gone up with such ceremony and substituted a taller one with no ceremony. And on top of a corner house they placed a symbol of domesticity, a dovecote.

Hamilton Moffatt replaced Mr. McNeill in 1859, but the building process had gained such momentum by that time that it rolled steadily along into the last years of the century.

CHAPTER 11

Potatoes

MOTHER SNAPPED SHUT the padlock of the tank house behind her, after hanging a hind quarter of venison within.

"You will just have to learn to keep your things put away after dark," she said to the three-and-a-half feet of steaming indignation that was I.

"But the varnish wasn't dry on my oars and I left them right by the kitchen door. They stole my swing board last year and my petticoat with lace off the clothesline. When I played marbles for keeps and came home with all Mary's glassies, you said it was stealing. You were very mad and made me take them back to her. But you don't do anything when the Indians steal from me."

Mother leaned against the boards and battens of the tank house and fixed her eyes on something far away and well above my head. She answered me but she spoke slowly, with long pauses, and I knew that she was answering herself, too.

"Perhaps the word 'steal' is the wrong one to use about the Indians taking your oars. After all, we don't say we are stealing when we take milk from a cow, an egg from a hen, a deer from the woods, salmon from a river, territory from the Natives. Just as our own early ancestors did, the Indians have always had to live by taking what they needed from whatever source was at hand. Neighbouring tribes were one source and when the Hudson's Bay Company built a fort it was the handiest hunting ground of all. That was only eighty-five years ago. It must be over three thousand years that our own race has been changing those same ways. Eighty-five years isn't very long."

The Hudson's Bay officers, even from the fort's first year, did use the word *steal* regarding their neighbours' depredations. It dots the pages of the journals like dandelions on the roadside. It is used with varying degrees of frustration and annoyance but never with more real anger than concerning potatoes, for besides starch, Fort Simpson's potatoes had a high content of "blood, toil, tears and sweat."

Potatoes preceded the Hudson's Bay Company to the northern British Columbia coast. They emigrated in Spanish ships from their Andean origins in Peru and Bolivia, to Europe and, it is thought, to the islands of the Pacific as well.

The Haidas told an old story of a canoe, fishing far off the coast of the Queen Charlotte Islands, caught in storms and driven farther and farther to sea. After a long time it reached an inhabited island. There the people took the crew ashore and cared for them. Eventually — and this part of the story is not as unlikely as it sounds for the north coast indigenous people were instinctive navigators and seamen — the canoe made its way home. The men brought tales of the wonders they had seen and at least one proof, in the form of rounded, brown roots that could be cooked and eaten.

Whether the story is true or not, there is no doubt that the Haida, never farmers, did cultivate the potato with success. It became for them not only a staple of diet, but also a valuable trade item. And that is why the story of Fort Simpson potatoes began two days after the Nass personnel had disembarked from the *Dryad* in McLoughlin's Harbour.

Those first potatoes arrived from the Queen Charlotte Islands in some eighteen Cumshewa canoes that were on their way to the Nass River. The Hudson's Bay people welcomed the potatoes happily and the Cumshewa warily; they put on an extra watch and "a gentleman in each division." But they did not eat potatoes with their salt fish that day nor for three days to come because, according to Native protocol, it would have been vulgar (and unadvantageous) to rush into trading immediately. When the formalities had been observed with seemly deliberation, barter took place at the rate of one measure of baize for two of potatoes. The product must have been satisfactory, for two months later the fort's men were hard at work digging a cellar in hopes that the "potato people" would return. The trade thus initiated continued right into my day, when it was the Nishga'a from the upper Nass who brought a boatload of huge, dry potatoes from their fields of volcanic ash, every fall. But traded potatoes filled only a portion of the Hudson's Bay cellars.

Under the sun that beat down on the wondrously fertile gardens and orchards of Fort Vancouver, on the bank of the Columbia River, Dr. John McLoughlin impressed on all the factors of his district Governor George Simpson's directive concerning gardens. The gist of the directive was: be self-sustaining, grow potatoes, grow fruits and vegetables. It was obviously a wise rule for that scurvy-threatened country but Hudson's Bay regulations were usually blanket regulations and the north coast did not fit under this particular blanket very neatly. There, forts had to be built on the shoreline that was rocky with, at best, a thin overlay of soil. Instead of Fort Vancouver's floods of sunshine they had floods of rain. That was an era of unquestioning obedience; the Light Brigade charged and Fort Simpson grew potatoes.

Fort Simpson might well have grown nothing more palatable than devil's club and thimbleberry had not John Work CT (chief trader) taken command of the new post in 1835. Factors coped variously with the hardships and loneliness of early fort life, some finding solace in liquor, some in religion, some in books. Mr. Work found solace in potatoes. He certainly did not eschew those other interests. He was Irish and warmhearted, and younger officers seeking out his company described him as well informed, but the items that leap off the pages of his journal have to do with his garden.

Gardening began with clearing, no casual undertaking in a primeval rainforest. The men worked and worried, burned and chopped the massive roots out of the ground and rolled them to the beach where they launched them upon the outgoing tides. "Had nine men and thirty-five Indians rolling stumps out of the garden. Many of them are so heavy that all hands that are about them have enough to do to get them hauled and rolled out with ropes." No sooner was a clearing under cultivation than Mr. Work dispatched his men to tussle with another segment of the shoreline jungle until he had fields and gardens stretching out from the fort, flat and smooth as prairie land, and all fenced with Hudson's Bay pickets.

Hard on the heels of the clearing crews came the planters. That first spring they planted seven bushels of potatoes. It must have been a favourable season for on October 19th, "In the afternoon took up part of the Potatoes say 50 Bush. [They] appear to be good & very large." This was not entirely beginner's luck. Over the years Mr. Work and his successors produced tons of good potatoes but it was never a simple matter of sowing and reaping. Fort Simpson gardening took some unique twists.

Potato work began early in the year while sleet flurries were still disappearing into the puddles that rippled on the surface of the soil. It began with trenching and draining. When there was more soil than water visible, Mr. Work assembled a crew and they set out by canoe prospecting for seaweed. There was no scarcity on the bay's indented shoreline. Once they had located the best supplies, fort workmen went out in canoes to harvest it. By 1837 tribesmen were going out with the fort men and by 1842 the seaweed industry signified spring. Up to four hundred Tsimshian canoes shuttled back and forth over the unsettled March surface of the bay, the outgoing, highriding craft skimming past the incoming canoes that were so low in the water their gunnels were nearly awash. As the loads were landed the Natives were paid off in "seaweed papers" and next day the trade shop was a mob scene of claimants exchanging papers for vermilion and tobacco.

Unlike dry land compost, fertilizer from the sea may be used without going through the decaying process, so that once it had been carried to the garden planting could begin at any propitious moment. In 1836 Mr. Work began planting on April 12th, but in 1837:

May 10 — "We intended to have commenced sowing potatoes but deferred doing so on account of the heavy rain which has so wet the ground that it is in Mortar."

That year he did not finish his planting until May 23rd when he tallied it all neatly:

"... 33 bushels of potatoes planted on 6461 Yards or 1 ⅓ acres of ground, English Measure."

In October he tallied his results:

"The people finished taking up the potatoes just as the heavy rain came on in the afternoon ... The whole produce of the garden is 651 bush. from 33 bushels of seed sowed ... which is over 19 ½ to 1 and 487 bush. per acre English."

And, in case you should ever wish to plant potatoes at Port Simpson, he left you meticulous instructions:

"The potatoes were sowed round ... They were planted in drills 3 feet apart, ... The ground was manured with seaweed which was put in the bottom of the drills and a sprinkling of clay put over it before the seed was laid in and covered up about two fingers deep ... The ground had been all well dug up before being sowed."

After the first few potato seasons, Native women, their babies folded within their blanket garments, their older children working beside them, took over the ever-expanding gardening chores, under fort foremen. There were always some weather-made emergencies when all hands were rushed to the garden as well. Sometimes it was for hoeing; during the course of their growing, or languishing, Hudson's Bay potatoes were hoed three times, come deluge, disease, mutiny or musket balls. At the first sign of a dry day in October every available harvester took to the potato field. In the heyday of Fort Simpson's gardening the crop exceeded seventeen hundred bushels so it was not too surprising to read that in 1861, in Mr. McNeill's time, "all hands and about eighty Indian women and children" were bent over shovels and baskets.

There were other crops, too. Fort Simpson grew vegetables, berries and apples , and the journals give us a glimpse of the hope and despair that grew with them:

April 19, 1837 — "Had some Cabbages, Raddishes, leeks and parsley Sowed."

July 2, 1839 — "Had 170 Cabbages transplanted making in all 1,420."

October 20, 1840 — "Got the Onions housed, 5 Bushels of them, and the same quantity of the carrots is all there is."

October 13, 1852 — "Picked the Apples from all the Trees, 'about half a bushel,' they are very inferior."

June 1, 1856 — "The garden has a fine appearance, the apple trees in particular ..."

May 24, 1860 — "Dull and cloudy. Cucumbers blighted."

August 12, 1860 — "Had potatoes and green pease on the table for the first time."

April 5, 1866 — "Hans employed in boxing in our apple trees to guard them from the Goat."

The garden's worst enemy was the weather. Sometimes it mounted sneak attacks as on May 2nd, 1859, "Heavy frost in the morning which has rotted all our pease in the garden."

But its usual form of attack was a barrage of rain:

July 8, 1859 — "The Garden is a lake and one-third of the seed potatoes have rotted in the ground the small seeds, all except the Turnips have entirely failed."

Other woes assailed the garden; the flood tides washed away one corner of the potato field, the crows methodically pulled up the seed potatoes by their sprouts, and the small birds picked out the vegetable seeds. (Mr. Manson in desperation engaged a small boy to chase them off.) Mr. Tugwell, a missionary of 1860, kept a goat that killed twelve apple trees. They had been the pride of the fort, having been coddled along from seed to the point of flowering. Intertribal warfare sent musket balls whizzing across the field so that gardening crews had to abandon their work for a day at a time, and Natives raided the garden regularly.

Potato raids were a food-gathering practice long before Fort Simpson planted its first potato. Mr. Work described one conducted by Chief Sabassa and his people that occurred in the fall of 1842. Sabassa had gone to the Queen Charlotte Islands to trade back the wife of a Tsimshian chief from the Cumshewa who had carried her off as a slave the month before. "It appears Sabassa did not come without plunder. The inhabitants of some village of the Haida which they visited fled to the woods and they [the Sabassa] took up all their crop of potatoes and brought them along with them."

Not all the fort potatoes that found their way into the Tsimshian lodges were there illicitly, for Fort Simpson observed a custom that was old in Biblical times, that of gleaning. As the last of the harvest was carried out of the garden, the gates were thrown open and enthusiastic crowds sifted the soil once more. As for the rest of the Hudson's Bay potatoes that the Natives ate with oolichan grease, they were loot.

Tribes from all over the north coast camped around three sides of the fort stockade, sometimes for a few days, sometimes for weeks, while many clans of the Tsimshian began to make their permanent winter quarters nearby. The tribes were violently disunited; they postured, they quarrelled, they fought. But they had many characteristics in common, and one of those was an appetite for potatoes. In time they developed quite an appetite for turnips, too, and one year made off with half the crop.

During the long, dark nights of fall, equally dark bodies slithered over the garden pickets and into the potato patch. Watchmen stationed in the garden rarely heard or saw them. Sometimes for a mass onslaught the invaders pushed over a section of pickets and walked into the garden. When harvesting was over they tunnelled into the blockhouse cellar where the crop had been stored. Late spring, between the oolichan fishery and the salmon fishery, was often a hungry time. Then they dug up the freshly planted seed potatoes. The infuriated fort officers fought back. They once stepped up their garden watch to twelve; they threatened; they discharged muskets into the blackness, but they were almost as powerless against the raiders as they were against the rain and the crows. On a very few occasions they detected marauders whom they attacked with fists, shovels, cudgels or muskets. More than once they took a prisoner who was put in irons for the night. Any punishment was sure to bring an angry crowd of tribesmen about the gates, a situation that could have exploded into shooting at the drop of an injudicious word or gesture. War was not productive of furs so the culprit was released, blacker threats were pronounced and within a few nights more potatoes were stolen.

With harvest over, farmers are expected to rejoice and relax; not so the potato growers of Fort Simpson. Once the crop was stowed away they faced a whole new set of worries.

The Hudson's Bay Company had always stored its potatoes in cellars and no one ever questioned that Fort Simpson must also store its potatoes in cellars. But the uplands sloped down to the fort so that, as the men dug cellars, Fort Simpson's phenomenal rainfall drained into them. Wetness rotted the potatoes. Some years they had barely been gathered in when that hostile wind from the north blew over Fort Simpson. Then frost rotted the potatoes. If the weather happened to be temperate, heat generated by the mass rotted them. Obviously the potato had not been designed for Fort Simpson but no one ever seemed to recognize that fact, so potato-preservation and potato-salvage held crisis priority over many other occupations.

Protection of the potato gave rise to an unlikely Fort Simpson undertaking — haying. Certainly there would have been no lack of waist-high grasses and weeds to cut. But how, where and *when* could they have been dried? The journals simply tell us it was done, year after year, and the potato crop bedded down in hay in those dank cellars. The ploy was not entirely successful:

March 22, 1852 — "Picking over potatoes. We find a large number have been touched with frost and now useless. We give them away by tens of Bushels to the Indians. We shall probably lose about 400 bushels in all."

The next crop fared no better: December 29, 1852 — "Our Potatoes are looking very bad in the cellars, I am afraid we will lose half of them."

Sorting potatoes ranked with cutting pickets and airing furs as a recurring part of fort life. At any time of the year, in one cellar or another, a troop of either workmen or Native women was likely to be squatted on the bottom of that dark, cold, wet hole in the ground picking over heaps of potatoes, sometimes for days at a time. Perhaps picking over potatoes still goes on in Simpson's decay-laden climate. I know it did in the 1920s because, on many a Saturday morning, I was sentenced to the store's spud-room where I sat on an orange crate sorting dirty potatoes into piles, recoiling and holding my nose every time my fingers plunged into a rotten one.

CHAPTER 12

Rations and Regales

THE FORT SIMPSON preoccupation with potatoes seems unreasonable until you consider the other available foods.

On Hallowe'en night, 1840, there were flickering lights and moving shadows in the Indian shop. The ghostly scene was merely a trading session. After sunset, canoes had arrived from Tongass and the Skeena with deer, some fresh, some half dried. At that time of year the Fort Simpson personnel, officers and men, turned out eagerly to spend half the night doling out tobacco, ammunition, and cotton, and stowing away venison, all by candlelight. They needed fresh meat.

Actually, the October of 1840 was a good month for provisions compared with Fort Simpson's first October when there was still the double complement to be fed, fifty-eight all told. Then meal times were not jolly events and there was no hint of thanksgiving. The journal keeper, no doubt after yet another skimpy dinner of salt salmon, commented sourly that it was the time of feasting for the Natives "... but with us the contrary — In order to participate in their joy we must receive a little more of the good things furnished by their woods & waters."

That was a powerful journal entry because the very next day some Tsimshian arrived with deer to trade and from then on fresh venison was frequently served in the officers' mess and occasionally to the hands. The deer were the small variety common to the north coast and a portion of them had to be salted down against the winter food shortage, so there was always a demand for more. The Natives seemed to kill deer in all seasons but it was the fall bucks that the fort people most ardently sought. Although the Tsimshian furnished the first deer, they furnished little of the fort's venison requirements over the years, for they were the Phoenicians of the northwest coast and their prowess lay in trading rather than in hunting, to which they seemed indifferent. They seemed indifferent to the hunger of the white men, also. Fortunately, the Tongass who lived across the Nass Straits were skilled hunters and better disposed to the Hudson's Bay people.

November 13, 1834 — "3 more canoes left this for Tongass, have been so fortunate as to prevail on one of the Young Men to remain in the Fort & to be occupied as Hunter."

This would appear to have been the perfect answer to short rations, but no, in the Tongass territory an internal feud erupted, taking the lives of four men and a woman.

November 18 — "... We are in consequence obliged to part with our Hunter whose Father is involved in it."

By this time the *Dryad* had sailed south with twenty-two passengers from Fort Simpson, thus relieving the victualling problems of the post considerably. Also, about this time, a trade in provisions began to develop. Each Sunday the entire trade of the week was recorded, first furs, then food, and finally such random items as cedar bark mats or whalebone. The list of provisions written up on the last Sunday of that 1834 October reads: "20 deer, 192 bbl. Grease, 16 gals. Whale oil, 187 Dried salmon, 10 Pieces of Dried Goat's Meat, Meat of 2 Dried Beaver."

As the years passed, so did the hunger. The lists lengthened until we are told of one hundred and ten deer being received in a thirty-day period in 1862. Geese and ducks were frequently traded and occasionally swans, plover, grouse, teal, widgeon and, horrifyingly, sandpipers. If the waterfowl had been shot in the Interior, they were a delicacy, but if they came from the fort environs they were likely to taste fishy. Entered in the trade record, quite nonchalantly, were the meat of bear, porcupine and seal and beaver tails for roasting. There were cakes of dried berries, fresh cranberries in November, and the eggs of gulls and wildfowl.

August 31, 1838 — "Some eggs were received from the Hanaga people. We don't know what kind of birds' eggs these are that hatch so late in the season." They ate them anyhow.

August 10, 1852 — "Kygarnies traded about 900 Eggs."

And what did the people of the fort do with nine hundred eggs? The journal gives us no hint.

Gathering seagull eggs was still a flourishing June industry in 1930. Within a radius of forty miles there were several bare rock islands rising out of the sea that were nesting grounds. A Tsimshian girl once described the gathering technique to me, her eyes shining. "We land on the rock. On top of it very hard to walk — so many nests all over. Some eggs roll out all the time. Those seagulls don't make good nests, just grass and little sticks on the rock. We have to break all eggs but my mother knows right time to go so not too many eggs and not too many seagulls chase us. They very fierce. Then another day we go back. All new eggs now. I take from one nest and run fast before the mother gull get me. Terrible noise of all gulls yelling. Terrible smell."

All such bounties of the land were welcomed for variety but Fort Simpson subsisted on fish:

May 27, 1836 — "about thirty small canoes started to fish, returned in the evening loaded with Halibut and CodFish. Traded 94 Halibut and 174 CodFish."

Herring, too, were salted down though they were not highly valued by either Natives or Hudson's Bay personnel.

The year-round staple of the north coast diet was salmon. One day in the summer of 1842 the Cape Fox Natives landed five hundred at the fort. They dried and smoked their winter's supply while the Company salted theirs; in fact they salted them twice, always. They did have a smokehouse but their smoked fish and game seem to have been supplementary. If the salmon fishery failed, as it sometimes did in those days, even as in these, some of the Native population died of starvation, and yet, in the lodges and within the stockade, it was the oolichan run rather than the salmon run that generated excitement.

The oolichans, swimming glints of silver, came to the Nass in the latter part of March. Then, while the ice drifted down the river, winter privations ended and a happy new cycle began. You may have your Easter bunny as a symbol of spring; mine is an oolichan, preferably smoked.

The north coast Natives, seemingly averse to preparedness, did make desultory preparations for the oolichan run. By February various tribes were assembling at Simpson to await the coming of the "small fish." Various tribes meant various troubles and those would have kept the waiting period lively even without the pre-oolichan activities. Year after year, insults, plunderings and shootings swirled through the camps with the March winds. In spite of the mayhem, it was the time for making and trading canoes, collecting gear and, when the skies filled with seagulls beating their way northward, the time for dismantling winter lodges and carrying packed cedar boxes into the company's shop for safekeeping. There was another early-warning device, a week ahead of the gulls: "A Tsimshian arrived in the evening from Skeena River where he shot a Seal in which he found some small Fish, the first seen this Season." During the exodus of 1852, five hundred canoes swept out of the bay in one day and by March 21st a total of seven hundred had left. The chiefs with their retinues took their departures after the masses had gone.

The fort people made preparations for the oolichans, too; they cleaned out every keg, cask, barrel, hogshead, tierce and puncheon that the fort could yield up, and repaired those that showed a tendency to fall apart. It seems that they never had enough. One year found them salting small fish in their large canoe and another in a scow.

There was a certain significance about the *first* of the oolichans:

April 1, 1853 — "... the first canoe of small fish arrived, we, of course, turned out and made the fellows welcome and were pleased that *the* fish had made their appearance."

It was usual to make a presentation to the bearer of the first oolichans and it was most important that the fort people ascertain that their fish were not the very first ones caught on the river. There was a powerful Tsimshian belief that the first take must be cooked with respect and in the traditional manner, otherwise the oolichans would take offence and leave the river forthwith. In 1843 an overzealous fisherman rushed his early catch to the fort where it was promptly cooked by the white man's method and gulped down unceremoniously. Of course the small fish were displeased and the run disappeared. For a long week the assembled tribes waited on that cold river bank. Eventually, the oolichans relented and returned but there were stories of irreverences of the past when the whole fishery had failed. This behaviour was not peculiar to oolichans; all up and down the coast Native people handled the first catch of salmon with deference.

Although the oolichan is a most delectable little fish, its supreme importance in those days lay in its willingness to render itself into oil. At first this process took place in canoes but Captain Snow, an early American trader, introduced vats that were more efficient. Oolichan grease was traded far to the north and south and into the Interior over the Grease Trail that was ancient by the time the first travellers learned of it. The

Natives carried and stored their grease in cedar boxes, having first caulked the very few joints with a doughy substance made by mixing grease with powdered rotten wood. They ate the oil in dollops on practically all Native foods, including berries and, as European foods such as hardtack and rice were introduced, they ate grease on them, too. Nature, having deprived the northern peoples of sunshine, thus provided them with lavish quantities of substitute vitamins A and D.

The officers of the fort at Simpson traded oolichan grease by the hundreds of barrels. It was the only fat available for their use except for intermittent supplies of whale oil, dogfish oil and tallow from deer and mountain goat. They needed it to lubricate the dried and salted salmon and venison that they ate, and for cooking, and they also needed it for their Native and export trade.

1866 — "Men Employed shipping Oolichans and oolichan oil on board the *Otter* for Victoria, Nanaimo and Fort Rupert."

By that date there was a wharf at Simpson but for years shipping meant ferrying goods out to the anchored vessels by canoe, small boat or raft. Unloading a ship was the reverse process and that is how the fort's salt, sugar, molasses, rum, biscuit, rice, dried peas, barley, wheat, salt beef and salt pork came ashore. Sometimes one item or another was missing from the fort diet for the next six months because of cargo damage, short shipment or a lightering mishap. Although every shipment produced some of these troubles, one, by the *Cadboro*, produced them all. In a letter to headquarters, October 22, 1841, Mr. Work wrote:

"The *Cadboro* arrived on the 16th. Owing to the vessel making water the lower sides of the tobacco hogsheads and sugar hogshead were wet and the sugar short weight 60 lbs., the fine biscuit was also deficient 280 lbs. of quantity charged. By upsetting of a canoe employed in unloading, 4 Kegs Shot, a Keg of rice and a roll of tobacco were lost and not yet recovered."

In the same letter he remarked with restraint: "Salt received by *Columbia* short by sixty-four bushels, thirty lbs. molasses for servants' orders did not arrive."

Fort Vancouver shippers seem to have been remarkably stupid or remarkably drunk, though they, in turn, suffered from shortages. Twice a year a ship arrived on the *Columbia* with supplies from London. What could not be packed into her holds, or was not deemed important in the London office, the West Coast establishments did without. The farms at Fort Vancouver and Fort Langley supplied amazing quantities of salt meat and grains but they, too, could have a bad season. Shortages at Fort Simpson might have been forgiven but overages — they were calamities that had no explanation. The most preposterous one is reported in a mild Work letter, 19th May 1842:

"The *Cowlitz* arrived on the 13th. It strikes me there must have been some mistake in sending such a large quantity of salt (3580 bags per ship a/c). We have enough now to serve this place 15 years. Perhaps it was intended for Langley."

The handling and storage of this mountain of salt, in a wet climate, was the subject of many a journal entry:

May 16, 1842 — "The men were employed with about 30 Indians carrying up salt landed by the *Cowlitz*."

May 23 — "... making a cellar for the salt."

May 27 — "Part of the men were carrying salt from the store to the cellar in the southern corner of the fort."

Food shortages came not only by boat. If the weather was particularly bad it ruined the garden crops; if the weather was particularly good it dried up the streams, which ruined the salmon fishing and the deer hunting. If the Natives were joyful and peaceably disposed they did not produce food:

December 18, 1841 — "In consequence of three Indian children being initiated into the mystery of *dog eating*, which appears to be a grand occasion among the natives of this place — none of our hunters Can be prevailed upon to hunt Deer of which we are sorely in want at present, neither do they fish; so that we have subsisted on salt Provisions for the whole of this week, which is the longest interval we were without a fresh diet since the Spring."

And if the tribes were in turmoil they did not produce food either:

July 3, 1837 — "Traded a sufficiency of halibut to give the People a day's Rations. We were entirely out of fresh provisions. The people have been living chiefly on pease for some time past. There are plenty of salmon at Clemencity but there are no Indians to catch them and bring them to us. The Cape Fox and Tongass Indians who used to fish there we have heard are still at variance among themselves and have been lately killing each other."

One year the Russian American Company chose to compete in more than the fur trade. They sent a ship to Tongass Harbour and traded all the fresh deer "when they were in the best order, too," from the Tongass whom the Hudson's Bay officers had long regarded as their own special hunters.

Even as the fort inhabitants sat down to their dried peas, the eelgrass along the nearby low-tide margins waved over a population of large, succulent, coldwater crabs that would have furnished gourmet meals for an army. Below the crabs a million clams sent up their water signals through the sand, and mussels bunched on rocks everywhere. Hudson's Bay people apparently regarded all shellfish as poison, which the mussels were on rare occasions. The red menace of those years was red tide.

September 2, 1842 — "About 30 canoes of the Chymsyans [Tsimshian] who have been up the canals to the E. and N.E. ... returned. They have come sooner than they intended owing to four of them having been poisoned by eating mussels. Two of them died almost immediately, the other two were very near going, too but are likely to recover ... Nothing but wailing and lamentation to be heard."

The fort's servants were no fishermen and outstandingly unsuccessful hunters, but their incessant work with provisions kept Fort Simpson eating. They carried, they salted, they stored, day after day, year after year, and they performed some irregular food tasks, too. These are random samples:

June 26, 1839 — "4 [men] building small apartments under the gallery for the men to keep their provisions in, keeping them in their houses causes a great deal of filth & stench."

September 28, 1839 — "... one [man] and an Indian grinding wheat."

April 22, 1842 — "Kateman and Pierrish weighing the Common Biscuit."

March 29, 1852 — "We filled the smoke house with small fish after washing them in strong pickle."

September 6, 1852 — "... starting Wheat and Rice from Bags into Casks."

November 11, 1852 — "... got 4 pigs in a pen to fat for Christmas."

September 24, 1855 — "Leplante Salting Cabbages."

July 9, 1856 — "Quintal & Kiona has been baking Biscuits for the past six days for the *Beaver.*"

May 16, 1864 — "Jeremie assisting in trade shop mixing molasses."

July 27, 1865 — "Men ... cleaning out under the floor of the small fish cellar, the drain having filled up."

July 10, 1866 — "Hans ... bottling some beer."

December 18, 1866 — "Mending the flour Sacks that has been Landed from the *Otter,* a Number of them being badly cut by Vermin."

The most regular of food occupations was the issuing of the men's rations on Saturdays. It was carried out with Hudson's Bay Company consistency as long as the journals were kept but it did not begin until the fort was past its actual hunger. During that lean period there was often a scramble for day-to-day rations:

October 31, 1834 — "...salted down 2 ½ Tierces [a tierce held roughly thirty-three pounds] Deer's meat & gave out 2 days' rations for all hands."

November 27, 1834 — "Traded 5 Prime Deer, and was able to give out a fresh Meal to all hands."

January 24, 1835 — "Gave out rations for next week mainly Salt Deers' meat and Barley for four days and dried Salmon for the three following. Any Pease and Grease to the sick."

There is a hiatus of nearly ten years in the journals, 1843-1852, so we do not know when Fort Simpson crossed from privation into plenty, but from 1852 onward the entries are more likely to tell of abundance:

May 8, 1852 — "Traded a large number of Geese and Ducks. We often give them to the men over and above their rations."

December 2, 1852 — "Goat Tallow and Fresh provisions plentiful in fact we are never out of them. I have been in charge here now over 12 months [Mr. McNeill, the efficient, writing] and we have had fresh provisions for the mess every day with the exception of about 10. Men also have had extra fresh provisions given them some 150 times."

February 1, 1862 — "Served out 4 deer each to the men."

Better trade relations do not entirely account for this contrast. By 1862 most of the work of the fort was performed by Natives and the complement of Company servants had been reduced. During the unknown ten years other changes had taken place. The men, now overseers as often as labourers, were no longer accepting whatever rations might be issued to them:

July 2, 1853 — "Most of our men this day came and asked for more Pork and Flour as rations which I refused to allow; 'Foot' said that they would be obliged to apply to the 'Man

O'War' for address [redress?]. I told them to do so, but that I would not allow them any more provisions, so the matter rested for the present."

July 4 — "This morning our men, or rather 11 of them, would not go to work without more Salt Pork and Flour. Of course I refused to allow any more, as their ration is more than sufficient for any one man. I however refer'd the matter to Captain Prevost of HMS *Sloop Virago*, now on the beach repairing. He recommended that I should allow our men 1 ¼ lbs. pork and 1 ¼ lb. Flour more than the rations now allowed, which I agreed to do, and the men all returned to their duty. The Rations of Flour & Pork per week is now 5 ¼ lbs. of each, the Potatoes are reduced from 10 Gals. to 7 per week and salt … from 3 to 2 gals. per week."

This was not the first strike on the Pacific coast but perhaps the first complete with mediation.

Although Fort Simpson's officers could hardly be accused of living in luxury a seemly contrast between their mess and the men's rations was maintained throughout the years.

February 8, 1839 — "Fresh provisions coming in very slowly, Notwithstanding the number of Indians about the place. We get barely enough for the Mess ashore and Cabin mess aboard the Steamer."

July 29, 1860 — "Fresh provisions for sometime back plentiful for the mess, none to the men."

How the officers fared on high days and holidays we are not told but the company's bounty toward the hands on these occasions is meticulously recorded. The officers dispensed "regales" for the three holidays of the year, New Year's Day, All Saints' Day and Christmas. If the foods seem a little less than festive we need not be concerned; after that morning glass of rum the men certainly were not.

December 25, 1834 — "Traded 6 Deer, a Glass of Rum to all hands in the morning & a half Pint of it to each at night.

Regale, 2 lbs. Pork, 1 ½ lbs. Beef, 2 lbs. Flour it being always customary to give a regale on Christmas."

January 1, 1835 — "Gave 4 lbs. of Deer Meat, Salt, 1 pint of Rice, 1 pint of Flour to each man as a regale, it being the first day of the New Year, they also got a pint of Rum each besides three Glasses in the Morning."

October 31, 1840 — "This being 'All Saints Day' the men were allowed ½ pt. Rum, 1 pt. molasses, 1 qt. flour and a little grease in addition to their usual allowance." [All Saints' Day seems to have shifted casually between October 31 and November 1. By 1866 the Roman Catholic Church was such a distant memory to the French Canadians in Fort Simpson that one journal keeper spoke of it as "Old Sant's Day."]

Frequently regales were followed by a day of recovery:

January 2, 1835 — "No work. Dried Salmon to the Men, in the evening each man got a half pint of Rum"

December 26, 1859 — "Gave all hands a dram at 10 a.m. to sober them."

There was sometimes an unofficial regale during the season of jollity:

December 29, 1842 — "This evening McAulay was detected stealing rum out one of the puncheons in the new store which he bore with a gimlet for the purpose."

Holiday excesses were taken for granted as were the work excesses on the other days of the year.

CHAPTER 13

"Men Variously Employed"

NOT ONLY THE BUTCHER and the baker but the candle-maker, too, evolved from the Fort Simpson workforce. Those voyageurs, Iroquois, Kanakas and derelict seamen became jacks of all trades and masters of more than a few. Sometimes real tradesmen washed up on the shores of Fort Simpson in the coastal ebb and flow of company servants and their accomplishments were reported with pride in the journals. Fort Simpson once had a cooper, quite often a gunsmith and always, the most exalted of workmen, a blacksmith.

The candlemaker? Each year he worked for a few days to produce the fort's lighting. He relied on the Native trader to procure tallow, usually mountain goats', and the gunsmith to turn out his moulds. Either he, himself, or Native women spent a day plaiting wicks and then he poured his candles. One year, with an assistant, he manufactured nineteen hundred candles in one and three-quarter days, according to Mr. McNeill's precise reckoning.

Made-in-Simpson products were diverse. Sometimes the fort was a munitions works. On January 15, 1853, the men were "running musket balls," on the 18th, one was making musket cartridges and on the 21st, matches for the big guns. In 1856, they were turning out grape shot. They made brooms, and rope out of cable junk; they made hand barrows and sledges to take some of the weight off their backs in their never-ending carrying. They made bellows and buckets and levers.

Sometimes the fort was a shipyard. In the winter of 1834-35 there was a boatbuilder in the complement.

November 30 — "Faniant went in search of timber for 2 Boats, found an abundance suitable for the purpose."

December 5 — "Faniant accompanied three men to cut down & square wood for the Boats, to the little river."

December 16 — "The Two Logs of wood intended for the boats brought to the Fort, ea. 14 Inches Square 40 Feet Long."

January 24 — "The Sawyer finished the wood required for the Boats."

February 10 — "Traded 2 ½ Barrels Gum .... One of the Boats finished today."

February 18 — "... The Second boat completed in the afternoon."

Making plaster and whitewash from shells began early in the fort's existence. By 1841 it was so well-established an industry that one day there were "23 canoes with 2 Indians in each, bringing home shells." In 1853 burning lime was a routine procedure except for one occasion. The lime makers had turned out a good quantity that day and were doubtless anxious to finish their job and get home to supper. They filled twenty barrels and departed. It was fortunate that February evenings grew dark early; when the lime barrels glowed and took fire they were quite apparent. With the passing of another decade the lime operation acquired a certain sophistication. A troop of Native women, supervised by one of the workmen, built a new kiln. It was twenty by fifteen feet, with four tiers of shelves, and at one firing could produce ninety barrels of lime to be stored in a special lime shed. For all that, the lime kiln was a minor interest in Fort Simpson compared to the charcoal kiln.

The charcoal kiln belonged to the blacksmith's domain and was piled, covered, fired, drawn, slaked and the charcoal stored under his supervision. The first kiln began in a small way with twelve cords of alder, a month after the Nass complement came to McLoughlin's Harbour. An 1836 account of charcoal-making tells us that on July 21st the blacksmith and four men began piling the wood, which was burned out by August 18th, and an 1837 production report notes:

"... We have in all from 41 Cords of wood 97 Bags of Coals each bag about 2 ½ bushels = 242 bush."

By the middle of the century Vancouver Island coal began to replace the Fort Simpson charcoal in the forge. Though charcoal was made and used for a long time afterwards, the kilns never again had such status among the fort's undertakings.

The blacksmith's status endured much longer. The journals leave one with the feeling that without the factor, or the trader, or the clerk, the fort activities could have stumbled along, but without the blacksmith they would have stopped dead in a matter of days. There would have been no axes for the pickets, no nails for the building, no tools for the garden, no parts for the muskets that sometimes had to be rebuilt after one firing, no traps for the fur trade, no tin porringers for the trade shop, no locks for the gates, no hinges for the doors, no emergency repairs for the ships and no daily problem-solving for all the areas of fort life. The blacksmith was engaged at a higher rate of pay than the other men and his work was usually reported first in the day-by-day list of occupations. He had his own assistant and, at least once, a blacksmith had special accommodations built for him. While most of the other company servants travelled through the journals, sometimes for years, as mere names, the blacksmiths acquired individuality and even character. And whereas the journal keepers frequently berated the labourers for inefficiency, they criticized the blacksmith's work only once that I could discover, and then in the gentlest of terms:

"The blacksmith though ingenious and a good workman does not succeed well at making trap springs, at least in tempering them. Some time ago he commenced a bundle of steel that cut up in lengths for 113 springs. Today he tempered the last of them and has only 66 good, all the rest broke, some in the forging but a greater part in the tempering."

There was another specialized job in the fort. It required courage, strength and a bulletproof hide. The gatekeeper, from the protection of the small gatehouse, regulated the flow of traffic into the fort. If the Tsimshian and the Cumshewa were at outs, he barred the Tsimshian while the Cumshewa were trading; if there were rumbles of hostility toward the Company he kept the admissions few and well spaced; if an aggrieved tribesman became violent, he removed the offender. And so, to all the Natives of all the camps, the gatekeeper was the object of their disaffection.

It was in the 1850s that the gatekeepers lead the most exciting lives. One day in that period, picket raiders were kept at a distance by two gatekeepers and a sentry on the gallery. Again, a long-time villain of the journals, named Cushwhat, took on the entire Hudson's Bay Company beginning with the gatekeeper.

Cushwhat was like a rogue bear, spreading havoc among his fellow Tsimshian and the Company people indiscriminately. When he arrived at the fort on this particular morning the gatekeeper, out of long and sad experience, refused him entry. Somehow Cushwhat found a way inside, only to be ordered out by the relentless guard. Cushwhat drew a knife and the gatekeeper, not the gentle sort, throttled him until he dropped it and then ejected him. When Cushwhat was able to breathe normally once more he decked himself out with a couple of pistols and returned to the fort. As the gate opened to admit another Tsimshian he took aim and fired at his enemy. The writer of the journal remarks in a detached way, "The ball passed through his coat and shirt, quite a close shave."

How the gatekeeper felt at this point is not revealed but the factor felt so uncomfortable that he dispatched the trader and a long-time servant and interpreter, Pierre Legace, to Cushwhat's lodge to get to the bottom of the affair. Cushwhat received them by seizing the trader and claiming him as a hostage. (Cushwhat was obviously a hundred and twenty years ahead of his time.) But the trader played by the rules of his century so he whipped out his pistol and was about to end Cushwhat-related troubles forever when the Tsimshian bystanders in the lodge grabbed his pistol arm. Then some rapid passing ensued: a tribesman got the pistol; Pierre got the pistol. This seemed a good moment to end the interview so the trader and Pierre took their leave. I am not sure who was the winner in this episode but certainly the survivor-of-the-day was the gatekeeper.

"I suspect a woman at the bottom of this," said Mr. McNeill concerning another near miss at the gate. This time the Native man's ball skimmed over the gatekeeper's head and whistled into a roof nearby.

Actually, no Fort Simpson gatekeeper was ever killed. In view of the point blank shootings that took place at the entrance this is difficult to explain. Unless St. Peter, Honorary President of the Gatekeepers' Union, personally deflected the shots to nonmembers, how do you account for the strange facts presented in the journal entry of August 17th, 1853?

"About 3 o'clock this afternoon a row took place between our GateKeeper 'Kiona' and an Indian. The fellow wanted to get inside, and the GateKeeper would not allow him. A scuffle ensued, blows were struck and Shirts were torn on both sides. A second Indian struck Kiona and I struck him. The affair appeared to have ended when, just as I had entered the Gate, the Indian that was engaged with Kiona got a Gun from another Indian and fired, he says at me. The Shot however wounded one of our men, Robert Reid, and a chief ... A Beaver

Shot went completely through Reid's leg and a Beaver Shot went through the flesh part of the Chief's arm and entered his body under the armpit. But the worst wound was one that a Tongass Woman, a Half Breed, got. She received a Ball in her body. She was standing at the door of her lodge. This poor woman it is expected will die, which would cause a row between the Tongass and Tsimsheans. The poor woman has an infant male child by one of the Steamer's men. The two opposite parties of Indians fired a number of shots at each other. Set double watch for the night."

While the gatekeeper stood between the fort and assailants' bullets by day, watchmen patrolled the gallery by night. Sometimes in a strange, dry spell of weather there were fire-watches: "Hans on watch all night. Roofs being very dry we are afraid of sparks from the Indian camp." And sometimes there were daytime watches, too: "One man on sentry for crows."

Both gatekeepers and watchmen had a preponderance of ordinary, boring shifts. Even in the turbulent 1850s there were days when five hundred Natives would be allowed inside the stockade at once. It was at such times of peace and good-will that the fort's sentry was expected to watch with one eye while he applied the other to odd jobs. Watchmen gardened and cut seed potatoes and cut and melted blubber. But there were plenty of days and nights when several pairs of eyes were fully occupied with watching.

When Mr. Charles, a Haida chief, was killed by one of his own men while retrieving a stolen axe for the Company, the wrath of the tribe fell upon the fort. "Kept 3 men constantly on watch." When canoes arrived simultaneously from three different villages, "Put 6 men on watch for tonight as there are a great number of Indians, to prevent stealing potatoes." When there were rumours of an attack on the fort the factor presented each of three chiefs with a suit of clothes but also took the usual precautions: "Put 2 additional men on watch tonight ..." The rumour turned out to be correct and the clothes unavailing, so next day, "Men all in the Fort ... Have put 12 Men on watch tonight divided into 3 watches."

There was one lively day in 1842 when all hands were watching and loading muskets. It began with a pedestrian Kyganie-Tsimshian quarrel over a slave, which erupted with the force of a geyser when a Kyganie stabbed a Tsimshian, wounding him seriously. Because the offender was a brother-in-common-law of Captain McNeill, Mr. Work granted him and his tribesmen sanctuary inside the fort. The Tsimshian armed themselves and came ravening about the stockade demanding that either their prey or payment for the injury be delivered up to them. The Kyganie, secure behind the pickets and the guns, refused to make restitution. Said Mr. Work, "... as the objects of their [the Tsimshian] vengeance are now residing in the Fort ... it cannot at present be anticipated how the affair will terminate." It did not terminate soon. Two days later, "The Kyganie Indians are still inmates of the Fort no compromise being made as yet ..." It was not until the fourth day that the siege was lifted when "The Big Faced Man [a Tsimshian chief] received 1 blanket, 1 sheeting sail and an Elkskin Robe for the wound one of his men received," and the fort people ceased their watch and went back to sawing, chopping, digging, carrying and "beating the bears."

The people of Fort Simpson bore Native attacks, hurricanes, death and privations with stoicism, but what raised a loud alarm was the discovery of a moth in the marten skins.

To the officers, the moth was a threat to their returns. Returns were the only reason for all the building, logging, shipping, victualling and First Nations diplomacy that made up their lives. To the men it signalled the undoing of days and days of work. Every fur pack that had been wrestled up the ladder to the Big House garret, or the store garret, had to be carried out of that pungent atmosphere to the gallery to be opened and its furs, one by one, closely examined. (Looking for moth eggs and larvae in the fur of a black bear makes needles and haystacks seem like fun.) Then every skin had to be aired on the gallery pickets — sunning was preferable but often impossible in Fort Simpson — and beaten. All those fur-lined pickets must have been an arresting sight, with men at intervals along the gallery flailing away at them. The process for the smaller furs, mink and marten, was called "dusting" and was presumably somewhat gentler. And then there was the sprinting. If the skins got damp they would mould and mould was only a shade less damaging than moths. As the heavens cleared, the furs were rushed out to the pickets; as the clouds gathered they were hustled back inside. The intervals could be perversely short. Once again the packs were assembled, compacted in wooden presses, lashed with thongs cut from deer skins, and, with heaving and grunting, stowed away to await the southbound ship.

Newly traded furs went through the same procedure, without the crisis factor. Sometimes, in his eagerness to procure certain furs, the trader would accept improperly cured skins and then the men would take on the odoriferous job of staking them out beside a fire. No sooner had they put all their furs in good order than the Company's trading ship would cast up and discharge her cargo of furs and, on occasion, the Taku and Stikine furs as well. Again the workforce aired, beat, packed and stowed.

The fort operated its own tan pit for deer and hair seal skins. It could be found with one sniff. The smells of fish, tar, whale oil, wet work clothes and skins were but a bland background to the smoke-and-rawhide odour that rolled out of the tan pit.

In the fall of 1837, "Had twenty buck deer put in tan. Forty more are getting ready to put in tan also." Tsimshian were employed to scrape the hair off the hides and sometimes to do the stretching. Deer skins were exported but there are also numerous journal entries regarding the cutting and twisting of deer skin cords for use at the fort. During the earliest years the men performed practically all the fur-related tasks but by 1855 platoons of women were cutting the cords and cleaning the furs under the supervision of one lucky employee. For centuries Native women had been responsible for all such chores in their villages. They worked dexterously.

For days at a time fort workers were longshoremen, for the Hudson's Bay Company's north coast trade was amphibious. Sometimes it went to sea and sometimes it hauled up on shore as in the case of Fort Simpson. This duality came about because Dr. John McLoughlin, head of the Columbia District, was an exponent of dryland operations while Governor George Simpson favoured ships. Governor Simpson never left much doubt about his authority so the fort in McLoughlin's Harbour was at the service of the Company trading vessels. Orders, supplies, personnel, work and worries shifted from ship to shore and back again in an ambiguity that the journals seemed to take for granted. Pages were devoted to the waterfront work — the following items are mere sprinklings of salt:

May 16, 1836 — "Sent 10 men to cut wood for the Steam Boat." [The *Beaver* steamed into McLoughlin's Harbour for the first time on July 9th, 1836.]

March 27, 1837 — "Articles were landed from the *Nereide* and the rest of the day occupied taking ballast on board. Some provisions were sent on board the Steamer *Beaver.*"

April 4, 1837 — "Busy most of the day preparing a trading outfit for the Steamer in order to send her off on a trading cruise as soon as she is ready for sea. Though she is not likely to make much yet, it is necessary to have a turn made to all the different trading stations before the Opponents cast up should any come."

August 15, 1837 — "The *Beaver* was hauled ashore to

have a piece put on the rudder to widen it and something done to the paddles."

August 17, 1837 — "… the blacksmith and assistant hard at work [on the *Beaver* and the *Nereide]*."

September 4, 1838 — "… 2 [men] melting and mixing grease and small fish Oil for the Steamer's Engines. It is mixed in equal parts and it is still pretty hard and it is expected will answer well as a substitute for tallow. This is the only resource we have to make sure of having enough to serve. By some overlook there was no tallow sent on from Fort Vancouver for her. Enough of tallow may be got here but like all supplies from Indians it is precarious and can't be depended upon."

May 5, 1842 — "One man Jolibois, and fourteen Indians collecting stones to ballast the *Cowlitz* when she arrives." [The *Cowlitz* required fifty to sixty tons of ballast.]

May 29, 1858 — "Rudland still on the spar for Steamer. We had the two sticks brought inside the Fort by 22 Indians."

March 31, 1866 — "Hans with Graham searching for the *Petrel's* Anchor."

November 24, 1866 — "Men receiving their rations at daylight. Afterwards Employed with Wm. Graham putting Ways etc. under the Sloop's bottom, and trying to get her up in the front Wood Yard, all hands wrought at her until 2 p.m., and when she had just commenced to Start, one of the Sliding Ways slipped from under her bottom. So Now she must stop where she is untill Morning, when another atempt will be made on her to get her up, and secured from the comming winter storms."

All hands wrought at mundane tasks, too, especially on Saturdays. Saturday cleaning was an inflexible rule at Hudson's Bay forts.

October 29, 1858 — " 'All hands' cleaning their houses inside, i.e. scouring with sand."

It seems to have been a strenuous type of cleaning that was also used on the gallery and even on the pickets. When sand would no longer do the job, a coat of whitewash was applied. The results were not perfect, according to a letter written in 1850 by Captain D. D. Wishart of the *Norman Morison*. Concerning Fort Simpson he said: "... the whole garrison both officers and men living in a most careless dirty manner, appearing almost to endeavour to forget civilized decency, and copy their neighbours the Savages."

Another regular occupation was that of factotum in the Indian shop. So many different languages and dialects were spoken there that a man with a knowledge of one or more was very valuable to the trader. This man did the fetching and carrying between storehouse and trade shop and prepared the stock for distribution, turning rum into "Indian rum" by diluting it one to three, thinning molasses and reducing tobacco heads to the leaves by which it was sold. He also handled the goods received, measuring whale oil or tallying fish.

"Rain. Employed as usual," says the journal, but some of the employment was quite unusual. Once Fort Simpson had a shepherd. Once a workman was sent into a Tsimshian lodge to dress the wound of a tribal-war victim. Frequently the hands were chimney sweeps or firemen or undertakers. And constantly they pitted their strength and wits against water. It was not enough that they battled the rain above and the sea before, they also had to battle the pleasant little brook behind the stockade. It had been one of the deciding factors in the July choice of the site. They painstakingly devised methods of bringing its water into the fort with water runs and spouts made out of squared logs. Then came a freshet and their energies were bent on getting its water out of the fort. When summer ended, its gurgle became a roar and it tumbled the drainage of the coastal slope right into the fort yard. The men dug new channels and ditches and drains and lined them with boards and cleared them and recleared them and repaired them and built a dam and still the brook flowed into the yard.

They carried sand and crushed clamshells into the low-lying areas of the fort and still there were ponds.

That small stream known as the brook, the rivulet, the burn, according to the various journal keepers, had become The Creek by the time I was big enough to jump across its narrowest reach and to pick the forget-me-nots that survived some long-past planting along its course. By then it had been tamed and confined within its deep banks. Nonetheless, it was the focal point for at least one small family drama and provided my first awareness of poetic justice.

CHAPTER 14

Port Simpson Pact

"CHICKENS SMELL," said my father, "and when you shoo them they run in the wrong direction. They squawk, too. I don't know why you want them, but here they are," and he deposited the crate of Plymouth Rocks on the back porch.

My mother gave the same ecstatic "ah" I had heard on Christmas morning when she unwrapped her turquoise brooch. She snatched the claw hammer from a shelf and began pounding and ripping at the slats.

"Not here," said Dad with a tinge of horror in his voice, as he backed into the kitchen.

Mother pushed the wheelbarrow up to the back steps and, motioning me to steady one end, heaved and pushed and pulled until the crate sat squarely on the wheelbarrow and its occupants clattered their indignation. Dad was right — they smelled.

As I followed Mother and the wheelbarrow through the drizzle to the newly erected chicken house on the bank of the creek, I asked, "Why didn't Dad help you?"

"Well, he couldn't, because of our bargain," said Mother, a little breathless from lifting.

My parents' pact was made on a fall afternoon when the gasoline lamps hissed indoors and the rain slapped at grey-black shapes outdoors and Mother and Dad faced another winter in our forsaken settlement. In British Columbia's north coast country of the 1920s, Port Simpson was not classified as isolated. The *Venture* called once a week and a disaster-prone telephone wire drooped over twenty miles of wilderness to Prince Rupert, to hold us loosely within the world. It was only in the depths of the autumnal gloom that my parents' zest for our remote life faltered. Then they mused upon Fate. Obviously, it was Fate that had snatched Mother from her beloved Oregon farmlands to live in a country where cattle foundered in the muskeg and gardens grew or mildewed erratically; that had brought my father from such a circumspect background that he donned a suit, stiff collar and tie, daily, to sell bacon by the slab to the missionary's wife, or pink flannelette to shawl-wrapped Native women, or gear to the trappers. Frustration halted Dad between the ribbon showcase and the potbellied stove. "Outlets, that's what we need; outlets that will use our interests. Haven't you some interest beside farming, Hallie? The teachers at the mission school are taking up china painting."

Mother hardly waited for Dad to finish. "Chickens," she said. "Every night when the Nass wind keeps me awake, I lie there working out ways and means of raising chickens on this place. I know I can handle it — just a few for our own use, way up by the creek, so they won't ever bother you." Then Mother's enthusiasm dipped. "But you need a business to satisfy you. What business could you ever launch in Port Simpson?"

The Nass wind must have disturbed my father's sleep, too, because he said, without hesitation, "Perhaps I've found it. There's a fascinating article in the last issue of the *Canadian Fur Trader*. Fur prices are higher than they have ever been. The idea of fur farming is beginning to look practical. All over the States and Canada, experiments with fur farms are succeeding. Imagine cultivating the best fox or mink or even marten, in the north." Dad threw a scuttleful of coal into the stove, kicked the door shut and hurried on, "I don't want to make a big, expensive mistake on this. I'll have to do a lot of reading and research. Why, I don't even know which animal I should raise. I won't have much capital to put into my ranch and worse than that, not much time."

"I can give you some time, Boyd. I can take over the book-keeping and most of the cleaning in the store. Of course, I still need a chicken house — there's a plan for a new type in my *Farmers' Monthly* and chicken wire to fence in that deep grass along the creek, and feed, and purebred stock. All that will cost a lot but we'll get eggs and chicken dinners out of the investment."

Dad's pacing grew slower and his grin began to work the corners of his mouth. "Hallie, we'll both have our projects." Then the pacing stopped suddenly and the puckers vanished. "You know I abhor chickens, don't you? I'll pay for everything you need for them but I won't go near the dirty things. I won't feed them or wring their necks or clean the chicken house."

The pact was sealed with a duet of laughter. Each of my parents was enjoying his or her own mental picture of Dad hauling manure out of a chicken yard.

The flock throve in its haven of lush grass and Mother's loving care. Each member was addressed by name: Calico was the dependable layer; Dimity, the dainty pullet; Doodle, the handsome rake of a rooster, and so on down the length of three perches. Their feet were examined and doctored regularly, as a precaution against their soggy surroundings; their mites were exterminated by sulphur dustings; their diet was supplemented by clamshells carried up from the beach. I even found Mother administering castor oil, by spoon, to Dimity, one day. Orange-yolked eggs became the star feature of our meals and we all looked forward to the summer when our fish-and-canned-meat regimen would be relieved by platters of fried chicken. Dad bore poultry no ill-feeling once it had achieved the status of food.

My parents were punctilious bargain keepers. Mother never asked for help — well, only once — and Dad certainly never gave any. Each morning Mother rose in the cold blackness of six o'clock to get the chicken house chores done so she would have time in the afternoon to sit at the desk in the store and make entries in Dad's full-scale set of ledgers and journals. On Saturdays, enveloped in a slicker, gumboots and sou'wester, she went out to clean Dimity's home. For two hours I would hear her voice dipping and rising in "Red River Valley" counterpointed by the shrieks of displaced fowl. Then she would return to the back porch, change into her store apron and wash show windows for another two hours, still singing. On his part, Dad provided handsomely and without question for Mother's pets. He even furnished a fishnet to cover the top of that huge chicken run against the hawk whose life intent seemed to be to gain access to them.

As spring released the creek from ice and filled the hens' hearts with maternity, the hawk was succeeded by a more efficient enemy. It was then that Mother lapsed, just once, into an appeal for help. "A rat got into Calico's brooder last night and broke two of her eggs," she told us at breakfast. "The chickens were in a terrible state when I got to them this morning. I don't think Calico will go back on her nest."

Dad brought Mother a rat trap and the battle for the chicken yard was on. Next morning Mother reported, "The rat trap's missing. It's just gone. I'd set it right outside the fence where the rat had dug his way in the night before. I've searched all round but there's no sign of it."

My father was interested. Exterminating rats was something of a specialty of his. Each year the store was raided by pack rats, bush rats and ordinary dirty-looking rats, and Dad dealt with each invasion with quick and remarkable success. "What you need," he told Mother authoritatively, "is a weasel trap. That's how I get the bush rats so fast. I'll lend you mine."

When he produced the contrivance of steel with the wicked little jaw, Mother shuddered. "You're so good at this sort of thing, Boyd," she murmured, "wouldn't you like to look after it for me? You wouldn't really be dealing with my chickens, only with Port Simpson rats. Please?"

The lid of Dad's large right eye slid downward in a wink directed at me so I would understand that he was teasing. "Oh, it's simple enough, Hallie. I'll show you how to handle it. Just think how many little Dimitys it will save. After all, a bargain's a bargain."

Mother set the weasel trap. The following morning it was gone. Mother followed its trail to the bank of the creek. "That poor, hateful rat must have been in such pain he didn't care if he drowned," she told us.

Dad remembered he'd once caught a bush rat bigger than a weasel. That fellow had dragged the trap clear across the warehouse. "Chain the new trap to the fence tonight," he urged.

Mother declined. But she had to admit that her hens were headed for nervous disorders. "I'm trying poison tonight," she said, "the kind with phosphorous, that sends the rat away in search of water."

That afternoon Gingham's eggs hatched. At dusk there was an outcry of terror and hate from the chicken yard. Mother reached the gate in time to see a rat streaking under the fence with a baby chick between its teeth. "He was the ugliest, heaviest rat I ever saw. His hind feet looked huge," she reported.

"Scared bush rat, no doubt," said Dad.

"No. The tail wasn't hairy. It was naked like a house rat's."

"Then definitely, it was a brown rat grown fat and ugly on its diet of eggs."

"Well, there are going to be a lot fewer brown rats, then," and off Mother went to the kitchen to spread slices of bread with the mixture that gave off the stinging odour of a whole box of matches freshly lit.

Each morning for a long time, Mother reported depredations, but always the disappearance of the poison. "That's not a family of rats," remarked my father, frankly impressed, "it's a pack."

Then one morning when the crabapple tree had got around to its late blooming, Mother celebrated victory. The chickens had not been molested and the poisoned bread had not been touched. From that day on, the hens hatched their eggs and reared their young in smug serenity.

While Mother waged her war, my father's venture was having a difficult birth. After the first few days of study he gave up his dream of a fox farm and settled for a mink ranch as more suited to the climate and limitations of Port Simpson. He reported his progress at the breakfast table, too. (Those were the days when families had three courses and conversation for breakfast.) "I'll need two employees — one on the farm and one out in a boat fishing. Each mink is going to eat from a quarter to half a pound of fish a day."

Dad kept piles of books and periodicals and pamphlets on his desk. They all had to do with mink or mink farming. He worked hours at a time over the two long sheets of yellow accounting paper, one headed, "Possible Income," the other, "Probable Expenses." It was the latter that fascinated me. Every day it seemed to have a surprising new item; such as, "galvanized iron for underground extension of fence." I spent much time around the store those days because Dad's exuberance made it seem rather jolly. He shied pilot biscuits at the mendicant village dogs; he slipped peppermints into the parcels of his child customers; he told jokes, in Chinook, to ancient Agnes Ward and they laughed together till her black head handkerchief had to be retied.

Then one day my father came to dinner without a smile or a wink or even a swing to his walk. His chin had fallen down to the very V of his wing collar. Mother said, "Boyd, are you having another bout of indigestion?"

He replied stiffly, "No, Hallie, I'm very well, thank you," and proceeded to leave his venison steak and his apple pie, barely sampled.

"Did the fur market drop after you made your shipment?" pursued Mother.

He shook his head.

"Have the wholesalers been overcharging you again?"

Another shake.

Mother crossed her arms high on her chest, thereby indicating that she was going to be calm and patient. After a remarkable silence in which my tea seemed to gurgle uproariously down my gullet, Dad said, "The mink farm won't work," and he rose without folding his napkin and headed for his office.

Mother didn't press the matter that night but a day or two later she explained to me, "Your father just hasn't the capital to start his mink farm. The stock is frightfully expensive — twice as much as he expected. And mink are hard to raise in captivity. A mink mother simply eats her young if they are disturbed even slightly. It might take years to build up a ranch."

I was so distressed that I dusted the notions showcase without being bidden. Mother tried such palliatives as a dish of freshly salted almonds placed on the desk and a new Sousa record for the phonograph, but we continued in gloom. When we reached the point where mealtimes became so oppressive that dishwashing was a happy relief, my mother acted. She loaded my schoolbag with jars of jelly for one of her periodic visits to the old and afflicted of the reserve. "I may be later than usual," she called to me from the gate. "Start the potatoes at five."

Mother was late returning and when she came in she didn't even glance at the range to see if the potatoes were boiling. She walked straight through to Dad's office. "Harvey Adams is back from his trap line," she said. "He'll be in tomorrow to sell some of the darkest marten skins I ever saw. He shot three bear. You can smell them cooking all over the village. Phew! I told Harvey you didn't think your mink farm would work out ..."

Dad interrupted, "Now, Hallie, Harvey knows everything there is to know about animals in the woods but he doesn't know a thing about fur farming. The mink farm is dead and buried. I wish you'd forget it."

"Harvey agreed it wouldn't work, so I asked him what would. He said, 'Muskrat.'" Mother dropped her rather flimsy veil of matter-of-factness and let her excitement flash. "Boyd, it's meant to be. We have the creek with the right kind of banks for their lodges. Harvey says he and his boys can stock your farm from Dundas Island and the creatures will practically feed themselves."

Dad was slow to kindle. "You forget that the creek bank is already occupied."

"We can move the chicken house over to the east side of the property. That's no trick."

"Muskrat pelts don't bring much."

"You know that the market for short furs is rising phenomenally. You told me so yourself. Muskrat will always be in demand — you told me that, too. And you will have quantity. They're going to multiply by at least four every year. Harvey says they're so hardy you'll never have to worry about them."

Dad did a spin on his swivel chair. "I'll look into it," he said, with the restraint suitable to a back-east businessman.

So began the bright era of the muskrat farm. New piles of books and papers grew on Dad's desk; new sets of measurements were transferred to new sketches; new lists of figures crawled down the yellow sheets. This time they all seemed to fall into place.

"I think I like a muskrat, personally, much better than a mink," Dad confided, as I helped him fill the apple bin. "A mink doesn't have endearing habits but a muskrat is downright home-loving, and enterprising, too."

Three almost industrious Tsimshian lads moved the chicken house to its new location and fenced the whole creek area. Then Dad began to make overtures to Harvey Adams regarding stock.

Harvey was thrilled with the idea of transplanting a muskrat colony. Over and over again he would say, "I like see this, Mr. Young. My boys and I go out pretty soon." In the best Tsimshian manner, he kept saying but not going. My father, wise in the ways of his Tsimshian tillicums, did not urge him. He raised the rewards for the undertaking twice, but as Harvey was the best hunter and trapper in Port Simpson, he already owned a fine house and a fine boat and was long past worrying about the material aspects of life. So Dad waited while Harvey and his boys went to Zayas Island for seaweed, to a distant rock for seagull eggs, to Prince Rupert for a good time, and finally to the Skeena River for the fishing season. "After fishing, Mr. Young," Harvey called cheerily to Dad as he departed on this last expedition. Dad let out a combined sigh and groan. "After fishing" was the phrase used by north coast Native people to cover "this year, next year, some time, never."

My father had gone too far with his preparations to give up now. Muskrat had never been farmed in our part of North America so he could not simply send out an order for stock. He cast about him in every direction for ideas and landed one that delighted the family. The Vancouver Exhibition listed among its entries in the new category of "Fur-bearing Ranch Animals" one exhibit of muskrat. "I'll probably be able to meet the fellow who entered them and find out all I need to know," said Dad. "Let's go to the exhibition."

Going to the exhibition involved a three-day trip on the *Venture*, a stay at a hotel that had potted palms complete with lizards, and city shopping, by elevator. We children gulped down all these pleasures without impairing our appetites for the main course, our day at the fair.

As the turngate at Exhibition Park clicked behind us, my father announced, "The fur farming exhibits first; then the poultry for you and the children, Hallie, while I wait in the main building for you; and after that, the midway for as long as the girls and Loyal want to stay."

In the Livestock Building I skipped along behind my parents, dodging a whirligig seller, a tearful little boy and a fat man carrying a megaphone. I knew without the help of signs when we were near the fur farming section. The farmyard odours gave way to a pungency and wildness in my nostrils. Thorough, even in the midst of swirling crowds and hot popcorn, my father insisted that we start at the entrance and work our way, cage by cage, till we reach the muskrat exhibit. The first cages held mink but, as the creatures practically refused to be seen, Mother and I grew a little restless. I simply stood and stared at the spectators but Mother kept darting ahead with glances toward the sign that read "Poultry — South Wing."

Dad was saying to us, "That's a mutation mink with the white tipped guard hairs. In some markets his fur would bring a fortune; in some it wouldn't sell for even . . ." when an agonized cry from Mother sent us hurtling through people and balloons to her. I thought she must have been bitten by one of the animals. When we reached her she was standing in front of a cage of brown fur hummocks, on her face the stricken look of a child who has slapped his mother. She grabbed Dad's shoulder.

"The rats in the chicken yard." She spoke as if her lips were numb. "I poisoned every last one." Her left forefinger tapped on the small sign near the bottom of the cage. It read, "Ranch Muskrat."

My father stood staring into the cage while people came, looked and went away. He appeared to be studying every individual hair on those animals; but when he turned around, he said, "Let's go look at the chickens."

PART IV

"To Prosecute the Trade"

CHAPTER 15

Beginnings

EIGHT BLUE GLASS BEADS rattled about in a tobacco can in the top drawer of my father's desk. They were survivors of the fort fire. Once I came upon Dad reflectively rolling them back and forth in his hand. "I came late," he said.

Dad had just come off second best in barter for some rare cross-fox skins from the Interior. Fur trading in Port Simpson was unlike the active, vociferous bargaining that we associate with marketplaces the world over. It consisted chiefly of super-charged silences. On this occasion the foxes were heaped on the counter and beside them a growing pile of ten-dollar bills. On one side of the counter the Nisga'a trapper stood immobile and on the other side Dad paced. When that particular silence reached a climax that threatened to explode, Dad opened the till, withdrew another ten-dollar bill, placed it on top of the pile and closed the till. That launched a further silence, and so trading continued while the store clock clattered. After many openings and closings of the till the trapper nodded, picked up the stack of bills and then he and Dad shook hands and conversed.

My father might have regarded the blue beads less disconsolately had he known that, contrary to common belief, the Hudson's Bay beads never did purchase priceless furs at Fort

Simpson. In fact, nowhere in the fort journals — and the journals covered fur transactions in detail — were they listed in payments for furs. Mr. Work mentioned returning some beads to headquarters as unsaleable and Mr. McNeill once discussed beads in a letter, so they must have been used as *somentaskins*, the little items given as a bonus at the end of a good trading session. Without a doubt, in some parts of Canada, at some time, Natives exchanged valuable furs for trinkets, but not the Tsimshian. They were shrewd and sophisticated traders before the Russian American Company and the Hudson's Bay Company broke into their trade routes that wound back in time beyond our reckoning.

The Fort Simpson journal keeper sat down with his goose or seagull quill to record the day's take, without an inkling of the stories that would emerge in glimmers and flashes from those disconnected entries. The ending of the sea otter story was written thus and suggests that not only my father but the Hudson's Bay Company before him came late. The world's most luxurious fur was already on its way to extinction when Dr. Tolmie set up shop under oilcloth in McLoughlin's Harbour. The sea otter story belongs to the Russians and, unreasonably, begins with the sable.

Of all the furs that clothed the people of the cold, Eurasian northland, from prehistoric times, the sable was the most desired. It lured the Russians farther and farther east, into and across Siberia until they reached the end of their world and salt water. Then they built crude ships and pushed out into the sea. It was in 1741 that one of those ships, homeward bound, its crew weakened by scurvy, piled up on a barren island only one hundred eighty miles from its home harbour. Vitus Bering was its commander. He died there on the beach along with thirty-one of his men.

Blue foxes swarmed over Bering Island, as it was later named, and sea otters played about its shoreline, thick as bulbs in a kelp bed. The mobile men killed some foxes to keep them from their sick comrades and away from their supplies. They killed the sea otters for food. The foxes chewed up numbers of the untreated sea otter pelts but the men managed to save nine hundred of them. They were even richer and more lustrous than the sables, many of them six feet in length and of such obvious value that the castaways lost interest in building their escape boat and spent the short daylight hours in gambling for skins. Their greed was slight compared with the greed that was unleashed in Petropavlovsk when the survivors and their wealth finally made port.

Those who pushed their way across Siberia to the new Kamchatka frontier were the roughest and the toughest, Cossack bandits and their ilk. As their boats were completed they sailed eastward to gather in the wealth of furs that lolled on the island rocks. They progressed from island to island in the chain, stripping each in turn. They preyed not only on the animals but on the humans as well. The Aleuts, a mild-mannered people, were almost defenceless against them. The traders, backed by a long tradition of Russian serfdom, enslaved them to make use of their hunting skills and raided their bands for women. Thus they worked their rapacious way to the mainland. They faced the same dangers that Bering had faced, and many died, but those who lived made sudden fortunes.

Eventually, the Russian sea otter trade became almost respectable to everyone except the Aleuts, Inuit, Tlingit and, of course, the sea otters — they all continued to decline in number, although less rapidly than in the wild Cossack days. The reform came about under a company that was a Russian version of the Hudson's Bay Company. By the time Fort Simpson challenged its trade the Aleutian sea otters had been exterminated and the remainder were doomed.

Another chapter of the sea otter story opens with Captain James Cook's voyage to America's northwest coast in 1778. He sailed through Bering Strait and the exploration and cartography resulting from that voyage became famous all over the civilized world. His seamen's pastime of bartering with the Natives for souvenirs became famous, too. With great acumen they acquired sea otter skins. Cook fled from the winter ice to the Hawaiian Islands which, conveniently, he had discovered one year before. It was there he was killed. But the expedition continued its work for another year and then, on its westward route home, touched at Canton, the one port of northern China open to foreign trade. The sailors sold their furs for unimagined wealth and the Western world followed Russia, pell-mell, into the sea otter trade.

CHAPTER 16

Barter

SEA OTTER SKINS became so rare and desirable that in 1837 Dr. Kennedy, the Fort Simpson trader, bartered for days for one lot that the Masset had brought. He raised the offer per skin to an unheard-of "7 blankets and somentaskins, or small presents, or 8 blankets without anything else for each large skin" but the Masset were unmoved and advanced their price to eight blankets and a gun. "Giving such a price was out of the question and they were turned out of the shop," wrote the journal keeper. Both sides were expert enough bargainers to know that the matter would not end there. The next day's entry reads:

"Mr. Kennedy busy all day with the Masset Indians, they traded 12 Sea Otter, all they had, at the prices we offered them yesterday."

There was another highly speculative method of acquiring sea otter furs. It was to outfit a Native hunting expedition. Over the years the Company interests set out in many a canoe and since the practice continued we can only conclude that in the long run it was profitable. The odds seem alarming, for the diminishing herds had become elusive; the hunters often returned without having sighted a single sea otter. Since this accomplished animal is able to submerge for ten to thirty minutes at a time, even a sighting did not mean success. The

best hunting grounds in British territory were in the wild
waters off the Queen Charlotte Islands, which sometimes
swallowed hunters, canoe and gear. And, although they
painted their canoes and paddles black to camouflage them,
alien tribesmen rounding any point or approaching any shelter took the risk of being set upon by the Haidas and
murdered. Sometimes they took the risk of being the setters-
upon as, for example, on May 15th, 1855:

"A party of four canoes left this about 15 days since to
hunt sea otter near Cuyou where they are in large numbers.
Niswaymot went in one of the canoes, he attempted to take
by force some women out of a lodge, the women defended
themselves assisted by some Indians. Niswaymot and his
brother were wounded together with some other Tsimshians,
one nearly dead. This affair broke up the sea otter hunt and
they came back with one otter only — yesterday."

Nine days later Mr. McNeill, never easily discouraged,
wrote: "Fitted out 7 canoes to hunt sea otter."

When the factor or his assistant entered the week's trade in
the journal each Sunday, he began with the most valuable fur
and proceeded downward in order of decreasing merit to the
humble muskquach (muskrat) although that item appeared
rarely in the days of the opulent furs. Sea otter likewise appeared
rarely so it was beaver that usually headed the lists from 1834
until the middle of the century when the beaver began to follow the sea otter down the road to extinction. In its day the
beaver trade of Fort Simpson gave rise to some anomalies.

While Natives are cited as the supreme ecologists, nobody
ever, ever attributed such leanings to the men of the Hudson's
Bay Company, especially in regard to beaver. In the country
south and east of Fort Vancouver, which they knew would
eventually be lost to them, they quite frankly pursued a policy of trapping out the beaver. In the north the Natives were
particularly enthusiastic about the spring beaver hunt. Just

after the females had whelped they were easy prey; the pups, useless for fur, were killed or left to die. And so we find factors of the Hudson's Bay Company pleading with them to abandon the spring hunt and the Natives stubbornly continuing the slaughter.

Though our national symbol had faced extermination for many years, it was not until 1907 that the killing of beaver was outlawed. Then the Company and the Natives were united in their anguish. Fortunately their protests received sharp replies from the Provincial Land and Works Department so that today beavers' lodges may be seen from many British Columbia roadsides. When their dams flood the roads perhaps there is a feeling that their well-known industry is a trifle misused. Still, we are happy to welcome them back.

During the decline of the beaver, the marten, a relative of the sable, took over the top of the trade lists. At that time black bear, in demand in England for busbies among other things, ranked high, while mink was a lowly fur. The trader could not be bothered with squirrel in the day-to-day buying and opened the market for it once a year.

May 6, 1856 — "Commenced today to trade Squirrel Skins at the rate of one leaf [tobacco] each."

He shipped twenty-one thousand squirrel skins that year but he much preferred his trade in fishers, foxes, lynxes, land otters, fur seals (never in any quantity at Fort Simpson), hair seals, wolverines, brown and grizzly bears to supplement the furs that headed his lists.

Tucked away at the bottom of the trade lists were the Company's purchases other than fur. There, provisions were noted, and building materials, and some intriguing items that were listed without a word of explanation, for instance, in 1835, "14 iron pots or boilers." The trader once bought a lodge that had been dismantled — odd boards and bark were common trade items but not entire lodges. He bought oil for the export trade, whale, oolichan, dogfish and seal oil, and tallow of deer and mountain goat. He bought whale bone, stone pipes, northwest hats (woven) and cedar mats by the hundreds. He bought bears' gall, bladder and all, for medicinal use in China, and beavers' castora, the glands that produce a musky odour. Traps rubbed with castora were irresistible to beavers, while in Europe medicine and perfume makers bid for castora. The trader bought paddles and canoes and once dickered with the Kyganie for a whaling ship's boat that had been stolen originally by deserting crewmen. In fact, all sorts of marine plunder turned up at Fort Simpson's Indian shop:

February 3, 1836 — "A canoe of Masset Indians arrived today from Pearl Harbour. A quadrant belonging to Captain Duncan was offered for sale but did not get it, though I offered 3 Blankets for it." (Captain Duncan was the master of the Company's first *Vancouver*, which had foundered on Rose Spit two years before.)

February 5, 1853 — "Robert Peel also arrived from Chatsina, he has brought the Bell formerly belonging to the '*Susan Sturgis*'. We will purchase it of him if possible." (The *Susan Sturgis* had been seized by the Haida, plundered and destroyed.)

May 14, 1853 — "The Kyganies and Massets have lots of property with them from the plunder of the *Susan Sturgis*. They have Gold Coins and dust, but we cannot get it from them as they ask the full value for it."

Also offered in trade from the *Susan Sturgis* were the captain and the mate. The Company bought:

"This day we paid 17 3-pt. Blankets, 8 Shirts, Powder, Tobacco and Cotton for bringing Captain Rooney and his Mate here from Charlott's Island ..."

Eventually Fort Simpson ransomed the entire crew.

The purchase of slaves for release to their own people was somewhat more direct and also more expensive. It happened occasionally when a Native of very high rank was captured by an enemy tribe and in the summer of 1857 when Victoria requested the return of eight Cowichan who had been captured in a raid by the Haida. Mr. McNeill was outraged at the price he had to pay for these men, "say 30 Blankets & one Gun each for them, besides a number of other articles." But three years later the journal keeper registered no shock when "Mr. Moffatt bought the daughter of Wawlish, a Quoquolth chief from Wehar for 80 blankets, 2 Guns and the stowskins."

While the fort purchases hint of stories never told, the goods it dispensed were of some interest, too. First and always there were blankets, which quickly replaced cedar bark garments and nakedness in that ungentle climate. They became the standard of coastal commerce and in that capacity measured the wealth disbursed at potlatches. They also purchased slaves and, in the 1860s, bought whiskey from the trading schooners in lieu of furs.

The Natives, understandably, placed great value upon cloth and clothing items. The Hudson's Bay Company supplied them with duffel (coarsely woven wool), cotton and baize. There were "common shirts" and apparently whole outfits of wearing apparel, for Mr. Work once presented each of three chiefs with a suit. Handkerchiefs were in demand. No, this does not mean that the coast peoples promptly embraced the white man's ideas of hygiene. They wore the handkerchiefs as scarves, on necks and heads. Then there were elk skins, which were not native to that part of the country, but were highly prized by coast peoples who made them into luxurious garments.

In the early years the fort did almost no grocery business unless you consider as such the exchange of potatoes for oolichan grease and grease for potatoes. By the 1850s, however, the Natives had discovered rice:

October 8, 1853 — (From a letter to headquarters) — "Require more Rice, pearl buttons, buckshot, vermilion and beans. All the rice you sent on the *Otter* will be bought by Cacas' people alone."

October 23, 1855 — "We could dispose of 5,000 lbs. Rice in coarse of the next month to the Nass people if the Rice was good. The Indians are 'mad' for it."

Equally phenomenal quantities of molasses were bartered, suitably diluted, for in the lodges the dish of the decade was rice-and-molasses. It was particularly favoured for feasts before the day of the rum feasts dawned.

Tobacco was traded sometimes by the leaf and sometimes by the head, as on January 6, 1860: "A canoe of Haidas arrived this morning. As Edensaw's brother is dead they wish to trade tobacco."

Firearms were originally traded as an aid to hunting and trapping. The Natives found them useful for this purpose but indispensable for avenging an injury or a death, raiding neighbouring tribes or waging out-and-out warfare. Fortunately the trade guns that the Company provided were notoriously inaccurate and prone to misfire and explode; they could be guaranteed to produce almost as many misses as hits. One of the Company's early policies on the coast had been the abolition of the sale of firearms to Natives but it had proved impractical in the north and so we find such quotations as:

September 21, 1836 — "Traded 2 Beaver Skins from the Tongass Indians, one of them entirely for ammunition."

October 18, 1855 — (From a letter to headquarters) — "I hope you will be pleased to send for the Percussion Muskets for our bastions as soon as possible. The old ones are not safe besides we can sell them at a great advantage for Fur."

October 21, 1856 — (There had been two days of tribal warfare. On one of them, firing had been continuous for eight hours. One man on each side had been killed and one man wounded.) — "Trade good in Furs. The Tsimshians take a large portion of powder & ball."

October 23, 1856 — "Gunsmith repairing Guns for the Indians. Trade good. Traded 5 Guns with the Cannibal's people, lots of Powder, Ball & Shot traded."

May 22, 1857 — "Trade good from the Kygarnies. They took one whole bbl. of Powder, paid 50 Bears, 16 Ld. otter, 20 Minks for it."

Fort Simpson seems to have been ahead of its time in the business of supplying opposing sides in the arms race.

CHAPTER 17

"In Spite of Opponents"

INFLATION MUST HAVE arrived on our coast in the hold of the second trading vessel. Once released, the little balloon grew and grew until it cast an ominous shadow over us all. Fort Simpson's traders never quite succeeded in spearing the young inflation though they never let it out of their sight.

The basis of trade was a blanket for a beaver, but that rapidly became theory rather than practice at Fort Simpson:

June 15, 1835 — "Gave a gallon of Mixing Rum with a Blkt. for a large Skin (Beaver). We considered it prudent to do so in consequence of an opposition casting up."

In 1839, when the brig *Thomas Perkins* was competing, Fort Simpson raised its bid to one gallon three pints of rum, two blankets and three-quarters of a head of tobacco, and prices were on their way. Sea otter cost six blankets each in 1836, eight blankets in 1837, ten blankets, one gun, one shirt and somentaskins in 1839, "and other furs in proportion." By 1865 the asking price was thirty-nine blankets and three guns each. Answering Mr. McNeill's concern over rising prices, Dugald Mactavish wrote from Victoria in 1861: "We anticipate that furs will cost more and more every year on the coast and if you can only trade plenty of prime martens and large, prime black bears at the tariff you mention, we will not do so badly."

Fort Simpson's fur prices were kept bobbling about, above the standard tariff, by what the Company referred to as the opponents. The original and everpresent opposition was the commerce of the merchant tribes. Though the Russian American Company and the Hudson's Bay Company established forts and built ships, the chiefs continued to push off in their canoes for the near and distant inlets and rivers where their forefathers had collected furs. They usually returned with their little flotillas piled high with reeking wealth. Some was offered at the fort's trade shop at a price that would look after the middleman's profit; some was paddled away to a more lucrative market.

The Tsimshian often intercepted furs from other tribes who had come to trade with the Company: "The Tsimshians encamped about and near the fort are occasionally buying in a few martens, and otter, etc. ... our prospects of trade are bleak."

It is likely that the Tsimshian profited from the fort's customers in another way, too. They exacted a tribute from all the tribes who brought furs — after all, the fort was in their territory. If there was resistance, the toll was collected with bloodshed. There is not a single direct reference to this practice in the Hudson's Bay journals. It is hard to believe that those hard-bitten factors did not recognize it, especially as they had Native or part-Native wives to interpret to them the action outside the stockade, and they wrote innumerable accounts of clashes and dashes that resulted from it:

October 31, 1852 — "Two canoes of Massets arrived, on their landing a row took place between them and the Tsimshians. Several shots were fired but no person was wounded."

March 2, 1856 — "A canoe of Kitsalas, ... arrived at 4 a.m. and were safely got inside the fort sometime before the Tsimshians were aware of their arrival."

At Fort Simpson, unless otherwise qualified, the term *opponent* meant the Russian American Company. To the Russians, the northwest coast was theirs. For nearly a hundred years before the Hudson's Bay Company arrived they had been pushing east and south along its shores and had even established a ranch in California as a mark of their intentions. The Hudson's Bay Company shoved west and north. The shock of the meeting of their interests at the upstart Fort Simpson might well have created tidal waves; in fact, it produced only an uncomfortable swell. The reason for the restraint on both sides was a common foe.

The two companies suffered equally at the hands of the Boston Traders. These ships made sorties up the coast, loaded with rum, guns and ammunition and other trade goods. They snatched the furs almost out of the companies' grasps, raised the prices recklessly, debauched the Natives and then sailed away leaving the forts to deal with the havoc they had wrought. Neither company had ever shaped a policy for any purpose other than profit, yet compared with the rum traders they appeared saintly. Thus it was the rivals decided to form a solid front by setting a standard tariff on furs. They kept it, too, in a loose sort of way. What would not fit inside the agreement could be given outside of it as presents. Hamilton Moffatt, in 1860, wrote to headquarters: "… even the few martens we have been enabled to obtain, have been got by sheer perseverance and the giving a few more presents than is usual especially in liquor, but this I trust the Company will overlook when I can asure them that without *this* the bulk would have gone to the south, the tariff on goods is still the same."

Indeed it was necessary for the officers at Victoria to overlook or perhaps close their eyes entirely to the giving of liquor for that also was covered by a Russian American-Hudson's Bay agreement. A letter from John Work, July 6, 1842, tells of his reservations about the new arrangement made by Sir George Simpson and Governor Etaling: "… renders rum unnecessary at Taco and Stikine. I therefore sent back whatever was intended for their places by the *Columbia*; but to guard against a visit from opponents I have landed what was intended for this place which with what we have will be a sufficient standby. We stopped the sale of rum immediately on arrival of the *Vancouver* [which brought the news]."

The problems of the two companies were so similar that they often worked toward the same end without formal collaboration. One day a Stikine chief arrived at Fort Simpson bearing a document written in English by the Russians, extolling him for foregoing the pleasure of killing his slaves. At Simpson, though the fort people observed a strict hands-off rule in matters of Native customs and behaviour, they could not stomach the practice of slave-killing for mere aggrandisement, and sometimes interceded. They, too, had some success. In spite of themselves, the companies were somewhat unified by the hostility of the people they had dispossessed:

September 25, 1866 — "The Schooner *Langley* arrived from the North with Mr. Malvivanski's Son on board. He has been Shot by the Indians through the breast and thigh. He comes for Medical advice."

Both companies operated steamers — the *Prince Constantine* quickly followed the *Beaver* into coastal trade — and in a crisis were known to appeal to one another for those rare engine parts. They were cheerfully supplied.

There was no unifying force on sea or land that could abate the enmity between Fort Simpson and the Boston Traders. In the 1830s, though fort people kept a sharp watch to westward for ships that did not belong to the Company, the sightings were few. During some of those years none of the competing vessels came north. When they did the fort trader set out to break them as speedily as possible. Whatever they paid for furs, he topped, thus exhausting the limited stock they could carry on board and decimating their profits. When the system worked, the intruders fled from the territory and the fort returned its prices to the Hudson's Bay standards.

In the 1840s and 1850s, after the Company had ceased to trade liquor, the system lost much of its power, and the Hudson's Bay people were compelled to watch the rum ships sail into "their" territory to take "their" furs and demoralize "their" Natives. Mr. Work reported in 1844 that the Natives were holding their furs hoping for rum and better prices from the American whalers who were wintering in the north. Mr. McNeill wrote the Board of Management in 1852 that American ships were buying furs on the Queen Charlotte Islands and that the fort had not received one skin from that area, and later that year qualified his hope that trade would be good if "no more interlopers or gold seekers pay us a visit." However, the Fort Simpson factors would have gone back happily to the light and sporadic competition of those years, once the next decade had loosed its swarm of whiskey-laden boats and unconscionable captains, mostly from Victoria.

When James Douglas became governor of the Colony he outlawed the sale of liquor to Natives. It was a fine law but almost unenforceable in the remote reaches of the coast. The traders dispensed their stocks from any sheltered cove or bay and sometimes, brazenly, from the beach in front of Fort Simpson. By this time whiskey, known locally and graphically as tangleleg, had superseded rum as the favourite vehicle for mayhem. In 1860, Hamilton Moffatt wrote: "The schooner *Nonpareil* owned or commanded by a man called Lewis is now lying in the harbour with spirits I presume for Indian trade ... I think that a magistrate ought to be appointed for this district or some person with full power to seize & condemn any vessel or parties selling liquor to Indians."

Eventually William Duncan of Metlakatla was appointed magistrate but even that man of indomitable will succeeded no better than King Canute in rolling back the tide of whiskey, except when he had Her Majesty's navy immediately at hand to bolster his authority. And even then, those naval guns were barely on their way southward when the sloops and schooners emerged to get on with the business of making a few fortunes before they should be driven out of the country.

Less than five miles south of Port Simpson a hard-packed beach curves around a bight that offers safe anchorage. I used to know it as Whiskey Bay, a spot frequented only by seagulls and once-a-year picknickers. Fort Simpson people of the 1860s knew it as Whiskey Harbour and it was filled with sound and action for it was a rendezvous for the tangle carriers and canoes from all the northern waters. The trading ships never tarried too long in any spot; they managed to cover the entire north coast, particularly the Nass River. The fort people could tolerate the rum schooners' trade under the shadow of the stockade better than their trade on the Nass, for down that river travelled the finest furs of the territory. Up to that point the Nisga'a (the Nass people) had shown a certain loyalty to the Company, inspired no doubt by the first Fort Simpson and by Neshaki, a Nisga'a woman of highest rank and wife to Captain McNeill. A factor's view of the illicit trade is revealed in a smattering of excerpts from journals and letters of the early 1860s.

May 15, 1861 — "All hands in camp drunk from liquor purchased from the *Saucy Lass* and *Langley*."

September 15, 1861 — "Schooners doing a good trade after dark."

December 17, 1861 — "The *Nonpareil* and *Ino* started for the south while the sloop *Eagle* arrived from Victoria. Now we have the *Antelope* and *Eagle* to remain here and retail out Tangleleg during the winter."

December 21, 1861 — "The authorities at Victoria shut their eyes at the barefaced smuggling of these craft or else are too lazy to perform their duty and seize the vessels as they all come here full of spirits and never go to New Westminster to clear."

March 29, 1862 — "Our Indians report that the Nass people have been fighting, that 3 were killed and 6 wounded ... rum traded from the *Nonpareil* and *Antelope* now at the Nass was the cause of the trouble."

June 17, 1863 — "The Schooner *Thorndyke*, Charlie, the man that smuggled Rum so long, and so successfully, on the *Langley*, in charge, passed yesterday for Chatsina. She has 200 g'ns spirits on board to trade with the Indians at the North. This fellow is a desperate character and should be either hung or transported, when he is taken *again*."

April 13, 1864 — "7 p.m. the Schooner *Carolina* arrived from the Nass. [The *Carolina* was no smuggler. She belonged to the Metlakatla mission and was in the charge of Mr. Cunningham who brought news.] ... He reports a Notorious whiskey seller named Jackson in the vicinity of Nass, trading and selling whiskey to Indians. So he has sent a few of his constables [Natives] on the lookout after the man, and caught him, and had him in their canoe; But much to their astonishment he demanded their authority which they failed to produce, so the man was set at liberty in consequence."

Another attempt, complete with undercover agent, to bring the notorious Mr. Jackson to justice ended in tragedy rather than comedy. Mr. Moffatt sent a Native, armed with a marten skin, to Jackson's sloop in Whiskey Harbour. The Native returned with a gallon of evidence. Then Mr. Moffatt sent word to William Duncan whose constables seized the sloop and headed it for Metlakatla and justice. It never arrived. Jackson retook his ship by killing one of the Native constables and wounding three, one of whom died later.

A year later Mr. Moffatt wrote: "Our trade for sometime back has been very bad, the camps round here being deluged with grog. We want another visit from the *Devastation* to put things on a proper footing." It was HMS *Clio* that finally arrived to establish the proper but temporary footing.

November 28, 1865 — "The Schooner *Non Pareil* arrived last night. At 8:30 p.m. the *Clio's* launch arrived in charge of the 2nd Lieut. who seized the *Non Pareil* and Sebastapol [the trader]."

December 12, 1865 — 1 p.m. HMS *Clio* arrived from Metlakatla. 1:50 Capt. Turnour landed 150 Seamen and Marines under the command of Lt. Carey. They arrested several notorious murderers and whiskey sellers. This will have a good effect in Keeping the Indians Quiet and friendly."

The following February the fort received news "that all the prisoners ... got off clear." Flaunting this official blessing, the whiskey traders bobbed up again cheekier than ever.

The last Fort Simpson journal entry available to us is dated midnight, December 31, 1866, so we are not able to enjoy the Hudson's Bay officers' exultation when the smugglers were finally swept out of British Columbia waters. It was such a thorough sweeping that the Port Simpson I knew fifty years later was essentially a quiet, sober, mission-dominated village, with no more evidence of violence than the sportsmanlike game of soccer that was the highlight of New Year's Day.

The fort staff gamely battled the competition from the Natives, the Russians and the invading schooners, and then they had to face further competition from some unlikely sources. The most threatening of these was William Duncan's mission at Metlakatla.

To understand why a new mission settlement, twenty miles distant, could be a threat to the mighty Hudson's Bay Company, one has to know something of the equally mighty William Duncan. He has been chronicled, extolled, criticized, eulogized, cursed and adulated to the point where I had resolved to leave him entirely to my predecessors. I soon found that trying to describe the mid-nineteenth century on the north coast without mentioning William Duncan was comparable to describing the final decade of the eighteenth century in France without mentioning the French Revolution.

Duncan was the young Church of England missionary who, nine and a half months out from England, preached to the Tsimshian in their own tongue; bested Legaic, chief of all the Tsimshian, in a contest of wills and survived; and led an exodus from Fort Simpson to Metlakatla by canoe, to save his followers from the 1862 smallpox epidemic and from the debauchery that was rotting indigenous life.

Metlakatla grew and thrived to become a veritable wonder. There Victorian English life was superimposed upon an ancient Tsimshian village — successfully. Duncan taught his people not only the white men's religion and ways but also their forms of law and government and their accomplishments, especially music. The community was partially supported by industries and trade, all conceived and directed to the minutest detail by William Duncan.

Unfortunately for Fort Simpson it was a glowingly successful career in business that Duncan had renounced at age twenty-three to enter a seminary. He knew exactly what he was doing when he opened a trade shop at Metlakatla to supply his converts with the materials of his culture. The business soon outgrew the village and took to the sea, as well, in the schooner *Carolina*. The *Carolina* held her own among the liquor traders and, with all the Tsimshian fur trade secrets to guide her, swooped in and out of the settlements, particularly the Hudson's Bay Company's favourite Nass settlements. Mr. Moffatt ended the 1863 journal with a dispirited note: "Mr. Duncan is doing us a great deal of harm and I fear his opposition more than the schooners'. In fact if he continues the trade much longer I see no alternative but for us to shut up our shop."

Three years later the fort was operating its own sloop on the Nass and the situation had changed, but not the iron-willed missionary. He proposed that the Company take over the Metlakatla store, which had become a deadweight. When the factor declined, Duncan wrote a letter that did not conceal his annoyance at being crossed and as the journal keeper relates, "also Censuring Mr. Wm. Manson severely for Sabbath desecration and violation of God's Laws because forsooth he took advantage of fair wind on Sunday to Start the Sloop down South on a trading Excursion." The fort's officers were by no means the first or only people to maintain strained relations with the man who, Moses-like, led the Natives out of barbarity.

Among the fort's unpublicized rivals was Her Britannic Majesty's navy. In the summer of 1853, HBM steam sloop *Virago*, newly arrived on the coast from Valparaiso, beached at Simpson for repairs. Immediately a rash of pained entries broke out in the journal.

June 21, 1853 — "The *Virago*'s people are trading our Furs right and left ... it was a 'dark day' for Fort Simpson when the *Virago* arrived 'back' here from Victoria."

June 22, 1853 — "Trade dull in fact the *Virago* is getting nearly all the Martens from the Indians and everything they can lay hands on in the shape of Provisions and curiosities."

June 25, 1853 — "We have lost our Marten trade altogether as the *Virago*'s people give one bottle of Rum for two Martens and four times our tariff for one Marten in Cotton, Shirts or Soap. As she will be here 15 days more We will lose about 500 Martens and about 80 bear skins by her. I wish to God that we could be allowed to *protect* ourselves, and let the Men O War remain at Valparaiso. As the case now stands we have to protect the *Virago*."

The largely Chilean crew and the officers, green on the northwest coast, were no match for the tribes who considered the beached ship fair game.

Mr. McNeill made black predictions about annual fur trading visits by the navy, but they were wrong. Some years later the Fort Simpson factor was sending out entreaties for a man-of-war. Over the colonial years HMS *Alert, Devastation, Grappler* and *Clio* all made sporadic voyages to the north to advertise law and order and sometimes to enforce them. Their officers also traded furs but the Hudson's Bay people accepted the inevitable and confined their rumblings to letters and the journal:

October 1860 (Letter from Moffatt to headquarters) — "HMS *Alert* during her stay here traded a great number of skins especially Martens and I really think that her visit did more harm than good. *Some* Men of War coming here would command respect and esteem."

There were rare and happy times when Fort Simpson could relax its vigilance against "opponents." The traders, even then, had worries. Extreme cold or stormy weather kept their customers inside their lodges and the trade shop empty. Epidemics that swept the villages, particularly the smallpox epidemics, put an end to trapping and the movement of pelts along the coast. Tribal wars that sometimes dragged murderously on for months occupied the contenders completely. Every year, during the winter feasting and medicine rites, the Natives lost interest in trade, and in times when liquor flowed far and free they were in no condition to sustain it. And the Company's own new Fort Victoria became a menace to the northern trade.

In the 1850s Fort Victoria's fur prices were higher than those allowed in the north and the rambunctious, muddy little settlement offered new attractions to the Natives — almost all demoralizing. In addition, liquor was lavishly available to them in the adjacent American territory. The six-hundred-mile canoe trips satisfied the Natives' nomadic urge and loosed waves of coastal plundering. Here are a few of the many journal references to the lure of Victoria:

May 14, 1855 — "Six Kyganie Canoes ... started for Victoria and Nisqually. About 60 women went in them."

May 23, 1855 — "25 canoes of Tsimshians started for Milbank and Victoria, half of them come back here and half go on to Victoria with the Fur they obtain at Milbank. Six canoes of Nass people also started for Victoria. Never so many Canoes went to the South as this year."

May 27, 1855 — "Most of the principal people in camp drunk and noisy. Rum from Victoria."

February 3, 1856 — "Our Indians will now soon make a start for Victoria, report says that at the least one half of the Tsimshians will leave this for Victoria between this date and 1st April [just at the time of the oolichan fishery]."

May 6, 1856 — "Four canoes of Chatsinas and Kygarnies arrived from Victoria full of property plundered from the Americans and others."

June 9, 1856 — "Six canoes of Tsimshians arrived from Victoria report that some Tsimshians have been killed at Victoria and That 'Estemele' had also been killed or taken prisoner with all his party by the Nicaltoes ... The canoes are thirteen days from Victoria."

June 22, 1856 — "Our men most all drunk, They get Rum from the Indians outside. It is now brought here in Canoes from Victoria by Casks ... Yates himself would stare at the cargoes that come here from Victoria."

February 9, 1859 — "About 19 Canoes started for Victoria one half the Crews composed of women, lots of them not more than nine years of age going to prostitute themselves at Victoria and in the American Territory."

Not all the setbacks were local. Even on the farthest fringe of civilization, Fort Simpson was jolted by the American Civil War. It sent the prices of tobacco and cotton skyrocketing and those were staples of the trade. Wherever and whatever the problem, Fort Simpson coped. The coping wrote a story of change.

Most changes crept into the fur trade. A few leapt in. Of these the most joyfully received was a sea-going trade in the fort's very own sloop, the *Petrel*. The *Petrel* came to Fort Simpson fresh from a life of crime. She had been such a successful whiskey smuggler that she was a prime target when HMS *Devastation* made a sweep through northern waters in 1863. She travelled south behind the *Devastation*, at the end of a towline. Apparently she could not wriggle free of the charges, for the next journal entry concerning her reads:

June 29, 1863 — "The Sloop *Petrel* was towed to this place from Victoria, having been purchased by the Company for the use of this post to oppose the Smugglers."

By this time the fort's fur-trading patterns had been completely disrupted by the many vessels that ran right to the source of the furs. Now the fort personnel gleefully prepared to run there ahead of them or in pursuit of them. All those ex-seamen, and landsmen turned sailors by their environment, worked and fussed over the *Petrel* as a household of adults coddles an only child. They referred to her as "the little sloop." Mr. Moffatt, who had served in former years on the company ships, took charge of the refitting personally and all of the fort work became secondary to it.

August 7, 1863 — "Took the *Petrel* alongside the *Labouchere*, hoisted her mast out to shorten and plant."

August 10 — "Rigged the *Petrel*, bent sails, and got a part of the ballast on board. The *Nanaimo Packet* is going to Nass, and we must follow her, to get a share of the Furs."

August 11 — "All hands loading and preparing the *Petrel* for a move after the *Packet*."

August 12 — "Captain McNeill started for Nass in the *Petrel* at 11 a.m. for the purpose of opposing *Nanaimo Packet*."

Captain McNeill returned in thirteen days with two hundred martens and a good take of other furs. The *Petrel* was a success. From that time until we lose track of her with the ending of the journals, from earliest spring until latest fall, she was kept busy. For the first three years she sailed chiefly to the Nass, but then came the year 1866 and another turning point.

Neshaki, daughter of the most powerful Nisga'a chief,

wife of Captain McNeill and stepmother of his many children, was, for all that, very much her own woman. She was a fur trader of some note and over the years had set forth in her canoe on many a Nass excursion. She sold her furs to the Company and by the spring of 1866 was being supplied with trading outfits from the fort, on credit. Under this arrangement she set up shop in her Nass residence. When her trade was well established, Fort Simpson sent Thomas Hankin to take it over from her. It seems this had been prearranged though we are not told outright that it was. However it came about, Fort Simpson now had a flourishing branch post.

Robert Cunningham, who had once commanded the mission's *Carolina*, operated a freighting service, by canoe, between the parent and offspring posts. Thus the *Petrel* was released from the Nass to ply the trade at other coastal points.

May 28, 1866 — "Our sloop *Petrel* Arrived this Evening from Kitkatla and Port Essington. She has brought a tolerable trade, but has Established the most important part, Viz. arranging regular periodical visits to the Indians for trade, so that they may Know when to Expect us and us where to find them."

In July of that explosive year, Mr. Cunningham replaced Mr. Hankin at the Nass establishment and by September was expanding it:

September 3, 1866 — "Despatched J. Jolibois to Nass to erect a Building under the superintendence of Mr. Cunningham for the Hudson's Bay Company. It is to be a dwelling House and trade Shop attached."

This sounds like a sophisticated operation compared with Mr. Hankin's next assignment:

November 16, 1866 — "Men Employed putting goods up for the Skeena River trade, for Mr. Hankin who is to start tomorrow Morning and winter about 75 Miles up the Skeena. He is to have one Man with him who has just agreed for one year, at the rate of £30 sterling per annum."

With the coming of the *Petrel* Fort Simpson had begun to fight off its slow death by liquor, and in three years was restored to such health and vigour that it could enter a new life as depot and department head for branch posts that eventually ranged from the Queen Charlotte Islands to Babine Lake.

PART V

The Port

CHAPTER 18

The Port I Knew

PORT SIMPSON PEOPLE led salty lives. Since the town was built on a peninsula we were almost surrounded by water. The Tsimshian were as much of the sea as of the land and the rest of us were only slightly more shore-bound. The sea was our highway and our usual communications system; it was our larder; it was our heavy-duty equipment for moving large loads, the extreme high tides of the solstices, especially, being put to use in floating machinery into place or beaching boats high and dry. And the sea was our playground.

All over Port Simpson mothers called after departing children, "And don't get your feet wet." They might as well have called these words to the crabs that scuttled under the tide-line rocks, for we were all on our way to join them. First we toddled to the beach behind older brothers and sisters, where we commanded the derelicts half buried in the sand, or slithered up and down the remains of the Hudson's Bay ships' ways, and fell in the water and were hauled out. When we had been properly initiated we were allowed to sit motionless on the bottoms of the small craft the older children rowed or paddled about the shoreline. These ranged through rowboats, dinghies, flat-bottomed skiffs, dugouts, right down to rafts and logs. There was no status and only one requirement for a craft to enter this fleet: it had to float at least some of the time. Our next promotion allowed us to row our boats alone — to the length of the bowline that was tied to a wharf approach piling or to a beach log. Those were the days of scrounging bits of rope to lengthen the painter. Eventually we won or seized the right to inshore paddling. The tide rose and fell while we raced and reversed and made landings, complete with vocalized ships' bells, whistles and engines, or practised Chinese rowing and the fisherman's push. We learned to read tide tables about the same time we learned to read *The Tale of Peter Rabbit*; where twenty-foot tides are normal it is just as well to know what they are doing.

The first day that I rowed around the point, out of sight of home and completely beyond parental control, I became an exultant explorer. Our coastline was lavishly set with islands, coves, creeks, reefs and narrow channels. Before I had hauled up on more than a sampling of them, with a sputter and a roar the outboard motor burst into our lives. I promptly shipped my oars and found my seaways lengthened by miles. My seamanship was stretched noticeably, too. Oars could never have won me the enmity of the entire Prince Rupert Yacht Club.

It was as a concession to my newly achieved teens that Ruth and I made our first trip to Prince Rupert on our own, by rowboat and outboard. The boat was a sixteen-foot clinker-built; we called her the *Blue Streak* and discussed her lines as though we were admiring a China clipper. Outboard motors of the early 1920s were not the behemoths that adorn the transoms of modern craft. Our motor was one of the breed that had a knob on the flywheel rather than a starting cord and was advertised to start on a quarter turn. The advertisements did not specify the *first* quarter turn and it was more likely to be a fifty-sixth that brought the thing to life. For one whole summer I wore adhesive tape on the knuckles of my right hand. When the motor developed a bad cough, as well, my father agreed that the Marine Engine Works in Prince Rupert should look into the case. We left Dad on the boat float shouting into the wind, "The shearing pins are in the tool box."

Prince Rupert was a three-hour run south. Dad had improvised a high seat in the bow and rigged tiller lines to it so the steersman could have a clear view in all directions. We had no steering wheel — we simply clutched a line in each hand and tugged on the appropriate one. Ruth, by seniority, was skipper, so it fell to my lot to keep the outboard kicking. I accomplished this through willpower, cajolery and a leaner-than-specified mixture of gasoline and oil.

Ruth and I tied up diffidently at the Engine Works' float in Prince Rupert harbour. The *Blue Streak* looked frivolous alongside the tugboats, halibut boats and trollers docked there. We arranged to pick up our outfit the next morning and then we set off up town — in Prince Rupert the town is literally up. We followed our usual day-on-the-town ritual, which included banana splits, the newest gramophone record, a movie and the night at the hotel. Next morning we were back at the float by ten o'clock. It was a Sunday so there was no one around the repair shop. We filled the gas tank, loaded our bags aboard and gave the flywheel an enquiring flip. When the motor stuttered into action we shouted in unison our amazement and joy, and were headed into the harbour before we had even buttoned our sweaters.

A fresh breeze swept the harbour into choppy little waves and dancing upon them, in a long, ragged line, were pleasure craft of every description, from luxury cruisers to dinghies with home-built cabins. While Prince Rupert possessed more of the amenities of life than did Port Simpson, there was still no road leading off Kaien Island and the people turned to the water for their recreation, even as we. Almost every family had some sort of boat and this was their day.

"It's the Yacht Club sailpast," Ruth bellowed above the noise of our motor and the harbourful of engines.

"Let's give them a wide berth," I bellowed back and there-upon the *Blue Streak* hit the wake of a heavy, old launch. The motor leapt off the transom into my scrawny arms, never missing a stroke though its roar was like artillery fire because part of the propeller was above water. There was I, held fast on my knees in the stern, my chest supporting the heavy motor, my arms locked about its gas tank, my ribs pinning the steering arm hard over, the corner of one eye intent on the whirring flywheel half an inch below my chin and my cries for help being whipped astern by the wind. And there was Ruth in the bow, pulling frantically on first one unresponsive tiller line and then the other while the boat began to describe a circle of majestic proportions.

Prince Rupert is famous for its spacious harbour, but the harbour was not spacious enough that morning for a sailpast and a sixteen-footer gone berserk. At first the circumference of our circle did not intersect the line of boats. From wheelhouses and decks, yachters waved jauntily at us. Ruth, always conscious of social niceties, dropped a tiller line to wave back, even as she flat-tened herself on the seat, for we were speeding toward the hull of a thirty-foot cruiser. By some miracle of navigation it turned aside to allow us to skim under the bow and our circle, in a long sweep, headed back to the line of yachts. They were scattering like apples out of a burst bag. Once again hands were raised in salute but this time they were clenched and shaking at us. The com-modore's yacht, all hand-rubbed teak and brassoed brass, was looming before us when there was a thud against our keel and a scraping along the bottom. Everything in the boat jumped. The motor shoved me backwards as a chunk of driftwood knocked the propeller right out of water. The vocal fury of the engine was increased but, mercifully, we were drifting. Ruth picked herself off the floorboards, came aft, and reached under my right armpit for the shut-off button. Together we eased the motor onto the transom and began turning thumbscrews.

Dad was waiting for us on the float as we pulled in. The moment I turned off the motor, he called, "Have any trouble?"

Waves slurped and glugged around the float while I rubbed on the engine with a piece of waste. Ruth finally rallied with, "The mechanic didn't fasten the engine on but we got it screwed down."

Port Simpson's harbour was a wide-angle screen on which its people watched snatches of large and small dramas. During fishing season the screen was filled with the rowboats of hand trollers, gas boats with doghouses and trolling poles and Easthope engines, gillnetters, seiners and packers. The spit-and-polished police boat from Prince Rupert and tugs with paint peeling berthed side by side at the wharf. The doctor's busy cruiser darted in and out. In the winter, season of inter-tribal visiting in potlatch days, we would sometimes hear band music blown across the water to us and rush to the window to see an Alaskan seine boat riding low in the water, flags and banners flying, a band drawn up on the forward hatch. To the tune of "Onward Christian Soldiers" it would disgorge its load of Tlingit for one of the religion-based exchanges that bridged the gap between ancient and modern First Nations ways.

Of all the small craft that used the port, we thought the *Northern Cross* was the loveliest. She was a raised deck cruiser with pilothouse aft and she enhanced the bay when she was merely riding at anchor. She belonged to the Anglican Church Mission Society and came in on a regular monthly schedule, her arrival signifying that services would be held in the Anglican church that stood, disintegrating, on a bluff. By the time my family had lived in Simpson for ten years there were few of the Anglican flock left but the clergyman-skipper was so popular with us all that even some Methodists attended his services. I have to admit, though, that it was the annual *Northern Cross'* picnic that left the deepest Anglican impression upon me.

Port Simpson picnicked expansively. Only for picnics would all those independent spirits tolerate concerted action. Women mixed and baked for days in advance and children cached balls and bats in readiness. Finally we assembled with our baskets and bathing suits and babies to be loaded onto a launch. Sometimes we loaded everything and everybody aboard a flotilla of open boats and rowed the few miles to the appointed beach. But *Northern Cross'* picnics were the most expansive, the most united, and were held on distant beaches where perhaps no one had set foot in years. One of these still sends out flashes from the muddle of my fourth year.

The *Northern Cross* took us to a little island separated from the mainland by a channel no more than fifteen feet wide at low tide. When the baskets had all been carried up above high tide line, everyone dove into the woods to put on bathing suits. The women emerged in black sateen — yards and yards of black sateen, gathered and ruffled and piped and collared. They ran into the shallow water where they splashed and joined hands to jump up and down. Not one of them swam, and just as well, too, since their bloomered garments would certainly have acted as nether water wings and plunged their heads down-ward. We smaller children, paddling near them, were utterly bemused by the sight of so many uncorseted ladies, the sound of their little screams and the smell of all that wet black sateen.

The ladies returned to being our normal mothers in time to unpack the food. Their skirts brushed the sand and their hats, small edifices of straw and silk, had to be repinned now and again as they spread white linen cloths on the logs and laid out their specialties. Our eating was not harassed by thoughts of calories, cholesterol or the Canada Food Rules.

When there was no more chocolate cake and the women began to exchange recipes, the older children set off to cross the island. The younger ones scrambled along behind, wriggling through brush, rolling over and under logs, yelping as they encountered devil's club. We all came out on the beach that was only a stone's throw from the mainland. It was more than my stone's throw but some of the big boys were hitting a cedar tree that stood well inside the opposite forest.

The end-of-day stillness was upon us when out of those near woods came a sound that has never quite left me. It was a threat and a lament, a raging and a wail. We had all heard wolves howling beyond the edge of town on a winter's night but this came from within fifty feet of us and was directed to us. There was a prickling in my upper body and my mouth felt as though I had eaten chalk. The other children were fixed in mid-motion, throwing arms still raised. I knew they were absorbed with the same sensations. We had not yet translated them into fear when the men of the party came crashing through the woods to herd us back to the picnic site. The wolf cried only once more.

Our long trip home took us into the night. I lay wrapped in a blanket, my head against a deck railing. Above me were stars and below me were stars that leapt and dashed and shot through the black water. The adults were saying,

"Lots of phosphorescence tonight."

"Is it really from jellyfish?"

"I think it's in the plankton."

"I was told that it isn't phosphorous at all."

I never guessed that their matter-of-fact conversation had to do with my submarine fireworks.

Less familiar, because they came only once or twice a year, were various purposeful craft. The *Thomas Crosby*, the United Church's hard-working mission boat, occasionally lay over at the wharf, and the *Lillooet*, of the Geodetic Survey, anchored her rakish lines and white paint well out in the harbour. The lighthouse tender steamed in to inspect and adjust the black buoy that marked the underwater extension of a reef. At intervals of some years, ships of the Royal Canadian Navy anchored briefly in our harbour and once we had a misplaced Navy Week.

Because the British Admiralty charts for the north coast dated back to the days when Simpson had been the important port, HMS *Delhi*, cruiser class, was routed there on a goodwill cruise of the coast when I was in my teens. Her size reduced our fine harbour to a pond. Apparently her orders for Simpson were the same as for Vancouver, to entertain the masses with conducted tours of the ship, and the elite at a band concert and a buffet. The people of the reserve were away at the canneries and no more than fifteen families occupied our side of the village. Let it never be said of the British Navy that mere circumstances could swerve it from the execution of its orders. Officers came ashore to blanket the population with invitations. On Wednesday we were the masses and were ferried out in ship's boats for the conducted tour. On Thursday, we unearthed the dress-up clothes that dated back to our various last trips south, and became the elite. This time we were ferried out in the captain's launch. The buffet was served to our motley troupe by officers who well knew England expected every man to do his duty. They bowed from the hip as they proffered French pastries to the fisherman who had tarred his boat that morning and had been unable to remove the tar from his hands. One, who offered a mission lady claret cup, merely coughed behind his hand when she answered in puzzlement, "Carrot top?" And when the westerly whipped my wholly unsuitable chiffon dress upward about my waist, the officers, to a man, were gazing impassively out to sea. Is it any wonder that the British navy ruled the waves for all those centuries?

There was one steamer whose arrival at Port Simpson produced immediate panic, in the days when we lived on the reserve. She was the *Old BC*, our coal boat. True, the lettering on her bow read *British Columbia* and, since she was built in 1903, her age could not have been greater than ten years when I first began to take part in the panic. Still, she was then and

continued for another six years to be the *Old BC*. She was completely black with coal dust and her crew, from bridge to bilge,
was black with coal dust, too. Mother said the blackness had
eaten right into their hearts. When her whistle sounded,
Mother clapped shut the day book she was totalling at the
desk in the store, grabbed the hands of her two small daughters and called to Dad, "I'm leaving, Boyd." She rushed us to
the house where she locked all doors and pulled the window
blinds. To Mother, drunkenness was the most horrendous sin.

The crewmen of the *Old BC* rolled ashore and made their
way to the store, brawling and shouting bawdy songs. Dad
insisted they were sent as a diversionary action to prevent his
checking the unloading of the coal. Usually, a few days after
she sailed northward, news trickled down from the Nass or
Alice Arm of remarkable bargains that had been offered there
on several tons of coal. The amount always coincided with
the shortweight of Dad's shipment.

In spite of all the villainy aboard the *Old BC*, my sister
knew that steamer had a heart of gold beating amidships on
the lower deck. The cook, who emerged miraculously from
his galley in white cap and apron, had made Ruth's acquain-
tance when she was a small child playing about Dad's feet as he
tallied coal buckets. He invited them to his galley to sample his
apricot pie to which Ruth reacted with dimpled enthusiasm.
For years thereafter, within half an hour of the *Old BC's* docking, there would be delivered to the store a small apricot pie
with r-u-t-h pricked out on the crust. The pies ceased in 1919
when the Union Steamship Company bought the *Old BC*,
renamed her the *Chilliwack* and made a respectable freighter
out of her.

The Union Steamship Company supplied the ships that
gave life to the small settlements of the British Columbia
coast. They were known as logging boats and cannery boats
and ore boats. They were called freight boats and mail boats

and passenger boats. They were also referred to as cruise ships and excursion boats and daddy boats. The last two classifications belonged wholly to the southern runs but in the north we expected any one Union ship to fill all the other roles and simultaneously, if necessary. In the out-of-the-way settlements we expected and received more.

In the first fifteen or so years of the century, while Simpson was still something of a centre, the Canadian Pacific's princesses and the Grand Trunk Pacific's princes called at our port. They abandoned us as Prince Rupert grew into a town and we never missed them for, by then, we had given our allegiance to the *Camosun*, the *Chelohsin* and the *Venture* and the Union Steamship Company had become an extension of our lives.

Every fall, from remote harbours and inlets, children who had passed their entrance examinations went away to school. Our educations were the product of northern homes, southern high schools and the Union Steamship Company. By the time I was making two round trips a year, "our boat" was either the *Cardena* or the *Catala*.

Captain Andy Johnstone, hero of a hundred coastal legends, commanded the *Cardena*. His ship was like a dancing partner as he docked her: slide, pivot, swing; glide, reverse and stop. The stop was always on her toes, dramatic, and to generous applause. If he had ever decided to command a barrel going over Niagara Falls any north coaster would have accompanied him without a second thought. It was Andy Johnstone who taught us, with much hilarity, how to splice rope and make Turk's heads for our oars. He taught us such assorted essentials as where to watch for blackfish, etiquette of the bridge, and coast history — he seemed to know a good story for every rock and point along the Inside Passage. He also taught us where to place our shuffleboard shots and never to pass up the Union Steamships' crab cocktails at dinner. Andy

Johnstone still had a boyish look and laugh when he went out of our lives to join the Pilotage Service after twenty-three years with the company.

Captain Dickson, commodore of the fleet, was master of the *Catala*. His style was a black-and-white contrast to Andy Johnstone's. He had no Christian name as far as we knew — we always used his title in full. He must have been young during the early years of the forty he spent with the Union Steamship Company but northerners could not picture him without white hair and moustache, and dignity. We never heard his mirth in guffaws; we saw it in his eyes, which were mariners' eyes protected by lines and creases and were of compelling blueness. To him I gave my first love bestowed outside of the family circle, as did all the other youngsters who made those September and June trips, and sometimes stormy December ones.

Captain Dickson taught us, too, although we did not immediately recognize the incidents as lessons. If, for fifty years, I have been able to refrain from gushing, it is probably due to an embarkation night aboard the SS *Catala*. The *Catala's* Friday night sailing from Vancouver always generated action and noise and excitement. One particular departure on a summer night was late and attended by a full moon, which intensified the passengers' ebullience and kept them on deck until long after the city lights disappeared behind Point Atkinson. Captain Dickson found me alone at the rail and since he felt personally responsible for every shy, northern schoolgirl who travelled on the *Catala*, led me off to the delights of midnight supper in the dining saloon. We were headed for the nearest companionway when a group of women tourists spied the three rows of gold braid on Captain Dickson's sleeve and, like a settling flock of crows, encircled him. They all talked at once.

"We think your boat is just lovely, Captain."

"Ship," said Captain Dickson.

"Now, are we on the port or starboard side? We can never remember."

"Port," said Captain Dickson.

"Those lights way off there, are they other boats? I mean ships."

"Those are the lights of Nanaimo," said the Captain.

"Nanaimo? Way over there? Imagine seeing lights on Vancouver Island."

"How far away would they be?"

"But we didn't see the lights of Victoria."

"If you are interested in seeing lights," said Captain Dickson, "look just slightly above the Nanaimo lights. Do you see those three bright lights?"

"Oh yes, I can see them."

"Tell us what they are, Captain."

"Those, Madam, are stars," and with that Captain Dickson hustled me into the companionway.

Captain Dickson had a Victorian sense of propriety. Once when he was taking me ashore at Anyox to show me the smelter, I met him at the top of the gangplank in my usual windblown state. He said, "You'd better wear your hat."

"I don't have a hat," I said, abashed.

The next year when I made the trip north, I owned and conspicuously wore hat and gloves. I never even slightly resented being nudged toward ladyhood by the captain until the year I turned eighteen and graduated from Normal School.

That summer it was quite obvious to me that I had become a woman of the world. The *Catala* took Port Simpson passengers north to Kincolith, Stewart and Anyox before calling in at our harbour on her southbound trip. At Kincolith a survey party boarded the *Catala*. These men had spent three months in the wilds of the Nass Valley and were exuberant as they returned to civilization as represented by the *Catala*. They were headed by a young engineer, distinctly shaggy in appearance, but, as I recognized instantly, of superior intelligence. As always north of Prince Rupert, the passenger list had dwindled drastically. I was the only female under forty aboard the ship. It was no great wonder, therefore, that when the stewards rolled up the rugs in the saloon and opened the big Victrola, the young engineer and I became dancing partners. There were only two records that were not scratched beyond use, but we found them quite adequate. We waltzed and foxtrotted alternately to them as the *Catala* glided up Portland Canal through the half-light of the summer night. The other passengers, no doubt desperate to escape those two records, drifted away from the saloon, but we waltzed on alone, having made the daring decision to dance into Stewart and then go uptown to view the night scene. (Stewart was a mining town and enjoyed a gaudy reputation.) The height of romance as depicted by the movies of those days was a couple dancing the night away. Jean Arthur and Charles Boyer did it, why not I? The engineer did not look quite like Charles Boyer but it was not his fault that there were no barber shops on the upper Nass.

At 1:30 a.m. Captain Dickson took a turn around the saloon as he seemed to do at intervals all day. He hardly glanced at our best twirl. At 2:15 he made another turn, this one much slower. At 2:45 he was back and this time he stopped and we stopped. "We're going into Stewart and Hyder to see what's going on," I told him by way of explanation.

Addressing himself to the engineer, Captain Dickson said in that low-pitched voice that had been smartly obeyed for forty years, "I think Stewart's too rough for Helen at 3:30 a.m. We're going down for a bit of supper before she turns in. Goodnight, Mr. Kendrick," and he held out the crook of his arm to me with the almost imperceptible bow that always accompanied that gesture. I placed my hand in it without any more question than I would have accorded the Ten Commandments.

As we turned down the stairs to the dining room I glanced back to see my friend standing where we had left him, his chin and lower lip seemingly detached from the rest of his face.

I found my coffee bitter that night, and refused the cold cuts, the McLaren's cheese in its white glass jar, and even the famous Union Steamship pound cake that came from Scotland, though they were all pressed upon me by the night steward whom Captain Dickson had roused from a nap at the end table. But the captain, who usually ate sparingly, had an amazing appetite that night. He drank two cups of coffee and sampled everything the steward brought forth, maintaining a pleasant, one-sided conversation all the while. When at last we ascended from the dining room, the Victrola was closed, the saloon empty. Captain Dickson escorted me to my state-room door and bade me goodnight. Obviously, Jean Arthur had not been protected by Captain Dickson.

The next morning the passengers clustered about the for-ward deck to watch the landing at Port Simpson. Slightly detached from the rest, in animated conversation, stood the engineer and a little redhead from Stewart. I craned my neck to look accusingly up to the bridge, and Captain Dickson, in the middle of a docking manoeuvre, caught my eye. He fixed it in his unwavering gaze as he issued an order in a voice more like a trumpet blast than the usual low growl that he used on the bridge. "Hold her hard astern," he called.

Once, on a visit to the bridge, I watched as the first offi-cer studied a lighthouse through binoculars. "There she is," he said, as he reached up to pull the whistle. I could make out a figure and a white object that moved. When the officer handed me the binoculars I saw that it was an elderly woman waving something. With each wave she bent nearly double. "What is she waving?" I asked.

"A bed sheet. She won't have another conversation with the outside world until our next trip."

At a logging camp at the head of a long, lonely reach, the camp tender met the steamer. From the gas boat a woman yelled, "Did you get my corset?" and on the freight deck the purser held aloft a long, slim box.

Tall stories were a specialty of the officers, and one chief engineer, Andrew Beatty, was famous the entire length of British Columbia for his. He told them in such an honest Scottish accent and with such earnestness that even old-timers were sometimes caught by them, though tourists were his favourite game. Once when the *Catala* was loading salmon at Alert Bay, a group of officers and passengers went ashore to explore the town and converged on the store. The door bore a notice, "Seal noses bought here." At that time there was a bounty on hair seals, the salmon's natural enemy, and it was collectible when a seal's nose was produced. Only the larger centres had bounty depots so storekeepers all over the coast paid the bounty, salted down the grisly proof in casks, and shipped them once or twice a season.

"Seal noses," said a female tourist. "Why do they buy seal noses?"

"There's a great demand for seal noses," said Andrew Beatty. "They're shipped straight to New York. Restaurant trade, you know. Of course they give them a French name and no one knows they are eating seal noses. Delicious sautéed."

"Well, fancy that. But the poor little seals — it must be hard for them to manage without noses."

The *Cardena's* hull is one unit in a log-pond breakwater at Powell River; the *Catala* ended her life as a floating hotel and restaurant at Grays Harbor, Washington, and the last Union sailing was in 1959. The white village of Port Simpson is gone and so are all but a few of the ports of call of the Company ships. All those deaths were related. Port Simpson's harbour, however, lives on.

CHAPTER 19

The Port of Canoes

HOW LONG THE NATIVES' canoes had sheltered in McLoughlin's Harbour before the *Dryad* cast anchor there is not known, for in the last few years the anthropologists have been busily pulling up the dates of earliest human habitation on the coast and setting them farther and farther back. One of the present estimates is twelve thousand years. We can peer into that distance only from the near edge and through the eyes of white men who often could not comprehend what they were seeing.

The arrival of canoes was noted in the Fort Simpson journal within three days of the Hudson's Bay Company's landing. Those were the first of thousands that would be recorded — canoes brought furs. The journal tells of arrivals in ones and twos, in twenties and hundreds. The canoes ranged from one- and two-man craft to those that rose eight feet out of the water and carried up to one hundred people, paddling in shifts of fifty. "… you have no idea of the quickness of their canoes, with sixteen paddles they literally fly through the water," wrote Lt. Charles Wilson, a young Englishman who reached Victoria in 1858. Canoes came to Fort Simpson from nearby islands and inlets and bays and from others as distant as Nisqually, which we know as Tacoma. They came and they went and they came again for they followed the patterns of food and trade and war and pleasure. Some routes converged in McLoughlin's Harbour and many new ones came into being because of the attraction of the white men's wares.

The most impressive of all the harbour scenes must have been the annual departure of the canoes for the oolichan fishery on the Nass. They assembled during February and early March. Then one day the seagulls would give the signal and the canoes would sweep across the bay and out of sight beyond Birnie Island. More than seven hundred canoes took part in this flitting that might occupy two or three days.

March 8, 1835 — "About 100 Canoes started for Nass this morning tho' it was raining heavily."

Rain was the least of the murderous weather that March hurled against the travelling Natives, year after year. They paid no more attention to it than did the oolichans they pursued. In 1865 the March weather began brewing in February with a stiff Nass blow. A storm went berserk on the night of the 26th, flinging the *Petrel* ashore — "the gale was so strong that divers ducks and codfish were driven on the beach and frozen to death ... We were in great fear of the houses in the fort being unroofed." By March 12th the wind had swung around but its nasty mood had not subsided:

"Blowing still from S.W. with sleet and snow, the most part of the day. 10 Canoes started for Nass."

March 17, 1865 — "Stormy with snow and sleet, throughout the day, Winds S.E. to S.W. Snow fell during the Night 6 1/2 inches. About 100 Canoes started for Nass."

March 24, 1865 — "Kithoon, the Kitselas Chief, with 2 men was drowned in Nass straits, his canoe having foundered in the heavy gale of yesterday."

The only explanation for the high survival rate was the wondrous affinity of sea, canoe and paddler.

In May and June the canoes rallied again at Fort Simpson, this time loaded with dried oolichans, grease and house boards. May 19, 1837 — "A great number of Tsimshians arrived from Nass, they were arriving from daylight in the morning till night, a continued stream of canoes crossing the harbour all day."

The returning Tsimshian were joined in McLoughlin's Harbour by people of other tribes who came to purchase oolichan grease with canoeloads of furs, potatoes and other barter. The waterfront seethed with arrivals, and canoe crews, including women and children, camped uneasily about the fort, for many dialects of many languages were spoken and many feuds smouldered. We have the story of one that turned the port into a battleground. It was chronicled in detail because the fort, contrary to Hudson's Bay policy, became involved.

By May 22nd of 1839, seven hundred and seventy-six canoes loaded with Tsimshian had returned from the Nass, and by May 25th a major Skidegate-Tsimshian row was in progress. It began as a trading quarrel and in no time at all flashed into warfare with shooting and casualties. "Mr. Kennedy exposed himself greatly to stop the firing and afterwards even went to the Tsimshian camp and brought a prisoner they had taken."

Like so many modern ceasefires, this one did not last through the night and once again the fort officers had to effect a peace so they could hustle the band of Skidegate into their canoes. Before all were embarked, Tsimshian opened fire on them and for once the haughty Haida panicked. Forty men, women and children who were still on the beach fled to the fort while, out in the bay, Skidegate were shooting and being shot, jumping out of canoes and being hauled into others. The most aggressive men and women abandoned their weaker comrades and commandeered craft with strong crews. Fourteen such canoes paddled to safety. Aboriginal civilization still hinged on survival of the fittest, in its simplest form.

The Tsimshian swooped down on the helpless canoes that were left and there was bloodshed and death in the harbour.

Some of the survivors were brought to the fort by friendly Tsimshian and some were ransomed by relatives already there. The fort was finally giving sanctuary to sixty-eight Skidegate. It was May 29th before another embarkation was attempted:

"At one o'clock in the morning, the tide answering and it being calm, We sent off the Skidegate Indians. We furnished them with Ammunition to defend themselves and gave them one of our canoes as the two they got back from the Tsimshian would not hold them all. They seemed to be very little obligated to us for all this attention and the care we have taken of them since they have been here and took the whole as a matter of course and were begging for many more things than they got. But this is their way, and nothing else is to be expected from them. [There are no words for *thank you* in the coast languages.] Everyone among them seems to be for himself. They were very much afraid when starting lest the Tsimshian would pursue them and bundled into the canoes as quick as they could, all the men got into the 2 best canoes and were going to leave the other one, with only 4 or 5 women and some children to get on the best way they could, till they were stopped and part of the men made to embark in it with the women. Notwithstanding all the lookout we kept, one of them a young lad, was left behind and is here yet ... They were soon out of sight and out of danger of being pursued."

Waterfront incidents were common during May and June. Usually the journal keepers disposed of them in a sentence or two, as on June 15th, 1857: "Two canoes from Nass arrived to a feast at the late Cannibal's house. The Tsimshian broke their Canoes to pieces also all their Boxes and other property." When July and the salmon run arrived, the Tsimshian moved on to their Skeena River fishing grounds and a blessed calm descended upon the shoreline of McLoughlin's Harbour.

Not all the harbour activities of the Native people were connected with work and war, though it was these that were emphasized in the journals. The social life of the villages depended on canoe traffic, too. When the chief known as Big Face gave a great feast, guests arrived from Tongass, Sabassa and the Nass. "We fired 4 big guns on the arrival of the illustrious fellows." Within a few days Kyganie, Chatsina and Milbank canoes brought more chiefs and their attendants to join the party, all peacefully and pleasurably disposed.

Bearskin, a Skidegate chief, made a dramatic entrance one day in 1837. His party of fifty or sixty people came in seven canoes but "on arrival they drew up in three canoes near the shore opposite the fort and had a dance and song before landing, they had themselves ornamented with feathers etc. and all painted for the occasion."

Kaw of Kyganie introduced himself with less tradition but no less colour:

July 30, 1837 — "Two canoes of Kyganie people arrived headed by a Chief named Kaw. He never was here before, he is a stout fellow and came with a flag flying and dressed out with a white beaver hat, white ruffled shirt and he has a good many furs with him."

A leave-taking, also, could be a spectacle. When Neshaki, she of great rank, celebrated the completion of her new house in the Nisga'a country, the departure of the head Tsimshian chiefs for the housewarming was an event in itself. Another send-off that must have been worth watching was Edenshaw's as he left to return to Masset with one thousand of his people. The factor was so impressed that he ran up a flag and fired a gun.

Ceremonies of all kinds were enacted on the shore:

June 8, 1838 — "Cacas came from Pearl harbour with two large canoes full of his people on a wooing expedition to the daughter of the chief Nesselcanooks, (the Cripple man). But it seems that the girl and her father were both averse to the match and would not listen to the suit, and the wooers had to return without their errand."

Had the girl and her father agreed to the marriage, their family and the wooer's would have engaged in a battle of stones, there on the beach, the wooer's being allowed to win, finally, and to carry off the bride by canoe. And again:

May 20, 1839 — "In the evening 6 canoes of them [Tsimshian] lashed three & three together arrived bearing the burnt bones and ashes of a principal woman who died some time ago, with great ceremony in the Indian way."

In Port Simpson there were always tantalizing mysteries that came by water. When I was eight years old the tones of the telling of them gave my spine cold sensations that no horror movie has ever been able to duplicate. "Every day, just at dark, some one see this black boat off Rose Island. Then a man walk in the village with a wolf behind him — bigger than any wolf we ever see. The man never speak. He never stop. No one see his face. A bad thing is going to happen."

In 1842 the omens arrived by canoe. There was one concerning a huge Tongass or Stikine canoe that came in the night. Her crew knocked on the door of one house, spoke Russian words, and disappeared. Simpson always seemed capable of fulfilling any portents of disaster.

Occasionally a canoe entering McLoughlin's Harbour carried white passengers. Early missionaries, fort people, gold-seekers, the Telegraph Company's personnel and the first Indian agent in those parts often travelled in that fashion. In fact, some owned their own canoes and hired Native crews. A few white brides reached their north coast homes by canoe. One was Alice Woods, daughter of the registrar of the Supreme Court of British Columbia. Her groom was Robert Tomlinson, B. A., from the Anglican mission at Kincolith, on the Nass River. He arrived at Victoria for the wedding in his fine Haida canoe. The marriage took place on April 24th, 1868, and on the 25th the couple was away on the honeymoon, twenty-four days northbound by canoe. Eight Nisga'a paddlers sped the canoe on its way and a Nisga'a woman accompanied them to attend the bride.

In the 1860s Robert Cunningham operated a freighting service on the Nass with his large canoe. He carried furs and goods to and from Fort Simpson on an almost regular basis.

It was via canoe that the port of Simpson entered its heyday of Skeena River freighting in 1866. That first transshipment was carried out by unseasoned northerners and was not a happy operation:

July 15, 1866 — "The Steamer *Mumford*, Captain Coffin, C.O. Telegraph, arrived here this Morning from the South with supplies for their Interior Stations and wires, in charge of Capn. Butler, who intends shipping them inland by the Skeena route. He purchased and hired quite a Number of Canoes and Indians here for this service & will no doubt push this business with Energy."

July 20 — "All the Indians, and Canoes that Capn. Butler hired here for going up the Skeena, returned to day complaining that they had been starved having got Nothing to eat but one dry Biscuit a day."

The beginning of the end of the canoe is glimpsed in a journal entry of February 28th, 1864: "Sloop *Kingfisher* sailed for Tongass, old Ibbets [Tongass chief] in tow." By the time I lived in Simpson the magnificent war canoes were gone and the Natives towed their only remaining canoes behind their gas boats, as dinghies. These were mean little dugouts, as cranky as their great predecessors had been splendid. I was forbidden to ever set foot in one. "No keel," said my father. One of the very last was Andrew's. While his fellows worked on their engines, caulked and copper painted, Andrew paddled toward his destination. One day he was bringing home a load of firewood (and when would one need firewood but in stormy weather?) when his canoe capsized. He was wearing gumboots that instantly filled with water, dragging him to the bottom in the manner of divers' boots. Andrew sat down on the rocks under three fathoms of water and removed his boots. As he sat there he must have done some thinking for, after he had struggled to shore and made his way to the village, he chopped up his canoe along with his firewood that had been washed onto the beach.

CHAPTER 20

The Port of Sail and Steam

THE GENTLEMEN ADVENTURERS on the northwest coast adventured chiefly by sea. Their ships came homing in to McLoughlin's Harbour to load and unload, to ballast, wood, victual, water, outfit for the trade and, on the hard sand beach that fronted the fort, to repair. The sailing vessels did not come without difficulty.

Port Simpson is tucked well inside the Inside Passage and while this route is a marvel of protected waters for modern shipping, the sloops and schooners, brigantines and barques suffered there from the loss of the ocean winds. They could make the crossing, Hawaii to Sitka, faster than they could coast San Francisco to Sitka, half the distance. They suffered also from the passage's freakish air and water currents and tight navigation. When gales blew strong and contrary the ships were almost at a standstill; when the winds died down they were becalmed. Dr. Tolmie described one primitive solution to such problems: "... the anchor was hoisted on board & as the breeze was very slight, the sweeps were manned. The sweeps are very large oars which work on an iron pivot at the forepart of deck, about 6 men were employed at each today, one pushing and guiding the sweep from before and the remaining 5 pulling on rope fastened to its handle from behind."

The *Beaver* provided another solution:

August 1, 1838 — "At 2 p.m. the *Columbia* came in sight off the North end of Dundas Island [seventeen miles north-west of Simpson] but the Wind being ahead and light she did not get into the harbour. There was not enough of wood on board the Steamer to admit of her going out to tow in the *Columbia* but should she not get in tonight the Steamer is ready to tow her in, in the morning."

August 2, 1838 — "The Barque *Columbia* ... had worked up to the entrance of the harbour by daylight. The steamer went out and towed her to the anchorage when she brought up at 7 a.m. Capt. Humphries and the people having been up all night these two nights past were fatigued and did not commence unloading today."

We have the details of another exercise in frustration that took place in the fall of 1841. The *Cadboro* was ready to leave Fort Simpson on October 24th but was "detained by calm." She was detained by calm on the 25th and 26th but sailed with a "fair breeze" on the 27th. By November 3rd she was back in port, being "unable, because of contrary winds to proceed."

Fort Simpson began recording port history with the brig *Dryad*. It was the *Dryad* that carried the founding party to the mouth of the Stikine River, retreated to McLoughlin's Harbour, survived the move from the Nass and flitted in and out of the bay as a protective presence while the builders were still encamped under canvas and boughs. In turn, she was the first of twenty or more vessels that would bring Fort Simpson's land activities to a halt while the fort people serviced them.

October 20, 1834 — "20 men employed wooding, ballasting & watering ship."

The *Dryad* was an early pioneer on the coast. She came in 1825, new from the shipyard. She was moulded, sheathed with wood and, as practically all the vessels of those days were, sheathed again on the bottom with five-pound copper plates.

She came complete with a figurehead, presumably a dryad, and a bowsprit that could serve more than one purpose. When her deck was in need of repairs and there was not an oak plank within hundreds of miles of Fort Simpson, a bowsprit (it must have been a spare) was sawed into planks that did the job neatly. The *Dryad* was considered a graceful ship but, as Dr. Tolmie discovered, a poor performer. "The *Dryad* makes no progress at beating unless with a 7 or 8 knotter," he remarked in his diary during one tedious trip. Whatever the reason, after carrying the Columbia Department's furs back to England in 1835, she was sold.

The brigantine *Cadboro*, the ship that ventured up the Nass River to locate the original Fort Simpson, also made the first entry into the Fraser River from salt water, in 1827. She was the first to cast anchor in Cadboro Bay and first to sail into the Canal of Camosack. From 1827 to 1860 she probed scores of unmapped inlets and dodged hundreds of uncharted rocks. In the winter of the fort's second year on McLoughlin's Harbour she was trading in northern waters:

December 15, 1835 — "About 9 p.m. heard the report of a Cannon which were answered by ours from the Fort."

December 16 — "About one o'clock this morning the *Cadboro* was at anchor & shortly after had the pleasure of seeing Capt. Brotchie on shore."

The *Cadboro* seems never to have passed up a chance to communicate or salute with her guns. She had six of them. And what were the specifications of this famous armed craft with a complement of thirty-five? Her length was fifty-six feet, her beam seventeen feet, the depth of her hold eight feet, and her tonnage seventy-two. She was the size of our gillnetters.

An enemy of the *Cadboro* became a frequenter of Fort Simpson harbour. McLoughlin, who was opposed to ships and dead set against sea captains, purchased the brig *Lama* complete with cargo, and hired her captain, W. H. McNeill, and two mates. As you might surmise, this was no routine transaction. The *Lama* was registered at 144 tons. She sailed out of Boston in 1830 but it was 1831 before she put in on the West Coast. When she did the Company became aware of her — she was rumoured to take the largest share of the ten thousand beaver skins that were traded annually. The *Cadboro* and her six guns were dispatched to rout the newcomer but the *Lama*, far from being intimidated, prepared to do battle. This was hardly what McLoughlin had in mind, considering freedom of the seas and international relations, so he abandoned guns and used instead five thousand dollars to eliminate a formidable opponent and further his own trade. Captain McNeill raised the Hudson's Bay insignia and continued to command the *Lama* and pile up furs, until 1837 when she was sold and he assumed command of the *Beaver*. But the *Lama's* story does not end there.

Captain John Bancroft bought the brig for fifty-five hundred dollars for his sea otter expeditions. Jacob Astor's fur trading organization had instituted the long-range hunt using Haida, chiefly Kyganie, as huntsmen and crewmen. Their skill was unique. The route took them to California and on to the Sandwich Islands before returning them, after long months, to their island homes. These trips, besides providing sea otter pelts for the Americans, provided abalone shells for the Haida. To them, gathering abalone shells was like coining money, for these iridescent shells were indeed a form of their currency.

Captain Bancroft was an Englishman who hunted for the American trade. He set off in the *Lama* on such a voyage with a crew of Kanakas and Kyganie, a first mate who was white and a wife from Hawaiian nobility. That was a volatile mixture. When heat, pressure and food shortages were applied, it exploded in a Kyganie mutiny. Captain Bancroft was shot dead, his wife, who had exerted most of the pressure, was wounded, and the mate was held captive to assist the Kyganie in sailing the ship to their Dall Island home. There the *Lama* was abandoned to roll and pound and break up in the surf.

One of the earliest ships in the Hudson's Bay Pacific fleet was a schooner built on the Columbia River and named *Vancouver*. There seems to have been a powerful marine curse on that name. This first *Vancouver*, a sixty-ton schooner, even smaller than the *Cadboro*, accompanied the *Dryad* on the 1831 expedition to establish the Nass fort. Three years later the *Dryad* was sailing north with another land party to establish another Fort Simpson when the barque *Lagrange* hailed her to relate the story of the *Vancouver's* end. She had run aground on Rose Spit, Queen Charlotte Islands, and all had been lost except the crewmembers. They had made their way to the Nass fort. The captain of the *Lagrange* noted sadly that the rum had been scuttled.

The nemesis of the second vessel named *Vancouver* was the Columbia River. She was a barque of three hundred thirty-six tons, built in the old country and brought out to this coast in 1838 by Captain Alexander Duncan who had survived the wreck of the previous *Vancouver*. The river gave fair warning to the new barque and weeks later and eight hundred miles away, at Fort Simpson, Mr. Work acquainted McLoughlin with the accident that had happened on Fort Vancouver's own doorstep, in a letter dated August 13th, 1843:

"*Vancouver* arrived 1st August and delivered outfits from Vancouver. The *Vancouver* had got on a stone or stump in the Columbia River. She was hauled ashore here to ascertain what damages she had sustained when it was found that 13 feet long and in places 3 feet wide of the copper and sheeting were gone and also 13 feet of the false keel at the stern carried away besides the false keel being injured and the copper taken off in other parts."

The repairs took fort and steamer men nine days of working by tides. They must have been sound because the barque sailed the England-Pacific run for another five years before the Columbia finally trapped her on a sandbar and wrecked her completely.

Refusing to bow to seamen's superstitions, the Hudson's Bay Company built its third *Vancouver*, a brigantine. She sailed north with the Fort Simpson outfit in the summer of 1853. Mr. McNeill recounts the interaction of Rose Spit, a ship named *Vancouver* and Fate.

August 23, 1853 — "The *Vancouver* is now no more, she was run on shore on Point Rose Spit early on the morning of the 13th inst. going seven knots. Mr. Swanson and Griffin [supercargo and mate] arrived on the 15th with the astounding news, about 10 a.m. The steamer was fortunately lying here with 25 cords wood on deck waiting the arrival of a vessel with supplies. Capt. Dodd ordered the steam to be got up immediately and started at 2 p.m. ... and arrived at the scene of trouble at about 10 p.m. The steamer arrived back here on the 18th ... having on board Capt. Reid, his officers, and crew, All the Powder, Six Cases Guns, a few Bales and Cases of Sundries and some of the stores ... I must mention that after all had been done possible to save the *Vancouver*, Capt. Reid set fire to her, ... The Indians had begun to plunder and break up the vessel."

That report was written to the Board of Managers. The journal account was less restrained and added such bits of colour as: "The *Vancouver's* crew behaved badly and cowardly ever since the Vessel struck, in fact the fellows have been drunk most of the time." Apparently the third *Vancouver's* rum was not scuttled.

The end of the story was written by McNeill the sea captain, rather than McNeill the fort commander, as he described the sailing of the *Beaver* with the *Vancouver's* complement on board, "... Poor Captain Reid went with a sore heart and no wonder. The *Vancouver* was his first command."

By the time she made that rescue, the steamship *Beaver* was a veteran on the coast. While we have managed to hide away most of British Columbia's brilliantly coloured past under the dust of political history, the *Beaver* is one feature that has escaped and made her way into our affections. We think of her, all one hundred and one feet of her, as the embodiment of the province's sometimes romantic, always robust beginnings.

The *Beaver* sailed to North America. Built in England, she was convoyed by the new barque, *Columbia*, on the journey that followed the usual trade route round the Horn and north by way of the Sandwich Islands. When she reached Fort Vancouver and an adequate supply of wood, in the spring of 1836, she broke out her engines, her boiler and her side-wheel paddles to become the first steam-powered vessel on the northwest coast. Her engines developed 70 horsepower and she had a speed of 9 ¾ knots.

The *Beaver*'s arrival at the port of Simpson that summer must have been an amazement of noise, smoke and churning water, yet it was none of these that the journal recorded. What was noted was the fact that she could make port one hour from sighting. Another feature that impressed the fort people was the steamer's appetite for wood. They had started felling, chopping, rafting and piling two months before she first anchored in the bay. Her large complement, twenty-six, allowed for wooding en route but, as that system meant two days of wooding for one of steaming, Fort Simpson was responsible for supplying a deckload whenever she reached port. In 1838 the fort hired Tsimshian to work on the *Beaver*'s wood supply: "There is not yet enough cut though 17 men have been busy at it these 2 days."

The hard, sand beach at Fort Simpson was the coast's dry-dock. The *Beaver* was making use of it little more than a year after her first arrival. During her life she was hauled ashore there for innumerable inspections, repairs and adaptations.

There seems to have been intense interest in whatever work was under way on her:

January 8, 1838 — "I had to set two men to, to saw wood for paddle blades for the Steamer, as none of her own people could saw such wide planks, 19 inches straight. Had also to send off 5 men to assist two of the Steamer's people to square timber to saw for deck planks. One of the beams over the boilers is broke and must be replaced ... with new ones."

January 10 — "The broken beam over the Steamer's boilers was examined today and found to be rotten more than half way through, and no doubt was so when it was put in which was a gross piece of Knavery of the builders. It is African oak and had it been sound when it was put in it would not have been rotten yet."

August 14, 1838 — (For two weeks the men of the fort had been scurrying to and from the two ships, *Beaver* and *Columbia*, with cargo, provisions, wood, stones for ballast and material for repairs and at last the *Beaver* was ready to sail.) — "But behold as these arrangements were made and about to be acted upon the Engineers discovered some defects in the Machinery which before it can be taken to pieces and put together again will require at least three weeks and perhaps longer."

At that time Mr. Work seemed a little vague about the steam engine but by the 1840s he had penetrated its mysteries and was ordering parts from the London office in technical detail: "In the overhaul the pistons were found to be worn too small for the Cylinders, to remedy which they would require to be reduced in size and hooped which cannot be done with the means possessed in the Country. A pair of new ones are required, having them sent out by the *Cowlitz* is of much importance." In those years Mr. Work was responsible for the *Beaver* and her engines along with the entire marine department *and* Fort Simpson. Worn pistons were the least of his troubles; mutiny was the greatest.

The *Beaver* wintered in Fort Simpson harbour her first two years. As the particularly cold, miserable January of 1838 drew toward its end so did the crew's tolerance of Captain McNeill's discipline. The west coast seems always to have attracted free spirits and nineteenth-century sea practices had nothing to do with freedom. When the captain resorted to flogging, the seamen and stokers revolted. For two days notes passed from ship to fort and back again but the sailors stood firm in their refusal to serve under McNeill. Then the engineers, the only people who could get the *Beaver* under way, joined the sailors' cause and Mr. Work was forced to grant the mutineers the victory. He managed to retrieve a scrap of victory for the Company also, by taking command of the *Beaver* himself with Captain McNeill beside him, officially as passenger. In this way the *Beaver* was returned to Nisqually and a change of crew, and in this way she went about her business for many voyages, various officers relieving Mr. Work as skipper on the ship's papers, but Captain McNeill always actually in charge. The mutineers had dug up the fact of his American citizenship, which made him an illegal captain for British ships.

The *Beaver* worked diligently at the trade. She made three trips north from Fort Simpson each trading season, as well as covering much of the rest of the coast. Her manoeuvrability made it possible to visit villages that the other ships had never reached, so she became explorer as well as trader. She was sent to "run up and examine all the canals between Johnstone Strait and this place," to search for coal on Vancouver Island, to investigate the Kitlope and Kitimat channels and, in 1837, to make the first search for a suitable fort site on southern Vancouver Island. Less gloriously, the *Beaver* towed:

July 31, 1838 — "The Steamer arrived at 3:20 p.m. She left Fort McLoughlin on Sunday last and towed the Company's Barque *Columbia* out of Milbank Sound so that she may be expected here very soon."

September 23, 1844 — "The report of a cannon was heard … The steamer went out early the next morning in quest of her and returned with H.M. Sloop *Modeste* in tow."

The *Beaver* did long-distance towing, too:

June 10, 1840 — (James Douglas had come north to establish a fort on the Stikine.) "About 3 o'clock a.m. the Steamer with the *Vancouver* in tow started for Stikine."

She was also known to tow the canoes of chiefs and, during the 1850s gold excitement, the craft of prospectors. In fact, it was as a towboat and freighter that she ended her career.

By 1863 the *Beaver's* best days for the Company were over and the Honourable Gentlemen leased her to the British government to pursue her explorations officially. Under Lt. Daniel Pender, RN, she spent seven years surveying the coastline that she had already made her own. A Victoria freighting firm purchased her in 1874 and for another fourteen years she was tug and carrier. Government had progressed from company to colony to province but through all the changes the *Beaver* steamed steadily on. Then Prospect Point claimed her one night and there she ended her fifty-two years as coastal expediter.

The *Otter* was another Hudson's Bay Company innovation. She arrived in 1853, also under sail, a steamer without a paddlewheel. Mr. McNeill referred to her as "the propeller." And Fort Simpson welcomed its third steamer six years after the *Otter's* arrival. She was the *Labouchere*, a paddle ship exactly twice the length of the *Beaver*. Her life was short, seven years, but full of material for the Fort Simpson journal.

Ever since the *Beaver* had reached the coast there had been a low rumble of threats against her from the Natives. She kept her boarding net either ready or lowered but never had to repel an attack. It was the *Labouchere* that received the attack. She was in Chilkat waters, north of the Stikine, her crew ashore wooding, when Natives boarded her and for hours held the captain and an officer captive on the quarter-deck. Then, suddenly and without explanation, the Chilkat took to their canoes. The chief, as he left, advised the captain to get away quickly. The two men who had been awaiting death considered that an excellent idea.

The *Labouchere* would seem to have been tempting disaster again, in 1862, when she rescued prospectors and miners of the lesser gold rush, from the Stikine's approaching winter:

October 24, 1862 — "The *Labouchere* took about 20 more passengers on board which will make at least 180 souls on board. We sold a large number of potatoes to the passengers on *Labouchere*." (The vessel was two hundred two feet long.)

There were other Company steamers and sailing ships, none without a story. Among them was the brigantine *Una*, first of all the gold questing vessels on the coast. We hear of her in McLoughlin's Harbour in 1851 when she brought Mr. McNeill north via the Queen Charlotte Islands. She had taken a gold-mining party to Mitchell Harbour, Moresby Island. The mining proved hazardous because the Haida were as interested in the gold of their island as was the Hudson's Bay Company. After each blast the Natives vied with the miners for the ore. As the game grew rougher and the Company's take smaller, the project was abandoned and the *Una* sailed for Fort Simpson. There, in the safety of the fort, McNeill wrote a report to James Douglas that is a study in viewpoints. The report complained that the Haida stole the ore from the Company.

That same report suggested that a cabin be built below decks to replace the *Una's* deck cabin as "musket balls would go through and through it." But it was without muskets that the Natives of Neah Bay destroyed the *Una* two years later. When she went aground there they plundered and burned her.

The Company ships were dwarfed in the Fort Simpson harbour by those of Her Majesty's Navy. The first naval vessel mentioned in the journal was HBM sloop *Modeste*, in 1844.

She arrived on the coast fresh from the Opium War in China to project the British presence during the determination of the British-United States border. As we have seen, the *Beaver* towed her into port so that she could haul up on the beach for inspection. A letter written by Mr. Work suggests that her supplies were running low: "Supplied *Modeste* with coals, candles and a log of wood for which they paid in dollars also some vegetables not charged, for which they were well pleased and grateful."

The next naval vessel written up in the Fort Simpson journal was the *Virago*, which arrived in 1853. By this time there was the crown colony of Vancouver Island to be defended. Beside the little *Beaver* the *Virago* was impressive, HM paddle-sloop-of-war, 1,060 tons, 300 horsepower. She was hauled ashore for repairs that continued for three weeks, sufficient time to send the fort people into a black despair. Not only did they resent the *Virago's* officers buying furs at reckless prices and with rum, but they also disapproved of the great *Virago's* show of helplessness at the hands of the Natives.

June 18, 1853 — "A number of the *Virago's* men were pushed down by the Indians while carrying Coals. A row took place in the evening, and was near being serious."

June 22 — "The Indians give them a considerable trouble. Many of her officers sleep on shore in the Indian Lodges every night."

June 29 — "*Virago* getting on very slowly with her repairs, and the Indians are stealing from her right and left. They also unshackled the Raft that had her large Guns on it. The raft went adrift and gave them much trouble. They have also lost 30 round shot."

Seven years later when HMS *Alert* was in port, though a different factor and journal keeper were reporting, Fort Simpson was still critical of the navy:

August 30, 1860 — "A grand Pow-wow was held in Legaic's house, this afternoon relative to the various grievances such as murder, drunkenness and theft, which in my opinion ended in *smoke*. This meeting was attended by Captain Pearse [of the *Alert*], Mr. Duncan and other guests from the *Alert*."

August 31 — "*Alert* exercising her guns to make an impression on the Indians which was a failure, the firing only so so."

The *Alert* was a propeller corvette and carried seventeen of those guns.

HM paddle sloop *Devastation*, 1,058 tons, 400 horsepower, six guns, won a glorious victory in northern waters in 1862. The details are enough to make a British subject crawl under a clamshell. That summer, singly and in convoys, an odd assortment of craft lay over in the port, readying for the last lap of the journey to Stikine — large and small sailboats and canoes, steamers and a barge, all carrying miners. To the ancestral owners of these territories this was an invasion and they set out to repel it in their own way. From all over the north coast came outraged accounts of harassment. Canoes were stolen, ships boarded, outfits plundered and finally, two men of a party of three were killed. On September 15th the *Devastation* steamed into the harbour to tidy up the situation.

September 16 — "At 4 a.m. the *Devastation* manned and sent 5 boats and took old Cacas and 9 of his tribe prisoners, took them on board and gave them to understand that they would be in limbo until the three murderers of Henry and one other man were given up. The Natives seemed to be astonished at this sharp practice. Mr. Duncan [magistrate as well as missionary] arrived at 10 a.m. We sent for him last night. Indians have not brought any of the murderers, are humbugging. Capt. Pike is getting tired and talks of burning the village. Sent a canoe to Dundas Island to make inquiries, etc."

Two days later the Tsimshian surrendered one of the murderers and naval reinforcements arrived in the surveying steam sloop *Hecate*, 860 tons, five guns.

September 19 — "Men o'War captains and Mr. Duncan had a long talk with the chiefs and others and told them plainly that the three murderers must be given up or the village would be burnt."

Next day the *Devastation* crossed to Dundas Island to pick up their suspects but not finding them "brought 14 canoes containing a number of women and children prisoners also a quantity of winter provisions. They fired on the Indians and drove them into the bush on Dundas Island."

On the 23rd the *Hecate* steamed to Pearl Harbour. "She did not find the third murderer but brought nine canoes from Pearl Harbour belonging to Cacas' tribe."

And on the 25th: "This morning the *Hecate* and *Devastation* sent a number of boats and about 100 men and took old Cacas prisoner on board the *Devastation* as hostage. The boats made quite a demonstration."

The Fort Simpson incident was the mildest of many examples of the horrifying deeds of Natives and the more horrifying retaliation by Her Majesty's Navy. Another was recorded at Fort Rupert in 1850. Three sailors were murdered by an equal number of Nahwitti. HMS *Daedalus* was dispatched to the scene. Finding the village deserted the ship fired at it until much of it was destroyed. The next summer HMS *Daphne* took up the cause. This time the people were home and ready for the attack. They fired first and wounded some of the sailors as the ship's boats approached the shore. Their chief was killed and three tribesmen wounded. The *Daphne's* men set fire to the village (cedar burns well and fast) and once again the navy departed, triumphant.

The episode at Matilda Creek, Clayoquot Sound, in 1864 revealed the Ahousat as savages and the officers of Her Majesty's ships *Sutlej* and *Devastation* as better-armed savages. The Ahousat murdered the captain, mate and a Native crewman of the sloop *Kingfisher*, then plundered and burned the ship. The navy replied by demolishing *nine* villages and sixty-four canoes, killing fifteen villagers and carrying off several prisoners to Victoria. These and a few similar naval actions were acclaimed as British justice.

The fort made no complaint about the navy when those ships towed captive whiskey smugglers out of the bay. Such rare discipline belonged to the 1860s when Victoria was the lusty homeport of the sloops and schooners that carried liquid havoc to the coastal peoples. They sheltered and repaired and traded in McLoughlin's Harbour along with the Company vessels. They were successors to the British and the Boston Traders of the eighteenth and earlier nineteenth centuries, those far-sailing vessels that originated the Hawaiian winter excursion so popular with modern British Columbians — they wintered in what was referred to as "The Sandwich Islands" or "Owyhee" or "Wahoo" or "Honoruru" and in the spring they came billowing back to northern Alaska to coast southward for another season's trade. Those early ships instituted the trading chase, also. It had been worked up to a fine technique by the 1860s. The vessels, great and small, chased one another all over the coast. Pursued and pursuer were stormbound together and becalmed together and, if the pursuer was successful, they found themselves bartering for furs in the same cove. The most enthusiastic chaser of all was Fort Simpson's swift little sloop, *Petrel*.

July 28, 1864 — "A large schooner passed up the Nass Straits."

July 29 — "Mr. Horne started in the *Petrel* for Nass to oppose the schooner seen yesterday."

There was one period in the turbulent 1860s when the fort people regarded any arriving vessel other than the Company's, the mission's and the navy's as a whiskey trader. They were usually right but their cynicism almost prevented their observing the beginning of the northern fishing industry:

August 3, 1864 — "Schooner *Gazelle* arrived from the south on a supposed cod fishing trip."

August 4 — "The *Gazelle* sailed for Kithoon, *cod catching* (tangle selling more likely)."

April 28, 1865 — "Schooners *Kate* and *Onward* left for the Fox Islands on a cod fishing expedition. Schooner *Gazelle* arrived from the Nass. The Captain says they have caught about a ton of Cod fish." (The salmon fishery so completely superseded the cod industry in the north that I grew up believing cod to be a throw-away fish.)

It was in that same decade and the latter part of the preceding one that some of the whiskey sloops and schooners became passenger carriers at least part of the time, and new and strange nontrading craft entered the harbour. The four-letter word *gold* had already altered the direction of development in the south and it brought changes to the port of Simpson also.

The germ of California's 1849 gold fever reached the north coast in 1850. The Queen Charlotte Islands saw British Columbia's first glint of gold and the mainland rivers the Skeena, Nass and Stikine were being prospected six years before the Fraser and the Thompson were associated with gold. Mr. McNeill was one of the coast's first victims of gold fever. His experience aboard the *Una* at Mitchell Harbour in 1850 reduced the fever slightly but was no cure. He did, however, make an early and complete recovery, writing the history of his case in journal and letters:

November 20, 1851 — "I have employed McGregor and Crittle blasting the rock where the gold Mr. Work took from here was said to have come from, to no effect. We have looked at other places near this establishment to no purpose."

April 8, 1852 — "This day one of the Chiefs from Skeena River that arrived here yesterday, brought a few small pieces of Gold ore to the fort, two large pieces of Quartz Rock with a few particles of Gold ore ... He tells me that the gold is to be seen in many places on the surface of the Rock for some distance, say two miles. This is a most important discovery, at least I think so, and may prove more convenient for us to work than the diggings on Queen Charlott's Island. I shall go, or send, to have a look and examine this new discovery so soon as possible … Who knows but this new discovery may prove more valuable than the diggings on California? W. H. McN."

A Company man made trips to both the Skeena and the Nass in search of the exposed veins but found nothing of note. Then came the first of the miners:

May 9, 1855 — "Baptiste Bottineau, two Canadians and nine Stikine Indians arrived from Fort Victoria, they are bound to Stikine to look for 'Gold.'"

For the next few years the journals reported the arrivals of many goldseekers and the trade lists mentioned such items as "10 oz. pure gold" or "a one-pound nugget" but these did not interrupt Mr. McNeill's cure. "The American Goldseekers are taking the world very easy," said he, "in fact Gold hunters live a very easy and idle life, if I am to judge from those that are here, they have been back from Nass since the 5th inst. and have not been ten yards from the Fort since."

Fort Simpson's wood yard became headquarters for a mining party that arrived in July of 1859. Even mining parties were divided into gentlemen and men and this one was made up of "Capt. Torrens, Messrs. Denman & Harry McNeill [the factor's somewhat wayward son] with a party of men on board bound to Queen Charlotte Island to look for gold."

August 5 — "At 1 p.m. Captain Torrens and party also arrived back from Q.C.I. They returned on account of the hostility of the natives. The Skidegate people fired eight shots at them. The party found Gold on an Island near the South end of Dundas Island."

August 6 — "Captain Torrans' [sic] party drying their bedding and provisions in the wood yard, having got very wet on their voyage to Q.C.I."

August 10 — "At 10 a.m. Captn. Torrens, Henry McNeill and four men of the nine that composed the party started for Q.C. Island '*again*' … This Goldseeking is a *reckless, lazy, idle*, Indian sort of life, the Gypseys are lords, in comparison to the Goldseekers. At all events I will take very good care that I do not become a Goldseeker, otherwise than by *regular* daily labour, and regular salary. [Signed] W. H. McNeill." When he expressed a personal opinion in the journal, Mr. McNeill would initial the entry. This one he signed in full.

Although that was the end of Mr. McNeill's gold fever, it was only the beginning of the symptoms that enlivened the harbour for the next decade. The Torrens-Denman-McNeill party from their base at Simpson continued to prospect in all directions with all kinds of results, such as:

October 13, 1859 — "Captn. Torrens returned from Nass late at night with ½ oz. fine Gold taken from the Canion some 75 miles up the River."

December 10, 1859 — "Mr. Denman arrived from Tongass having been cleaned out and fired at."

Encampments filled the wood yard and prospectors arrived and departed in large and small parties and in craft that ranged from steamers to canoes. Mr. McNeill's sardonic eye kept watch over the harbour. In June of 1862 he concluded, "… at least a ½, say 100 men will leave soon for Victoria. This ends the Stikine speculation."

Within a few days that assumption seemed to have been proved false for passengers for the Stikine were streaming into the harbour aboard the sloop *John Thornton*, the stern-wheeler *Flying Dutchman*, the *North Star* and six unnamed sloops and schooners, a whaleboat and canoes. And on the last day of the month, "Last evening the Sloop *John Thornton* arrived from Stikine and has famous news. The captain reports that 2 men obtained $700 in dust in 6 days, others getting from $11 to $50 per diem."

But that was June. August bore out Mr. McNeill's earlier opinion:

August 3 — "All the miners and schooners left for Victoria afraid to proceed to Stikine."

Hundreds of prospectors passed through Simpson in the fall exodus but unfortunately not all of them:

June 6, 1863 — "The *Nanaimo Packet*'s people report that 8 or 9 White men had died at Stikine during the past Winter of scurvy, and that the Russians had taken some few men that were still sick to Sitka, and would send them to Victoria."

That summer some of the discouraged miners returned to try their luck on the Nass and Skeena Rivers but this miniature gold rush never gained momentum and Mr. McNeill closed the season with:

October 8, 1863 — "We now have about 24 miners, and gentlemen loafers, about the place ..."

By the time the 1898 gold rush exploded, the port of Simpson was an old-timer at accommodating goldseekers and transshipping outfits.

PART VI

People of the Fort

Mrs. John Work, Josette Legace, daughter of a French-Canadian father and a Native mother of the Spokane country, was Fort Simpson's second first lady. Her fame as a hostess spread even to England.

The Irishman John Work was in charge of Fort Simpson and the Marine Department 1835–1851. Thereafter he was a member of the Hudson's Bay Company Board of Management and the Vancouver Island Legislative Council. He was warmhearted and much esteemed by those he commanded.

This painting of Fort Simpson by Gordon Lockerby — sea captain, artist and a turn-of-the-century employee of the post — was copied from a painting done by Pym Nevin Compton, who was an officer at the fort in 1866.

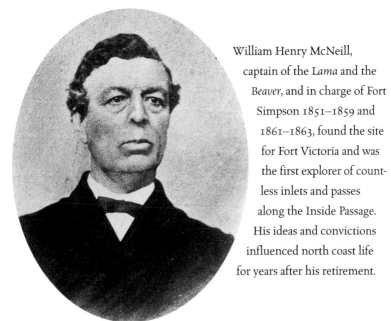

William Henry McNeill, captain of the *Lama* and the *Beaver*, and in charge of Fort Simpson 1851–1859 and 1861–1863, found the site for Fort Victoria and was the first explorer of countless inlets and passes along the Inside Passage. His ideas and convictions influenced north coast life for years after his retirement.

Hamilton Moffatt, in charge of Fort Simpson 1859–1861 and 1863–1866, had trouble with the Natives and with his own men — his departure was celebrated with a bottle of rum to each employee (a beneficence unheard of elsewhere in the journals).

Mrs. Hamilton Moffatt, Lucy McNeill, daughter of Matilda and W. H. McNeill, occupied the *Labouchere's* VIP cabin as she came north to take her place as the first lady at Fort Simpson, but she was equally at home in a canoe on a trading expedition.

The last traditional Tsimshian house at Port Simpson (on Rose Island).
It stood until after 1910.

The Hudson's Bay Company post at Port Simpson. The whitewashed building was the store; the old building adjoining it was the Big House and the rocks in the foreground were marble leftovers from the stonecutter's lucrative trade in tombstones. (c. 1900.)

Port Simpson before 1900. Pictured are the Native village (mainland) and the bridge to Rose Island. The firehall and bell tower are at the left end of the bridge, with the first Methodist mission house on the hill behind. At centre is the Methodist church.

The buildings of the post skirted the shoreline and extended to the reserve boundary. The wharf approach, though one-third of a mile long, had no railing until there was a drowning in 1907.

A Native funeral march to the graveyard on Rose Island, led by the band, which also led wedding processions and highlighted all manner of ceremonial events.

The SS *Princess May*, here seen steaming out of Port Simpson harbour, was famous for a series of disasters, one of which sliced off one end of the Port Simpson wharf.

The *Port Simpson* was queen of the Hudson's Bay Company's Skeena River fleet for four short years and was beached in 1912 by the completion of the Grand Trunk Pacific Railway to Prince Rupert.

Camping down the coast from Simpson were, from left, mother (holding Loyal), Helen, Ruth and Beatrice Brentzen. Mother chose camping to mark an end to a winter of serious illnesses. Dad commuted by boat. (1916.)

In 1912 Mother took her daughters to visit her Oregon family. There we were starched and curled and photographed —Helen aged two, Ruth aged six.

The general store was built on the leased Hudson's Bay Company property where, from 1915 to 1932, my father bought furs and sold whatever Port Simpson needed — gasoline (in five-gallon cans), peanuts, flannelette, pencils, coal, crackers, coffins ...

The original Methodist church was built in 1874 by Rev. Thomas Crosby and his converts. The spire, rising to a height of one hundred forty feet, was composed of more than one hundred hand-hewn, fitted pieces. It burned to the ground in the 1920s.

At the Crosby Girls' Home, the girls received intensive training in religion and other classroom subjects from dedicated, over-worked teachers. This original site of the home was another victim of fire.

"Home Girls" went for a daily in-line walk. (c. 1912.)

Dinah was believed by the villagers to posses supernatural powers for evil, but it was by brain power that she survived.

The 24th of May was the day that crowds assembled, flags flew, the band played, children ran races, teams played games and summer clothes came out of storage. (c. early 1920s.)

In the early twentieth century, Columbia River Boats, such as this one, were the gillnetters of the north coast. They were powered by wind and oars. Rose Island forms the background. (c. 1910.)

In 1921 there was no available colour film to record a sunset over Port Simpson's harbour.

In 1917 the family spent some time in Victoria, where the streets were full of khaki uniforms, and war bulletins were posted at frequent intervals. We youngsters from a north coast village gleefully discovered Beacon Hill Park and ice cream parlours. Our father discovered a photographer. Clockwise from top: Helen (seven), Ruth (eleven), Eva (Hallie) Young, R. B. Young and Loyal (two).

CHAPTER 21

The Factor and Life and Death

FOR ME, THE FORT at Simpson will always be a dim living room full of children playing blindman's buff, and magical bubbles floating overhead. The bubble pipes were made of clay and smelled of earth and stuck to lips a little. The year was 1913. You must pardon my carelessness in failing to observe an era drawing toward a precipitous close. I was three; it was my first birthday party and the fort's last.

Early recorded impressions of Fort Simpson were more comprehensive but almost as personally coloured as mine. To the youthful Dr. Tolmie, camped in the clearing, in the fort's first construction days: "it was a lovely evening & I Think a landscape painter would have found a good subject for his brush in our encampment 'under the greenwood tree' — the ample bay with its woody islets and rocks & the surrounding peaked & snow dappled mountains — the felled trees — grass and herbs had then the freshness & verdure of life …"

To Captain D. D. Wishart of the *Norman Morison*, lying over at Fort Simpson in 1850, it was "a most miserable place, surrounded by the Indian Lodges — and the fort gates secured from Sunset to Sunrise, and locked during meals,… It rained incessantly the whole time I was there, and that they tell me is mostly the case all the year save that it will occasionally vary the scene by sending a little snow."

The *Victoria Colonist* published more professional reports. One was written aboard HMS *Sparrowhawk* bound for Sitka and appeared under date of July 10th, 1867:

"The fort is a quadrangular enclosure stockaded round with beams, about 20 feet high, driven into the ground and has a bastion at each corner, while on the inside at the height of about 12 feet from the ground a gallery runs round. The buildings within consist of a chief trader's house, stores, trading room, etc. The village stretches on each side of the fort the lodges being built on piles of the height of 8 or 10 feet and are at high water inaccessible except by canoes the tide circulating underneath."

The tight little clump of humanity that was locked inside the gates each night was made up of several entities: the factor, the gentlemen, the men, the Native wives, the half-Native children and occasionally slaves who belonged to fort women. Dependent upon one another, sometimes for their very lives, those segments still maintained their nineteenth-century class separateness. This produced disparate viewpoints. The one most readily available to us is the factor's for, by the light of his goat-tallow candle, he wrote up the journal each night.

What the factor wrote in his copperplate hand were reports of the fur trade and everything that affected it, summaries of the days' occupations and the state of the physical fort. The lives behind the stockade went their ways almost unrecorded. Regarding them, the journals and letters dropped a revealing phrase here, a sentence there and, rarely, the climax of a story. When these are tacked onto the framework of Hudson's Bay Company routines that were carried out at all forts come hurricane, ice, death or disaster, fragments of events and lives take shape. The factor's chief concern with those lives was preserving them.

"Everyone suffering from dejection and colds," wrote Mr.

McNeill during a particularly malevolent fall that followed a summer of "shocking bad weather," and again, that year, "Just the weather to kill anyone who is not made of iron." Fort inhabitants were indeed made of iron for most of them survived not only weather-induced colds, rheumatism and lame backs, but innumerable waves of influenza that laid them low for a week at a time. They survived exposure, frostbite, boils, piles, stricture, fits, fever and ague, chronic dysentery, the effects of "rot gut" whiskey and heart attacks. Not all the women survived childbirth and not all the children survived epidemics of European diseases, measles, mumps and chicken pox that so rapidly found their way to that isolated community. And not all the men survived the effects of venereal diseases. Many of them seemed to be afflicted with these and there were month-long periods when one or more of them were sick because of what one factor delicately termed "ladies' fever," "the particular disease" or "large pox" (smallpox being on everyone's mind in those days).

Smallpox first arrived on the coast in the late eighteenth century. That epidemic was only a story told by the older Natives when the disease struck Fort Simpson, from the north, in 1836:

October 16 — "One of the men's wives in the SmallPox, this is the third case that has occurred in the Fort. The two first [cases] did not remain in the Fort."

November 18 — "The three cow inoculations on Wednesday the 9th I am sorry to say has not had the desired effect owing I suppose to the matter being old. It was tried twice on the same individuals."

April 28, 1837 — "William Kennedy's Wife is recovering from the smallpox but within these four days two of his children and an Indian boy and girl that he has, have all been taken ill with the same disease only one of his children is now clear of it. He has his hands full with so many sick about him."

That one epidemic alone wiped out one-third of the north coast indigenous population, according to Company estimates.

The 1862 epidemic arrived from Victoria by canoe. While it swept through the village dealing out death, the stockade seems to have repelled it (or perhaps this time there was fresh vaccine for fort personnel). At any rate when an ex-employee arrived on the *Labouchere* to take up residence in the village with his Native wife, rules were waived and they were admitted to the fort and safety from the disease.

Fort Simpson's harsh work habits accounted for nearly as much illness as did climate and epidemics:

April 9, 1839 — "X. Kateman still sick, it is the fever and Ague he has probably brought on by being wet all day on Friday last landing the casks from the Steamer."

Neither the officers nor the men themselves ever seemed to give much thought to improving working conditions but they did give consideration to those who fell ill from those or any other causes. A seriously sick man had another assigned to care for him and the best of available foods were rationed out to him, even if that meant "pease and grease" during the fort's hungry first year.

A few treatments have been detailed for us. When Pierre Legace was very ill, "copious bleeding" gave him relief. When Mr. Work had a sore lip that Dr. Kennedy's remedies failed to cure, the two surgeons of HMS *Modeste* came ashore to treat it. "They immediately ordered carrot poultices." The lip, being cancerous, did not respond to carrot poultices, so, "Captain Bailley's 2 surgeons and Mr. Kennedy on 26th of September removed the diseased part of my lip, nearly the half of it. It is doing well. They attended me daily while they staid here."

And when Mr. Weynton was stricken with "headache caused by a rush of blood to the head" his head was shaved and mustard poultices applied to his feet. Mr. Weynton recovered.

Mr. McNeill learned to accept Fort Simpson's sick list with equanimity:

January 14, 1852 — "All hands on duty for the first time since I took charge" — and he had taken charge the previous November. But neither he nor any other factor could view the fort accidents calmly. As heights were achieved in the construction of the fort, people tumbled off them. Mr. Work was one of these. A scaffold on the store roof gave way and dropped him to the ground, injuring his knee and leg. No bones were broken so, though he could not walk, it was considered a fortunate accident. Two workmen fell off the top of the Big House; one broke his thigh and injured his wrist, the other damaged his head and chest. Men fell from the pickets and, during a Christmas celebration, one fellow *jumped* from them, none without injuries. The men put up a gallery ladder that showed woman-hating tendencies. It was built on the 23rd of February. On the 27th, Mrs. Work fell from it and "hurted herself seriously." On March 30th, "A little girl whom Mrs. Kennedy keeps to take care of the children fell from the top … with Jenny in her arms. And hurt herself very seriously. Fortunately the child was not much hurt." Eventually a railing was added to the ladder.

Blood flowed throughout Fort Simpson's building and logging days, chiefly from wounds inflicted by the axes. Gashed feet were common and a few of the men limped from lack of toes.

There were saltwater mishaps:

March 8, 1852 — "I learnt this day that Mr. Ogilvy upset in his Canoe yesterday and was nearly drowned with an Indian lad. He lost his Gun and if a canoe had not fortunately been at hand to rescue them they would soon have gone down. I have forbid Mr. Ogilvy from ever going in a Canoe again without some White man being with him."

And there were saltwater-and-alcohol mishaps:

December 20, 1856 (during a Nass blow) — "this morning when we turned the hands to work found that Ole Engebretson was missing on inquiry found that he had been on board the *Otter* in the evening and on coming on shore in a Canoe he fell overboard and drowned, this was the report of an Indian woman in the Canoe, he was very drunk at the time and has been so ever since the *Otter* arrived here. Someone on board had been selling Rum to our men."

Trees attacked Ignace. In the fall of 1836 he "injured one of his feet very severely by a log of wood falling on it ... I suspect he has fractured his fibuli." No sooner was he hobbling about than he was off to the woods again.

January, 1837 — "Ignace received a very severe injury of the head today by a tree falling on him."

Ignace was not the only accident-prone workman. Raymond, the blacksmith, in a two-year period cut his foot with an axe so badly that he could not attend his forge "for a length of time"; fell, while skating on the lake, damaging his hand; and "... had, by the bursting of a Gun, his hand injured but not seriously" (though he was on the sick list for some weeks).

That last accident was no amazement to the fort people. Lacking our dispenser of death, the automobile, they had instead gunpowder, the musket and the cannon. Their weapons made little distinction between friend and foe as they unleashed mayhem. Matches were a rare commodity, so: "This morning McAulay in endeavouring to light a paper with Gunpowder was near blowing out his eyes fortunately he had not much powder in his hand at the time and his eyes are not severely injured tho' it will deprive me of his services for some time to come."

It seems that the British musket had a bad reputation everywhere. Certainly at Fort Simpson throughout all the early years there were protests about it. The replies, like this one from Mr. Mactavish in Victoria were never much comfort:

"The two guns have been repaired and are now returned and we have sometime since called the attention of Their Honours to the inferior quality of the guns now sent out for trade which your remarks on that subject confirm."

Meanwhile trade guns were shooting wide, misfiring, and bursting.

December 11, 1834 — "Today one of our Common Trading Guns burst in the hand of the Chief (Nashoots) son which injured his left arm considerably this has been the third Gun that has burst since February last & will much lower the estimation of them."

December 10, 1839 — (Dr. Kennedy writing) — "Today I had the misfortune to blow 2 of my fingers off by the bursting of my Gun when firing at a deer of which there is still an abundance of about the Fort tho' we cannot get any."

The accident in no way interfered with Kennedy's writing up the journal that night and the loss of his fingers had to share a sentence with a report on deer hunting. Of course, this was a minor wound compared with the one he had received six months earlier at target practice. In that affair a ball ricochetted off a gallery post and hit his head. Said Mr. Work, "The wound appears very ill and bled profusely but as he was not knocked senseless it is hoped that the skull is not injured. The wound was sewed up and the bleeding stopped and he is apparently in a much better state than could be expected." Twenty years later trade guns were still treacherous. Then a workman's gun accidentally discharged, giving Mr. Moffatt "a slight contusion."

The cannons could do more serious damage to personnel. There was one at each corner of the fort and all the Company ships carried them. Since naval engagements were few they were fired chiefly in salutes.

May 23, 1843 — "About 10 a.m. the Steamer *Beaver* with the *Cadboro* in tow was ready to start for Fort McLoughlin. The fort saluted the vessels with 7 guns in returning which one of the steamer's men had his hand blown off which required amputation a little below the elbow joint."

May 24 — "I was obliged to open the sick man's stump today as the bleeding was profuse, and again secure the arteries by ligature."

May 25 — "The man who had his arm amputated on Tuesday feels much worse and appears to be sinking."

The sailor, however, recovered and left Fort Simpson and the life of the sea to become an interpreter at the new Fort Victoria. He was luckier than the two men who were injured in the firing of salutes, one at Fort Victoria and one at Fort Langley. They died.

It was not Hudson's Bay men alone who gave their lives and limbs for the sake of saluting by cannon. In 1866 George McKay, an educated, part-Native employee was left in charge of the Simpson fort and journal during the absence of all the officers. In almost Biblical prose he reported the death of a chief and the aftermath: "on the event of his death [the chief's] a small cannon was loaded to the Muzzle and a young Man stood by with a hot Iron to fire it off, So it Burst in a thousand pieces, taking the young Man's head clean off on the spot. So his father got angery at the death of his son and seased his Musket and Shot a Man with Buck Shot, [the man] belonging to the Kateseesh, [shot him] in the leg and arm which caused disturbance throughout the camps and at 1 p.m. they commenced to fire on one another. But just as they had got well started, the W.U. Telegraph Steamer *G.S. Wright* hove in sight from the North, which brought H.M. Ship *Clio* home to their Memorys, and in a moment all was quiet."

The fort cannons did take aim and fire in warfare on a few occasions, though never with any degree of earnestness. They were powerful as threats but less powerful as weapons, partly because the shots were usually directed *over* the targets. One day in 1837 the fort, the *Beaver* and the Tsimshian indulged in a small shooting war.

"As we saw our shots did not do much harm we thought it prudent to cease firing about 5 [o'clock] least they [the Tsimshian] should depreciate our Great Guns for I must say we managed them very badly and had it not been for the able support of the Steamer *Beaver* we should have cut a poor figure in the eyes of the Indians."

Within two days, the Tsimshian, compulsive traders that they were, had collected the round shot and grape and sold them back to the fort and the fort had served out four gallons of mixed rum to them and there was goodwill all round.

The great guns were used more effectively as a means of communication. When the fort's personnel sighted a ship far out and apparently off course, they fired a cannon to apprise her of her location. In fog and foul weather when a passing vessel fired an enquiring shot, Fort Simpson's guns replied, guiding her into the harbour. At least twice, men from the fort who had gone hunting became lost in the woods. The booming of a great gun brought them home. And when trouble with the tribes flared up at the fort while a work party was outside it, a cannon shot warned the men that they were in danger.

Fort Simpson celebrated by cannon, too. The very last entry of the last available journal ends it in fine style:

December 31, 1866 — "Fired off 8 Guns at 12 O'Clock and Gave the men a 1/2 pt. of Rum each to Welcome in the New Year, 1867." Dramatic as it must have been, that New Year's Eve pales beside the fort's first New Year's Eve, which was also observed by cannon.

In that fall of frantic building, Mr. Birnie had managed to roof the bastions and to hoist the cannons into place on the 11th of September. It was later in the year that proper housings and ports were completed for them. Then came December 31st. The men received their rum *before* midnight. A watchman, out in the lonely night, fired his musket (accidentally, says the journal). The ball hit a cannon. The cannon fired. The new gun port erupted in splinters and half that side of the block-house exploded into the night. It was difficult to find out just what had happened because the watchman's hand was badly injured and "he soon became incoherent and at times quite delirious."

Dr. Kennedy patched up the watchman's hand and returned him to health as he did so many others over the years 1834-1840. John Frederick Kennedy had arrived at McLoughlin's Harbour with the Nass complement as doctor and trader, the Company being much inclined to combine those two positions. During Mr. Work's annual winter absences, Dr. Kennedy took charge of the post, also. He was the son of a Company officer and had been educated in Scotland and sent to Edinburgh for his medical training. The Company placed limited confidence in the part-Native sons of its gentlemen and Kennedy himself deferred to other doctors. Yet, among the journal keepers he alone showed a social con-sciousness that we can comprehend today; he saw the Natives as people and expressed concern for the men's coldness, tired-ness, hunger and thirst. After he left to command Fort Durham at Taku, Fort Simpson was without a doctor. Then the factor, or sometimes one of the gentlemen, dispensed the contents of the medicine chest and staunched the blood. The Company forbade their officers and their doctors, too, to treat indigenous people. Had death ensued the chief would have felt entitled by custom to claim a life from the fort, or at the very least, repa-rations. There were times when the doctors, out of simple humanity, broke the rule.

As a reversal, we have the case history of a white man who was treated by a Tsimshian doctor. The tribes had their own medicine men who sometimes wrought cures and sometimes did not, through the use of herbs and native drugs, suggestion, hypnosis, sleight of hand and elaborate mumbo jumbo. The

Frenchman (the journal's only name for him) was put ashore at Fort Simpson as the schooner *Explorer*, with forty gold-seekers aboard, hurried on to the Stikine.

March 27, 1862 — "He had permission to remain inside the fort ... He shot himself in the leg accidentally and cannot stand. It will be a long time before he recovers."

April 4 — "The stranger's leg ... is doing well. An old Indian woman is his doctor. She uses grass and roots from the woods."

CHAPTER 22

The Factor and Rescues

ALTHOUGH ON THE 27TH day of March one of the fort men was dying and another was sick, the factor admitted the Frenchman who would also need care. The factor never thought of doing otherwise. He exercised the Hudson's Bay Company's godlike authority over thousands of square miles of land and sea and he accepted the Company's equally god-like responsibility for every non-Native who might venture within that area and sometimes for Natives who grievously needed help.

The gold flurry of the 1860s brought many badly pre-pared, inexperienced travellers besides the Frenchman to Fort Simpson. When the ships could not proceed for want of repairs the fort people showed them where to beach, sup-plied them with iron and allowed them the use of the forge. When mining parties were delayed the factor opened the wood yard to them so that their camps would have some secu-rity from the original residents who were openly hostile to miners. He even provided those in distress with firewood. He admitted the *gentlemen* who headed such expeditions to the officers' mess. And he did his best to protect them all from their own ignorance and unreadiness. Major Downie's party was one of his recurring worries.

In the summer of 1859 the Major's eight-man expedition explored the various rivers by canoe. When he went south in the fall some of his miners wintered at Simpson.

November 9, 1859 — "Two of Major Downie's party requested permission to live in the Fort, as they were nearly frozen and starved outside, the Indians also having commenced their 'Medicine' work had given them notice to quit the houses they were living in. I have engaged them both to work making packing cases for the Interior as one is a tolerable good carpenter."

The following April Major Downie returned — with a scow.

April 9, 1860 — "Stored a few provisions for Major Downie as his scow was very leaky."

Apparently the factor stored the scow, too:

April 11 — "Major Downie intends to go to Nass River by Canoe. He is afraid the Indians would plunder the Scow if he took her up."

The next summer the scow *was* towed to the Nass.

June 16, 1861 — "2 canoes of Kitimats arrived. Report the Hydahs to have killed the crew of Mr. Downie's scow in the vicinity of the Rapids."

Long before that minor gold rush the fort had succoured many a seafarer. Since Simpson was the nearest approach to civilization between Sitka and Victoria, or Fort Vancouver in the earlier days, ships and sailors in distress headed for its friendly bay and stockade. In 1840 the schooner *Unity* limped into port. She had set out from Oahu with a party of Tongass sea otter hunters aboard.

The winds that blew the ships so swiftly from Hawaii to Alaska must have turned contrary toward the end of the 1839-1840 winter for the *Unity* was damaged and her crew laid low by scurvy and "in a most pitiable condition in every respect." The factor dispatched three of his men to cut spars and four tribesmen to cut firewood for her. The spars were brought in with the help of another five Natives, and the fort carpenter and four men immediately set to work "reducing one of the spars for the main boom." But the men were used to cutting spars for larger ships than the little *Unity* and the other two proved too big. The men went back to the woods, and within three days three new spars became two booms and a sweep. Then the carpenter made a new anchor stock, and the fort was able to send the schooner off to California in fair condition, after twelve days of tender, loving care. She must have sailed with fresh provisions — the fact that they could raise the anchor proved that the crew's health was at least partially restored. Please note that the *Unity* was a rival trader.

Mr. Work wrote a large drama in a few lines in a letter to Dr. McLoughlin dated September 16, 1844: "Five men here (two Americans and 3 New Zealanders). They belonged to the French whale ship, Capt. Smith, which they left about 13 Nov. and remained with the Kyganie Indians all winter. Gill, (one of the Americans) was 2nd mate and left with the captain's consent and brought his chest and things with him. The other 4 all deserted. They were in miserable condition for want of clothes and half starved when they came here. They would willingly enter our service. I shall send these men to Vancouver but not by steamer. It would not be proper as the less strangers know about her routes and trade, the better."

In Mr. McNeill's 1852 journal, rescues and rehabilitations tumble over one another. On November 7th, after relating by letter to the Board of Management the fate of the *Susan Sturgis* and his efforts on behalf of the crew, he summarized the year's services to other distressed seamen:

"This year we have relieved i.e. clothed, 'paid Indians for bringing captives' and fed the following ships' crews: Four men from the wreck of the *Georgianna* clothed and fed for one month. Supplied and gave passage to five men who ran away from an American Whaler — Supplied and protected the Brig. *Pandora*."

Mr. McNeill wrote with finality because he could not guess that his work with the *Susan Sturgis* would extend into 1853, which would also bring him his biggest rescue operation of all, that of the crew of the Company's third *Vancouver*.

The American cutter *Georgianna* was wrecked on Moresby Island in the latter part of 1851. It was on December 11 that four of her crewmen arrived at Fort Simpson by canoe. Mr. McNeill took them in, gave them food and clothes, assigned them to a watch and had the problem of shipwrecked sailors well in hand when the *Damariscove* arrived on January 6th to rescue them. The problem that Mr. McNeill could not keep in hand was the rescuers.

The *Damariscove* sailed from Nisqually, U.S.A., carrying an army officer and six soldiers to uphold the rights of the United States. Captain McNeill, the strict disciplinarian, wrote a series of shocked comments:

January 7 — "The Crew and Voluntary on board the *Damariscove* are a most disorderly set and the Captain has his hands full to get work done. A row took place on board this day, the Captain was struck several times. I had to send a note to Captain Balch and Lieut. Dement, complaining of their people bringing Rum on shore and on bringing it out among the Indians etc. which is against the Regulations of the Post and will give us trouble with our Indians."

January 8 — "About 18 of the Schooner's crew sleep on shore nightly with the Indian Women and bring Rum on shore to them. The pay for a night's lodging is five dollars and one blanket!!! tolerable fair pay. They keep us in continual hot water with the Indians and our own men."

Worst of all, crewmen of the *Damariscove* brought rumours from the south that they used as a large spoon to stir up dissension among the fort workmen. When the schooner left for the Queen Charlotte Islands with the four rescued Americans aboard there was relief all round.

The next item in Mr. McNeill's summary of aid to mariners, the story of five deserters, was actually the story of six — there was one Canadian with them who was immediately employed in the fort. The five were Americans and all were from the whaling vessel *Mary & Martha* out of New Bedford, U.S.A. Two Kyganie canoes brought them to Fort Simpson in August. They told a moving tale of their ship's sinking, their lifeboat being separated from the others, and their boat, sails and equipment being seized by the Kyganie. Old salt McNeill wrote it all down in a letter to headquarters and then added a skeptical note: "This is their story." His doubts were later confirmed. The men had deserted.

As for supplying and protecting the brig *Pandora* — we are not told why this was necessary. We are told, however, that she lay in the harbour four months and eight days, an unheard-of delay in trading season. During that time she took on a cargo of eighty spars. A small Fort Simpson crew could have cut and loaded those spars in two weeks. Also, her captain went searching for ice, for the California trade, at the end of June. There is no more accessible ice on that part of the coast in June than there would be off San Francisco. The *Pandora*, previously a surveying ship in the Queen's Navy, seemed to have become an unsuccessful trader. Mr. McNeill set his men to baking biscuits for her on one occasion and, all in all, it seems just as well that Fort Simpson did supply and protect the *Pandora*. One service to that ship that Mr. McNeill did not include in his summary was easing the death of her passenger.

Those were the days when physicians sent patients of means on long sea voyages to regain their health, particularly consumptive patients. Mr. Gaskill, designated as an English gentleman, took passage on the *Pandora* from England. Apparently the salt air worked no cure for him. On June 28th he came ashore at Simpson to die in the rugged comfort of the fort. He was admitted to the quarters and consolation of the officers though it was a difficult time for them to accommodate a patient. Mr. McNeill was rebuilding the fort and the Big House had to be taken down. In July the gentlemen moved into temporary housing in the bastions and whatever odd nooks were available but Mr. Gaskill was moved into Captain Dodd's new quarters.

August 10 — "Mr. Gaskill ... is getting worse, his will is made and in case of death all his money and effects are to be sent his Mother in England."

August 20 — "About 11 p.m. Mr. Gaskill ... departed this life."

The *Susan Sturgis* episode, the climax of Mr. McNeill's year-of-the-survivors, was a matter of piracy. The Masset were well aware that the schooner carried a complement of only seven. They waylaid her four miles off Nass Harbour. "The natives stripped and plundered the Vessel of everything they could lay their hands on, cut the Sails to pieces, threw the Guns overboard," wrote Mr. McNeill. "There was about 1,800 dollars on board in Gold and Silver also Powder, Cotton, Blankets and other articles of trade."

When the Massets had sacked the ship they burned the hull and carried her company off to the Queen Charlotte Islands. There they seem to have done a brisk trade in loot and captives with the other island tribes; three different chiefs disposed of spoils and collected ransoms.

September 29, 1852 — "About 4 p.m. a Chatsina Canoe arrived from 'Masset,' Q.C.I. headed by 'Scowal'. Captain Rooney and his Mate formerly of the Schooner *Susan Sturgis* [aboard] ... The remainder of the Crew five in number are still in the hands of the Massets. They may however be brought here by Indians in hopes of getting payment."

October 2 — "Captain Rooney rather unwell."

October 3 — "Capn Rooney sick in bed."

October 4 — "This day we paid 17 3-pt. Blankets, 8 Shirts,

Powder, Tobacco and Cotton for bringing Captain Rooney and his Mate here from Charlotts Island. Our own Indians are much excited seeing the Chatsinas obtaining so much property for bringing Capt. Rooney and the affair may cause us trouble."

October 7 — "About 3 p.m. Edenshaw the North Island Chief arrived with one of the men formerly of the *Susan Sturgis* ... Four others still remain in Captivity among the Masset Indians."

November 3 — "About 8 a.m. Three more men that formerly belonged to the *Susan Sturgis* were brought here by 'Scowal,' a Chatsina Chief. He brought them from Masset ... We shall be obliged to pay about 40 Blankets for their release from Captivity, and they will go to Victoria on the Steamer. We have had much trouble on account of these men many ways ... We gave the three men before mentioned a Suit of Clothes and one Blanket each, as they were naked."

November 16 — "About 3 p.m. Robert Peel arrived from 'Q.C.I.' he brought James Cordon, one of the Crew of the late *Susan Sturgis*. He is the last of the crew that remained on the Islands. We have now relieved, and received inside the Establishment all the crew of the unfortunate Schooner. Five have gone away on board the Steamer, one on the *Pandora*, and one is here. The poor fellow will be obliged to remain with us all winter. He will be of no use to us as we have our full complement of men and Cordon does not understand how to do the work we require to be done here. We clothed him from head to foot."

March 9, 1853 — "Jas. Cordon who came here on the 16th Novr. Last ... went in Robt. Peel's Canoe to Victoria."

The fort even liberated some of the plunder from the *Susan Sturgis*.

November 17, 1852 — "Robert Peel brought 309 dollars into the Fort and bought 2 Guns and 54 Blankets of us. These dollars came from the unfortunate *Susan Sturgis*." At that time dollars were rarer than sunshine at Fort Simpson.

These incidents were by no means the last of looted ships and naked sailors at Fort Simpson. Long after Mr. Work and Mr. McNeill were living on their respective acres on Vancouver Island, Fort Simpson journal keepers were reporting vessels attacked by Natives and weather, and Hudson's Bay Company aid to them. George McKay, he of the Biblical style, told of a seafaring man brought to the fort by the Kitimat natives, in 1866:

"Captain Stephens of the Schooner *Non Pareil* arrived in a canoe last Night. He reports having been caught in a heavy Gale with the Schooner some short distance from Kitlope and was blown over on her Beamends and there She lay with him, his woman and another man on her side for one whole Night, it Snowing and blowing a terriffic Gale from the S.E. At daybreak they managed to get on shore in his little boat, but could not manage to make a fire during that day. They managed to go to the Schooner when it calmed a little, She only being about a hundred yards from the shore and let go one anchor in 30 fm. water. Towards evening 2 large canoes of the Kitlopes arrived and as soon as they saw the Vessel in that state they went off to her and commenced on her top side with their axes and cut a large hole in her and when Stephens saw them commencing to cut up the Vessel he sung out to them to stop, but he says they would not, and in a short time the drygoods commenced to float out of her and the Indians canoeing them off to the Bush and as soon as they had secured all they could well get they came back and cut the Masts and all the Rigging and carried away all the sails and everything that they could lay their hands on. They would not even give him a Blanket. But by Chance there came a Kitimat Canoe to the place where they was and gave them every assistance that they could do, afterwards brought them up to Metlakhatla where he laid the case before Mr. Duncan."

CHAPTER 23

The Factor and Indian-Fort Relations

THE FACTOR'S RESPONSIBILITY stretched over Indian-fort relations. The Company maintained a policy of detachment regarding Native affairs; the Natives held no such policy regarding the fort. The factor went his impassive way while the Natives dragged a corpse to the fort gates and that season's initiate into the Cannibal Society exhibited his new accomplishment. He merely stayed indoors when two tribes, camped on opposite sides of the fort, opened fire on one another across the yard. Yet, for special reasons he bent Company policy enough to place a firm hand in the middle of aboriginal activities. One such reason was peacemaking when a prolonged quarrel deprived him of a region's furs.

Mr. Work did not tell us much of the delicate diplomacy that succeeded in 1838 when he led the Tsimshian and the Kyganie, who had been feuding for years, toward reconciliation. The first step was the meeting, offshore, of seven incoming Kyganie canoes and a Tsimshian welcoming committee sent to invite the arrivals to lodge with them. The Kyganie were dubious "and after a good deal of haranguing on both sides Five hostages from each party were exchanged when the strangers came and landed at the fort and all so far seems quiet."

July 10 (next day) — "The Tsimshians and Kyganie people are visiting each other but still retain their hostages on both sides. The hostages seem to have great attention shown them, New blankets wrapped about them, their faces painted and their hair dressed etc. and feathered in the best style of Indian fashion."

July 11 — "They [the Kyganie] are a good deal occupied with the Tsimshians making peace, whether it will be permanent or not is a question. There are none of the head men of the Kyganie people here."

July 12 — "The Kyganie people and Tsimshians passed the most of the day dancing. They appear at present to be on good terms. They have returned their hostages."

That peace lasted somewhat tenuously for three-and-a-half years.

Sometimes the factor called a summit conference. It usually progressed in the manner of a twentieth-century summit conference and attained as few results. One, however, that Mr. McNeill engineered in 1856 turned out rather well. His method of breaking a stalemate was simpler than any in modern use. The conferees were the Tsimshian and the Kitiwash, a band of Haida who had arrived in the night and had been hustled into the fort before their enemies knew of their presence.

March 11 — "At noon there was a large muster of Tsimshians at the Front gate demanding the Haidas to be delivered up to them — of course this was refused. They threatened however to seize them on their departure, provided they do not make reparation for the thefts committed on the Tsimshians some few years since. Property appears to be the object these latter have in view and the Haidas will be very fortunate if they get off by sacrificing a few Blankets. Deeming it advisable to make the two parties friendly, if possible, I prevailed on one or two of the chiefs to come to a parley with the Haidas in the Fort, which they did, but arrived at no satisfactory conclusion. It will be rather a difficult matter to settle and wish the Haidas were away. There is at present, 9 p.m., a strong party of Indians watching around the gate. Gave Legaic half a bottle of Rum and the others a glass each which had the effect apparently of inducing them to lower their demands."

March 13 — "The Haidas and Tsimshians came to terms this afternoon in the Fort. I gave the latter, ten in number a small present each to seal the compact."

Over and over again factors intervened in another touchy area of indigenous life. They bought slaves.

September 22, 1838 — "We traded a young woman, a slave, from a Tsimshian to prevent her falling into the hands of the Stikine Indians and that she may be returned to her friends. She is the daughter of Kilome a Newittie chief and was taken with 19 other women and children last summer by the Sabassa Indians. Their friends have been frequently applying to Capt. McNeill to try and get her back and they would pay the expenses. She cost the value of nearly 20 blankets which is probably more than her friends will be able to make good. Capt. McNeill has no doubt they will pay it. Taking her back will have a good effect on the Queen Charlotte Sound Indians. The poor woman pleaded most pitifully not to be allowed to fall into the hands of the Stikine men."

The Stikine had a bad reputation concerning slaves:

December 2, 1839 — "Traded a Skidegate woman from the Tsimshians to prevent her falling into the hands of the Stikine Indians who had already made an offer, indeed paid for her, but on my interfering the articles were given back & she returned."

Once, the factor forced the Tsimshian to release a whole canoeload of Cape Fox people they had captured offshore and on many occasions he interceded for the life of a slave.

July 16, 1838 — "Two of the Kyganie women ... quarreled today and had a fight. They both held themselves up as women of consequence and as is customary among them on such occasions proposed killing slaves on each side in order to make up the matter by showing who was the richest and could best afford the loss. But on hearing of the circumstances we interfered and pointed out to [them] the sin, inhumanity and uselessness of such a step and used every means in our power to dissuade them from such an atrocious act ..."

July 17 — "The two Kyganie Women ... instead of killing slaves as they were preparing to do last night, threw away, as they term it, a quantity of property, one of them 10 blankets, the other 7 blankets and a gun. The blankets were torn up in pieces and distributed among the Tsimshians who were about them. The Tsimshians seemed well pleased and I dare say would be much gratified were there frequent quarrels to be made up the same way. The parties who disposed of the property also appeared satisfied and said their hearts were good."

There was one Tsimshian who must have approved fort intervention in the happenings of the camps. At the time of the 1839 smallpox epidemic he was a baby. His father contracted the disease and as he approached death somehow felt he must take his only living son with him. He strangled the child with a cord and then died. The mother was laying out, in the traditional manner, both father and son when Dr. Kennedy arrived to confirm the father's death. His trained eye detected signs of life in the baby. He and Mr. Work rushed the child into the fort, revived him in a warm bath and within a few days reported that the little Tsimshian was playing happily. His rescuers had dressed him in fort clothing and named him Joseph. The sequel to the story is confusing to us: "Legaic [the head chief] asked for a Capot, a Pair of Trousers, a Hat and a Shirt for having saved the Child's life and for our trouble, with which request we did not feel inclined to comply."

The factor was not at all confused by such a request. Indian-fort relations like intertribal relations, depended to a large extent upon compensation and retaliation. Compensation, of course, served a useful purpose though we cannot always grasp the logic that lay behind the complicated Native system. (No doubt the Natives were equally mystified when they encountered the white man's strange custom of insurance — paying money to unknown people because of misfortunes by death or fire that had not yet happened.) Retaliation ran deeper and darker through aboriginal lives. It seemed to be a North American variant of the Asian concept of maintaining face and accounted for much of the coastal warfare. Its channels were even more hidden and convoluted than were those of compensation and often the two systems became completely entangled. The factor dealt with them, sometimes in the proper Native spirit and sometimes in the spirit of an outraged white man. There is no need to search for examples since the pages of the journals offer them freely. In June of 1836 Ancago from Stikine celebrated his arrival with rum. Then, during the fort dinner hour, he found a way in and, befuddled, entered a house. It was the blacksmith's and no doubt the blacksmith was surprised and frightened. He reacted by attacking the Native who "became very much exasperated and threatened to kill one of our men unless we would give him 30 Blankets and 2 Guns." The factor demurred and suggested a soberer meeting next day. It was a long meeting:

"Shortly after breakfast Ancago arrived accompanied by two of his brothers and Cacas [a Tsimshian chief who was consistently hostile toward the Company]. He appeared to be very cool but was still firm and demanded 30 Blankets & 2 Guns or 50 without the Guns. We explained to him that it was partly his own fault and that the affair occurred without our knowledge that we would give him clothing and a Keg of

Liquor and that we wouldn't give more. It was late in the evening before he came to our terms."

And again: June 27, 1853 — "About 3 p.m. an Indian died inside the Fort. He was grinding wheat and dropped down dead suddenly. We paid his friends 1 Blanket, 3 Shirts, 3 Hkfs. and 7 Yds. Cotton, 2 lbs. Tobacco, which made all right."

Or: April 1, 1857 — "Cusetar tells us that the Stikines intend to take one of the Fort or Steamer's people prisoner on account of their friend being killed by the Americans last fall in Puget Sound."

Fort and Native attitudes toward one another were not always grim. There were times of accord and times of real friendship. One April day in 1859 the whole fort personnel were loading muskets and cannons, for rumour had come faster than the Masset canoes and it suggested that the Islanders were on their way to avenge the death of a tribesman at the hands of a white man at Victoria. The Massets came ashore, affable and amazed at the warlike preparations. That night Edenshaw and Wehar, the Masset chiefs, had dinner in the officers' mess and the journal keeper wrote a wistful note: "I think our men would have stood well to their guns in case of a row."

There were simple acts of kindness on both sides. When a Nisga'a expedition of four canoes landed after a cold night trip, Mr. McNeill supplied tobacco, rice and molasses to warm the half-frozen people. The Tsimshian stowed their boxes of belongings inside the fort as they left for the oolichan fishery and this reciprocal act of good faith was repeated year after year. The Natives were givers of presents. None was more acceptable than the one that Ibbets, a chief of the Tongass, gave Mr. Work. It was a chart of the coast from Simpson to the Stikine, drawn by Ibbets himself. But of all the neighbourly acts, the one by the Tsimshian on an 1852 June evening was the most appreciated.

Before the fort was seven months old, Cacas arrived on the scene with seventy canoes. He was a Tsimshian chief who wintered at Pearl Harbour and he came to proclaim his ancestral rights to McLoughlin's Harbour and the surrounding territory. When the fort people continued their hammering and digging he assured them that he would burn down their fort. The fort was completed without incident by fire; after all, it is not easy to burn down rain-soaked buildings. As the years passed, Cacas was relentless in his antagonism toward the Company, and the fort people were relentless in their watchfulness of the Tsimshian, especially in dry and windy weather.

In the early summer of 1852 the Sabassa were raiding the Bella Coola; the Stikine were shooting the Sitkan; the Nisga'a were fighting Interior tribes, but the Tsimshian were at peace, and feasting. This generated a brisk trade at the fort where, contrary to custom, they were admitted in large numbers. On June 3rd at six o'clock in the evening, there were five hundred armed Natives inside the stockade.

When the cry of "Fire" rose, the fort inhabitants knew that they were doomed. Mr. McNeill who had been helpless in his bed with rheumatism emerged on crutches to try to save his fort and his people from the Tsimshian. He found the smokehouse, a corner house and a hundred feet of gallery and pickets all ablaze. And certainly there was concerted action among the Tsimshian. They were drawn up in a column that extended from the tide line to the fire. They were passing the cooper's wooden buckets from man to man in unbroken rhythm, and thus directing a steady stream of water to the flames. (People who lived in cedar houses with open fires in the centre had to have a system of coping with sudden blazes.)

It took two hours to control the fire. Then it was found that the culprit was not Cacas but a Kanaka hand who had piled too much rotten wood in the smokehouse where oily oolichans and fat bear meat were in smoke. The Natives were not all heroes. By the time the excitement had died down twenty pounds worth of stock and a large portion of the men's clothing were missing, and even some of the Tsimshian' possessions that had been stored for safekeeping. But, as Mr. McNeill remarked, the losses were a trifle "considering how matters stood at the time."

CHAPTER 24

Gentlemen

WHEN MY SISTER AND I went to the fort to play with the little girl who lived in the old Big House, we knew her father as *the factor*. But at Fort Simpson in the early days there was no such title; there was *the gentleman in charge of the fort*. There was little danger of that gentleman's becoming obsessed with power. His responsibilities, the country, the weather, the tribes, the unruly workmen, the opposition, all tended to trim his ego. As well, there were frustrations that arrived by Company ship or Native canoe, sealed in packets. Letters from headquarters in Fort Vancouver or Victoria could bring good news or they could jar the factor right out of his Windsor chair.

In the fall of 1860 when the liquor trade was tearing north coast life apart, Mr. Moffatt received a letter from Mr. Mactavish at Victoria. At that time Moffatt was dealing with internal thefts, strikes by the Native employees, insubordination of the Company men, falling stockades and declining trade. Inside and outside the fort tribesmen were shooting at each other and at him. Mactavish's letter reproved him for sending in documents that were deemed "informal" and enclosed "3 sets of papers which you will copy in duplicate and return them to the Board here by the first opportunity after you have signed and dated them as marked in pencil."

Almost twenty years earlier, Mr. Work, his Irish dander up, replied to a letter from Dr. McLoughlin:

"I have received your letter dated 13th July last relative to loose women being admitted into the forts on the Coast to sleep with the men contrary to orders. I am not aware of any orders existing on the subject, I supposed that such matters, and as I conceived very properly, too, were left to the judgement of the person entrusted with the charge. When I came on the coast the practice was common but I broke it off and for a length of time nothing of the kind has been allowed at this place. So far from any instructions existing on the subject it was proposed to me last fall and in 1840 to provide accommodation for the sailors and their Quandum Wives, which I objected to."

The factor's lot seems to have been an unenviable one. Why then, did English and Scottish young men struggle so hard to attain it? Commissioned officers — chief traders and chief factors whose names had the letters CT or CF appended — shared in Company dividends. According to W. F. Tolmie's 1839 explanation, a chief trader might receive some three hundred pounds and a chief factor six hundred pounds, each year, in addition to his salary, with the prospect of these returns diminishing steadily in step with the fur trade. He was also assured of full pay for his first year of retirement and half pay for the next six, after which a nineteenth-century gentleman was, presumably, expected to die. Perhaps hopes of such rewards brought young men into the Company but there must have been something more to keep them on those forlorn posts, sometimes for years. Perhaps it was adventure, for in spite of the journal's matter-of-factness, that was an epoch.

Little is known of the clerks and assistants who were making the Company ascent, except that they were gentlemen and never, never to be confused with *men*. A symbol of this distinction was the title "Mister" which belonged to officers only. It seems to have outranked "Captain" and "Doctor" for it was conferred upon Captain McNeill when he came ashore permanently and was sometimes accorded Dr. Kennedy when he was acting factor. Thousands of miles from the world of civilization, trapped between rainforest and sea, facing dangers and privations together, the gentlemen addressed and referred to one another as "Mr. Finlayson" or "Mr. McDonald." (I found it quite unseemly when I tried to do otherwise in this narrative.)

At Fort Simpson the number of gentlemen varied for they moved from fort to fort and from ship to fort as need arose. Often there was only one beside the factor, and seldom more than two. A bachelor officer moved his wooden chest into his quarters, one small room in the Big House, and was at home. He had access to a common room that was also an office. It opened into the large central hall and a constantly changing view of fort life. This was where the factor received visiting chiefs, the men made their Christmas and New Year's calls, men and ships' companies and officers turned out to dances, and it was here, three times a day, the officers attended their mess. They sat on severely straight chairs at a deal table, according to rank, and took part in conversation led by the factor. They were served from the steward's pantry at one end of the hall, though, for the first few decades, the cooking was done in a detached kitchen behind the Big House.

Beyond the hall, the factor's apartment occupied the other side of the main floor. It consisted of a living room and two small bedrooms. Since Mr. Work had ten children, a nightly ritual must have been the herding of a troop of them through the hall and up the stairs to the garret.

Married officers had their own houses in the fort yard but were required by Hudson's Bay protocol to take their meals in the mess, no women allowed, of course. This system did not facilitate the teaching of English and the ABCs to their children that was also expected of them, a carryover from the old Northwest Company rule. As their working day was ten hours

long, six days a week, and they were subject to call at any hour
of the night for a trading session, the arrival of the Company
ship or a disturbance in the camps, education must have been
administered in very small doses.

The young gentlemen managed to work diversions into
their schedules. They paddled for miles to hunt deer, mountain
goat and bear. They were not sports fishermen but when rations
were scarce in 1835 they descended upon Salmon Creek as the
salmon started up to spawn and *killed* four hundred. In the
1860s they discovered cod fishing, still ignoring the salmon
jumping in the bay almost beneath their windows. They crossed
the harbour, by canoe, in freezing weather, to skate on the
nameless little lake where Port Simpson people were still skating a hundred years later, and they swam in front of the fort in
water that never lost its chill. Family parties made Sunday canoe
excursions to nearby beaches or to favourite berry patches.

Such recreation was not to be taken for granted, however. It depended chiefly on periods of slack trade. Angus
McDonald who had succeeded Dr. Kennedy as trader, in
1840, found himself with the entire fort on his hands when Mr.
Work suffered an illness that lasted for months. The day that
Mr. Work resumed his place at the mess table, Mr. McDonald
wrote: "Had a turn round the Bay in a Canoe myself in the
forenoon, the 1st time tho now 8 months here I have been
out of sight of the fort."

How did the young gentlemen spend their evenings after
the factor rose from the dinner table to dismiss them? They
took night strolls on the gallery; they played cards for shillings;
at least one officer, Pym Nevin Compton, painted. Regarding
his four-month posting to Fort Simpson's beginnings, Dr.
Tolmie wrote: "Did not find the store a comfortable dwelling.
We generally lay in bed in the morning till breakfast time
and at night each after supper turned in and being provided
with a candle betook himself to reading." It was impressive

reading: Paley's *Moral and Political Philosophy*, Adam Smith's *Wealth of the Nations*, Cowper's poem on Truth. True, Dr. Tolmie was a remarkably studious young man, but his taste in reading matter was not unique in the posts. When he exchanged books with other Hudson's Bay gentlemen the titles he received were far from frivolous, Goldsmith's *Animated Nature* and *The Life of Edmund Burke* as examples.

For some of Fort Simpson's gentlemen rum was the prime diversion. Their drinking habits were of endless concern to their superiors at headquarters who dealt with enough drunken sea captains to sink their whole fleet. For this reason, though the journals commented often and freely on the men's drinking, they were more than discreet about the officers'; men got drunk, while gentlemen became "incapacitated through inebriety" and even that phrase was forced out of Mr. Moffatt's pen by a direct enquiry from Victoria.

Fort Simpson's social life made few demands on the gentlemen's time. When the Company ship arrived there were fresh supplies and mail and most important of all there were the vessel's captain, officers and sometimes passengers who were eager to talk to shore people. During Mr. McNeill's regime he put on dances in the hall for the officers and crews of newly arrived Company ships, even though he could be sure that his workforce would be sadly reduced next day.

Before whiskey smugglers had soured the relationship, fort people and the few traders who had been long on the coast maintained a mutual understanding that amounted to friendship. Whenever the *Bolivar Liberator*, the *Lagrange* or the *Thomas Perkins* anchored in McLoughlin's Harbour the factor invited the captain and supercargo to dinner in the mess; the captain entertained the fort gentlemen aboard his ship, and they all enjoyed the companionship and did a little covert spying. Thereafter, visitors and hosts tried every trick known on the coast to ruin one another's trade.

The fort fulfilled its social obligations to Her Majesty's navy more formally:

June 19, 1853 — "Several officers from the *Virago* took Tea with us."

Christmas Day was a holiday but New Year's produced the celebration of the year. The big event of 1839:

January 1 — "... at 8 o'clock a.m. fired a Gun and hoisted our flag ... At sundown fired another and took it down. The men fired three rounds of Muskets, wished us the compliments of the Season, on which occasion each of them received Four or five glasses of Grog."

January 2 — "Gave each of them [the men] a dram in the morning. At night had a dance in the Big House in which Mr. Sangster and I joined. The men I am happy to say conducted themselves with respect & propriety though they had four or five glasses grog each."

The early dances on the posts were all-male affairs at which officers and men danced with one another to vocal music. (Imagine singing *and* dancing an eightsome reel.) Obviously those celebrations fell short of the purpose of a dance. By Mr. McNeill's time the dancing partners came from both inside and outside the fort, with a purpose. Of all the gentlemen's diversions, finding a wife was the most absorbing. At Fort Simpson there was romance as well as rain in the air.

A directive that had its origin in the old Northwest Company continued to be observed: it instructed the gentlemen to take mixed blood rather than fully Native wives. The senior officers therefore provided many of the brides for the juniors. Mr. Work and Mr. McNeill were extremely cooperative in this matter, Mr. Work having eight daughters and Mr. McNeill six. Roderick Finlayson and Dr. Tolmie chose Sarah and Jane Work when they were very young girls and waited for them to grow up; Dr. Tolmie even arranged for Jane's "finishing" in the home of missionary friends in the

Oregon country. Governor George Simpson, no romantic, held a different view of officers' marriages. Gentlemen, he admonished, should make "connubial alliances" with the leading local tribe immediately upon joining the fort. The officers seemed to suit themselves as to which precept they followed; at any rate Fort Simpson had mixed blood wives and it also had its share of resident Native princesses. For years the "country marriage" sufficed for Hudson's Bay personnel, but after his own was legalized, Dr. McLoughlin pressed for formal marriage and in the north Mr. Duncan's mighty will bore down on the subject. Gentlemen at Fort Simpson began to take their wives according to the Anglican Book of Prayer, in the latter 1860s.

CHAPTER 25

Men

WHILE THE GENTLEMEN'S LOVE lives were never shown
in the journals, the men's, if they were noteworthy, were sometimes sketched in lightly. Certainly Raymond's was
noteworthy, being no less than the Fort Simpson version of
Romeo and Juliet. You will remember Raymond, the blacksmith, who was accident prone. The worst accident that
overtook him was falling in love. It happened to him in the fall
of 1839 when he was innocently engaged in the project of
making tin porringers for the trade.

Raymond's love was a girl in the Tongass camp. Alas, she
had a husband so that neither the fort nor the Natives would
sanction the match. The lovers met by night and that was not
easy since locked gates and high pickets separated them.
Raymond reached the trysting place by wriggling through
one of the drains that had been dug to carry the rainfall under
the stockade. Before daylight he wriggled back inside.

Raymond must have felt suspicion upon him (or perhaps
there had been a heavy rain) one evening in October, for he
asked Dr. Kennedy's permission to go to the lake to hunt.
That was his undoing for it soon became known that he had
not gone to the lake. He returned to find Dr. Kennedy, usually lenient with the men, assuming the role of irate father

and barring his love forever from the fort.

Raymond was known as a resourceful blacksmith. He was also a resourceful wooer. That day was a Saturday, a point in his favour. He organized a hunting party of six fort men who received permission to leave the fort that night to return on Sunday night. Raymond was casually among their number. Before ten o'clock he had managed to slip away from the party and by the time the hunters returned to the fort on Sunday evening, he and his Juliet were triumphantly on their way to the Stikine where he knew the Russians would welcome a blacksmith.

It was on Monday that Tongass canoes overtook the fleeing couple, bundled Raymond into their canoe and paddled back to Fort Simpson to collect the reward of ten blankets, two-and-a-half gallons of rum and three heads of tobacco that Dr. Kennedy had offered. Raymond's bleak return was somewhat brightened by the girl's insistence that she accompany him and be put in irons with him. Dr. Kennedy decided against irons ; he couldn't find a convenient spot for a jail anywhere in the fort and besides, he was already shorthanded and much preferred forgiveness. But he sent the Tongass girl away on the threat of clamping Raymond into irons if she stayed about. She went, and, as his movements were drastically restricted and well watched, Raymond could not even go to the gallery to witness her departure. Worst of all, iron gratings made by the assistant blacksmith had been fastened into all the drains.

True love being what it is, the girl did come back — twice. Both times the night watch was doubled, Raymond more closely confined, and she sent off. The last time, Dr. Kennedy refused to trade with the Tongass people until she had gone her slow, sad way. It was no wonder that on October 11th, Raymond was ill. Since Raymond's love story was enacted in Fort Simpson instead of Verona he recovered and there were no corpses on stage for the curtain — only Raymond alone at the forge making tin porringers.

If you had thought it the prerogative of Victorian *ladies* to languish for love, consider, also, the case of Kiona.

January 4, 1853 — "'Kiona' deserted from the fort to be with his Indian Wife in camp."

January 5 — "We found 'Kiona' in an Indian Lodge this afternoon and brought him to the fort. It would appear that the fellow is over head and ears in love with an Indian Woman, and she will not remain inside the Fort with him, which drives him nearly mad, and it is 'possible' he will be useless to the Company in consequence."

And so he was for some time. At least, nine days later he was still on the sick list.

Kiona was one of many Hawaiians who, to alohas, sailed from the idyllic islands for the less idyllic Columbia District. Most of them lived out their lives as fort labourers, always sensitive to the cold, but contented, we are told. What had gone wrong in Paradise for these young men is hard to imagine but it is known that the factors, in requesting reinforcements, often specified Sandwich Islanders. They seemed to have a steadying influence on the near explosive fort crews.

Raymond, in contrast, belonged to the excitement of the fort. He was a French Canadian who had reached the coast perhaps as a paddler with one of the overland brigades. The voyageurs were the backbone of any fort's workforce. Many were second and third generation Hudson's Bay and Northwest Company people. They wore their prestige in blue capots, tasselled caps and woven red sashes. In those days bilingualism was not argued — it was practised. Buildings were erected in French, salmon was salted in French, and a new clerk arriving at Simpson had to learn fort French before he could tell the hands to dig the ditch deeper or press the furs tighter. Some eastern Natives, mostly Iroquois, also arrived with the overland brigades. They were known as the

Canadians. They had their troubles with the other men, with the west coast Natives, and after Fort Simpson's shores were washed with liquor they had trouble with everyone. There were sometimes a few Orkney Island men and the rest of the fort's company came from the assorted humanity that collected on the world's newest frontier. These men were adventurers and sailors and refugees from their pasts.

The Natives regarded the fort workmen as the gentlemen's slaves. They treated them accordingly, pushing them out of the way, snatching at their clothing and their tools, and flinging insults at them. Their attitude caused many a fierce incident.

One day in 1839, Barker, a Tongass chief, taunted Pierre Legace with the word *slave*. Pierre was an in-law of Mr. Work's and occupied a position of trust and some importance. He replied with a blow that cut the chief's head and knocked him down. Barker, of course, immediately demanded payment and Dr. Kennedy immediately refused it. The last we hear of that affair is: "He [Barker] still continues sullen and was preparing his gun."

The situation had not improved by 1853 when "One of the Kyganie Indians came to the fort and told me that he wanted to take Alexander Lecompte away with him, as he was his slave etc. I told the fellow that he had better try it on and that he would find that he would not get away with a whole skin, in fact the fellow was sent out of the Fort with a Revolver at his head."

And then there was the case of the bridegroom. Jeremie deserted from the fort to live in the encampment with the wife he had taken. One month later he was back at the fort gates begging admittance. His father-in-law had welcomed him — as a slave, and had kept him cutting wood and carrying water and being the camp menial. It did not seem to matter what fury the factor and the men loosed against the Native attitude, the Natives were unshaken in their conviction that the men were slaves. And perhaps they were.

A man was engaged for a period of one to three years and for that length of time his life belonged to the Company. The stockade that kept the coast people out of the fort, kept him in. The gentleman in charge granted him permission to go out for specified times and specified purposes. The permission was neither lightly sought nor lightly granted.

Six days a week the fort bell jolted the Company servant out of sleep at six in the morning; fifteen minutes later the factor or postmaster assigned him his task for the day. He piled logs or baled furs or dug the garden until the bell called him to breakfast at eight. For that meal he was allowed one hour, and for the midday meal, another. At six in the evening the bell released him from his labours and he returned to the Men's House or, if he had a family, to his own quarters. To the north, employees of the Russian American Company worked from 5 a.m. to 7 p.m. with one meal hour but in turn, they had sixty-one holidays per year. When winter closed in on Fort Simpson and a man went stumbling through darkness at 6 a.m., the schedule was relaxed slightly. Then he was permitted to eat breakfast before going to work, and when he could no longer see the log he was chopping he was allowed to shoulder his axe at 5 p.m.

Wages for the men averaged about twenty pounds a year in the 1830s and over a thirty-year period rose to the dizzy heights of thirty pounds. There were fringe benefits: a man received drugs from the medicine chest, basic Victorian remedies such as castor oil and chamomile, and whatever medical services were available. These ranged from Dr. Kennedy's ministration to a fellow-worker's watch over his deathbed. Besides housing he received subsistence rations and during some rare periods a daily grog ration. Luxuries such as rice, molasses, tea and soap he ordered from Fort Vancouver or Victoria six months in advance, to come by the Company ship, the price to be deducted from his wages. He was charged at a rate of "fifty per cent advance on prime cost" which was a great improvement over the standard markup of one hundred percent. But without buying more than the meagrest necessities of food and clothing he usually found himself in debt at the end of his term of contract and so had to sign up again — and again, and again. Mactavish at Victoria urged McNeill at Fort Simpson to try to keep the men out of debt. Perhaps if he had urged increasing rations this goal might have been more attainable.

Any misgivings a man may have felt concerning re-engaging were hastily drowned in rum:

January 3, 1842 — (Just as the New Year's rum regale was wearing off) — "Ten of the men engaged today for two years, each of whom got a pt. Rum."

September 20, 1855 — "Five or six of the men unable to work on account of re-engaging." This particular drunk lasted for four days.

Discipline was relaxed for the re-engagement celebration, for Christmas and for New Year. For the rest of Fort Simpson's days it was taut enough to snap; for example, when Alexis was overheard telling the Native employees that they were being underpaid, "he was reprimanded and got a slap with a caution." When Pierre Turcot slept outside the fort without leave, his grog was cut off and when he stole three heads of tobacco he was boxed on the ear. When a gatekeeper, no doubt frightened of the Natives' musket balls, "refused to keep the gate," he was imprisoned in the bastion in irons. One factor of the 1860s was prone to violence:

"Had occasion to give Louis Maurice a good thrashing for insolence to Messrs. Dobbs and Compton. At 11 a.m. he deserted and is now in camp."

"Mr. M. had occasion to give Celeste Antoine a good thrashing for stealing and other like offences. He has therefore deserted."

There were so many desertions and firings in this period that there must have been a small colony of the men in the Tsimshian camp. The Company servants received a bottle of rum each to celebrate the departure of that factor and another the next day to celebrate the arrival of Mr. Manson. Then the new factor rehired all the deserters and discharged men.

The men were right; they were not quite slaves, they were nineteenth-century employees. And when Mr. McNeill wrote, on January 1, 1856, "Men all enjoying themselves, they paid us a visit in the hall when they received a few drams, and wished us a happy New Year, etc. *We* took dinner with them in one of the houses, which looks well between Master and man," he was displaying the standard nineteenth-century viewpoint. Among its peers the Hudson's Bay Company was in many ways a benign employer, ranking well ahead of Scrooge and the British Navy.

CHAPTER 26

Women

THE RUSSIANS INSTITUTED fur trade and Native wives almost simultaneously on North America's west coast. Through shipwreck, Aleutian weather, scurvy and the hatred of the Tlingit they pursued the sea otter. The survivors were usually those who had Aleut or Inuit wives to teach them how to shelter from some of the fiercest winds that blow over the earth, how to find food on the bleak shorelines, how to build baidarkas, and how to dress in waterproof mukluks and parkas.

A hundred years later and a thousand miles to the southeast, at Fort Simpson, Native women were still sustaining white men. For the primary and obvious purpose of the country marriage they were well qualified. Coast Native children grew up in communal lodges where up to twenty-five families bedded down with only three-foot partitions between them. Courses in human sexuality were about as necessary for them as courses in breathing. The girls matured early and were given, sold, loaned or rented by their fathers. But women of the West Coast tribes were well qualified for other important aspects of the fur trade marriage — their hands had a characteristic deftness, their voices a comforting softness and they were adaptable to a degree that few humans in history have been called upon to equal. They stepped with dignity across the chasm that separated the Stone Age from the Industrial Age as though it were a hairline crack in time.

On the domestic side, the fort women were usually faithful wives, forever appreciative of the consideration shown them by their husbands; however little it may have been in some instances, it far exceeded that shown by Native husbands. They were proud to bear fair-skinned children and this they did at a truly Victorian rate. They were good mothers, though indulgent, having an easy, gentle, loving approach to child rearing. Housekeeping hardly existed in the Native lodges but the women learned to keep house in the forts because they were accustomed to doing whatever work was done in their community, apart from fishing, hunting and canoe-building of which they handled only the drudgery.

In the overall fort life the women played a subtle and wholly unacknowledged role. Even as the journal keeper wrote down the strictest facts he was maintaining a fiction — that one half of the fort population did not exist, the half that consisted of women and children. It was not only in the journals that women were suppressed. Said gossipy Captain Wishart with some disappointment, after spending a few days at Fort Simpson in 1850, "... the wives of the officers I know nothing about." Visible or not, the women were there, a regular information centre for puzzled Company personnel. They showed their men where the tallest stands of timber could be found, the fastest method of bailing a canoe, how to make nettles palatable when the garden failed and a thousand other tricks of north coast living. In the various languages they could translate the nuances that the fort interpreters sometimes missed and, more importantly, they could interpret the behaviour of the fort's more baffling customers. They could explain why an otherwise friendly chief took his furs and made a glowering exit — his dignity had been damaged because the trader's assistant had behaved flippantly. They could even dredge up reasons for the action of Cushwhat, enemy of gatekeepers:

January 15, 1853 — "Cushwhat threatening to Shoot both Mr. Work and Myself, as well as the gate Keeper, how this affair will end is more than I can forsee. It would appear that some time since he paid 'Robert Reid's' Wife some Blankets and Cotton to sleep with her. He had done so but a short time, when Reid came on shore from the Steamer, and as a matter of course his Wife came inside the Fort with him. This prevented Cushwhat from getting the value of the property he gave the Woman and he wishes now either to get the property back, or the woman outside of the Fort."

The women could predict the movements of the tribes because they had access to information that would never have reached the Indian shop: the Masset would be arriving in a few days (bound on revenge); the Tsimshian would leave early for their fishing grounds (they feared a Cumshewa raid); the Tongass would not bring their furs for the season (they were plotting war).

Conversely, the fort wives could explain to the tribesmen the crazy actions of the Hudson's Bay people: the white men wasted so much time shovelling fish heads and offal out of the fort because they were sensitive to the smell; they brought all that water into the fort because they washed themselves and their clothes in their houses instead of in the sea or a lake; they worked all day long six days a week because their great chief to the south insisted upon it and would be very angry if they did otherwise. The women, in fact, maintained a sort of liaison between the fort and the Native camps.

Of all the women's contributions to fort life, probably the one that mattered most was contentment. Dr. Tolmie, aged twenty-two, less than a year on the coast and obviously troubled at the thought of a Native marriage, had to admit, "Manson I am sure is much happier with his wife and two pretty children around him than were he a lone bachelor &

leading the sensual life, indulged in by most of the gentle-men, who live in single blessedness."

Some Hudson's Bay marriages were outright trade alliances. Dr. Kennedy's was particularly effective in this way since his wife was a daughter of Legaic, the highest chief in the Tsimshian hierarchy. The marriage forged an evident bond between Legaic and the Company which, in spite of temporary lapses, lasted as long as his life. His role of head chief made him head trader also. He collected furs from his domains, north, south and inland, and the fort could count on receiving a good portion of them, at a tidy profit to Legaic, of course.

Mrs. Kennedy knew her place in the fort — it was sec-ond from the top. The class-conscious north coast peoples and the class-conscious British understood one another very well in matters of rank. Mrs. Kennedy maintained a slave woman to serve her and a nursemaid for her children, and in no way did she renounce her position within the tribe when she moved inside the stockade.

November 27, 1841 — "Mrs. Kennedy who intends to give her relations a Regale, in commemoration of her deceased brother, traded a few Beaver skins this evening for Rum."

In spite of her well-defined positions both inside and out-side the fort, her social season was enlivened by the same challenges that a Washington, D.C. hostess might expect:

November 29 — "Madame. Arthur [Peter Arthur was engi-neer on the *Beaver*] came in this morning and traded 6 Large Beaver for Rum to give the Indians a regale in opposition to that of Mrs. Kennedy's. Another Tsimshian (Bibeau's brother-in-law) traded 4 Large Beaver for Rum. He is likewise to give a feast to his relations, commemorative of his sister's death."

First lady of the first Fort Simpson was Julia Ogden. Peter Skene Ogden's life in the early Columbia District is a flaming story of adventure, hardship, bravery and glory. Julia's story is of the same adventures, greater hardships, equal bravery, little glory, motherhood and constancy. It reveals attitudes — hers, her husband's, the Company's. Those same attitudes shaped the lives of every Native and half-Native wife in every fort.

Julia met Ogden at Spokane House where the young veteran of the Northwest Company concluded his first assignment with the newly merged companies. They had an unsatisfactory courtship conducted in the European manner and a satisfactory wedding conducted in the Flathead manner. It involved the payment of fifty fine horses. As for living happily ever after, there were ups and downs, some of the downs being the result of separations as long as two years. The nature of Ogden's work caused most of the separations but the nature of the man caused the longest one. Yet the union endured for thirty-one years till death did them part and was an example of the fur trade marriage at its best.

Immediately after the wedding Ogden sent for his two half-Cree children whose mother had vanished during one of his year-long absences. Julia enfolded them in her love and they became an instant family. The following year Ogden set out on his first Snake River expedition with fifty-eight men, thirty women, thirty-five children, two hundred sixty-eight horses, three hundred fifty-two traps and twenty-two leather lodges. Julia was one of the women and the two little boys and their new brother accounted for three of the children. The baby, strapped to a cradle board and enclosed in a fur bunting bag, joggled along happily, attached to the pommel of his mother's saddle.

The fur bag was important because Governor Simpson deemed fort wintering a foolish waste of time and money and decreed that the Snake River brigade should winter on the trail. Thus it was December 20th, 1824, that the party broke camp at Flathead Post where they had assembled, and headed out to trap beaver over a route that wound through country that is now known as Idaho, Montana and Utah, some of which had been explored, much of which had not, and all of which was Native territory.

The Flathead Natives were friendly; the Nez Percé, the Blood and the Piegan Natives made night forays on the horses; the Blackfoot cut off scouts, captured trappers and killed. Most of the journey was through Blackfoot country. It was not the Blackfoot, however, who threatened to shoot Julia.

The trappers of the brigade were chiefly freemen; that is, not engagés to the Company. The forts outfitted them, at advanced prices, on credit against their take that was paid for at reduced prices. A few were French Canadians, most were Iroquois. They were irresponsible, unmanageable, and, under-standably, at least half hostile. The brigade trapped its way south to a location that is now marked by the town of Ogden, Utah. There it encountered American traders who sought to lure the freemen over to their camp — fourteen deserted. It was not a quiet desertion; the freemen forcibly took their furs and, while holding Ogden at gunpoint, tried for the horses by stampeding them. While this was happening, Julia was desperately searching the camp for the two little boys. She brought them back to what safety the lodge would offer only to discover that her horse, with cradle board, bag and baby, was missing. She made a dash for the American camp where she found them. She mounted and was galloping out with them in a cold fury when she caught sight of another brigade horse carrying Company furs. She grabbed its lead rope and immediately muskets were raised and cocked. She stormed on out with such defiance that not one shot was fired.

Since Native knives and American guns were no detri-ment to family life as practised by Julia, it is not surprising that weather was not allowed to interfere with it. She shep-herded her children over mountain passes clogged with snow, across rivers full of floating ice and rivers in flood, up icy inclines where the horses slipped or in mud that mired them, through days of mountain cold that withered bodies and prairie heat that scorched them. At daybreak she roused the children and helped them mount; at dusk she fed and bedded them within their home of hides. Sometimes the brigade camped for a few days or even a week while the horses grazed and rested or the men trapped and hunted buffalo and chased their stolen horses, or while a blizzard imprisoned them. Once it tarried a whole day after a freeman's wife gave birth.

On one such occasion the company paused on the bank of the Snake River after three nightmarish days of struggling across the snow and mud of spring thaw on the Snake Plain. Charles, the six-year-old, had been travelling wrapped in a blanket on Julia's saddle because she was worried about his chest cold and fever, which was growing worse. She knew exactly what was prescribed for such a condition — a goose. She persuaded a freeman to shoot one but it fell into the far side of the river that still carrying break-up ice. The freeman was apologetic but there was nothing he could do. Julia peeled off her excess clothing, swam across the river, picked up the goose and swam back though the current carried her, along with the ice, downstream. She brushed off the wafer ice that had formed on her neck at the waterline, then she hurried to the lodge where she prepared goose grease to rub on Charles' chest and goose soup for his stomach, and they both survived.

Families were not allowed to accompany Ogden's second Snake River expedition; Governor Simpson forbade the squandering of food and horses on women and children. Had she not been seven months pregnant Julia might have caught up with the brigade, casually, when it was several days along the trail, as some of the men's families did. As it was, Sarah Julia was eight months old before she took over the cradle board on Julia's pommel as the whole family set out with the third Snake River brigade in September of 1826. They were along on the fourth and fifth brigades also. These were all called Snake

River expeditions although the third was an Oregon journey.

Along with new thrills of exploration, these trips added new terrors and sorrows to the family's experience. The most unshakable was starvation. The brigade lived off the land. At one time the band ate six meals in ten days and a woman was known to have gone eleven days without food. Horses were killed and eaten but this could not happen often as the horses, too, were dying of starvation and cold. On one windy October night, Natives set fire to the dry grass on the edge of the encampment. A watchman roused the people and a clump of willows slowed the fire enough so they could overcome it. One March, in the Siskiyou Mountains, for an unrecorded reason, everyone spent a night in the open, in heavy rain, without even a blanket. Bad water and beaver meat that had been poisoned by water hemlock caused illnesses so desperate that the men were willing to swallow the cure, pepper and gunpowder mixed in water. Ogden himself spent ten helpless days in the lodge with Julia nursing him. The fourth expedition was marked by the birth and death of an Ogden. It had been an on-the-trail pregnancy for Julia with at least eight months of hardship and hunger. The baby was born in a teepee-like shelter during the cruellest cold that the expeditions ever experienced. All Julia's wisdom and determination failed to keep the baby boy alive for more than two weeks.

At the end of the fifth brigade Julia found herself relegated to her mother's lodge at Fort Nez Percé with four children. Ogden made his sixth and last Snake River expedition without her and ended it at Fort Vancouver, two hundred miles from Fort Nez Percé. There he proclaimed his bachelorhood. Julia waited. She waited another year while a disease known to the people as intermittent fever swept through Fort Vancouver. It delayed Ogden's next assignment by six months and perhaps helped to cure him of his surfeit of family life. At any rate, when he sailed on the *Cadboro*, in the spring of 1831, to establish a fort on Aemilius Simpson's Nass River site, Julia and the children were with him. Julia's credentials for first ladyship at Fort Simpson were impeccable.

While Julia could not have been at the new Fort Simpson for a full two months after the move from the Nass, her successor had a long tenure. Josette Legace Work also came from Spokane country and a background of buckskin and horses. She was the daughter of a French-Canadian father and a Native mother and her husband was another leader of Columbia District expeditions. John Work's career sometimes paralleled and sometimes intersected Peter Skene Ogden's. They had made the journey from York House to the Columbia together and while Ogden and Julia starved in the Snake country, Work and Josette starved on expeditions closer to the coast. When Ogden sailed for the north, Work took over the Snake River territory; when Ogden left the north, Work took over Fort Simpson and the marine department.

Josette and her older daughters pined for their sunny southland while the rains drenched Fort Simpson for weeks at a time but they managed to maintain a happy atmosphere in the Big House. Young officers found the Works' apartment a joyful place to visit. Roderick Finlayson wrote to his friend, John McLoughlin, Jr., of the good times he had there and eventually married one of the "young ladies." The same spirit pervaded Hillside, the Works' Victoria home after Mr. Work was promoted to the Board of Management. Young Charles Wilson, lieutenant in the engineers corps that was out from England for the border survey, wrote of it several times in his diary, as on September 3rd, 1859: "Directly I landed I started off to spend the evening with the Works and thank them for all their kindness; you can imagine how astonished they were to see me open the door and walk in. They got up an impromptu hop immediately and we danced till Sunday commenced ... The Works are about the kindest people I ever came across; 'my western home' I call it." Josette, of course, is not mentioned. But who else set the happy tone of that household?

Two of Fort Simpson's resident princesses were wives of W. H. McNeill, successively. During the time Captain McNeill was commanding the *Beaver*, this note appeared in the Work-Finlayson journal:

April 18, 1843 — "Capt. McNeill's family who arrived by the steamer landed this morning and occupied the house where the school was kept."

The mother of that family came from Dall Island, the home of the Kyganie. She accepted the English name, Matilda, and English dress and customs, but she remained always a princess. Queen Victoria bore herself no more regally than women of Native nobility.

In 1851 Mr. McNeill came to Fort Simpson as factor but this time he did not have his wife and family with him. Matilda had died the previous year after giving birth to twins. Helen, their eldest daughter, had been married to George Blenkinsop of Fort Rupert, some five years before, and the rest of the children seem to have been settled in Victoria. Family ties were strong within the milieu of the forts and Mr. McNeill's position in the company was strong, too. Together they brought about the transfer of the Blenkinsops to Fort Simpson, which provided the factor with family life once again. Helen even presented him with a new grandson during that tour of duty. But Mr. McNeill had his own resources, also, and some time in the years 1853-56 Neshaki became his second princess. Her father was the top-ranking Nisga'a chief. Neshaki, too, had an English name, Martha, but it was never used at Fort Simpson. There she was either Mrs. McNeill, the factor's wife, or Neshaki, the royal fur trader. As the former she presided over the McNeill apartment and as the latter she maintained an official residence on the bank of the Nass River. She would set out from Simpson in her large canoe, large because it accommodated her crew and her stock that had been purchased from the Indian trade shop. Eventually she would return, her canoe loaded with those coveted, inland, cold-weather pelts that she traded at the fort. This system worked admirably; the Company got the Nass furs and Neshaki got rich. It worked so well that it continued after Mr. McNeill retired to Victoria. In 1866 Neshaki came north, apparently to expand the system.

February 5 — "Mrs. Wm. McNeill came in the Fort to Stop."

March 18 — "Mrs. McNeill arrived in a Canoe from Nass. She brings letters to Mr. Manson from Mr. Doolan [missionary] and Cunningham. (All Well.)"

March 19 — "Mrs. McNeill paid up her a/c in Furs to date (Viz) 72 Martens, 16 Beavers, 2 land Otters, 2 Minks and 5 Bears."

March 23 — "Mrs. McNeill got a fresh supply of goods on credit and left in her Canoe for Nass against a strong head wind." (I have the feeling that many of liberated Neshaki's activities were launched against a strong head wind.)

May 2 — "Mr. Cunningham arrived from Nass in a canoe on his way to Metlakatla … He left Mr. Hankin quite well at Nass and doing a good trade in Mrs. McNeill's house which Graham has fitted up for that purpose according to Mr. Manson's instructions."

On one of Neshaki's 1863 trading expeditions Lucy Moffatt accompanied her. We do not know in which capacity she went: as wife of factor Hamilton Moffatt; as educated daughter of W. H. McNeill, CF; as stepdaughter of Neshaki; in her own right as a Kyganie noblewoman, daughter of Matilda; or as a miraculously unfettered Victorian female. Perhaps Lucy did not bother about these categories — after all, she was so adaptable that she could occupy the VIP cabin aboard the *Labouchere* on the trip north and then set off in a canoe for weeks of weather-exposed travel to Nass River villages, her back braced against a bale of blankets. Lucy makes the balancing of two heritages look as effortless as riding on a teeter-totter.

One of Lucy's childhood companions was a Scottish-Tongass girl. She married Pym Nevin Compton, Fort Simpson gentleman, who whisked her off to his homeland to live. How she reconciled Victorian England and her Tongass upbringing we are not told but it is certain she did it unobtrusively and with her head held high. It is a relief, however, to learn that within a few years the Comptons were back in America to stay.

Mention of an officer's wife in the journals was rare. Mention of a man's wife was a mere slip of the pen. One exception to the rule was the formal recording of births, which were frequent at Fort Simpson:

July 11, 1852 — "About 3 a.m. the Wife of Jeremie Sururier was delivered of a female child."

It was difficult to exclude a woman from the matter of childbirth but thereafter she was excluded entirely from official parenthood. Seven days after the above entry, "About 8 p.m. the infant Child of Jeremie Sururier died."

This attitude was not reserved for vital statistics alone:

March 28, 1842 — "Maurice's wife deserted this evening, on account of a drubbing he gave her for misconduct and took one of his children along with her."

In spite of the odd drubbing and a zero status, the Native women usually preferred life in the fort to life (and sometimes violent death) among their own people. There, unless they belonged to the small pampered nobility, their status was even lower; as, for example:

February 20, 1843 — "This morning a woman was shot by Cacas' brother for declining to go for some firewood."

Among the fort couples were many devoted partners who spent a lifetime together. The wives, with their children, camped out in the snow and rain with the picket cutters, eked out Company rations with native foods, raised their children by what they chose as the better of two standards, and followed their restless husbands from their own villages to forts located in alien and often enemy territory. Such ordinary domesticity was not journal material and we hear of it only indirectly. But when liquor inundated the north coast in the 1850s and 1860s the resulting violence in the men's quarters was written up quite directly:

"All hands more or less under the influence of Liquor. St. Arnand with drawn sword charged our black Cook with giving Liquor to his Woman which the other fearing the consequences, if acknowledged, as stoutly denied."

"Tailor laid up the past 2 days from the effects of Rum brought here from Victoria by his wife." Later in the month, the same man, showing no gratitude, "… gave his Wife such a severe beating that all inside the fort cried shame and I had to interfere and put a stop to it."

"A row took place between Turcot and his father-in-law. Turcot had beaten his wife unmercifully. The father struck Turcot and took his daughter away with him. I gave the Indian 2 bottles of Rum or he would have done mischief to Turcot sometime or other."

It was a bad time for the women but they survived it in their individual styles:

"Mrs. McAulay [mother of Mrs. Compton] left the fort this morning on her own responsibility and has gone to Tongass."

"Lac Kar's son died this morn' of course a grog feast was given. Underwood's wife got drunk and thrashed her husband and broke 11 panes of glass in the men's house window."

McNeill felt that a woman lurked behind each of his personnel problems. He had some justification. In the winter of 1855–1856 there were two desertions within a period of a month and a half. In both cases the men, with their loves, set out by canoe for Victoria. One made it and one returned rather abjectly after three days of storms. McNeill's explanation:

"The Women of this place have some '*way*' to turn men's brains, more so than I ever heard in any other part of the world. W.H. McN."

Though the women appeared submissive to the men and to the Company rules and to their fate, there is one McNeill journal entry that makes one wonder if they did not feel the very same resentments that modern women would feel under such conditions. The entry is dated May 24th, 1859:

"About 3 p.m. the roof of my house took fire, supposed by smut from the Kitchen Chimney, the Shingles caught in six places, with the assistance of some women outsiders and some six Native men we fortunately got it under in a short time. The women of the Fort with the exception of two did nothing, in fact they would have been pleased to see the Fort consumed."

CHAPTER 27

Children

ALL OF LIFE WAS A HAZARD in the days of early Fort Simpson but the greatest hazard was being born. It is one thing to read nineteenth-century infant mortality rates and quite another, a much more personal experience, to read the births and deaths that followed one another down the pages of the journals. Still, enough babies survived to become the cherished half-Native children who tumbled about the fort yard and grew up to be the new country's wives and gentlemen and work-men and Natives in good standing in their mothers' tribes.

Each of those children must have felt the tug of his other heritage as he settled into either the white community or his Native village. The father usually determined which life lay ahead of his children by taking or leaving his family as he moved about the district or out of it, though in a few cases the mother made the decision by refusing to leave her people. The Fort Simpson factors and traders, as far as the record goes, seem to have been responsible husbands and fathers and with their progeny established some of the colony's enduring and respected families. Usually the ships' officers and crews did not threaten the tradition of the sea by being overconstant, and the fort labourers came and went, some accompanied by their families but more accompanied by their memories. Their children, for the most part, were allowed to make casual adjustments to whichever condition they might find themselves in, but children of the gentlemen were subjected to some cruel pressures. Their fathers, having forfeited their own attachments by coming to the remoteness of the west coast, lavished affection upon them. Mixed with the affection were great dollops of ambition for the children. The fathers seemed delighted to have their young lady daughters marry ranking Company officers, though we would call the young ladies children. Sarah Julia Ogden became engaged at age thirteen but waited until she was fourteen to marry. Regarding their sons, the fathers were overly sensitive, since they well knew the Company's attitude toward mixed-blood employees: they were considered undependable. The family dramas that resulted have been concealed from us. One exception is the story of Henry McNeill, second son of W. H. McNeill whose stony convictions overpowered his journal reticence.

Mr. McNeill came as factor to Fort Simpson in 1851 and a year and a half later young Henry, known as Harry to his family, arrived on the *Beaver* to become a fort hand. By 1853 Mr. McNeill was campaigning by letter to have his son given some status. It was a tough campaign because neither Henry nor the Board of Management showed any enthusiasm. However, by June of 1855, the young man was acting as interpreter and assistant in the trade shop and was granted a clerk's salary without a clerk's standing. This was not good enough for Papa McNeill who sharpened his quill and set to work once more. His correspondence with James Douglas on the subject was gaining momentum when all his soaring hopes were shot down — by Henry. Mr. McNeill did not spare himself when he wrote up the journal on three December nights while the rest of the fort personnel were preparing the Christmas celebration. Any parent knows what those entries cost him:

December 21 — "I learned a day or two since that Harry McNeill had been in the habit of sleeping *outside* nightly for a long time, and gave the keys of the Gates to the Watchman or the Steward, to keep until morning, I immediately ordered him not to do so any more for the future, when he said he would not do any more duty. I told him that he might go to the Devil his own way."

December 22 — "This morning I asked Harry McNeill if he intended to attend to his duty in the Indian Shop. He said No. I ordered him out of the Fort to act as he thought best, he endeavor'd until night to get a Canoe to take him to Victoria, none could be procured, the Indians being fearful of the cold weather, and did not see clearly when they would be paid for the voyage."

December 23 — "About 2 p.m. Harry McNeill managed to muster a Crew of nine Indians for his Canoe and started for Victoria, *The* woman also went in the Canoe. I rather think they will have a long and cold voyage of it."

Henry did not shake the mud of Fort Simpson forever from his feet for he kept reappearing in adventurous roles. During the little gold rush of 1859 he arrived with Captain Torrens and Mr. Denman and a party of nine miners. W. H. McNeill was still factor and would not relent toward Harry enough to invite him into the fort, though he did allow "the three gentlemen" to make camp in the wood yard. All that summer and fall and well into the winter it was their base for sorties that brought them every kind of danger the north could supply and hardships beyond recounting, but no mineral finds of value.

When Henry came again, in 1866, he was attended by a personal servant and was received with some deference and lodged in the Big House. (His father had retired and Hamilton Moffatt, a brother-in-law of Henry's, commanded the fort.) "Mr. Butler of the Collins' Overland Tele'h Company accompanyed by Henry McNeill arrived this forenoon in a Canoe from Nass. They are from Bulkley House, Lake Tatla, New Caledonia district And have come by Babine Lake and Skeena River." That was a daring trip, one of the first made by white men over that route, but it was just a segment of the whole daring venture that pushed through the northern Interior toward Bering Strait to lay a cable, and then fell dead in its wilderness tracks, killed by the fast completion of the rival Atlantic cable. Though the loss to the Collins Overland, by then known as the Northwest Telegraph, was total, there was a gain to British Columbia for the new trails and clearings encouraged penetration of virgin country. I hope that W. H. McNeill was not too proud to acknowledge Harry's service to us. Along with his brother, William, and his brother-in-law, George Blenkinsop, he had furnished the local knowledge of Natives and techniques and terrain that the American executives so sorely needed even to unload their equipment at Fort Simpson.

We do not know how the young Henry McNeill was educated but we can be sure that he received some schooling. Gentlemen believed in education for their sons and many were sent, at about twelve years of age, half a continent away to the school for officers' sons, at Red River. The boys were not likely to see their Columbia District families again until they had grown into young manhood. A few went on to universities in Scotland, England and Paris, but most entered the Company service.

Perhaps Henry was one of the three McNeills in attendance at the Fort Victoria school for gentlemen's sons and daughters. It opened in 1849. The Company had brought the Reverend Robert John Staines from England as chaplain and schoolmaster. His school dispensed lessons in all the gentlemanly subjects, including Latin, to boys who arrived usually more fluent in a native language than in English. It also dispensed scanty meals (breakfasts and suppers of bread and treacle and clear tea) and Spartan sleeping accommodations (one covering blanket per pupil though the water for washing their faces often froze in the bucket beside them).

The education of daughters was extremely casual until the opening of the Staines' school. Then Mrs. Staines took charge of them and Deportment became their most important study. The whole school was contained in the Staines' quarters in the fort. This put the young ladies directly over Bachelors' Hall, a circumstance which provided endless distractions to both upstairs and downstairs residents.

You may not have thought of Fort Simpson as a seat of learning but in 1840 it was — it had a schoolhouse and a teacher. Apparently the schoolhouse was one of the little-used fort buildings and when it was required to shelter personnel, education moved on to another location, in the manner of a floating crap game. The teacher was Edward Alin, a French Canadian whose professional status was not exalted; he ranked as labourer. On Saturdays he was assigned light work such as painting doors and windows, and on Sundays he read the Bible and prayers to the men, in French. He was still at Fort Simpson in 1843 but how long thereafter is one of the many unwritten sequels. There is more information about Simpson's second school since it belongs to the famous William Duncan story.

James Douglas, in Victoria, introduced W. H. McNeill, at Fort Simpson, to the missionary by letter of September 21st, 1857. The firmness of the tone suggests that he was not at all certain of the ex-captain's reaction to a man of God. "He [Mr. Duncan] had a free passage from England to this place by Her Majesty's ship *Satellite* and now proceeds by the *Otter* to Fort Simpson where he will be placed under your kind and special protection. Mr. Duncan is a gentleman of pleasing manner and with every disposition to make himself agreeable. He will be an acquisition to your society and I have no doubt he will receive every kindness at your hands and through your judicious counsels and earnest assistance he will under Providence be enabled to effect much good among the native tribes. It is understood that Mr. Duncan is to take up his quarters in the establishment and to be maintained at the Company's table in the same manner as any of the Company's officers. You will please to provide him with a comfortable apartment and every other accommodation in your power."

Mr. McNeill received Mr. Duncan into the fort on October 1st, assigned him a two-room apartment and with some wonderment began to note his activities in the journal. Almost immediately there was a school for fort boys — and Clah. It was held in one room of Mr. Duncan's apartment and began at noon each day. From ten until noon Clah tutored Mr. Duncan. He was the exceptional boy from the Tsimshian camp whom Mr. McNeill had selected to teach Mr. Duncan the language.

In addition to the boys' school: "Mr. Duncan commenced a School this evening to teach all the *Men* inside the Fort that think proper to attend it. He intends also to give lectures three times a week to them on dift. Subjects, and to continue the School and Lectures through the Winter, he appears to be indefatigable to do good to all, both Whites and Indians."

Those evening lectures were surely the very first of the nightschool classes to which British Columbians now flock for instruction in everything from Wok Cookery to Relativity. By the end of June Mr. Duncan had defied the traditions of his age and of the fort by recognizing that there were women within the stockade: "Mr. Duncan commenced to keep School for the men's Wives this evening from 7 to 8 p.m."

Now Duncan felt secure enough in his use of the Tsimshian language to open a school in the Native village. It was held in Legaic's lodge, a location that established it as a worthy institution. It began with thirty children and an unspecified number of women. Meanwhile, fort hands and Natives worked for over a month and a half to cut timber to build a mission house and to raft it to the village. Another fort hand showed a gang of Tsimshian how to build a road to the site. Then, in November 1858, "Mr Duncan commenced keeping school for Indians in his own house on the 18th inst."

Mr. Duncan's school had many of the problems that still plague education departments:

August 18, 1859 — " 'Cushwhat' got drunk and broke all the windows and doors in Mr. Duncan's Schoolhouse. He is a great scoundrel."

June 8, 1860 — (While Duncan was visiting other northern tribes) — "Had occasion to put all Mr. Duncan's forms etc. in the Bastion as the Indians had broken into his School and plundered it of a part of the furniture."

The school had some specialized problems, too: "The Espokelots kept Mr. Duncan from keeping school as they were carrying on medicine jugglery."

That first mission building served as Mr. Duncan's residence as well as the school. By winter of 1859 he had an attendance of two hundred that must have crowded the little bit of selfless living in which he indulged right out of the door. Duncan needed another schoolhouse and this time he and his Tsimshian followers built it without fort assistance. He finished it in December of 1861, a building that was adequate for his classes and his church services and an object of pride. Six months later it stood empty. The smallpox epidemic had precipitated the exodus of Duncan and his followers to Metlakatla.

By the time I crossed the Hudson's Bay field and climbed a knoll to go to school, Port Simpson boasted three separate schools. There was the Indian Day School whose two classrooms held up to a hundred and forty children in the coldest part of winter. The Natives had always found the white men's notion of arising briskly on frigid mornings a ridiculous one, so peak attendance occurred only in the afternoons. Even before spring was recognizable the nomadic movements of the Tsimshian were under way and by the end of June there were no pupils to celebrate the school closing. Apparently no one ever thought of adapting the educational system to the coast peoples' life style. The second school had perfect attendance. It was the classroom in the Girls' Home. The third was designated as the "white school."

Our school was, in many ways, a typical country school of the 1900s' second decade. I know this because the old school tie is as nothing compared to the bond that exists among us survivors of one-room schools. We ask each other eagerly:

"And did you have a waterbucket with a dipper for drinks to relieve boredom?"

"And double desks with glass inkwells that overflowed?"

"Did Queen Victoria still look down on you with disapproval from the front wall, though George V had been on the throne for years?"

"Did you learn by heart whole cantos of the 'Lady of the Lake' by listening to the Senior Fourth class instead of doing your primary sums?"

"And Gray's 'Elegy'? And 'The Burial of Moses'?"

There were some ways, however, in which the Port Simpson Elementary School was a little unusual, as a long succession of teachers discovered.

One of these was a rite of spring. When the creek shouted and rolled out of its lower bank onto the field that had once been the Hudson's Bay potato patch, we began to jump. With a run and a leap we took off from the high bank, and with our knees hiked up to our chins made flights to the opposite shore. At the end of recess we scrambled up the knoll and piled into the schoolroom, gasping for breath, wringing out the hems of our dresses and squishing inside our shoes. The nervous Scottish woman who was our teacher one year was distraught by our condition. She pulled at her grey hair and cried, "Ye've been to the bur-r-n again. I forbade ye. I forbade ye." We could not understand her reaction. Were robins forbidden to fly in the spring?

When one teacher enquired the birthdate of a new first grade pupil, the little girl answered with a winsome smile, "When the hens lay eggs."

"But can you tell me the day?"

"Oh yes, when the plum tree blooms."

That little girl was being brought up by her Tsimshian grandmother and though she was a white child in every other way she had the Native turn of expression and the Native approach to time. More than half of the pupils shared these with her for they were descended from Hudson's Bay-Native backgrounds. They were all potential artists and during drawing lessons, while my eraser was rubbing holes in my paper, they were effortlessly producing true and beautiful lines.

The purest white backgrounds disconcerted the teachers, too. When we were learning an Irish gavotte, a demure little one-and-two-and-three-kick number for the school concert, an all-girl dance, mind you, the Methodist missionaries raised eyebrows and voices and demanded that their children be spared from this shame. And once our new teacher turned out to be a girl with an Irish lilt to her voice and an almost perpetual smile. I thought she was the most beautiful lady I had ever seen and would willingly have memorized my entire primer for her. Soon after her arrival, the mission doctor came into the store, marched straight up to Dad and said, "Things have gone too far, Mr. Young. We've got to band together. It's the new teacher."

"What's wrong with her?" asked Dad who had noticed only that she was a pretty girl.

The doctor, catching sight of me sweeping up the rice I had spilled, leaned far over the counter to direct a stage whisper at Dad, "She's an RC."

Dad replied with a startled, Presbyterian, "No."

Miss Rafferty had to battle her way through that school year but, being Irish, held out till June.

PART VII

People of the Village

CHAPTER 28

Dinah

DINAH WALKED PORT SIMPSON'S roads and pathways alone. She walked in men's boots, steadying her steps with a driftwood cane and turning aside the rain with a gunnysack across her shoulders. Little Native boys, romping along in a pack, fell silent and decorous as they overtook and passed her in an arc through the grass at the side of the road, their faces averted to protect them from the evil eye, for Dinah was a witch.

Dinah would have been an outcast even if she had never cast a spell nor hurled a curse. In her old age she had come from another village to live with relatives on the Port Simpson Reserve. The loneliest people there were the few Haida, Tlingit and Kitimat who were fated to dwell among the Tsimshian; whether they had been slaves or descended from slaves, or whether they arrived through mishap or disapproved marriage, they were fiercely scorned. In Dinah's case the scorn was tinged with fear and horror.

I think Dinah must have come to Port Simpson when I was about eleven. My parents, considering themselves immune to Indian witchcraft, were intrigued by her aura of mystery. She seemed to walk all day, every day, at a gait that never varied from slow. She did not encourage my father's Chinook conversation, though he and all the village ancients considered him fluent and entertaining in Chinook. She knew as many English words as my mother knew of Tsimshian, perhaps thirty, yet they could reach a fair understanding and even rapport in seconds.

My own fascination with Dinah was: what is an evil eye? And so, one day when she and I were on a collision course, I stopped squarely in front of her, muttered, "How do you do?" and raised my own eyes slowly upward from the gunnysack. They didn't have far to go for Dinah, though stocky, was hardly taller than I. They travelled up that imperturbable face and at the nose they wavered before leaping straight into Dinah's eyes. There they found the usual brown-black gaze that conceals a Native's soul from the world, but, indeed, there was a difference. These eyes held the merest flicker of amusement.

After I had thus entered the Dinah-Mother alliance I became the keeper-of-the-kettle. A small aluminum pot with a tight lid and a bail for safe carrying had somehow become Dinah's kettle. When Mother cooked our large midday meal a portion went into this pot to stay warm on the back of the ever-burning coal range until Dinah's perambulations brought her close to our back gate. Then I ran out and thrust the bail into her hand that was not engaged with the driftwood cane. This manoeuvre was like passing the baton in a slow motion relay race because it had to be accomplished without impeding her progress. If she had stopped at our gate it could have been construed as begging. Later in the day I would find the empty kettle, scoured clean with sand and seawater, just outside the gate.

Summers in Port Simpson had a feeling of unreality. The rains abated and there were days of sunshine warm enough to send the grass rampaging waist high and the raspberry patches into frenzied production. Days meandered along from four in the morning till ten in the evening and nights darkened only to silver. Stranger still, the village was deserted, so that the sound of our footsteps bounced along beside us on the hard-packed gravel. The people sailed off for the salmon canneries in late June, leaving behind only four or five of the very elderly, usually each with a child to carry water and run errands. Dinah remained but no child accompanied her.

While the white population basked on the beach and revelled in summer, Dinah's gait grew slower. In time, Mother induced her to rest on the bench outside our back door. She would never come into the house — few of the older Natives could bear the high temperatures of our homes — but would sit for an hour at a time, breathing in puffs and perspiring in trickles. Mother and I ana-lyzed her clothing and decided that much of her bulkiness was due to layer upon layer of skirts and blouses and sweaters. We found a cotton dress that would surely be cooler for her and she accepted it with more gratitude than she had ever shown. It seemed rather a frivolous garment for Dinah, being a green and yellow print with triangular, yellow buttons. She wore the dress con-stantly — on top of the layers of skirts and blouses and sweaters.

That summer, at least, there was good reason for Dinah's excessive clothing, the same reason as for her excessive walk-ing. I discovered it the day she knocked on our kitchen door with her cane. Mother handed me the spoon with which she was stirring up sweet, fruity odours from a pot of black cur-rant jelly. At the door she and Dinah held a discussion of few words and many gestures. Finally Mother took the spoon out of my hand. "Dinah seems to need some help at home. You'll have to go — I can't leave the jelly now," she said.

We knew that Dinah lived at her nephew Henry's house. It was one of the more substantial houses in the village, painted on the front and one side. Dinah and I reached it at her pace and in profound silence. She led me to a window and tried to shove up the lower sash; when it didn't budge she stood aside in an invitation to me. I tried and concluded that the window was nailed shut inside, so we went on to the next window and the next, and next, until we had tried them all, as well as two doors.

"No key?" I asked.

Dinah showed me empty hands.

I went back to the kitchen window and peered inside. There was a patch of rust on the range, a pool of water on the floor from a leak in the ceiling, and a look of abandonment that told me no one had entered that room since the exodus to the canneries, weeks ago.

"Where have you been staying?"

Dinah began a Tsimshian reply in a low monotone but as she went on anger entered her voice and her body until she was fairly hissing and shaking. Of the entire harangue I could translate only one word that occurred repeatedly: *unduh* — go away. Her speech ended abruptly and, sagging under all her clothing, she started around the corner of the house. I followed her to a place where the ground fell away in a slope leaving a crawl space no more than three feet high under the house. I knelt to look in. There was the empty aluminum kettle, as yet unwashed, three hardtack stacked on a board and a depression in the earth, strewn with moss and rags and showing the contours of Dinah's body. There was nothing else.

I ran home, propelled more by my indignation than my legs. Mother, washing up the jelly-making dishes, asked, "What did Dinah want?"

"She wanted me to break into Henry's house. They've locked her out."

"I hope you did," said Mother.

"I hope you didn't," said my father who had come in from the store in search of a snack. "There's a law about that, you know."

"I couldn't. She's pretty mad. She's living *under* the house."

"There should be a law about that, too," Mother said, "poor defenceless, old soul."

"Defenceless? Not Dinah," said Dad, rummaging in the food cupboard. "Old Oliver made it over to the store this afternoon, not so much for a pound of sugar, I think, as for some reassurance. He's scared. I gather the people had been putting pressure on Henry to get rid of Dinah so when they all left he locked the house and told her to go. She went into a fury and called down all evil upon Henry and his family. And last night there was a boat in from Wales Island Cannery — that's where the family's working this summer. The news is that Henry's daughter has gone crazy — stark, raving mad."

"Hmff, that Cora. You know what's wrong with Cora. She's a bad girl. She's not possessed of evil spirits; she's possessed of syphilis."

"Would you like to try to tell that to any Tsimshian?"

Mother's hands in the dishwater were still. "We never hear of the medicine men practising any more. Perhaps the people don't believe so much in witchcraft nowadays."

"Perhaps they don't, but was it five or six years ago that Stephen Morris died? You remember, he had a row with a Kitkatla Indian at the cannery. Somebody in the Kitkatla's tribe willed that he would die and so he came home and took to his bed. The doctor couldn't find a thing wrong with him but he turned his face to the wall and died. I don't think we've heard the end of Dinah's strong magic."

My father was right, for the grapevine was soon writhing with messages. How it could operate in an empty village with the residents scattered over a hundred miles of coastline, we could only surmise, but old Oliver, who apparently was its receiver, began to make frequent trips to the store.

"Police boat take Cora to Prince Rupert Hospital," he told Dad one day.

"Cora maybe die," a few days later.

"Cora dead. They bring her home Friday. Lots of people come back."

When that news broke Dad knew Oliver's jitters had been vindicated. During the winter, funerals were dramatic productions with a thirty-piece band playing perhaps the slowest Dead March that ever issued from brass. All the evident

Christian ceremonies and all the furtive Tsimshian rites were similarly prolonged, sometimes for days. But a death during cannery season meant the return of only a handful of relatives to witness a hasty burial. Within the day they were gone again for the salmon runs tarried neither for the living nor the dead. A crowd returning at the height of the season had significance.

The morning of the funeral, Mother and I stood at my bedroom window watching the boats come in. Henry's family had arrived the previous night with the coffin and the wailers. As the cacophony of the single-cylinder engines diminished to sputters, Mother's hand on my shoulder pressed harder and harder. Below us we could hear Dad pacing in the store. He was a compulsive pacer but these were not the slow steps that accompanied conversation or contemplation; these steps were fast and jerky. As we started downstairs to discuss the situation with him we met him coming up.

"They're starting to dock," he said and his voice was as staccato as his pacing. "If Lewis Gray is with them you'd better worry in earnest."

Lewis was the last acknowledged shaman. He had ostensibly put aside his medicine rattle and headdress and retired at the missionaries' behest, but it was only half a secret on the reserve that he still had instructional visions and maintained liaison with his special spirits.

As the throng took shape on the wharf approach, Mother groaned. "Lewis is there, right in front. And this certainly isn't the usual funeral gathering. They're hurrying. Dinah didn't come past the house at all yesterday. I went looking for her but she wasn't to be seen. Do you think she's in hiding?"

"She'd better be. But I can't think of any place on that entire reserve where she'd be safe from such a grim-looking crowd."

We watched the stream of men and women flow past the store and fan out on the village streets. Not even the remotest path nor the most overgrown trail was undisturbed; there was movement everywhere but hardly a sound. I shivered so much that Mother made me put on a sweater. At two o'clock the church bell tolled and the streets emptied, but after the funeral we could see knots of people moving toward the wooded hills behind the town. With evening they returned to the wharf and one by one the boats pulled out, some heading north to the Nass River, some south to the Skeena, and some northwest to Wales Island, leaving us baffled.

There was no sign of Dinah next morning, and her kettle sat on the back of the stove until the corned beef hash had toasted. Dad waited in vain for Oliver to bring him news, while Mother took a walk right around the beach that skirted the village. Toward evening Dinah hove in sight on her usual course. Mother dropped the salmon she was cleaning, splat, on the floor and ran to the gate.

"Dinah, we didn't see you for a long time."

"Maybe rain today," replied Dinah without bringing her men's boots to a halt.

When Mother reported this conversation, Dad said, "It's all beyond the ken of white people. We'd best resign ourselves to never knowing what happened." And so we did, but only until lawncutting time, which occurred the next day.

Our back yard had been a tennis court in the latter days of the Hudson's Bay fort. That fact alone may provide a clue to Port Simpson's decline as a trading post. It must have been someone straight out from England (with a tennis racquet) who rolled and seeded that flat expanse without realizing that one could not play tennis in the ten rainiest months and that in the two summer months the grass sprang up in overnight leaps that defied any lawnmower that had yet been devised. About three times during the summer my father took down the scythe that hung on the warehouse wall and attacked the growth. It was my job to go over the yard ahead of him to pick up toys, swing seats, clothes-pins and whatever else might be embedded in that miniature jungle.

On this plot of grass and just behind the house and store, Dad had built an enclosed water tower known as the tank house. No more than eight feet beyond it, and parallel with it, stood a storage shed that housed oakum and tar and coal oil and yellow ochre and other odoriferous and messy stock that was banned from the warehouse. When trade was at its summer low there was no reason to enter either shed.

As I reached the three-sided enclosure between the buildings, on my picking-up rounds, I noticed that there was one area of grass that was grey-green in contrast to the lush green of the rest of the lawn. It was perhaps five feet by three and right against the wall of the tank house. I found that it had been crushed and flattened. A bear? I mused. Impossible — bears had not been seen inside the town in years. I had started toward Dad to ask for a solution to this puzzle when my running shoe came down on something hard. I bent down and picked out of the grass a triangular, yellow button.

That September's homecoming was a jubilation. It was the year of the big-run in the sockeye cycle and it had been a phenomenal big-run. The Natives were rich — at least until the opening of the Prince Rupert Exhibition. The village hummed with hundreds of softly spoken Tsimshian greetings and the store stayed open far into every night. Through the clusters of people unloading boats, exchanging news, showing off babies or kicking footballs, Dinah and her cane walked her customary routes at her customary times. Dad watched and shook his head as he did over his chessboard.

"You have three choices," he said. "The Indians' old beliefs are still so strong that they are terrified of Dinah, or their old beliefs are so weakened that they can accept a medical report, or the present atmosphere of joy and goodwill is large enough to include Dinah."

Mother said, "All I know is that Dinah is wearing a brand new pair of women's shoes."

CHAPTER 29

Johnny Naismooht

ON ANOTHER GHOST TOWN summer day, my father was over-hauling the outboard motor on the grocery counter when six-year-old Joshua burst through the store door. He stood there panting for several seconds before he could say, "You come quick, Mr. Young. Johnny Naismooht make cry very loud."

While Joshua struggled to reunite his pants and his half suspender, I grabbed the propeller shaft and Dad, pliers in hand, sprinted in the direction of the reserve. There was good reason for my father's reaction for Johnny was old and crippled and alone. He was a boatbuilder and worked around the large square opening in his floor that looked down very directly into high tide. With only one functioning leg, he scurried up and down the ladder that connected his shop to the sea. Unlike his Tsimshian fellows, in both body and soul he had the characteristics of an oversensitive mousetrap. He was fiercely Naismooht though all the Native people, some generations back, had turned in their Tsimshian names for new missionary-assigned Wesleys and Knoxs and Sankeys and other English appellations.

Dad pounded along the deserted shoreline road, his middle-aged heart and lungs shocked into a tumult of wheezing and pain. Before he reached the bridge he heard the sounds that had sent Joshua running. Full-throated roars they were, scarcely diminished by the wall of Johnny's shop-home that stood fourth in a line of buildings fronting on the bridge and backing into the bay.

My father always insisted that he had to peer through vaporized smoked salmon, herring eggs and oolichan grease to locate Johnny in the thick odour of his home. On this occasion he found him squatted on the floor before a cookstove that was partially assembled and still unctuously black. At that moment Johnny was releasing a bellow out of all proportion to his wizened rib cage. When he saw Dad he thwacked the length of his cane on the floor so that a line of dust rose to join the murkiness.

"Johnny, are you sick or hurt?" Dad asked with all the voice he could raise between gasps.

Johnny brandished his cane over his head. "I make hell with them. I make hell with you, too, Young," and the cane shot toward Dad's bald head.

Dad ducked, picked up the weapon and tossed it outside. Johnny threw back his head and started another roar but it deteriorated into a wailing "e-e-a" and ended in a sharp, "Young, you bring my tobacco?"

"No, I didn't. I came to find out what's wrong with you."

Johnny began to rock to and fro in anguish. "I tell you, March my stove all a time broke. You say, 'Sure, Johnny, I get Indian Agent say for new stove for you. You cold, poor Johnny.' April, no stove yet. You say you write two letter to Indian Agent; stove come by 'm by. May, no stove come. You say big Vancouver company going send some day quick. June, no stove come. You show me letter that say have to send back east, no stove for Johnny in Vancouver. Then yesterday stove come. You bring him my house on wheelbarrow, boards all round. I not let you set up my stove, Young. I want set up my stove. Very nice stove, very rich stove. I like. I put here. I put fancy top on. I look for legs. I look in boards and paper, I look in oven, I look in part where fire go. No legs. NO LEGS — stove burn up house, burn up lame Johnny Naismooht. From March I wait for stove no legs. E-e-e-a."

My father sagged where he stood. Johnny's story was accurate as far as it went, but Johnny didn't know of the filing folder that held page upon page of correspondence with the obstinate Indian Office in Prince Rupert on the subject of "1 only Little Dandy Cookstove," nor the Indian Department forms filled out in quadruplicate, nor the long-distance calls, nor the orders and back orders and enquiries to the wholesaler, nor the tracers sent out by the Union Steamship Company when the shipment went missing. Clearly, the stove had been cursed. For a moment Dad was tempted to join Johnny in a prolonged wail. Instead, he said through his teeth, "I'll write a letter to Mac & Mac."

Johnny, missing his cane, brought his hand flat down on the floor in a blow that must have tingled to his shoulder. "No, Young, your letters no good. I write Mac & Mac."

Dad grinned. "Okay, Johnny. I'll pick up your letter and mail it tomorrow, after I close for the day." He retrieved Johnny's cane, placed it within reach of the sufferer and retreated rapidly.

As he returned to the store with much more dignity than he had left, my father speculated on Johnny's letter. He knew that Johnny could write, because from time to time he received missives delivered by apprehensive-looking Native children. They were terse and extremely clear:

"Mr. Young
You send me rong tobacco.
Give kids other kind.
          I am
Mr. John Naismooht"

or

"Mr. Young
Glass for lamp you sell me no dam good.
He brake. Send 1 more.
    I am
Mr. John Naismooht"

The next day Dad closed up shop ten minutes early, so interested was he in seeing Johnny's masterpiece. Amid the shoulder-high nettles of the roadside, he paused to listen but there was no sound from Johnny's abode. When he opened the door he stepped smartly aside, but no trajectiles came at him. Johnny was seated at the table. On the oilcloth top, along with a block of dried seaweed, a sleeping cat, a pan of soaking trolling spoons and a pot of cold rice, sat a bottle of ink and a steel-nibbed pen, but Johnny was not writing. His hands were clasped and he looked utterly spent.

"Is your letter ready, Johnny?" asked my father, in what he hoped was a bland tone.

"No letter. No more paper."

Dad was surprised, since he had supplied Johnny with a small writing pad not more than a week before. His eyes roamed the room in search of that pad and found it on the floor, near Johnny's chair, in some three hundred shreds.

Johnny followed Dad's gaze and explained without a hint of apology, "I start letter to that Mac & Mac Company and I get mad again. Mebbe you send me some nother paper?"

"To tear up?"

"No, I write this time."

"I guess I'm a nut, but I'll send another pad over with Joshua. I'll pick up your letter tomorrow. Good night, Johnny."

The next day Day did not close shop early and he sauntered to Johnny's house. He had an envelope in his pocket but very little hope that he would find anything to put in it. Inside the house there were no signs of violence. Johnny was bent over a half-filled page and looked up almost absently to say, "How you spell goddam?" Dad wrote his version on a scrap of paper and handed it to Johnny who compared it with his script and scratched in a change.

"Are you just about ready to have your letter mailed, Johnny?"

"Not ready yet. I write this letter very strong, very strong. You go now, Young. I make finish tomorrow."

My father came home and told the family that we might as well expect him to be late to dinner every night that week.

On his next trip to the bridge, Dad stopped short of the fourth building, in amazement. There, in the doorway, basking in the glow of the early evening sunshine, sat Johnny, a beatific smile upon his face, a kindly greeting upon his lips. "Good evening, Mr. Young. You are a good man for come to Johnny. I have letter here for you send to Mac & Mac." In his shirt pocket he separated his epistle from a lumber bill and cigarette papers and handed it over to Dad. "You think this good, strong letter, Mr. Young?"

Dad opened the sheet and read:

"Dear Mac & Mac

I wait from March for my stove. He come July 17 — I try to set up. No legs come. I say damn. I look all over for legs and I say holly God damn. The Indian Agent pay for stove with legs. So now you send legs right away quick. If you don't send legs you come Port Simpson and get this stove no legs out my house. I call police but they gone for canry.

I am

Mr. John Naismooht

p.s. Don't send legs. This day I find legs in clean out ashes part of stove."

"You think that strong letter, Mr. Young?" Johnny asked again.

"I do. I certainly do, Johnny," said Dad with conviction. "But you don't really want me to mail it, do you?"

"What else you do with letter that take three day to write? You put in mail tonight."

My father mailed the letter that night.

CHAPTER 30

Slavery

JOHNNY NAISMOOHT WAS the fiercest Native I ever knew, though five hundred Tsimshian were my neighbours. My memories are mostly of people like Charlie Abbot who came to our house, as surely as the fourth of July rolled around, to present Mother with a bouquet of roses and tiger lilies and peonies from his garden, because she had once described Independence Day in the United States to him and he thought that she was homesick on that day; or Joshua Moody who sat by the hour on a wheelbarrow in front of the store with my little brother, carving cedar chunks into boats for him; or David Johnson, in whose store of novelties and knickknacks I shopped for my parents' birthday gifts while he waited patiently and cheerfully for me to examine every item of his stock; or the choirmaster whose studious manner would have graced a university, or our customers in general, who transacted their business with a natural courtesy and dignity. I did know one fierce woman. She was famous in particular for her row with the Wales Island Cannery manager. She ended it by throwing eleven salmon at him — she was a remarkably good shot with a salmon. But from those days until now I have been unable to reconcile the gentle people of our village with the fragments of the Native past that came to us in stories of treachery and barbarity. Still, there stood the guest-house posts in all their horror.

It was a pleasant enough site that the chief had selected for her guest-house, at least half a century before my childhood. It faced the sunsets across water and ended at the rise of a green hill. It was still level except for the toppled log beams that lay parallel to one another, well wrapped in grasses, but children never played there. Only four posts remained upright. They had been magnificent specimens of cedar when the chief's canoe towed them to that place. Though time had knocked them askew they still marked the four corners of what had been a great lodge.

At the potlatch that celebrated the beginning of construction, the chief lavished blankets and guns and grease upon her guests. She hurled a copper into the fire and finally, as the crowning magnificence, commanded that a bound slave be dropped to the bottom of each of the deep pits that had been dug as postholes. The upright cedar logs were then driven into place.

The Hudson's Bay people estimated in the 1840s that one-third of the coast's Native population were slaves, which means that one-third of the men, women and children could be sold, abused or killed according to their owners' whims. Of that number some had been captured but most had been born in slavery. Slaves ranked with coppers as the most valuable of trade goods and were bartered from California to Taku. At Fort Simpson the slave trade had an adverse effect on the fur trade and was accordingly reported in the journals:

August 15, 1839 — "The Stikine people, notwithstanding the high prices they are getting still seem loath to part with all their furs. probably they hold them up in hopes of getting slaves, who sell very high where they go to trade and yield a much higher profit than any other articles they take."

April 12, 1862 — "The Stikenes traded 3 Indians who were slaves here to the Tsimshians, mother, daughter and son belonging to a tribe in the interior of Stikine upriver."

There was a variation of the slave trade that took place annually on the Nass when the tribes assembled for the oolichan fishery. Then the half-starved people from the Interior brought babies to sell.

Slaves were not only bought and sold — they were stolen. Twice, in the year 1840, Tsimshian got possession of Kyganie slaves. In the first instance the Hudson's Bay factor stepped in to prevent the ever-smouldering Tsimshian-Kyganie feud from flashing into a conflagration. He paid "the value of a beaver skin of rum" to the Tsimshian and returned the slave to the Kyganie. The Tsimshian perceived that they could not lose at this game and six months later pounced on an unfortunate slave who had made his escape from the Kyganie. They held him for a ten-blanket ransom. The Company remained aloof from this transaction and the Kyganie replied by capturing two Tsimshian who were travelling in the choppy water west of Birnie Island. The only ending we have to this story is the next day's journal entry: "5 Tsimshian [canoes] off after the Kyganies."

Of all the sneaky methods of acquiring slaves the most abhorrent seems to have been the one reported in 1838: "One of the Queen Charlotte Islands' Indians got a Tsimshian girl for a wife when he was here some time ago [and] no sooner did he get home than the scoundrel sold her for a slave."

An enterprising Native had no need to barter or steal. He could procure slaves in the time-honoured manner, by violence. In the summer of 1842 Haida canoes were on the prowl for captives and the fort people did their best to keep the journal abreast of the action. They recorded that the chief, Nislameek, was heading for Tongass with a small war party to find the Haida who had carried off his daughter. Two days later: "Late last night Nislameek arrived with his men from Tongass and brought the deceased Coukolt's wife captive instead of his daughter who was captured by the Kyganie Indians."

Within two weeks:

August 12, 1842 — "The old Tsimshian chief, Neeselcanooks, went off yesterday towards Pearl Harbour ... accompanied by his two wives and two men and one of their wives and was fallen upon this morning by a marauding party of Queen Charlotte Island Indians who took away one of the old man's wives and the other woman and killed and cut off the head of one of the men which they also took with them and made off."

August 16 — "Neeselcanooks started for Tongass with two canoes to endeavor to get the Tongass people to use their influence to find out who took his wife and get her back."

August 22 — "Neeselcanooks returned without finding out by whom she was taken. The Kyganie people deny any knowledge of the affair."

September 1, 1842 — "The Sabassa people who arrived yesterday bring intelligence of Neeselcanook's wife who was taken [a] short [time] ago. It appears the marauders were a party of Cumshewas or their neighbors from the S. end of Queen Charlottes Islands. The woman is represented to be stripped naked and in miserable plight. A Skidegate Indian who had known her family ... happened to be there, took pity upon her and gave her his own blanket."

And years later:

April 15, 1853 — "Two more canoes ... returned from a marauding excurtion to the South'd ... brought two Prisoners i.e. slaves; He says that he killed four of the same people."

May 14, 1855 — "Niswaymot arrived with 2 canoes from his sea otter hunt. He got into a row with the Kake Indians and was wounded with his brother and one more Indian in his party. He has brought a boy that he stole on his voyage, I suppose from the Kake people."

August 19, 1855 — "We learned this day that Nistuil and his canoe of Massets have brought 9 Nisqually women as prisoners with them."

In fact, one tribe of Haida, the Cumshewa, had the reputation of neither fishing nor hunting but of making its livelihood by capturing and trading slaves.

The conditions under which slaves lived varied from tribe to tribe and from owner to owner. Our best account of northwest coast slavery is contained in *The Adventures and Sufferings of John R. Jewitt, Captive Among the Nootka 1803-1805*. True, Jewitt was an exceptional slave, being an Englishman and a blacksmith, and his owner, Chief Maquinna, was an exceptional master, but *The Adventures* gives us an idea of the attitude toward slaves. In many ways their living conditions were no worse than those of the lowlier members of the tribe. However, inconsistencies made their existence precarious. Sometimes Maquinna treated Jewitt as a well-loved son; sometimes he left him to suffer through cold weather in near nakedness. Always death lurked within sight. In Jewitt's case it was the tribesmen who would have killed him. Usually it was the chief who destroyed a slave's life to glorify his own or to atone for a wrong however unrelated to the slave. At Fort Simpson the crisp journal entries softened noticeably when recounting the state of slaves.

August 29, 1837 — "Seix and Quatkie returned from Sabassa with a number of the poor Newittie women whom the Scoundrel Sabassa men took Slaves during the Summer. The poor Wretches, one of them in particular, the daughter of a A Chief and the Wife of a Chief, imploring Capt. McNeill … to trade her and take her back to her friends, When she and another were ordered to carry up some boxes from the canoe and another who had probably been a slave before, showing them how to do it, their looks poor wretches were pitiable in the extreme."

Under the aboriginal system of reprisals, the slave was a very handy fellow to have around. As the aftermath of a rum feast, the great Chief Legaic was shot in the hand. For obscure reasons, probably political, he was not able to take revenge upon the guilty tribe. For two months he brooded over the shame that had come upon him. Then he cancelled out the whole matter by shooting his slave in the hand. That slave was comparatively lucky:

August 28, 1839 — "One of the Tongass men is very ill and not expected to recover. He and his friends attribute his sickness to one of his slaves having given him bad medicine or conjured him. They have had the poor wretch of a slave some days tied with his hands behind his back with the intention of killing him as a sacrifice should his Master die or perhaps before, should the whim take them."

The changes in Native life that had been put in motion by the establishment of Fort Simpson in 1834 were like the outside waters of a whirlpool, circling imperceptibly at first, gaining in force during the 1840s and 1850s and spinning furiously into the vortex around the end of the 1860s when Father Duncan's influence was strong. Slavery was one of the practices that whirled out of sight forever about that time. And yet, in the Port Simpson I knew, there were old people who were outcasts — they had been slaves half a century before. Dad referred to them as "your mother's Indians." Certainly Mother felt responsible for them as no one else did, and when she did not see them about for long periods of time she went to their shacks. She never talked much about what she found there but when she returned she took a bath with carbolic soap and washed her hair and changed all her clothing. "They can't help themselves," said Mother, "they have been completely abject for sixty or seventy years and now they are feeble and cold and hungry, too. No Tsimshian goes near them."

CHAPTER 31

Status of Women

SCARCELY DISTINGUISHABLE from slavery, in the lodges about the fort, was the status of women. Chiefs had slaves and the rest of the men had wives.

A girl was subject to her father's bidding until he sold her in marriage (though the negotiated gifts were never considered a cost price), perhaps while she was still a child. When she took up her position as wife she was subject to her husband's bidding. Mostly he bade her do the work that was beneath his dignity. She loaded and unloaded his canoe, cleaned the fish he caught, skinned the animals he trapped, made gear and clothing and mats and baskets and she carried. She carried home firewood from distances of two miles; she carried baskets and cedar mat rolls full of possessions and cedar boxes full of food. Among the people past middle age, she was still carrying in the 1920s when I would watch a gas boat land at the wharf and its occupant couple make their way up the wharf approach that was one-third of a mile in length. The man ambled along, completely unencumbered, while a few paces behind him his wife laboured under a load of sacks and suitcases.

In the early days women prepared food for their men; if the men were away on an expedition, the women and children subsisted on snacks and cooked almost nothing. In day-to-day life families ate together but feasts were usually all-male affairs. Lavish quantities of food were offered so that there was always some left to take home to the women and children. There were some feasts that included the entire clan and to these women were admitted.

For those who did not own slaves, women often had to serve as scapegoats in matters of reprisals:

September 13, 1857 — "A large Rum feast was given to the Indians by some of Cacas' people ... about 2 p.m. a poor old woman was deliberately shot dead by a young scamp by the name of Clah on account of one of his friends being hurt by a stick of wood falling on him."

Marriages were easy, comfortable arrangements for the husbands:

December 4, 1852 — "The *Cannibal's* Eldest daughter, Dag, died. She was formerly Wife to 'Legaic' but discarded."

March 9, 1858 — "Two Tongass canoes arrived, Ibbets and his gang of Wives and Children."

Marriage was a less comfortable arrangement for the wives who could no more discard their husbands than slaves could discard their masters. And should a wife displease her husband he took care to disfigure her, before dismissing her, so that she could not remarry. As for polygamy, it does not seem to have been distasteful to the women, probably because it was usually the chief who could afford multiple spouses, and being one of any number of wives to a chief brought distinction and some security. We lack statistics for the Fort Simpson area but we know that in the year 1803, the illustrious Chief Maquinna of the Nootka had nine wives. Women of the tribe were not regarded as trade goods as slaves were. However, the Natives were gift-givers, thus they showed goodwill and welcomed strangers; the favourite welcoming gift was a daughter or a wife. Some such gifts were made on a temporary basis, others were permanent.

The women did have one defence, which was still evident when I knew them. It was a silent and granite obstinacy. When they stiffened into it their faces lost any trace of expression, their bodies set in heavy lines and they became, in every sense, immovable.

It seems that grandmothers had no less responsibility than mothers for the children, but in turn the children, from six years of age onward, took some responsibility for the grandparents. There was no trace of the empty-nest syndrome in a Native village. Aged women performed the least strenuous tasks. Eventually they did nothing but tend the fires in the lodges where they lived in perpetual smoke (there were no chimneys, only gaps in the roof boards to serve this purpose), so that numbers of them groped through their last years in blindness.

Not all the women were near-slaves. There were women who owned slaves:

July 28, 1837 — "A Canoe of Kyganie people arrived in the evening with 33 beaver belonging to the woman named Howan who seems to be the head of the party."

There are a few other references to women who headed their clans and we know of one Tsimshian woman who occupied the highest chieftainship. Amor De Cosmos was aboard HMS *Sparrowhawk* when she put into Fort Simpson in 1867. He wrote at length about the Indian village for his *Victoria Colonist* and of the Chieftainess Shoudal whom he reported to be head of the Tsimshian and living in a house that was clean and tastefully arranged, in part, with European furniture.

Then there were the close female relatives of a chief — wives, daughters, sisters — who enjoyed honour and servitude from the tribe. After witchcraft and potlatches and canoes had all but disappeared from the Native village of Port Simpson, the missionary ladies of the Crosby Girls' Home were dismayed to find their routines completely scrambled by a new student. The girls were no longer dressed when the breakfast bell rang because they were engaged in lacing the high boots, braiding the long hair and buttoning the pinafore of the new girl — she was a princess and had never performed these tasks for herself and had no intention of ever doing so. The other girls were even more distressed than the princess when democratic rules were enforced.

As late as the 1930s a young teacher in the Indian Day School was brought to her knees by the ancient system of rank. For the Christmas concert she had chosen a musical play, "The Princess of London," which had a few solo parts and could accommodate the entire school enrollment as courtiers. The children, every one of them full of rhythm and music, practised the songs with gusto. Then came the day of assigning roles. For the part of the princess the teacher selected a little girl who had a good voice and a flair for acting. At the next practice the young star stood immovable, her eyes cast down, uttering not one sound. The courtiers refused to bow, the prince steadfastly did not proffer his arm to the princess and the rousing opening song of the chorus was delivered as a dispirited hum. The following practice was even glummer. Then the teacher took her problem to various townspeople.

"What does *Amelia* do in the play?" asked an old-timer.

"She's in the back row of the chorus."

"That just won't do. Amelia is the highest princess in the village."

The next day Amelia, stately at age ten, was made a queen upon a throne, centre stage, and the whole cast burst into song and action.

CHAPTER 32

"Singing and Going-on"

THE DAY SCHOOL CONCERT had to compete with many entertainments for mid-winter was the one time when all the people were in the village and was, by tradition, the theatrical season as well as the social season. Their own concerts were popular. They had put away their masks and rattles and given up their dances and what the factors termed jugglery, in favour of solos and monologues and skits performed in the English manner with Tsimshian undertones. As well as being natural musicians they were natural mimics and comedians.

Only once did I regret attending a Native concert. I persuaded my father to take me and we found seats well to the front in the crowded hall. The band played the "Light Cavalry Overture," the singers rendered solos and duets, girls in white dresses went through the figures of a drill and then there was a hum of expectation as two men came on stage for a skit. They had no special costumes and no props and they spoke Tsimshian entirely, but within seconds I was uncomfortable and after the first minute I knew beyond a doubt that they were enacting a fur-buying scene. One actor represented the trapper, and the other my father. He made his identity known simply by his stance and the way he moved his head and hands. The audience tittered. Then the actor inspected the imaginary fur, neglecting none of my father's mannerisms; he passed the palm of his hand over his forehead, he paced, he stopped suddenly to look again, he shook the fur and pulled its length through his fingers, and in the audience shawls jiggled up and down and mackinaws swayed in almost silent laughter. The two actors discussed price rather sadly and then my-father-on-the-stage seized the pelt and, bending it double, blew into the fur. He solemnly spoke words that could have meant only—*not prime* and everyone in the hall with the exception of Dad and I rocked forward and back and groaned with mirth. We were able to laugh with restraint. Since then I have often wondered why our society failed to utilize the indigenous peoples' highly developed theatrical skills. After all, Chief Dan George as a good actor was only one of thousands.

Partially replacing the potlatch was an institution known as the Indian sale. It was a pale shadow of its predecessor but to a little white girl entering the hall it was a sensory explosion. The door was still closing behind me when the steamy heat hit my face and the odours pierced my throat — fish and smoke, deer skin and smoke, bodies and fish, iodine and salt of the sea, molasses, twenty-five cent perfume, tobacco, gumboots, wet woollen mittens. The sounds of the crowd were low and even of tone and the auctioneer's voice rose easily above them to wheedle and urge in Tsimshian and English, with a Native deliberation that would have dismayed a rapid-fire, English auctioneer. He stood on a stage with the goods piled about him. An assistant handed him a tablecloth embroidered in green and yellow and pink, and when that disappeared into the audience, a block of dried seaweed; fish eggs dried to a beige colour on evergreen branches; a lamp complete with rose-painted shade; salmon, smoked to a fire red; oolichan grease in a five-gallon gasoline can; a raisin cake; a cedar bark basket in the characteristic coarse weave of the Tsimshian; heavily beaded moccasins; and what I had come to bid on, a shoe-box full of smoked oolichans, stiff and hard as kindling sticks but most deliciously black-brown and oily.

Sometimes the sale took the form of a bazaar with the wares displayed on long tables. Then I could poke a block of seaweed to discover how tightly packed it was, or run my hand over the crocheted doily that was sewn onto blue tissue paper, or walk right up to a cedar bark mat to test the smoothness of the weave.

Another descendant of the potlatch was the Native feast. When my parents first came to Port Simpson feasts were based on the spirit of the potlatch if not, at times and surreptitiously, the substance. In my early childhood a few white people were sometimes invited, or more accurately, summoned, to special feasts. The day of the event, a well-dressed delegation of three or more tribesmen would arrive at the store to issue the invitation. Sometimes it included my sister and me. When we arrived at the hall, while Ruth and I were adjusting our noses to the heavy odours, Mother and Dad were whisked off to places near the head of the table and we were relegated to the far end where the children ate and played and peeled Japanese oranges. We did not eat much because the food tasted strange to us but we peeled oranges along with the best of the little Tsimshian and when the speeches started I fell asleep with them, much to my sister's consternation.

I never intended to sleep through the speeches. Even though they were in Tsimshian and very long, I was intrigued by the tingling sensations they evoked in me. Almost any Tsimshian used his voice masterfully. He was in complete command of the singing or sobbing words, of the rising inflection and the quickening tempo, of the dramatic pause, of the suddenly lowered voice, and had no need for the shouting and gesticulating that characterized the English speechmaking of that era. I drifted along on the flow of words until some trick of the speaker's voice rippled a thrill down my spine and

I opened my eyes to make sure that Ruth was still beside me and then returned to my slow ride on sound.

When the night was late I was roused to be helped into coat and toque and hoisted onto my father's shoulder. All around us women were loading their head handkerchiefs with morsels of food from the table. Mother took some, too, in a white linen handkerchief brought for the purpose — it would have been a slight to the host to take nothing. Then the sleeping babies were secured within their mothers' fringed shawls by some marvel of folding, and we all went out into the shock of the winter night.

The Hudson's Bay people of the previous century recorded snatches of what they saw and heard of the Tsimshian entertainments. Their methodical classifications and literal translations often broke down before the intricate net of songs and dances and feasts and potlatches and atonements and commemorations and initiations and rites and shamanism and excursions into the supernatural, but few other non-Natives were ever permitted to observe as closely this mesh upon which Native life was woven.

A smattering of journal entries reveals some of the diverse purposes of the events:

May 20, 1837 — "A grand feast is to be given in memory of the late Cacas by his brothers when the Indians all arrive, and the most of the Indians are said to be holding up their furs to then to buy liquor to contribute to the entertainment."

Eleven days later, when the name Cacas had been bestowed upon the new chief: "Cacas wishes to set himself up as a man of great consequence, to effect which giving these feasts is generally one of the means employed."

June 2 — "Early this morning Sabassa and his brothers with a party of their people arrived from Pearl Harbour and traded 12 beaver and land otters and returned again to Pearl Harbour immediately to be present at Cacas's feast and ball. Several of the Tsimshians who are encamped here also went by invitation and returned again in the evening. It appears it did not turn out such a grand affair as was expected. There was a lack of both food and drink for the number of guests invited."

A new chief in 1866 seems to have "set himself up" more successfully: "Neastohyah, the New Chief of the Keenakangeak has been giving away the property of the deceased chief Allaimlakah and a Keg of Liquor of his own containing ten Gallons. So Now he takes the name of WeShakes."

At the time of a disaster the gatherings, beside commemorating, could soothe and comfort a disturbed populace:

March 11, 1853 — "Two of Nistoack's people were drowned by a Canoe upsetting. They had been away hunting Seal on one of the Islands that lie off Browns passage and had killed 40 which made the Canoe so deep that she capsized. There were 4 men in the Canoe, two reached the shore and two were drowned. It caused quite a ferment in the Camp for a while when the news first arrived. Nistoacks traded a large quantity of Tobacco and invited all the Indians of the Camp to have a smoke at his house."

Then there were the lavish housewarmings. As the Native camps about the fort grew into a village, houses were erected and celebrated at close intervals. Mr. McNeill made some observations regarding a housewarming potlatch that lasted for seventeen days:

February 6, 1853 — "The Big face man is making great preparations to entertain his guests, and the Tsimshians are [in] high glee."

February 7 — "The Tongass, Sabassa and Two Canoes of Nassgars arrived at the Big face man's house."

February 13 — "The Big face Chief burnt a quantity of Oil in his new house this day, 'which was a house warming.' All the Tsimshians Chiefs were present. They threw a number of large 'Coppers' into the fire together with Muskets, Blankets, Elk Skins, Duffil Blkts trimmed with pearl Buttons etc. The common people also destroyed much property. Several Slaves were taken to the house with the intention of killing them, but were spared, and no lives were taken."

February 15 — "The Indians all engaged at the Big face Chief's house, he has given out to them about 310 Boxes of Small fish Oil and Berries, 'so we hear'."

February 19 — "Indians engaged in the Big face man's house. He or his people are giving away Cotton etc., Tomorrow he gives away Elk Skins, Coppers, etc. to his guests. We hear that he has 500 Elk Skins ready to give away."

February 21 — "A large quantity of Cotton, Tin Kettles, Elk skins etc. were given away at the Big face Chief's house. 'Three difft.' lots of Cotton reached from Elgaic's to the Big face Chief's house."

February 23 — "The strangers who were invited here by the Big face Chief took their departure, he having finished his ceremonies etc. He and his people have destroyed and given away a vast quantity of property. Chatsinas, Sabassas, Nassgars, Tongass and Lacatte were the strangers that started this day."

Many functions had no purpose other than enjoyment. In 1861 while the fort people were celebrating our midwinter festival, the Natives were celebrating theirs. There were some similarities:

December 22 — "Shudal gave an entertainment at her house this evening say dancing and sleight-of-hand work."

December 27 — "Shudal gave away to the chiefs some 300 Elk Skins and blankets also 6 coppers."

December 31 — "Indians dancing and feasting and giving away property."

There was nothing in the white man's life that corresponded to the grim initiations and the rituals of the secret societies.

May 15, 1841 — "The Sabassa Indians had today a grand

ceremony though to us a most disgusting one. It began in the following manner. The body of a man who died last night was carried into the bush — instantly one of their principal chiefs commenced devouring his remains — when the monster had his dirty belly [full] of this he fell at Eating the living-man or woman that came his way. [They] had to undergo the painful operation of having a mouthful or two torn from [their] arms. As soon as he was done of his Butchery a second followed his example only that he confined himself to the flesh of the living."

Today, many anthropologists have come to the conclusion that Indians did not actually eat human flesh. The men who were on the scene at the time felt differently:

February 29, 1860 — "This afternoon we had a Cannibal exhibition in front of the Fort performed by a Kitsamackalen Indian."

March 3 — "This afternoon 4 cannibals had a feast from Taulth's slave who died a few days since."

December 9, 1856 — "Medicine work still going on in the camp, 'dog eating etc.' "

There were and are no doubts about dogeating. The frenzied, or purportedly frenzied candidate who had been sequestered in the woods without food for days came ravening into the village, seized a dog, pulled it apart and ate thereof.

Cannibalism came under the heading of "medicine work," which covered a large territory, some of it well shaded from white men's eyes. The more beautiful aspects of aboriginal life also dwelt there, the creativity and arts and rich mythology:

December 9, 1852 — "Indians making 'Medicine.' The 'Big Crow' arrived this morning. It was formed on a Canoe and resembled that bird very much. The Medicine Bird was taken into Elgaic's house."

At the very centre of medicine work was the witch doctor with his ministrations, spells and incantations and not far removed was preventive medicine:

July 31, 1839 — "The Queen Charlotte Sound Indians it appears have exerted themselves less hunting and trading than formerly which is attributed to their employing a great deal of their time singing and dancing, conjuring to keep off some sickness attended with great mortality which is said to prevail among the Natives farther to the southward."

During the devastating smallpox epidemic of 1862 — "Medicine work going on all over the camp and a piece of stick with red medicine on it stuck on top of every house. This of course will keep the smallpox from entering the house."

Somewhere in this area were the mystical and psychical experiences that were not phenomena to the coast peoples. It is certain that the Natives of the last century had not yet smothered their psychic abilities as completely as we have. Said Hamilton Moffatt in 1859: "Indians still at the Nuckuuck. Legaic's daughter gone to the clouds."

It is equally certain that some of the mysticism was staged to achieve devious ends:

February 10, 1839 — "A considerable commotion among the Indians on account of a woman who is both a great Chieftess and a great Medicine woman being either dead or dieing. It is said she was once dead before but came to life again."

February 11 — "The great Medicine Woman who was said to be dead yesterday it seems has come to life again. She reports having seen while dead a number of the Indians who have died for sometime back and that they asked her with great surprise what had taken her to where they were and desired her to return again and that some other personages she saw in the other world had laid an injunction upon her to take another husband a young man. She has already two husbands, brothers but they are both like herself advanced in years."

CHAPTER 33

Survival

DEATH OF A MORE permanent kind than the chief's lurked in every Native camp. It pounced on the feeble, the hungry and the near naked when winter assailed the lodges. At Fort Simpson, in the harsh weather of 1852, fifteen Natives had died of exposure before the middle of December. European diseases such as influenza, that sent the fort people to bed, killed the Natives outright, and smallpox tore whole families and clans and sometimes whole communities right out of existence.

While there were always many women in the camps whose long hair had been cut to form veils over their faces to signify mourning, cures were wrought, also. The medicine man used legerdemain, prescriptions, dances, rattles and chants with some success, and the people had their household remedies, as commonplace as the bottles of aspirin in today's medicine cabinets. Instead of the mustard plaster, they used cedar bark from the fire. For a healing application they used warm, roasted frog that had been cleaned and pounded and spread with fir pitch. The skin of the frog was considered even more efficacious and was reserved for serious illnesses.

Death came from the sea, for the Natives respected their canoes more than the elements and seldom allowed violent weather to interrupt their trips to potlatches in other villages, to the seal hunting grounds far northward, to the sea otter waters to the west, to their fishing grounds or their favourite sites for drying seaweed, hunting, trapping or pursuing any of a dozen other occupations. No other deaths desolated the entire village as drownings did and the people made desperate attempts, in the same weather that had taken the lives, to recover the bodies. Apparently a lost body to them meant a soul lost forever and was an almost unbearable thought.

The Natives' other element, the forest, could also bring death. Their usual method of obtaining cedar for a canoe, a totem pole or the wide boards of a lodge was to bring the giant tree down by setting a fire at its base. They had small tools but their logging was accomplished more by ingenuity than force and the trees sometimes took revenge upon them.

At the very time nineteenth-century coastal peoples were fighting off death by disease and accident, they were embracing death by warfare. (Twentieth-century populations all over the world seem to have suffered from the same inconsistency.) Conflict between the tribes was a state rather than an event. It was like a fire, lit in ancient times and kept smouldering through the ages by the heaping of fresh grievances upon it. At unpredictable times it blazed up, hot and red, in skirmishes and raids and massacres. The factors wrote hundreds of observations, as pointed and clear as icicles, concerning the fighting that popped and sputtered outside their stockade. They leave us with the feeling that although some enmities were deeper than others, there were no two tribes on the coast who would not shoot at one another at the drop of an insult or less. An account of the hostilities is like a roll-call of the tribes. During 1836 and 1837 alone, the Tongass, a band of Tlingit, were embroiled in turn with the Tsimshian, the Stikine, the Skidegate and the Chilkat—casualties: twenty-four killed, an uncounted number wounded. In those same years the Tsimshian took on, beside the Tongass, the Skidegate and the Kyganie (both bands of Haida) and the Stikine. Meanwhile, all the other tribes were equally active.

Intertribal battles did not account for all the bloodshed; division of the tribes into clans and bands and totems and extended family units made for internal warfare, and it seems that the Natives were not too fussy about the tribal relationships of those receiving their musket balls; for example:

May 11, 1839 — Kyganies came to the fort to trade ammunition and reported "that the Kyganie Indians who left this place some time ago quarreled among themselves and that the great woman Scutsay[,] her brother and three of her slaves were killed."

A month later some Tongass arrived with the news "that Cape Fox Indians have been fighting among themselves, and that Jack the chief and four women have been killed."

And at the end of that summer, "One of the Canoes of Tongass people who arrived yesterday after trading their meat went off. As they were going off they got into a quarrel with some of their own Tribe who were ashore, they fired upon each other and kept up the fire from both sides till the canoe was out of reach."

Then there was the rather confusing affair of September 1841, that began as a Tsimshian-Haida engagement and ended as a Tsimshian-Tsimshian shoot-out. It started when the Espokelot, the Tsimshian whose home territory was the country around the mouth of the Skeena River, and a band of Haida quarrelled, to no one's surprise, over a trading transaction and "... had recourse to firearms and exchanged several Shots on both Sides — and are still hard at action at this moment (11 o'clock p.m.) whether any are killed or not, cannot learn, but had occular proof of 2 or 3 getting broken arms & legs." There was little sleep at Fort Simpson that night for trade guns peppered the camps until noon the next day. By this time the Tongass had joined the fray because a Haida ball, intended for a Tsimshian, had wounded a Tongass man. This complicated the factor's attempt to negotiate a ceasefire but by noon he had arranged an acceptable three-cornered peace and the combatants threw themselves, as vigorously as they had fought, into the ritual of the blowing of down and feathers upon each others' heads and the making of long speeches.

The moment the last word had been uttered the Espokelot and the Haida rushed back to their bargaining. The trade was lively for the Tsimshian were eager for the Queen Charlotte Island potatoes and the Haida, their ammunition now depleted, were anxious for powder and shot.

At this point, Cacas, the Tsimshian chief who ruled over the north end of the Tsimshian Peninsula, came upon the scene. With horror he and his band watched the Espokelot handing over ammunition to the arch enemies of all Tsimshian. They registered their protest by firing at the Espokelot who dug into their trade goods to fire back. "While this was going on," says Mr. Work, "the poor Haidas made off with themselves (it being perfectly dark at the time) in 2 canoes leaving 8 behind and a quantity of potatoes which the Tsimshians soon took possession of— the number killed & wounded as far [as] we could learn, 3 Tsimshians & one Tongass wounded & 3 Q.C.I.rs killed."

While trading quarrels brought on many a bloody clash, the Native code that made revenge mandatory accounted for even more. It bound the tribes hopelessly in chains of atrocities. Every outrage called for a retaliation, which called for a counter-retaliation, which called for ... until we have a proliferation of entries similar to:

September 24, 1841— (Two days after the Haida "made off with themselves") — "All quiet among the Indians — one of the bodies whom we buried yesterday had the head cut off and Scalped and disfigured in many respects by the Tsimshians — a Tsimshian Chief who visited Queen Charlotte's Islands a few years ago was shot and his body mangled in this inhuman manner by the identical person."

August 24, 1840 — "The Cogueles came upon a party of Sabassa Indians (28 in number) who had been 'Sea-Otter' hunting and cut the throats of the whole of them as a retaliation of the great haul they kidnapped of Newitties 2 years ago."

Witchcraft or suspected witchcraft could precipitate a fight any day.

June 24, 1856 — "An Indian was treacherously shot in the bush, he was a Medicine man & was *supposed* to been the cause of the death of a young woman. His friends and the murderer's friends at each other in the evening, by *understanding*."

And gambling, even in 1842, was a violent sport:

"Two Indians gambling quarreled, a Spachaloid and one of Neeskamek's men. Two shots fired which wounded 2 men and a woman. Another woman had her head fractured with a stone and died. At present firing occasional shots in order to show that they are on their guard."

Slaves were an inflammatory element of coast life. Tribes from north, west and south and from the east by way of the rivers converged on Fort Simpson, bringing their slaves with them. Painful meetings and desperate rescue attempts were inevitable. In one case the Hudson's Bay Company stopped the altercation just short of shooting but also just short of a happy ending.

In the early 1830s the Skidegates had attacked a party of Tongass. They had killed all the men but had taken the little son of one of their victims, as a slave. On a day in May 1837, some Tongass people discovered the boy in the Haida camp at Fort Simpson and set about rescuing him. Guns bristled on both sides. The Skidegate had a strategy for such occasions. They launched their canoes, the boy confined in one, leaving a war party on shore to cover their retreat. As the Tongass prepared to shoot into the canoes and the war party prepared to shoot into the Tongass, the fort rolled out its big guns and promised to send a ball into whichever side fired the first shot.

Meantime, the Skidegate canoes paddled out of musket range.

Mr. McNeill's theory that women were the root of all west coast evil was upheld from time to time by small woman-instigated wars. Austine's face (before it was mutilated) may not have launched a thousand ships but it certainly sent forth a few canoes. In July of 1837, a party of Tongass arrived with news of their battle with the Port Stewart Chilkats. They told of eight Tongass and fifteen Port Stewart warriors killed. It was not Mr. McNeill but Mr. Work who wrote up the report:

"It appears that the quarrel and all this bloodshed was occasioned by a woman named Austine, who had been the wife of Quintal, one of our men, sometime. She had a quarrel with a Port Stewart or Cape Fox Indian about two blankets which she affirmed he had cheated her out of, and about 8 or 10 months ago at the fort here she ripped open his cheek with a knife. In order to make up the matter, her friends (for she has powerful connections), had paid him blankets and other property and he appeared satisfied but it was only in appearance, for, on meeting her with her friends — some time ago he attempted to cut open her Cheek as she had done his, her relations interfered to prevent him and a quarrel ensued in which he was shot. His friends took up the cause and this battle and the loss of so many lives have been the result. The affair is not yet settled — Austine and 2 other women are said to have been taken captive by the opposite party the other two were stripped naked and released but she was retained to be cut and mangled and treated without mercy as the cause of so much mischief."

While a war could simmer for months, completely disrupting the lives of two tribes, it was not as horrifying as the single, hit-and-run canoe raid that was the specialty of coast peoples. Once, an elderly woman of our village was moved by my size and age, four or five, to reach back into her memory for the bright pieces of *her* fifth year and to show them to my sister and me. The most vivid were of a Haida raid on a fishing camp — of her mother grabbing her off the beach where she was playing; of the sight, over her mother's shoulder, of black canoes with black paddles sweeping around the point; of her hiding place between two logs, in the woods behind the camp; of the long and silent, cold, hungry, frightened wait for her mother to come back for her; of the return to the still camp with the other women and children; of the finding of their smashed canoes, their plundered boxes; of the three bodies of their men rolling in the light surf where she had played; of the wailing through the night. Her memories were corroborated by many a Fort Simpson journal note and letter:

"A short time ago a marauding party of Haidas from south end of Queen Charlotte Island fell treacherously on a party of Cape Fox Indians, killed 10 men and carried off all the women and children and took their property."

"3 canoes arrived from Victoria and Nanaimo, 17 days … They killed 4 men and brought 4 women prisoners belonging to the Kwakiutls."

"Yesterday a canoe of MacKenzie's people arrived from a war party. They brought 3 women prisoners also 2 heads."

It is plain to see that the depleted and deserted villages cannot be blamed wholly on the white man's diseases. Not quite so clear is the proportion of blame that should be attached to the white man's liquor.

In Fort Simpson's first decade rum rippled through the Native camps, if not gently, at least in a somewhat controlled flow. The factor kept a firm hand on the shut-off valve and used it occasionally. Those were the days when the Company traded liquor officially and accepted some responsibility for its consequences. In recording the case of a double murder the journal keeper ended with a contrite note: "Rum I regret to add has been the cause of these 2 peoples' deaths."

The second decade brought the Russian American Company-Hudson's Bay Company pact that ended their sale of liquor to Natives. It did not do away with rum in the villages — there were a few Boston Traders and other ships dispensing liquor and there was the odd Hudson's Bay Company "gift" of rum to a chief. But the flow of spirits was reduced to a trickle and alcohol-induced atrocities were uncommon.

Then came the 1850s and the north coast peoples' discovery of Fort Victoria. Their canoes slipped down the Inside Passage, plundering as they went, and returned laden with prisoners, spoils, disease and whiskey. When the sale of liquor to Natives was banned in Victoria, the tribesmen simply moved on across the Strait of Juan de Fuca to American territory where whiskey and loot were easy to come by. Before the 1850s ended, Victoria discovered the north coast peoples. It loosed its fleet of rapacious tangle sellers upon them and simultaneously the canoes and the sloops gushed alcohol that turned Fort Simpson into a sea of violence. In those times, every night in the village was like a night of modern television programs; there were beatings and stonings and strangulations and axe attacks and drownings, natural or otherwise, and shootings and stabbings, but the blood was not ketchup.

By the 1866 ending of the journals the flood seemed to have crested and the men-of-war to have reduced the flow, at least sporadically, but the horror of what had happened to the Natives is still with us.

PART VIII

Departures

CHAPTER 34

The Life and Times of My Father's 74

MY FATHER'S MOTORCYCLE was once held captive by a totem pole. But then, my father's Harley-Davidson led a rather unusual life.

In the Vancouver showroom the dealer straightened himself into a human exclamation mark.

"You did say, 'our fastest model,' didn't you?"

My father nodded.

"And you did say, 'to travel government trails?' "

"Yes, but that's just the official term for four-foot-wide dirt roads. I want it for going over wooden walks built above the muskeg, too, and for the paths on the Indian reservation."

"How do the cars manage?"

"There aren't any. My motorcycle will be the only vehicle within a radius of thirty miles."

"You must be very isolated."

"Certainly not. We have a boat from Vancouver once a week and telephone communication with Prince Rupert except when storms knock the line out. Say, this is a beautiful machine."

"Top of the line."

"I'll take it."

Even in the 1920s the dealer was not accustomed to doing

business in this manner — he dropped his fountain pen onto the battleship linoleum. Dad handed him cash to close the transaction and then, since he had run practically every type of gas engine that had ever powered a boat on the north coast, he asked casually, "How do you start the thing?" The dealer explained; Dad kicked mightily and roared off into Vancouver's traffic.

My father was a dignified, middle-aged speed demon. He operated the fastest motor boats that were available on the coast in those days, always at top speeds. He never slowed for a landing until he was within a breath of a crash. Mounted on the Harley-Davidson, he turned the throttle with enthusiasm. He shot out of the business section, through two residential districts and found himself in Shaughnessy Heights. In those days, Shaughnessy was Vancouver's undisputed seat of wealth and prestige. Opulent homes hid behind screens of shrubbery and streets formed a labyrinth of boulevards and crescents. Dad felt that he should pause and get his bearings but nothing in his marine experience had taught him how to stop a motor-cycle. As matrons with dogs on leashes scattered before him and chauffeurs and gardeners dropped their tools to stare, he tried one movable device after another within reach of his hands and feet. Though the machine reacted with surprising sounds and puffs of smoke he never did hit on the hand brake or the ignition switch. He drove around crescents until his Harley ran out of gas and Shaughnessy Heights was in a state of shock.

When my father and the Harley-Davidson reached Port Simpson, the whole population turned out to witness the motorcycle's trial run. Dad had learned how to stop his mount but had still not learned how to travel at half-speed. He started the machine with a flourish of noise and exhaust, waved to the throng, and before his hand had time to return to the handlebar hit an upright on a wooden bridge. He and the motorcycle described a magnificent aerial arc and landed

twenty feet below the bridge. The crowd bore Dad, uncon-
scious, to his bedroom. They pushed the Harley-Davidson,
unscathed, into its new garage. Mother locked the garage
door and collected all the keys in her apron pocket.

During Dad's convalescence Mother often jingled the
keys in her pocket. She also talked about responsibility, maturity, and safety. Dad must have listened to either the keys or
the conversation because, when he was once again able to
kick the motorcycle's starter, he turned the throttle as gently
as he handled our day-old kittens. He toured every road and
walkway in Port Simpson at a demure speed. Then he was
ready to break in his vehicle to its job.

My father operated an extremely general store and the
Harley transported its extremely general stock — twice: once
from the freight shed on the wharf to the store, and later from
the store to the consumer. He had a box sidecar cut down to
fit Port Simpson's lanes and byways. On any ordinary, dull
day that sidecar might carry coal, eggs, putty, ribbon, radios,
raisins. On more exciting days, Dad removed the sidecar and
bolted a wooden cradle in its place. Then the Harley was
ready to transport fifty-gallon gasoline drums and lumber
and coffins. The coffins were usually empty. But during the
summer salmon season, if a lonely fisherman died in the hilltop hospital, half a mile from the cemetery, there were not
enough strong men to carry the casket to the graveside, as
was the Port Simpson funeral custom. Then Dad's motorcycle, washed and polished, bore the deceased to the
churchyard with all the slow solemnity of a Cadillac hearse.

Each Monday the Harley had one shining hour. *The
Catala*, our passenger-mail-freight boat, would utter four
steam screams and slide in between the islands to the wharf.
Then Dad leapt onto the 74 and the 74 leapt onto the wharf
approach and they raced over that third of a mile of cross
planks that chattered and banged behind them. Dad caught

the ship's lines and by the time she was made fast Port Simpson's population was streaming down the wharf approach. Passengers came ashore first, followed closely by a slingload of mail. The sacks were tossed into the motorcycle's sidecar and Dad roared them up to the store where Mother waited in the glassed-in post office, stamping hammer in hand. The trick was to get the mail sorted and distributed to the people before they had to wind back up the roads and trails to their homes. That mail brought us the world in catalogues, magazines, newspapers and letters. Mother never commented on the Harley's speed on boat days.

There was another occasion when Mother failed to notice how fast the motorcycle travelled. It was the first day of each month. On that day, the aged, the handicapped and the hapless of the reserve came to the store to order the month's supplies granted them by the Department of Indian Affairs. Timothy, bent and blind, arrived first. "New moon?" he would enquire. Dad would reassure him and set chairs by the counter. There would be conversation in Chinook and a slow and thoughtful selection of groceries. Then Dad would load Timothy and his order into the motorcycle and return him to his home, where his granite tombstone, completely inscribed except for the date of death, stood expectantly at the front door.

Not all Dad's new moon customers accepted rides. Some shook their heads and cackled. Some covered their ears and fled. But Matilda Moody was far more interested in her ride home than she was in the tea and pilot biscuits and canned milk she had bought. Matilda, her relatives assured us, was eighty-seven. Arthritis had twisted her hands so that she could hardly hold her cane. But once her order was ready Dad hoisted her into the sidecar, she pulled her shawl tightly about her, and they were off for the ride of the month. Down one road and up the next they hurtled until they had covered every street in the town — Matilda's black silk kerchief straightened out stiff behind her head, a smile of ecstasy pushing her wrinkles right up to her temples. However deep my father's love for the Harley may have been, Matilda's was deeper.

If the 74 had its days of glory, it also had its day of disgrace. In our Indian village, by the 1920s, the rule of the chiefs had given way to the rule of an elected council. One day an eager new council took office only to learn that the treasury was empty. The members knew that taxation was the answer to this problem but they also knew that very few of the villagers could pay taxes. Obviously they would have to assess someone outside of the reserve. A road tax was the very thing. As the band's needs were many and taxable vehicles only one, the impost on the Harley turned out to be staggering. Dad gave notice that he would not be paying it. The next time the motorcycle made a delivery on the reserve, special constables seized it and chained it, with many chains and a padlock, to the leaning bear totem pole in front of a chief's house. The old bear had long since worn a hat of moss and blueberry bushes that sprouted from cracks in its cedar head. For years we had been expecting it to topple. But for two days it leered down through the rain at the motorcycle's humiliation, while Dad smiled stiffly and the six hundred members of the Port Simpson band made pilgrimages to view the prisoner. The situation had all the elements that the Tsimshian inherently enjoyed — humour, symbolism and degradation of the enemy, and, though the tax was found to be illegal, no one could deny that for forty-eight hours mythology had triumphed over mechanism.

In the 1930s my parents decided to retire to the gentler climate of southern British Columbia. Dad sold the store and, since he didn't see how Port Simpson could continue to function without the Harley-Davidson, he sold it with the business.

On the day of their departure Mother and Dad stood on the steamer's deck as she churned into reverse and bore them away from the waving crowd on the wharf. Mother's tears bounced on the rail — they were leaving their home of more than a quarter century. Beside her Dad was beaming. He said, "That new fellow can handle the Harley all right. Look at them go."

Since that day there have been many departures from Port Simpson. The hospital, the Crosby Girls' Home, the one-room school that I attended and my father's store are long, long gone. But the First Nations village has prospered and grown. It is homeport to a fleet of powerful fishing vessels that bristle with electronic gear. In the bay before it stands the First Nations cannery, now devoted to custom processing, and a new road crosses the Tsimshian Peninsula to Tuck Inlet, a ferry ride from Prince Rupert.

The Lax Kw'a alaams Band *purchased* the Hudson's Bay Company lands that, in 1834, was seized from then chief Cacas by right of the Company's four great guns. The band has spread out into the "white" village and southward, to accommodate a population of twelve hundred in modern homes. Meanwhile the non-Natives have spread out into the reserve so that modern Port Simpson is a village united under the name of Lax Kw'a alaams.

Cacas has won. McLoughlin's Harbour is once again the territory of his people.

Bibliography

ORIGINAL SOURCES

The Hudson's Bay Company Archives:
The Fort Simpson Journals — July 14, 1834–May 11, 1842; January 4, 1852–August 30, 1853; May 1, 1855–September 15, 1859; January 1, 1863–December 31, 1866.
Western Department Letter Book — Victoria Letters Outward — September 25, 1860–September 25, 1863.
Three Letters from John McLoughlin, Jr. at Stikine to Roderick Finlayson at Fort Simpson, 1841 and 1842.
Letters Inward to Archibald Barclay, London, 1846–1849.
Letters Outward from Victoria to Port Simpson, 1896, 1897.
Letters Outward from Victoria to Port Simpson, 1907.
Telegrams from Port Simpson to Victoria, 1907.
Log of Brig *Dryad* coasting, 1832.
Log of Schooner *Cadboro*, Captain Scarborough, From Fort Victoria Towards Sitka, 1844.
Log of Steamer *Strathcona*, Port Simpson-Stikine, 1899.
Reports *(Inspection* and *On Clerks and Postmasters)* — 1886, 1890, 1894, 1895, 1897, 1899, 1900, 1901.

The British Columbia Archives:
The Fort Simpson Journals — May 12, 1842–June 22, 1843, kept by John Work and Roderick Finlayson; September 15, 1859–September 30, 1861, kept by Hamilton Moffatt; October 1, 1861–December 31, 1862 kept by W. H. McNeill.
Correspondence Outward, September 6, 1841–October 11, 1844, Fort Simpson Letter Book signed by John Work.

Correspondence Outward, November 20, 1851–November 2, 1855, Fort Simpson Letter Book signed by W. H. McNeill.

Correspondence Inward, October 1854-September 1857, from James Douglas, Victoria, to W. H. McNeill, Fort Simpson.

Correspondence Outward, Fort Rupert (1859-1861) and Fort Simpson (October 26, 1863-October 24, 1865) Letter Book signed by Hamilton Moffatt.

Letter, D. D. Wishart to Dr. J. S. Helmcken, August 17, 1850 (Helmcken Collection).

Diaries of William Fraser Tolmie, 1830-1842.

Autobiography of Roderick Finlayson, 1818-1891.

Manuscript — *A Tale of Northern British Columbia (1880–1956)* by Martha Washington (O'Neill) Boss.

Manuscript — *My Memories* by Wiggs O'Neill.

The Journal of John Work, January-October, 1835, with introduction and notes by Henry Drummond Dee, reprinted from British Columbia Historical Quarterly, Vols. 8 and 9.

Statement of the Origin, Organization and Progress of the Russian-American Telegraph, Western Union Extension, Collins Overland Line, Rochester, N.Y., 1866.

PUBLISHED ORIGINAL MATERIAL

McLoughlin's Fort Vancouver Letters, Publications of the Champlain Society, Hudson's Bay Company Series — first series 1825-1838, Toronto, 1941; Second series 1839-1844, Toronto, 1943; third series 1844-1846, Toronto, 1944.

Anderson, James Robert, "Schooldays in Fort Victoria," *British Columbia: A Centennial Anthology*, ed. Reginald Eyre Watters, McClelland & Stewart Ltd., Toronto, 1958.

Helmcken, John Sabastion, *Reminiscences of Doctor John Sabastion Helmcken*, ed. Dorothy Blakey Smith, University of British Columbia Press, Vancouver, 1975.

Jewitt, John R., *The Adventures and Sufferings of John R. Jewitt, Captive Among the Nootka 1803–1805*, ed. Derek G. Smith, McClelland & Stewart Ltd., Toronto, 1974.

Mozino, Jose Mariana, *Noticias de Nutka*, trans. and ed. Iris Higbie Wilson, McClelland & Stewart Ltd., Toronto, 1970.

Simpson, Sir George, *Narrative of a Journey round the World During the Years 1841 and 1842*, H. Colburn, London, 1847.

Tolmie, William Fraser, *Physician and Fur Trader: The Diary of William Fraser Tolmie*, Mitchell Press, Vancouver, 1963.

Wilson, Charles, *Mapping the Frontier; Charles Wilson's Diary of the Survey of the 48th Parallel 1858-1862, while Secretary of the British Boundary Commission*, ed. George Francis Stanley, Macmillan Company of Canada, Toronto, 1970.

BOOKS TO WHICH I REFERRED CONSTANTLY

Duff, Wilson, *The Indian History of British Columbia*, Anthropology in British Columbia, Memoir No. 5, Department of Recreation and Conservation, Victoria, 1964.
Walbran, John T., *British Columbia Coast Names*, The Library's Press, Vancouver, reprinted 1971.

BOOKS THAT SUPPLIED VALUABLE INFORMATION FOR ONE OR MORE TOPICS

Barbeau, Charles Marius, *Pathfinders of the North Pacific*, Caxton Printers and Ryerson Press, Toronto, 1958.
Binns, Archie, *Peter Skene Ogden: Fur Trader*, Binfords & Mort, Portland, Oregon, 1967.
Inverarity, Robert, *Art of the Northwest Coast Indians*, University of California Press, Berkeley and Los Angeles, 1950.
McKechnie, Robert E., *Strong Medicine; History of Healing on the North West Coast*, J. J. Douglas Ltd., Vancouver, 1974.
O'Neill, Wiggs, *Steamboat Days on the Skeena River, British Columbia*, Northern Sentinel Press, Kitimat, B.C., 1961.
Pinkerton, Robert E., *Gentleman Adventurers*, McClelland & Stewart, Toronto, 1931.
Rickard, T. A., *Historic Backgrounds of British Columbia*, Rickard, Victoria, 1948.
Rushton, Gerald A., *Whistle Up the Inlet: The Union Steamship Story*, J. J. Douglas Ltd., Vancouver, 1974.
White, Howard, ed., *Raincoast Chronicles*, Harbour Publishing, Madeira Park, B.C., 1976.

BACKGROUND BOOKS

Anstey, Arthur and Sutherland, Neil, *British Columbia: A Short History*, W. J. Gage Ltd., Toronto, 1957.
Howay, Frederick William, *British Columbia from the Earliest Times to the Present*, Vol. II, S. J. Clark Publishing Co., Vancouver, 1914.

Innis, Harold, *The Fur Trade in Canada: An Introduction to Canadian Economic History*, University of Toronto Press, Toronto, revised edition 1956.

Large, R. G., *Drums and Scalpel*, Mitchell Press, Vancouver, 1968.

McKay, Douglas, *The Honourable Company: A History of the Hudson's Bay Company*, McClelland & Stewart Ltd., Toronto, 1949.

McKelvie, B. A., *The Pageant of British Columbia*, Thos. Nelson & Sons (Canada) Ltd., Toronto, 1957.

Pethick, Derek and Im Baumgarten, Susan, *British Columbia Recalled: A Picture History 1741-1871*, Hancock House Publishers, Saanichton, B.C., 1974.

Pethick, Derek, S.S. *Beaver: The Ship that Saved the West*, Mitchell Press Ltd., Vancouver, 1970.

Rich, E. E., *The Fur Trade and the Northwest to 1857*, McClelland & Stewart Ltd., Toronto, 1967.

Scholefield, E. O. S., *British Columbia from the Earliest Times to the Present*, Vol. I, S. J. Clark Publishing Co., Vancouver, 1914.

Zaslow, Morris, *The Opening of the Canadian North 1870–1914*, McClelland & Stewart Ltd., Toronto, revised 1949.

"The Works of Hubert Howe Bancroft," Vol. I and Vol. II, *History of the Northwest Coast 1543-1886*, San Francisco, 1884.

NEWSPAPERS AND PERIODICALS

The British Columbia Archives:

Na-Na-Kwa "Dawn on the Northwest Coast" edited and published by Rev. George H. Raley, Kitimat, B.C., 1898-1907.

The Colonist, 1858-1917, including its variously titled publications; e.g., The *Daily British Colonist, Semi-Weekly Colonist.*

Excerpts:

Alcohol and the Northwest Coast Indian by E. M. Lemert, from University Publications in Culture and Society, University of California Press, Berkeley, 1954.

Introduction of Intoxicating Liquors Amongst the Indians of the Northwest Coast by F. W. Howay, from British Columbia Historical Quarterly, 1942.

Debtor and Chattel Slavery in Aboriginal North America by William Christie MacLeod, from the American Anthropologist, 1925.

The Use of Iron and Copper by the Indians of British Columbia by T. A. Rickard, British Columbia Historical Quarterly, 1939.

The Beaver, Hudson's Bay Company, Winnipeg, various issues, 1921-1979.

Index

HELEN MEILLEUR was born in Port Simpson in 1910. She lived on the Tsimshian reserve for the first five years of her life and on the adjacent Hudson's Bay Company lands for the rest of her childhood and much of her adolescence, her father's general store dictating the locations. After careers in teaching and business she became a wife and mother of five. She didn't start writing until 1967 when she won an Indiana University scholarship for non-fiction. She was 70 years old when the book conceived in her childhood was completed and published. She now lives in North Vancouver.

Cabin at Singing River
Chris Czjakowski • Foreword by Peter Gzowski
This redesigned new edition of a classic account of frontier life presents the story of how one woman accomplished the task of making a slight, human indentation in a remote and uninhabited place. In her late thirties, with only rudimentary carpentry skills, Chris headed into the interior of British Columbia and, in the pristine wilderness of Tweedsmuir Provincial Park, cleared a piece of land and built her own home.
1-55192-463-3 • $21.95 CDN / $15.95 US

British Columbia: An Illustrated History *Revised and Updated
Geoffrey Molyneux
The perfect book for those who want a short, engaging history of Canada's westernmost province, this title is now available in a revised and re-designed edition featuring updated text and a decade's worth of new material. Brought to life by more than 100 archival photographs, this eminently readable history offers an entertaining introduction to the characters and events of British Columbia's history — from before the arrival of European explorers to the signing of the Nisga'a Treaty.
1-55192-420-X • $21.95 CDN / $15.95 US

Alone in the Appalachians
Monique Dykstra
A city girl's trek from Maine to the Gaspésie. This new addition to Raincoast's popular Journeys series is the tale of one woman's adventures while hiking the entire length of the brand new International Appalachian Trail. This extremely funny narrative includes local history, plus Dykstra's vivid descriptions of the many characters she meets along the trail. Includes 50 of her fascinating photographs.
1-55192-477-3• $29.95 CDN / $19.95 US

Hiking on the Edge *Revised Third Edition
Ian Gill, photographs by David Nunuk
A journey in pictures and words along the West Coast Trail. With a revised section on the Juan de Fuca Marine Trail and updated information, this book is the definitive resource for both the armchair traveller and veteran hiker interested in venturing to the western edge of British Columbia's Vancouver Island.
155192-505-2 • $29.95 CDN / $19.95 US